The White Rose and The Lady

Richard de Methley

First Published by White Boar Publishing Enterprises: October 2012
Second Impression: August 2013

Copyright© Richard de Methley

www.richarddemethley.co.uk

Cover design by Michael Craig and Richard Lyne-Pirkis

ISBN 978-0-9557480-3-5

.
Printed by Belforts Information Press, Stevenage. 01438.312777
www.belforts.com

Dedication

This book is dedicated to all those who have helped put it together, not least to Michael and Rosie Craig…and to my dearest love, Diana Mary Stirling. Michael, who has worked with enormous skill and goodwill on the new covers and has advised stalwartly on presentation; Rosie, for her unbounded enthusiasm for the project, her critical eye, her sharp intellect and her editorial skills…and Diana for putting up with me, especially when it was not going well, or the damned computer 'stole' vital bits! Outstanding…and gleaming!! Especial thanks go also to Diana L-P who typed every word and helped with the original story-board, to 'Nicky' of Nicky's Seeds for her unstinted help with plants and herbs of the period, and to Simon Carpenter without whose expert knowledge Gui would never have reached story's end! Thank you all *so* much.

Richard de Methley: August 2013.

Chapter 1...On board the *Mary* after *El Nazir's* attack.

Surrounded by the debris of their brutal fight with the Corsairs, Sir Gui de Malwood stood on the *Mary's* shattered forecastle, stunned, as he watched El Nazir's great fighting dromond pull steadily away from them.

Unable to accept what had happened, his armour running with the blood of all those he had killed, he stood there transfixed, still calling out his belovèd's name even though he knew she could no longer see or hear his words, while beneath him the ship wallowed sluggishly, hove-to with her sails reefed-up and tied to her topmost spar.

Torn sheets and halliards flying free in the wind, some trailing in the sea, the *Mary's* smashed and battered timbers graunched and tore against each other as if the ship herself was groaning, and crying out in pain...while the sea flooded in and Thomas and his crew fought to save her; struggling to turn the *Mary's* bows towards the distant shoreline and away from the wind and the landward waves, without her sinking beneath their feet. And all the while Gui just stood there, oblivious, cursing his men on *the Pride* whom he had charged with Alicia's life, and who had so cruelly failed to protect her.

Below him, along the bulwarks and across the blooded deck, while some continued to rage at their attackers, stamping their feet and roaring out their challenge; others of his command sat slumped with exhaustion amongst the litter of discarded weapons and the butchered remnants of their enemies. Here a severed arm, there a battered head, hands hacked off and left like discarded gloves, some still clasping weapons, and everywhere the deck was thick with congealing blood, fragments of bone, scattered brains and human faeces; or slimed with the greasy coils from some poor wretch's carcase, like a butcher's fresh filled sausages. From almost every surface there were arrows sticking up like porcupine quills, all slip-slopping amidst the water, swirled with blood and mucus, that continued to gush in from the great hole smashed in the *Mary's* side.

And in those few moments Gui knew real, sinking despair. It felt as though his heart were being torn from him, his mind ravaged by anger and grief, until all he could do was shout out in impotent rage and pound his mailed fists on the shattered timbers of the *Mary,* face filled with blood, powerless to stop El Nazir from taking Alicia from him.

"I will find you!" he roared across the sea, his voice echoed by the screaming gulls that swooped and wheeled above him. *"My love, we will come for you!"* he cried out again in his heart's agony. *"We will!"* The words carried

away by the wind as the great dromond pulled away from him faster and faster, the beat of the hortator's drum fading as she did so, while he stood, motionless in shock, shouting his misery to the seabirds and the open skies.

He could not believe what had just happened... *Dear God, what will they do to her?...and poor Agnes? And where are they going? Fucking heathen, infidel bastards!*...Rape, murder, destroy. That was all those barbarians understood, and they hated Christians more than any other, torturing them to death for fun, burning them alive on crosses...and Christian women? It did not bear thinking of...*Bastards! Bastards!*..And de Brocas?...*Filthy, murdering French swine. How dare he murder and attack those I most love. First my parents, and now my beautiful Alicia. Forced into marriage with that French bastard?...Unthinkable!*...And his heart and spirit groaned at his imagining the Baron touching his Alicia, pawing at her, entering her as Nazir had said he would, sullying her with his lust for an heir from her womb. And he cried out again, the pain twisting his bowels until he bent over in agony, his arms wrapped around his belly, his lungs tightening until he could barely breathe, "No! *No!*"

For Sir Richard and Father Matthew, as much as for many of their men, the sight of Alicia and Agnes dragged below the decks of the great galley had been no less shocking and, powerless to stop the great Corsair warship leaving, many had rushed to the sides and shaken their fists and roared out their defiance at El Nazir as his galley had rowed away.

Oblivious to the sea spouting in through the *Mary's* smashed bulwarks, they stood and raged against their enemies until brought to their senses by Tommy Blackwood's enormous voice.

"*Ho there, my Lords!*" their huge shipmaster shouted, beckoning violently at Gui's commanders, his booming voice breaking in on their thoughts. "Sir Richard, de Beaune...*John Fitzurse*, damn your hide man! *Wake up!* If we don't shift ourselves we will be food for the bloody crabs and fishes. This fucking tub is sinking! My lads can't do this on their own! *Get those idle bastards bailing!*" he roared, stabbing his fingers furiously at where their men were slumped about the deck.

"Chain of buckets...fucking helmets. Anything, my Lords! *Just get those buggers moving,* Every time we heel to port, the sea's bursting into her. If we don't get rid of this bloody water," he shouted, kicking his feet at it sloshing around him, "we'll lose her! God be praised the day is calm. If any kind of sea had been running she'd be gone...and us with it!

"And we must lighten her as much as we can, my Lords, and raise that gash further out of the water. Get rid of all these bastard bodies, and anything else you can think of. And will someone catch that fucking horse, before it's the first to go overboard!"

With that, and the bellowed orders from Gui's commanders, all now roused to urgent action by the Master's fierce demands, everyone seemed to jerk back into life and move at once. Some to bail, some to pump, some to shift and clear the debris from their fight; and in short order, with Gui's massive Master-at-Arms, John Fitzurse, calling them on, and his commanders adding their encouragement, the deck was swiftly sorted. Smashed bodies were tossed overboard, alive or dead, the living screaming and thrashing for their lives in the bloodied water. Broken timbers and torn rigging followed, and box after box of supplies and assorted weaponry were dragged up and also thrown over the side until the sea immediately around the *Mary* was covered with bobbing wreckage, discarded stores and bloodied corpses. The only things saved were the barrels of longbow shafts and bodkin heads that could not easily be replaced in France.

Merlin was caught and tethered, Beau, Sunburst and Gillygate taken from their stall the same, and then the partitions knocked down and also cast into the sea. But it was not enough! Though the huge gap torn in her side by El Nazir's artillery was now further above the waterline, the sea still bubbled and spouted into her every time Thomas tried to turn the *Mary* towards the shore, and she was already listing.

"What more can we do, Thomas?" Sir Richard called out. "My lads are all pumping and bailing like fury, but we cannot hold the water back. Much more of this and we'll be in it up to our necks."

"*We must try and fother that bloody hole, Sir Richard!*" he shouted back, and turning to his Mate: "Adam, muster all the crew you can find, and break out the winter canvas, and all the ropes you can lay your hands on."

"Oakum, Master Thomas?"

"No, lad! We don't have the time to do a proper job, but if we can just cover that bloody great hole, we may be able to make Houat at least, maybe even Nantes itself, it's only fifty miles or so, and once in the Loire, and out of these waves, we should be fine. Now, yarely, my lads, *yarely!*"

"What's 'fothering' my Lord?" Fitzurse asked Sir Richard anxiously.

"It's an age-old sailing method for patching holes in desperate circumstances!" Father Matthew interrupted tersely, coming up beside them both. "Usually you take a big sail and stitch it all over with oakum, the tarred shreds from old ropes, until it looks like a huge matted beard; tie a good hawser to each corner and pass the whole thing under the ship until the hole is covered! Then suction holds it in place. Only they haven't the time to do all that, so they're going to do the best they can with just a heavy, winter sail."

3

"God aid us," Fitzurse burst out, shaking his head. "Like patching a barn door with a handkerchief! They must be bloody mad!"

"Better that than drowning, John," L'Eveque drawled at him. "Go now, and give de Beaune a hand, and keep the lads moving. Keep them busy, and their minds occupied, we don't want 'em getting lazy now, do we?" And they both laughed.

"What about Sir Gui, My Lord?" Fitzurse asked then, jerking his head towards where the young man was still standing gazing out to sea. "He needs someone too."

"What indeed about Gui, Father?" Sir Richard asked, pointing to where his friend was still standing on the shattered forecastle, while his Master-at-Arms barrelled away amongst the men. "We need him here, busy amongst us," he said urgently. "I know he is wracked by what's happened. We all are! But brooding will do neither him, nor us, any good. I cannot lead these men the way he does," he argued strongly. "We all love Alicia too, Father...but he needs to snap out of it and get *'doing'* instead. The lads need him amongst them...and so do I!!"

"Leave him to me, Sir Richard," the tall Benedictine said in his lilting, Spanish voice, patting L'Eveque across his shoulders. "He will come-to shortly, I assure you. The trouble will not be to get him 'doing', it will be persuading him to stop! To take time to plan things properly and not leap about like a herring on a griddle," he added, making Sir Richard laugh. "Meanwhile, do all you can to help Master Thomas, and see if we have any swimmers amongst us? Ask Jean as well. If so, make sure Thomas knows. We are all in this together, Sir knight," he added grimly, "and somehow that fother has to be drawn under the *Mary* for it to work...or she'll go down like a stone and us with her!" And with that, and a final clap on the big Guard Commander's armoured shoulders, he strode off to join Gui on the shattered forecastle.

*

With the *Mary* heaved-to and drifting with the current, her sails brailed-up out of the way, everyone worked like fury, either bailing with anything they could find, working the crude leather pumps that the ship carried, or struggling with the thick winter canvas that the crew had dragged from its stowage beneath the sterncastle. And within the hour they had the bulk of it ready to drag over the side, three of Thomas's crew and three of Gui's command ready to plunge over and attempt to swim under the *Mary's* fat, scarlet bottom, each dragging a light line that would then be used to pull the heavy hawsers, now firmly attached to each corner of the fother, and elsewhere on its leading edge, right under the ship and up again on the other side like a massive bandage.

By then, despite everyone's efforts, the *Mary* was appreciably lower in the water, so it was now or never and with a *splash!* the men chosen for the task went over the damaged port side, with their lines in their hands. Then, after a moment's pause bobbing up and down in the swell to get their breaths, they dived, and all who could be spared from other tasks rushed across to the other side of the cog to watch for their return.

A minute passed.

Then two…then longer!

Until with mighty gasp, the first swimmer porpoised from the surface holding up his line, then another and another, until four had safely made it, scratched and torn where the barnacles on her keel had scored them, but alive…but that was all. Two were lost. Their lines snagged on the barnacles and weeds that clung to the Mary's fat bottom. Too far to go forward…too far to go back, swept away by the currents, never to be seen again, and all were saddened by their loss.

But then was not the time to mourn, and with the light lines recovered, the heavy hawsers were pulled safely under the *Mary* and up again over her starboard bulwarks. With that the swimmers were drawn-up out of the water, running across the deck to jump in again on the port side ready to guide it, while the whole unwieldy mass of the fother was then pushed over the gashed hull and into the sea. With all those neither bailing nor pumping now hauling steadily on the ropes, helped by those swimmers still starboard-side in the water, the huge fother was dragged down and under the Mary. The crew and Gui's men heaved on the ropes with all their might until the heavy canvas came up as hard against the jagged hole as it could be forced, and with a shout of triumph the crew lashed the heavy ropes down around the starboard rails, while John Fitzurse and half-a-dozen of his lions pulled all those overboard safely back onto the deck.

It was done!

And not a moment too soon either, for already the *Mary's* bilges were overflowing, the water sloshing and swirling over her bottom boards and over their feet. It had also seeped in around the rock still embedded in her starboard side; another hour and she would have gone. Even with the fother in place the water still spurted in little jets around the sides, but nothing compared to how it

5

had been, and once the bilges were cleared, Master Thomas reckoned that with constant bailing and pumping, the *Mary* could still be saved.

"Bravely done, lads! *Bravely done!*" Thomas roared out, hands on hips, his eyes alight with pleasure,. "Shame about Johnny Swales and the young Frenchy, for sure. But bravely done! Wine all round from my own stores, you whoreson bastards! Then let's see if we can get this old tub to move herself. Yarely done m'boys! *Yarely done!*" Patting the Mary's tall mast with an affectionate smile as he swung round, he went across to join his crew and check the lashing that now held the fother tight against the broad gash in her side.

Chapter 2...Father Matthew puts Gui straight.

Up by the shattered forecastle Father Matthew put his hands on Gui's shoulder, and turned him so he could see his face.

"Gui...I cannot really know how you feel, but I can imagine it: anger, despair, hatred, revenge? All of those and more probably. And fear? Fear of what may be happening to Alicia, and Agnes? Where are they going now? And how to catch up with them at Gruissan...and kill de Brocas?"

"Yes, Father. All of those. But mostly rage, at myself, for not doing more. For putting Alicia in such danger, when she begged me not to. For not being with her when she needed me most. *Everything!* And the thought of de Brocas forcing himself on her, marrying her out of hand, is just too terrible even to contemplate. That *bastard*, Father! That absolute, double dyed, wicked, fucking *bastard*. And those two French traitors," he added spitting the words out in disgust. "Those *Cousins!*" and he groaned and leaned his head against Matthew's chest.

"Gui," he said gently, cradling his hands around Gui's head. "Truly he is a bad man, even evil. If there was one man I would pick up a sword against, it would be de Brocas...He is everything you say, and more. But, my son, we cannot know everything beforehand. Sometimes, despite all we can do, or plan for, bad things happen. But God can give us strength, Gui. Remind us we are not alone, show us the way to get things done. Give us friends to help along the way...and courage to carry things through even when they look impossible. Look around you," he said, turning the young man by his shoulders to face down the *Mary's* battered deck. "See how your courage and that of your men and their commanders have defeated your enemies," he said giving his shoulders a shake as he spoke, "and with only a handful of good lives lost, against the hundreds of your enemies who were slain today, or drowned chained to their oars!"

"But El Nazir has taken Alicia, Father!" Gui replied in anguish, looking down across the ship's broken timbers and blood stained decking, at the battle scars, the human debris, the arrows still sticking up everywhere...and at the men struggling to fix the heavy hawsers to the fother now spread across the deck. "Despite all we could do that bastard still seized her from us, even right out here," he went on gesturing at the sea all around them. "And soon he will have his filthy hands on her, and Agnes Fitzwalter, and we are weeks away from Narbonne, *weeks!* Even more now that the *Mary* has been so badly smashed up..."

"Yes, my son," the tall priest went on quietly, turning the tall knight back to face him. "All that is true…but mooning up here away from your command that needs you to lead them is *not* going to get Alicia back! For that you will need every drop of the courage, determination and brains that God and your parents gave you the day you were born. Now listen, Gui," he went on firmly, pointing to where his men were now struggling to heave the fother overboard. "Down there you have a command that respects you. Even people who love you! More on the *Pride*. Though God knows what has happened to her. You want Alicia back, and to bring judgement to de Brocas?"

"*Yes*, Father."

"Then pull yourself together, Gui," he said sharply. "And get down there and lead them, they need you! Sir Richard, de Beaune, John Fitzurse, good as they are, are not in command of this expedition. *You are!* And frankly, right now, you are neglecting your duty. You're wallowing in your dismay over Alicia, when you should be down there with your men," he said definitively, as a great shout went up from below them. "Not up here indulging yourself in self-pity, and tearing yourself apart over something you can do nothing about…at least not as long as you are stuck on board this battered, leaking ship!

"Life is hard at times, Gui. Sometimes it is easier to herd cats! But you never know what you can achieve until you try…nor who will come out of the woodwork to help you. Look how Allan-i-the-Wood came to us, wholly unexpected, with the remainder of his verderers at Beaulieu. How many others may yet join us on this quest? The cherries will not really fall unless you shake the trees! If all you do is sit beneath them feeling hopeless and sorry for yourself, and wait for them to fall…all that will come down will be empty stones on stalks, rotten fruit and wasps to sting you! *Right?*"

"Right, Father!"

"*Good!* Then there is hope for us all yet. So be done with moping, dear boy, and let us join the others…they have done quite enough without you. What's needed now is plenty of zap and bustle, my fine Lord Baron of Malwood and the Forest! Everything forward and trust in the Lord!" And drawing Gui towards him he kissed his forehead, and blessed him, before turning him to walk back down to the deck and join the others, now gathered below the mast and waiting…*And let's hope that does the trick, because we all need him like a hawk in screaming yarak…not one that's deep in moult!*

*

"**S**plendour of God, Gui," Sir Richard L'Eveque drawled later, as they leaned across the torn bulwarks beside the *Mary's* shattered side. "I'd not want to go through all that again in a hurry! That must be one of the swiftest, most dangerous actions that I've ever taken a hand in. Sea fights are definitely *not* my favourite occupation!"...*You either win or you're overboard. Dead or alive and no second chances!*

"Yes, O my noble Guard Commander, "he replied with a mock bow. "The lads did well. Great fighting spirit, Richard, great determination...and great courage. So did Merlin, bless him, with his hoofs and teeth," he went on, looking down at Sir Richard's great charger, now meekly pulling at a bag of hay. "Picked one of those bastards up and shook him like a rat." And there was a pause then as they both looked across to where the *Pride* appeared to be still struggling, Gui's eyes steel grey and, his brow furrowed...*God knows what happened over there, but it has cost us everything. What did Robert Christchurch think he was doing?*...He sighed then, and turning quietly said: "Richard, I owe you and the lads an apology,"

"Apology?" the big man said slowly. "From my ever present Lord and Master?"

"Yes, my friend," Gui replied with a rueful grin. "Your present Lord and Master should never have left you and the lads, and Thomas of course, to have done all this on your own," he went on, gesturing across the cleared deck, and down at the fothered hole in the *Mary's* side still squirting water. "All I could think of was Alicia, that *bastard* de Brocas, and my own pain: leaving you and the others to cope! Bad leadership, Richard; won't happen again. Sorry!"

"Gui," his friend said turning to him, his hand on his arm. "You and I have known each other a good few years now. And you have covered for me with Sir Yvo on more than one occasion. Remember," he added, in his usual laconic style, "when I was absent from duty? Chasing after the delicious Laura, and your father nearly caught us in the hay barn?"

"Yes, you hid, she ran out, and I took the rap, you rotten bastard!" And both men laughed.

"Well, Gui. This is just like that. You would have done the same for me. And I haven't just watched the very love of my life being dragged kicking and screaming across an enemy's deck, powerless to do anything about it. The point is you are here now!"

"Thank God for Father Matthew!"

"Mmmm, in more ways than one, dear boy. That man knows more tricks to fix a wound than a squirrel does to eat a nut! Without him we would all be in a far worse case, leaving more injured men behind than I care to think of.

9

His stitches are neater than the Lady Margaret's, bless her soul." And they both laughed.

"What's the damage?"

"Don't know clearly yet. Better ask Fitzurse. He's coming across now."

"So, John?" he queried as the big Master-at-Arms came across to join them. "What's the butcher's bill? I haven't had time to check the lads myself."

"Ten slain my Lord, and six badly injured," the big soldier said, wiping his bloodied armour with a damp rag. "But Father Matthew is with them and says most will live, and should be able to travel with us. But two are badly hurt: Jamie Burke and Tommy Baker; and Thomas lost several of his crew as well as the lad drowned just now under the *Mary*. Other than that, there are some nasty gashes and not a few bumped heads and bruises, but nothing worse. Considering how many attacked us, we got off lightly"

"Lightly, indeed, John!" Gui exclaimed, with a grin. "I had expected it to be much worse."

"Who have we lost?" Sir Richard asked heavily.

"Robert of Burley and John Ditcher, my Lord," Fitzurse replied, looking at the tall knight. "James Goodchild, Peter Miller, young Robbie Cooper, Ned Bowyer, 'Donkey' Adams and…and…"

"Charles Lafitte, Pierre le Gros, Raoul de Cluny to the corsairs, and young Jean Letour under this ship," de Beaune chipped in, as he too joined them, cleaning his sword blade as he walked. "Four of mine from Burgundy, leal men all, Sir Gui. They will be missed."

"Robbie's mother will take it hard too, my Lord," Fitzurse growled softly. "She has none other to care for her now, not since her Simmy died last winter. The Lady Alicia will be sad, too. He was a favourite with her!"

"And young Adams!" Gui sighed. "Remember how he and that old jackass of Father Gerome's had a tussle over the old boy's straw hat and Adams ended up in the moat covered with duck weed?"

"That's how he got his name," Sir Richard said with a sudden grin. "'Donkey' Adams…and he'd offer a swift bunch of fives to anyone who teased him about it too. He was always up before me for scrapping, that one." Adding with a sigh: "But he was a good soldier for all that. A bit rash, but still a good man."

"Well, he's had his last scrap now, poor little bugger," John Fitzurse said sadly. "Some bloody great pirate took his head off! A single blow, blood everywhere. But I sorted the bastard out good and proper. Hacked his shoulder clean off, and dragged his gizzards out on the deck. Lovely job!"

10

"Well, they're both over the side now," Jean de Beaune said grimly, adding after a pause: "Yours, mine and theirs. All food for the bloody crabs and fishes."

"It's the living I care about," Sir Richard said then, looking at where his command were all bailing or pumping like demons. "In one swift engagement we have lost a tenth of our strength...let alone Lady Alicia and young Agnes Fitzwalter. And we still have hundreds of miles to travel, and a castle to seize at the end of it. Oh, don't fear, Gui...the lads are even more determined now than they were before, but they are anxious about those at home when the news reaches them of what has happened here. How they will cope with their rents, dues and so forth?"

"Don't worry, any of you," Gui replied, his eyes flaring at the mention of Alicia's name. "Malwood will always look after its own, so I will make sure old mother Burley is properly cared for, our little Lady would insist on it. And all the others too. And Sir James is the best of men. He will not let anyone starve, or lose their homes. Be certain of it...and be sure to tell the men that also. They will fight all the better knowing that their loved ones will be cared for."

"That's good, my Lord," Fitzurse replied with a grin. "And the lads will have the usual sale of effects, not that any of them had much about them, mind you, but it will all help. What about their bodies?"

"Over the side like poor 'Donkey' Adams and the rest, I am afraid, John," Gui answered him, jerking with his thumb. "We can't afford the luxury of a burial, and I don't want the stench of death around us either. I am sorry, but that's the way it has to be."

Then, while all his other officers returned to their jobs, he turned away and walked past the damaged side of the ship, towards the forecastle, to look again to where the *Pride* was still rolling her fat yellow girth from side to side, his thoughts racing as he thought of Alicia and all that might be happening to her, his hands clenched, white-knuckled on the ship's railings.

"Are you alright, Gui?" L'Eveque asked, coming up beside him, looking out across to the Île de Houat, and the hard line of the mainland beyond.

"No...not really," Gui replied over his shoulder. "Just thinking about Alicia. Wondering what in God's name is happening to her. I am so angry, Richard! *So bloody angry!*"

"I know, dear boy," he drawled. "I know. But we *will* get her back," he said, putting a long arm across Gui's armoured shoulders. "You *have* to believe that. I do! That filth will not escape these murderous assaults. We may have lost some good men today, Gui, but as I said, that has only served to make the lads that more determined. And anyway, dear boy, you never know what's

11

round the corner…who may come forward to join our expedition…nor whom we may find down there in Gruissan who are just waiting for the chance to pitch their current Lord and bloody master off the nearest cliff!" And he banged him on his shoulders with his hand. "We *will* bring him to justice, Gui…and his hell-born daughter. We have all sworn it!"

"I know, my friend. I know. But it is very hard to accept her loss to us, and Agnes, too," he added swiftly. "Especially when we had planned things so carefully!" Then, forcing all thoughts of Alicia aside, he said: "Anyway…what's next, Richard? We cannot afford to lose any more time between here and Narbonne. Nor any more men either!"…*And, God's Blood, where can I get some reinforcements?*

"We got off lightly, as I said," his Guard Commander replied with a grin. "I thought the boys fought bloody well today, the first real fighting that any of them have ever faced. They kept their heads and did what they'd been taught. What they really need Gui, is some heartfelt praise from you. For the lads fought for you, as much as for themselves, and so far you've said sod all to them!"

Gui groaned and dropped his head. "You're so right, Richard, and I hang my head in shame. First, a right bollocking from Father Matthew, and now one from you!" And he grinned ruefully, "This has just not been my day! No matter, you are quite right, and on all counts. I will speak to the troops soonest, and I expect a few flagons of wine, if there are any still unbroken on board, would not go amiss either…and a handful of extra silver in their pockets when we land. All of them, Tommy's boys as well. They've earned it."

"That would be a grand gesture, Gui. That'll put a bit of extra heart in 'em! Though they'll lose the money to the first sloe-eyed whore they meet," he said with a grin.

"Or in the first tavern they come to," Sir Gui added, smiling.

"Same thing, really," Jean de Beaune said with a grin, joining them by the side. "Taverns equal wine, that equals tavern wenches…and tavern wenches equal whores. At least they do where I come from!" And there was a brief gale of laughter. "And you will get warm thanks from my Burgundians also, My Lord," the tough war-leader added. "Mercardier always dashed us a little extra after a hard won fight, as you are going to. We will not let you down!"

"I never thought you would, Jean," Gui added, flexing his left shoulder. "Now, away and find that wine Master Blackwood was talking of earlier, you have all more than earned it. And I'll break out the flagons when we reach land, or they all be as soused as herrings and just as bloody useless!"

12

But before anyone could move there was suddenly a great shout from Fitzurse, who was standing over one of his men, urgently beckoning. "My Lords! Come quickly, and Father Matthew. This lad, Davy Coulter, has found something you ought to see."

Chapter 3...The Baron's message is found.

In moments they had all swiftly crossed the *Mary's* tilting deck to join them. "What have you found, Davy?" Sir Richard asked his young soldier quickly.

"Come on, Davy, lad," the huge Master-at-Arms encouraged him, laying a massive hand on the young man's shoulders. "Nothing to be afeard of. We all know you lads go through the bodies for coins and such. Things you might sell. That's spoils of war, Davy, that is. Done it myself afore now. That's normal after a battle. Just show Sir Richard what you found. He won't take the box from you."

"W..well, my Lord," the young man stammered slightly, shocked to be confronting his Commander. "I was..was going through one of those bastard's pockets, quickly like, to see if there might be s..something there, 'specially as his armour was far better quality than any others we'd been throwing overboard, and..and I..I found this my Lord." And with that, his large grey eyes dark with anxiety in his round face, he gingerly opened his hand to reveal a beautifully chased silver box, inlaid with gold and studded with finely polished green stones.

"Emeralds, no less, young Davy Coulter," Sir Richard said, picking the box up and drawing in his breath. "And gold. That is certainly a very fine box, Sergeant," he drawled, his eyes suddenly grown hard. "But nothing worth calling us all over for, surely? Just spoils of war, man, as you said."

"No, Sir Richard. That's right. But it's not the box that's important, my Lord. It's the message inside it!"

"Message, Fitzurse?" Gui questioned him sharply.

"Yes my Lord. Inside the box."

"I..I thought there might be c..coins inside it, my Lord," Davy Coulter broke in, petrified to find himself before his Lord Baron as well his Guard Commander. "But..but there weren't. Just a small piece of rolled up paper..."

"Paper?" Sir Gui questioned instantly.

"There's nothing in here," Sir Richard said, holding the box open for all to see.

"No, my Lords. N..no," the young soldier stammered, his face wrought with anxiety. "But there was when I opened it. I would have thrown it away, like. But the Sergeant saw me with that," he said, his voice shaking a bit as he pointed to the chased silver box still in Sir Richard's hands. "I..I was showing what I'd got, Lord. To..to my mates like. And to the Master-at-Arms. He

14

glimpsed the..the paper inside, and thought you should see it also. So..so he called you over," he added, his voice trailing away.

"When I saw how lovely that jewelled box was, my Lords," his big Master-at-Arms said calmly, "and then caught sight of the paper inside it, I thought that if anyone kept something written inside so valuable a box, it might be important."

"Well done, Master-at-Arms," Gui said, quietly. "Well spotted."

"Now, lad, show us the message," Father Matthew said softly, holding out his hand. "No-one is angry with you, Davy. But these are difficult times and that message might be very important. You have done well."

"It was the Master-at-Arms who spotted it, Father, not I. I would have thrown it overboard with his body and all the rest of the rubbish. Here it is," and fumbling underneath his surcoat, he handed over a tiny roll of the finest paper. "Can I go now, Father?" he asked the tall Benedictine anxiously.

"Yes, Davy. Of course. Go now and join your mates. Sir Richard will see you later I expect, and give you back your box."

And while the trooper ran off, his brow wet with nervous sweat...*Oh my God! Oh my God!*...to be surrounded by his friends, all eagerly questioning him, Father Matthew very carefully unrolled the message that Fitzurse had rescued for them.

"Now, what do we have here, I wonder?" And stretching it out, he held it up to the light. "Six words and one bunch of numbers...and all in tiny writing."

"What does it say, Matthew?" Gui asked him sharply.

"Mmm, not easy to read. Still: 'Rouge. Hoedic. Jules. Lucas. Vert. 4/5. Bordeaux.' That's it!" And everyone was silent for a while as they all took in its significance.

"*Sweet Wine of Christ!*" Gui swore at last, letting his breath out in a sudden swoosh. "That's us, isn't it? *That's us!* The 'Rouge' is the Mary, on its way to Bordeaux...which we were. And those two bastards need no recognition..."

"And Hoedic is over there, Lords," Master Thomas boomed at them suddenly, from over their shoulders. "From where those bastards jumped us!" he added, pointing over the Mary's shattered port quarter. "The island next to the one where the *Pride* is still struggling; and those numbers are the days we could expect to take in getting here!"

"And 'Vert' is the green colour of Islam that was hung off the stern of the *Pride* as she sailed away," Father Matthew said softly.

15

"Seems to me those fucking bastards knew all about us from the moment we left Brest," Thomas added in his deep voice. "Even sooner. Maybe even from Malwood!"

"Except which boat the girls were on," Sir Richard said sharply, smacking his hands together, making everyone stare in sudden surprise. "Our little trick would have worked beautifully, because those wild buggers attacked the wrong ship. It was only our misfortune that we put those two French bastards with them on the *Pride.* "

"Yes," Father Matthew growled tersely. "That spread of green silk did for us all!"

"One thing's certain, Lords," Thomas snarled. "Someone had all this planned. It *was* a trap, Father. As you thought!"

"But how?" Gui asked, astonished.

"Pigeons, Sir Gui, I expect," Father Matthew said suddenly, lowering the message.

"*Pigeons*, Matthew?" he exclaimed, stunned. "*Pigeons?* Are you mad? You eat pigeons, not fly 'em about like a kite on a string!"

"No, Gui. The Arabs have been using them for generations to keep themselves informed about troop movements throughout the Holy Land. Most Crusaders are too hide-bound with their own supposed superiority to barbarian infidels to give it a thought. But that's what this is," he said, holding it up again. "A message to be carried by a pigeon. I've seen them before during my time in Persia. Tiny, very fine paper, rolled up and placed in a minute brass cylinder and tied to the pigeon's leg or behind its wing. And a pigeon can fly as fast as a falcon. Same sickle shaped wings, hundreds of miles in a day some of them. Have to be trained though, and expensive! Someone surely wanted you stopped, Gui. And very badly."

"That bastard, de Brocas." Sir Richard cut in. "The *so* good and friendly Lord Baron of Narbonne and Gruissan!"

"Sir Richard is right, Gui," the tall Benedictine said in his soft Spanish lilt. "There is no-one else on whom this disaster can be pinned. I think that we will need to be extra careful as we journey south from Nantes. If Baron Roger can get at us out here, on the very edge of the Atlantic, and I'd wager my best woollen cloak that it's him, he can probably get at us anywhere!"

"Dear God…is there no end to his wicked scheming? He got two of his people into Castle Malwood that we now know of, so how many others, I wonder? For surely those two fucking 'Cousins', could not have done this," he said, taking the tiny roll from Father Matthew's hands. "They had neither the brains nor the patient skill!"

16

"No, no finesse," Father Matthew, agreed softly. "This took precision and brains...and expertise. And I think I know who," he added to everyone's surprise. "Mmmm, very clever. I saw what they wanted us to see. *Monsieur le Baron* is very good at that..."

"Who?" Gui asked, astonished.

"Those two we watched from the gatehouse roof the other day. The ones with the goose on a string..."

"And a box of pigeons on a donkey that you thought were chickens!"

"By God and the Pheasant, so we did!" Gui exclaimed then, banging his hands together. "And it was Alicia who put us right. The clever bastards!"

"No matter, dear boy," Sir Richard said calmly, "there's no point in getting excited now. Forewarned is forearmed. They will not take us by surprise again. That lad of mine, young Davy Coulter, and John Fitzurse, bless him, deserve a gold coin each for this day's work. That knowledge could yet save us all!"

"Right, my friends," Gui said then, "Back to work!"

"That's right, Lords," Thomas said, giving him a terrific buffet as spoke. "If we don't keep bailing...and pumping, this old tub is going to go down! And it's time I got some sail on her. God knows what Robert is doing on the *Pride*, she looks like a drunken whore at a wedding...and we're not much better, but if we are to make Nantes before dark we need to get this old girl moving. Yarley, my boys! *Yarely!*" he roared out then, throwing his arms wide as he did so. "Come on you whoreson bastards, move yourselves, or I'll throw the next man overboard!" And with that their meeting swiftly broke up.

As the others left, Sir Richard watched Gui flex his left arm and massage his shoulder again where the Baron's arrow had been cut out. "How's the wound?"

"Oh, not so bad," Gui said, wincing as he rotated it. "But I could do without that bear of a man thumping it the way he does!" he added with a grimace. "God's blood, but he has a hard hand," he added with a rueful grin. "Matthew said it would be stiff. He has some sort of foul ointment to rub in later. Smells like horse shit!"

"Well," Sir Richard laughed, "in my experience the worst a medicine tastes or smells the better it often does you. Stop moaning. A little more of this sunshine and you'll be fine. I thought you moved well today. Not much wrong with you then!"

"Well, there goes the sail," Gui said, still rubbing his shoulder as the great mains'l came down with a clatter. "Surely now we can get moving? And what in Heaven's name is happening over there?" he added, pointing at the *Pride*, still showing little sail as she rolled about near the shallows, sheets

17

flying everywhere. "Those bastards will be aground in a moment if they're not careful!"…*And serve them right after losing Alicia to El Nazir and his gang of bloody murderers! Just wait 'til I get my hands on them!*

"Never fear, my Lord," Thomas Blackwood boomed at him, his rolling walk carrying him lightly back towards him across the Mary's deck. "Adam and the crew have been busy. See, the mains'l is down now," he pointed to where his men were even then running back down the ratl'ns. "They'll have it sheeted hard and under control again in moments, and I shall have the old *Mary* back under command again at last.

"But gently, gently, Sir Gui. I have no wish to rip anything away, and we are still half-a-day's sailing from the Loire, and the best part of the rest to Nantes. And as for the *Pride*? She seems to be under command herself now," he said, pointing to where she was manoeuvring herself through the channels between the rocks. "Robert Christchurch's a good Master, my Lord. Knows what he is doing. He'll be up to us shortly, you'll see. Then we will know more! Meanwhile keep your lads pumping…*and bailing*!" he roared at the men over his shoulder as he rolled away to take the tiller, adding: *"Don't want to be fish food before dinner!"*

And with a great burst of laughter, he bent to hurl a whole shattered section of the *Mary's* sterncastle over the side as if it were mere kindling from the forest, before laying his great hands on the tough tiller bar, to turn her broken head towards her canary consort, now at last moving to join them, and away from the drifting corpses and smashed debris that marked their desperate struggle with EL Nazir's corsairs.

Chapter 4...How the Red and Yellow Cogs set sail for the Loire.

Four cables away, on board the *Pride*, there was a deep feeling of dejection and shame.

She had not been as badly damaged as the *Mary*, just her forecastle smashed about and a great chunk taken out of her starboard side...but she had not been holed on the waterline. There was no water pouring in. And while the men had fought like demons, leaving the deck littered with bodies, great splashes and pools of blood everywhere, they had still lost the two most precious charges for which they had been especially chosen, and all felt the loss of honour keenly.

The Lady Alicia de Burley and Mistress Agnes Fitzwalter had been ripped from amongst them as if they were children, and they had been unable to prevent it. Men they had trusted had proven to be traitors, and they all felt responsible, not knowing what to say to Sir Gui, nor how he would take the vicious theft from amongst them of someone so special to him, and of her close companion.

One moment they had been cheering on their comrades on the *Mary*...the next they had been under attack themselves as the great dromond had swept down upon them, almost from nowhere it seemed: had hurled two great rocks into them, boarded them, seized hold of Alicia and Agnes, cut herself free...and then was gone in a moment! *Dear God...what will Sir Gui think of us?*

The men couldn't believe it.

Allan-i-the-Wood, and Hordle John, couldn't believe it. The Lady Alicia gone...Allan's little Agnes gone too!...*Poor, lovely lass. What will they do to her? How can we get her back? And, God's Blood! What will Sir Gui say to us now?*

With the great dromond now gone as swiftly as she had appeared, Allan looked around at his command. Many were still stood staring, dazed, after their attacker, now pulling rapidly away from Sir Gui's ship. The *Mary* herself, now left wallowing in a following sea, sterncastle battered, forecastle almost demolished...and with a great rent in her side low-down across her port waterline...was already listing. What it must be like on board her now, the young Under Sheriff could only guess at!

As for themselves, with the *Pride's* Master slain, and the ship herself still not under anyone's command, unless the crew did something soon they would pile up amongst the rocks and all would be lost...*Not for me a watery grave today!*...So, swiftly turning, Allan-i-the-Wood roared at the mate, then standing motionless looking down at the vast pool of blood around Robert Christchurch's broken body: "*Simon Cooper!* Are you the Master's Mate on board this fucking tub, or just a bloody loafer?"

Hanging by a mere thread of gristle, truly The Master's head was a gruesome sight, and the two shattered carcases of the men so brutally hacked down on either side of him were not much better. Blood and tissue everywhere, shards of bone and gobbets of flesh. Altogether they were enough to stun any man. Now shocked out of his trance, the Mate replied sharply: "*Aye,* Sir!"

"Then jump about, *damn your eyes!* Do you want to walk ashore?"

"*No*, Sir!"

"*Then don't just stand there, you idle bastard!*" Allan roared again, jabbing his hand furiously at him. "Get the fucking crew working! *NOW!* Before we pile up on those bloody rocks and become part of the scenery!"

"But...the Master..."

"The Master is *dead*, Simon! *You* are in command of the *Pride* now, until Tommy Blackwood says otherwise. So, jump to it, man. The *Mary's* in a bloody mess and needs us. And right now this tub is wallowing about like a drunken whore at a wedding! *So get your bastard lads working!*" He shouted at him in frustration. "Hordle John, *to me!*"

With that, as if stabbed with a hot iron, Simon snapped back to life, shouting at his crew, themselves no less laggard, who ran to the sheets and halliards to bring the sail under control; while two of the Lions dragged the Master's body to the rail in a long smear of blood and swiftly tossed it overboard, followed by the bodies of the two men who had been told to guard him. Then, as the *Pride* continued to drift helplessly towards the shore, driven by the tides and currents, Simon took a firm hold of the great tiller bar. Shouting to his men to seize the quants, kept for the very purpose of poling her off any rocks that she might draw close to, he furiously worked the rudder to and fro to try and keep some way on the *Pride* until her sails could fill and real way be got on her once more.

Meanwhile, on the main deck, the Under Sheriff and Hordle John also got their men moving: dragging the corpses to the side, there being none living after the action, and quickly throwing them over. Severed limbs and hands the same, while the crew swabbed down the decks with buckets of water drawn up from the sea, 'til there was a bloody froth all round the Pride's fat hull.

20

"How are we doing, John?" the burly Under-Sheriff asked the giant swordsman, coming up to him as he finished mucking out his horse. "Oh, fair to middling, Master Allan," Hordle John replied, turning to lean back against Caesar's stall. "The lads have cleared the decks. Helped got rid of the bodies, plucked out the arrows and are now trying to keep out of the way of the crew. After you gave that sodding Mate such a fucking bollocking, his lads have been up an' down those ratl'ns like squirrels after nuts!" And he laughed

"And about time too! If I hadn't bawled at that stupid bugger, we'd've been on those bloody rocks in no time! Dear God, John. What a fucking mess!"

"Yes, Master Allan. Not clever, is it? Gawd alone knows what Sir Gui will say when we get up to him. Sweet Jesus, Fitzurse was right..."

"Right? What about?" Allan asked him sharply.

"About those two bastard Frenchmen. They bloody Cousins. He said he didn't wholly trust 'em. But what else could I do? Sir Gui told me to put the girls in their care, and the moment that bloody great galley came at us, that's what I did. Put 'em in the Master's cabin and told those two sods to guard' em with their lives! Those were my orders. Then we were hit by their bloody artillery, next Lady Alicia was screamin' her head off, with two of your lads hacked down and the Master almost cut in two before her eyes, blood everywhere, and a moment later we was boarded! I dunno' Master Allan, if there were anythin' more we could've done?" And they both paused then, their minds filled with the violent images of the attack.

"I saw all that, John, and came running. But by then there seemed to be hordes of the buggers between us and the girls. No matter how many we killed or shot down, Bouncer going for them tooth and claw, Agnes screaming out, *To me, Lions! To me!*" and kicking and biting for all she was worth. But those two fucking bastards had them both trapped and off onto that bloody great galley before we could even get to the stern rail. Then they were gone! Hate what happened as I do, that was the swiftest piece of piracy I've ever witnessed! But how can we explain that all to Sir Gui and still keep our heads...I don't know? Anyway, John, what's the butcher's bill?"

"You may find this hard to believe, Master Allan. But, apart from the Master and those two poor bastards either side of 'im...We've only lost eight other men, and two of those were crew! Lots of cuts and bruises, some of them really nasty that might yet turn sour, and a few bites!" he added with a grin, looking down at Bouncer, now frolicking among the men. "But no more lives. And even those badly hacked about might be saved once Father Matthew can get a hold of 'em."

"That's a gift from God if ever I heard of one," Allan-i-the-Wood replied, eyebrows raised. "Given the numbers we slaughtered, I thought we'd been really hammered! Someone up there must love us. So, well done the lads…yours and mine! Sorry about Bouncer, he just got a bit carried away!"

"No worries, Sir. The lads love 'im; they'll not take a few bites amiss. And, yes Sir, they did do well! Really well, especially as this is the first time in a proper fight for most of 'em. Different from a dust-up outside the George and Dragon on a Saturday night, that's for certain," and the two men laughed. "But right now they're feeling as fucked-up about Lady Alicia and Mistress Fitzwalter as we are. Taken it real bad. No matter how you look at it we failed in our duty. It will take a lot to cheer 'em up, I can tell you."

"Well, we will just have to see what we can do. Sir Gui is as fair a man as I have ever met, and Sir Richard too. It may not be as bad as we are all thinking," and he banged the big man on his shoulder. Then turning to look outboard at the *Mary* listing more heavily to port even as he watched, he growled tersely, "What the hell is that bloody Simon up to? Surely we should be moving properly by now?"

And so they were, but for all his initial hesitancy at the start, Simon was a good Mate. He had been with Master Robert for some years, and knew the *Pride's* ways, and how to handle her in cramped waters, so he had kept the sail well brailed up, enough to give him steerage way, but not enough to allow her to run onto the rocks that were all around them. With a man up in the main chains by the anchor with a lead and line to call the depths, and others standing by with the long, thick quant poles to fend her off any rocks, he was confidently feeling his way through the narrow channels around the base of Houat, but only moving slowly, before spreading more sail and turning towards the *Mary*, now well down by the head.

Even from four cables out, everyone could see she was in serious trouble. Her forecastle practically demolished, sterncastle badly damaged, and a great gash in her port side right on the waterline…and with those on board running about throwing things into the sea, the *Mary* looked beyond saving.

"What are they doing, Simon?" Allan asked urgently, striding across the deck. "And why aren't we sailing faster?"…*Sweet Jesus, if we lose Sir Gui now it will all be over!*

"They're lightening the ship, Master Allan. Trying to get that gurt great hole above the water line. And until we are clear of they rocks, and out of these narrow channels, we can do no more. Then we can let the old *Pride* have a bit more sail and we'll be up to the *Mary* soonest, I assure you. I might have been a bit slow off the mark at the start, Master Under Sheriff, but I know the old *Pride* well and I know what I'm doin'. Me and my lads'll not let you down. Trust me!"

"And so I will, Simon. So I will!" And Allan gave the man a confident smile as he spoke.

"What're they doing now, Master Simon?" Hordle John called to him moments later as they twisted out of the last channel. "What's that they have hanging on her side?"

"Looks like a fother," Simon called back to him, shading his eyes against the sun and the flickering glare off the sea. "Their spare winter sail I expect. Thicker canvas. Master Thomas has done it before. When the old *Mary* got holed below the waterline off Falmouth roads some years back. If they can get that over her port side, pulled under her and hauled up tight the other, they can cover that hole. That'll stop most of the water coming in. Look! There it goes. Now we'll see. We're clear of the last channel now. Bravely done, lads, *bravely done!*" he shouted to his crew. "Loose some more sail, and let's get this fucking tub moving."

*

Moments later they all heard a great roar of triumph burst out from the *Mary*, and shortly after saw her crew race up the ratlines, her sail begin to break out and her head gently come round towards the distant shoreline. Seeing which, Simon shifted his tiller over to meet her, ordering his crew to spill the wind out of the *Pride's* sails and heave-to so the *Mary* could meet up with her consort at last.

Releasing the tiller to another senior crew member, Simon ran to the rail where Allan-i-the-Wood and Hordle John swiftly joined him, both ships settling down less than a fifty yards apart, neither Master wanting their ships to be too close for fear of doing further damage.

"*Ho there, Simon!*" Thomas Blackwood roared out. "Lost a bit here and there then? Where's Master Robert?"

"*Dead!* Cut down by those two French bastards who took the girls. One moment all was well and we were nearly there, the next moment Robert and the two men beside him were hacked down, we were bombarded out of nowhere, and all hell broke loose!"

"That's bad, Simon. He was a good man," Thomas shouted back to him. "So that's why you went out of control?"

"Yes, Master Thomas! The moment Master Robert was cut down he let go of the tiller, the *Pride's* head came up into the wind, and she was in irons."

"What happened then?" Sir Gui called across, cupping his hands so his voice would carry above the crying gulls dipping and wheeling above, as they swooped onto the sudden harvest floating all around them.

"Alicia screamed!" Allan-i-the-Wood shouted his reply. "She saw Master Robert and two of my men hacked down before her eyes, and screamed her head off! But before we could reach her those two French bastards had seized her and Agnes, the galley grappled us athwart the tiller, and hordes of the buggers poured on board."

"The lads fought like demons, Sir Gui," John of Hordle bawled across at his commander. "You would have been proud of them, Sir Richard. They fought like the lions on their chests! And we drove them back right to the stern. Thought we were winning, slaughtered them, bodies everywhere, while all the time they were just withdrawing."

"Yes! We saw that. Saw them all leaping off you...thought you were winning!"

"So did we...But by then the infidel bastards had what they'd come for, my Lord," Allan-i-the-Wood shouted. "Jules and Lucas had seized both girls right from the start. And despite doing all we could, with the girls shouting, kicking and biting, they carried them across to the other ship like washing bundles.

"Why didn't our archers just shoot the buggers down?" Gui roared out at him.

"Because they couldn't get a clear shot, my Lord! Dared not with the girls so kicking and wriggling in the way. Then they cut themselves free, outed their oars and were off like a fox after a rabbit. We all feel dreadful, my Lord. *Shamed by it!* But the lads did all they could. Truly. It just wasn't enough!"

"But I blame myself, my Lord," Hordle John shouted again. "As soon as they attacked I did as you had ordered and put the girls in the Master's cabin and told those two buggers to guard her with their lives. *But they were traitors, my Lords!*" He exclaimed in great distress. "Tied some green silk on the stern, put on green arm bands, slaughtered the Master and grabbed the girls. If I had kept them with me they would have been safe. I'm so sorry, Sir Gui. Bastards! *Bastards!*"

"Don't feel so bad about it, John, though I admit I cursed you all at the time...but they nearly did for us too. You can see what damage they did, and we had twice the men on board. You can't be blamed for carrying out my orders. We both trusted the wrong men! Take it off your backs, all of you, and stop beating yourselves up. None of that will help Alicia...nor Agnes. What

24

we've got to do now is get to land. Anywhere if necessary, but Nantes if we can. Master Thomas thinks that's possible as long as we don't go too fast and rip the fother off, the sea doesn't suddenly get up, or the sky fall on our heads!" And there was a general laugh.

"What's the tally, Master Sheriff?" Matthew called to him. "Do you have many injured?"

"Lots of cuts and bruises and several nasty wounds. Even some bites, I'm afraid. Bouncer got a bit carried away. But they'll live till you can get to them. But, with God's Grace, Father...Sir Gui...apart from poor Master Robert and the two men beside him, we only lost six more troopers and two of the crew! Good skills and training, and a lot of luck! How about you?"

"Only eight altogether? That's excellent. We thought you'd been slaughtered. Much the same, here. We lost twelve...and six badly injured. Thomas lost several too when their stones took out the forecastle. Seems we both got off lightly!"

"So, Master Thomas," Simon Cooper hallooed him. "Where away next? With that fother you'll need to go gently. We should be able to keep close to you all the way."

"With the wind where it is, and how it is, we ought to make the Loire. It's only fifty miles or so, and the sea and currents are with us hereabouts. We'll steer for the Horse Islands and then turn in closer to the coast...but as you say, we must take it slowly. Once we're into the estuary, and out of the sea, we should be safe and able to show a bit more canvas. With God's Will, we might still actually get in to Nantes tonight as long as we don't lose the wind. So harrow away, lad. Get your boys on their feet. *And you lot,*" he roared, turning back to his own ship, and the cheerful faces of the men she carried, "*keep bloody bailing!*" And a wave of laughter burst from them all.

And as his crew leaped to do his bidding, so the giant shipmaster strode back to the *Mary's* great tiller bar, and with the wind steady in her coat-tails from the north-west, the sun tilted over the meridian and the sea still a deep shimmering blue, crests foamed with white, the *Mary* finally turned her fat scarlet body towards the shore, her yellow consort close to hand.

*

Behind them, on that hot July afternoon, the scattered wreckage of their fierce encounter with El Nazir's corsairs wallowed in the long Atlantic rollers as they lazily swelled towards the shore. For as they swept

25

towards the land they gently turned it all up and over: an arm, a leg, a box of stores; oars and whole pieces of shattered hull...and eyeless corpses, hundreds of them, the sockets empty, stark black holes within each white and water-wrinkled face. And above and all around them the gulls screamed and swooped and gabbled over the human debris left in the *Mary's* wake as she pushed towards the Loire, the *Pride of Beaulieu* by her side.

Chapter 5...Sir Gui arrives at Nantes.

B y the time the sun began to sink through a cloudless azure sky towards the far horizon in a blaze of crimson-orange flame, the two great cogs had long passed the Horse Islands and the Cardinals, and turned their fat bellies to draw closer to the shore.

With the *Mary* leading, her crew and Gui's command still furiously bailing, both ships sailed slowly down the coast, dipping their shoulders into the long rollers from across the Atlantic, their wakes leaving a torn blue-white track the mewling seabirds still followed.

Behind her The *Pride*, too, dipped and swayed across the edges of that great ocean, the shore a mottled green and brown line of rolling downs, white sands and rocky coves as she reeled steadily past. Small groups of houses, like squares of white cheese on a coloured plate, their red roof tiles a brilliant splash of life, showed where villages and hamlets lay half-hidden amongst the hills. And from time to time small fleets of fishing boats, their brightly painted hulls like darting rainbows beneath white and dun coloured sails, bustled around the not too distant shore, nets cast between them or long lines hanging over their sides.

The Bay of Biscay, so often wild and turbulent, was more kindly that day. The sea sparkled beneath the westering sun, the deep troughs shark-blue and green, as the *Mary* pushed her shattered stem up the wide estuary of the Loire that would take them safely up to Nantes at last.

Beneath the ruined forecastle, Father Matthew was still busy plying his trade, binding the wounds of those who had come to him for help, rubbing in salves and herbal oils, and stitching and splinting those few who had been more seriously injured, his hands and apron red with blood, his brow furrowed with concentration and concern. Soothing and encouraging, he moved amongst the men, especially those now coming to him with torn and blistered hands from the constant bailing and pumping.

Seeing Gui and Richard beckoning him as they left the hustle of the main deck, back to the damaged sterncastle, he smiled, acknowledging their invitation with a helpless shrug of his shoulders as he gestured around him at the many men he was still tending, too busy just then to talk. And it was a while before he could leave what he was doing and come across with Jean de Beaune to join them.

"How are things, Gui?" he asked calmly, dipping his bloodied hands into a bucket of salt water before drying them on a piece of rough linen at his side.

27

"And how is the fother holding?" he added, pointing to where Thomas Blackwood and Adam were looking at it over the side.

"It's alright, Father, still there, just about. But the lads have to keep at the bailing and pumping, turn and turnabout. He's more worried about that rock still in her side," he added as their ship master moved to examine it. "If that comes loose we'll be in trouble all over again!"

"We're lucky it's not worse! Our boys are now producing blisters for me to salve as well as wounds. Much more and you'll have no fit men left to command."

"Fine Job's Comforter you are, Father," L'Eveque drawled at him, stretched out on a pile of leather byrnies and hauberks, arms behind his head, the sun flickering off his blood stained armour and soiled cyclas. "You're just the rain cloud I need on a picnic afternoon! At least we're still afloat!"

"For the time being at least!" de Beaune said, picking his teeth as the *Mary* suddenly lifted and bobbled over the tumbling race that marked where river met the sea, the *Pride* following her, dipping and tilting as she too crossed the bar; the change in water, from deep, rolling swells and chopped waves, to the more gently, ruffled surface of the estuary easing her motion enormously.

At that their Ship Master, like the great bear he was, came booming up beside them. "Well, my Lords? Well? We bloody made it!*"* And he banged his hands together with a mighty *clap!* "And despite a few mild panics along the way, that fother held too. And with the quieter water at last we can now show some more sail."

"Thomas, I owe you more than I can say," Gui said, grasping the Master's great calloused hand with a huge grin. "Well done, my bully! *Well done!"*

"Thank you, my Lord! I said I'd get you here…and I have done. And, Sir Gui, you owe me nothing. I did it as much for your father, God Bless him, as I did for you."

"All the same, Thomas, I will leave you with plenty to repair both ships. That's the very least I can do. And money for the families of those lads you lost today. How much longer before we reach Nantes?"

"And can the lads stop bailing?" Sir Richard added, sitting up on his elbows.

"It's thirty miles up this river according to my charts, Sir Gui. And if this wind keeps steady, and nothing finally carries away, about three hours, four at most. About Vespers, I'd say," he added looking at the sun. "And about the money, my Lord. Thank you!"

"And the lads, Thomas?"

"Right now, Sir Richard," and turning, he roared across the deck. "*Avast bailing you idle bastards!* And you can stop the pumps too unless I think she needs it. All right, my Lord?"

"Yes, Master Thomas, and thank you," he drawled with a smile.

"Right, my Lords. Now we're in smooth water at last, I'll chase my men up those ratlin's and get some more canvas on her!" And tipping his head he turned and rolled across the deck, shouting and roaring as he went, his crew galvanised into action as he called their names, his Mate, Adam, taking the *Mary's* great tiller in his own hard hands.

And as the men shook out the reefs that had held her sails back, Gui and his commanders watched as their men threw down their bailers at last. Some came to the *Mary's* side to watch her sail up the broad expanses of calmer water and gaze at the distant banks on either side, like open arms ready to enfold them, cheerfully exclaiming at every new and unusual sight; while others just fell back and lay slumped and exhausted on the torn deck. The *Pride* too, in all her bold, canary glory sailed close behind them, her broad sail, with its great ram's head, also spread further to catch the wind.

"So!" Gui exclaimed, rubbing his hands together briskly, his chain mail mittens hanging from his wrists. "A few more hours and we'll be on our way at last!"...*Off this tub and away after Alicia. I can't wait!*

"Is that wise, Gui? Father Matthew questioned him quietly, gesturing to the many men behind him slumped across the deck.

"Those lads are pretty beat-up, my Lord," de Beaune added. "And we need 'em fresh. I've campaigned in France, Sir Gui. It's not England!"

"Oh, come on, Jean," Gui sighed. "You're as bad as our good Benedictine here. What's the matter with you all?"

"Oh, just feeling a bit weary, I suppose. Lost four of my best men too!" the swarthy Burgundian sighed ruefully, leaning against a broken stanchion. "But nothing, I suppose, that a jar of warm red, a hot tasty meal and a pretty girl wouldn't cure."

"And a soft bed!" Sir Richard added with a groan. "This has been a real bugger of a day, Gui! We are all worn out and fed-up. Bruised, battered and ashamed. We've lost the girls, most of our stores are bobbing about the Atlantic, and the men are crocked. Look at them," he urged him, gesturing over his shoulder. "They've shot their bolt, dear boy!" he exclaimed, picking up a dropped crossbow and shaking it at him with his lazy grin. "We've lost over a tenth of our forces today, and many are wounded. There must be the best part of four hundred miles still to go from here to Narbonne: over half the length of England! And you ask what's wrong?"...*For God's sake, man, use your bloody head!*

29

"Gui...Sir Richard's right," Father Matthew said firmly, standing up. "Especially now we're so nearly there, despite all that the good Baron has tried to do to us," he added bitterly. "I know you want to press on as fast as you can. So do we all. But even if we make Nantes tonight, it will be after sunset. We have neither horses for the men, nor wagons...and we need them, Gui. And we need to replace the stores we threw overboard as well. And, above all, we need a good meal and a proper night's rest. These men will be no good to you if they are faced with another fight like today's without it."

"Same for the horses, my Lord," Fitzurse added, as he came to stand before him. "They won't come off easy after all this, not Beau and Merlin...Sunburst and the rest. Give us twenty four hours at least, my Lord. To get properly sorted, replace lost equipment and rest the lads...then leave the day after tomorrow, first light."...*Come on Sir Gui. For pity's sake, do the right thing. The old Lord would never have risked everything at the first throw.*

There was a pause then, as they all looked at Gui, and waited, Sir Richard in particular looking at him with a wry smile, remembering what Father Matthew had said earlier about getting him to stop!

Gui looked at their serious faces, his mind already half made up: Matthew, steady, looking at him through half closed eyes; Richard with that quizzical, raised eyebrow of his; Fitzurse concerned, de Beaune resigned...and grimaced. "Oh...very well!" he exclaimed, standing up to look out across the *Mary's* bows as she moved in towards the river at last, the huge estuary now behind her. "I value what you've said, and you are all quite right, of course. Sir Yvo would never have pressed on regardless at the start of such a long campaign."

And smiling at the sigh of relief that had swept around him, he took a deep breath he said. "So...we'll take *three* days here, not one, and leave on the fourth morning.

"But look, all of you," he went on as they gasped in pleased surprise. "It's obvious that de Brocas has no intention of letting us get to Narbonne if he can possibly avoid it. So whatever you do once we've landed, keep the men under arms...and under control. Brittany is still a part of the Empire that Henry left to Richard. After all, his third son, Geoffrey, was Prince of it so we should be quite safe, but de Brocas may have spies everywhere. Anything could happen...just look at today? And don't waste it, for this will be the last stop before Bordeaux."

"It's a shame we can't all sleep on board," Father Matthew said, getting to his feet.

"No, Father!" Sir Richard said, stretching lugubriously. "No! *Absolutely not!* Before we set out for the best part of three weeks' filthy, dusty travelling across half of France, maybe more with wagons in tow, and no doubt sleeping on hard ground, come rain or shine…or in whatever bug-ridden, disgusting flea pit we can find along the way, I want three decent nights between the sheets. You may be used to a stone cell and Spartan living, Matthew, and you can sleep here if you like. *But not me!*"

"Well, some will have to," Gui said tersely. "We brought four wagons loaded with gear when we set out, and while most of that may well be bobbing about the Atlantic just now, the sumpters and their panniers are still with us on the *Pride,* along with Sunburst and Gillygate. And if we leave any of that unguarded… then by morning it will all be gone.

"We need stabling for the horses, those we have with us and those we will need to buy…and they will need to be watched too. Fitzurse, you, Jean, and our good Under Sherriff, can sort out who goes where amongst the lads. But leave Hordle John in charge on board, it will be good for him, and choose another of your likely lads to be with the horses. Then you and Allan-i-the-Wood must come and join Sir Richard, Father Matthew and me at the sign of the Angel on the north bank of the river, just across from the Île de Nantes."

"How do you know of such a place?" the tall Benedictine asked astonished. "You've never been there before!"

"Goodness me, Father," Gui grinned broadly, "a hole in your knowledge at last? I am almost bereft of speech!" and he tilted his head. "Tommy Blackwood, of course. He knows *everything!*" And they all laughed.

"How are we for money, Gui?" L'Eveque asked him lazily. "It will not be cheap to stay at an inn, feed the lads, buy horses, especially good ones, and carts, if we can find 'em. And there is no point in buying a collection of broken-winded, spavined old nags for the job we have in hand either. We'll need good solid mounts…and with a turn of speed in 'em too if possible!"

"That won't be a problem in Nantes," Matthew said, leaning over the side, watching as the *Mary* entered the river proper at last, the wind still creaming her along nicely, no water now spurting from around the fother. "They are famous horse breeders here."

"And how do you know that, Father?" Gui asked him, surprised.

"Oh," he said with a grin, tapping the side of his nose. "I know everything, remember?" And they all laughed. "In all truth, Gui," he added a moment later. "I have been through here before. There is a Benedictine Abbey at Vertou, just outside the city. The Abbot there, Father Hugo Gravier, will give us all the help we need. He'll make sure you're offered good horses to buy, and will put us all up for a night or two as well if needed. Don't forget I have the authority of the Holy Father in my scrip!"

31

"And those two horse doctors of ours," Sir Richard broke in. "Paul of Bartley and William Fisher, they can go with him. About time they earned their keep."

"That's excellent," the tall monk said, flicking back his cowl. "Abbot Hugh will be delighted. He is horse mad for all his calling. And there's also a castle of sorts. But its gates will be closed by the time we moor-up. And there is no curfew in Nantes because of the port. And because you hold the King's Warrant, we won't have to pay port dues or local taxes either!"

"That is excellent news! Is there anything you don't know, Matthew?" Gui asked him with a smile.

"Apart from dockside inns," Sir Richard said laconically, with a quirked eyebrow and his lazy smile.

"Oh, this and that," the black monk replied, looking at Sir Richard's long sprawled figure with a laugh. "How about you, my good Lord of Malwood?" And he tilted his head gravely while the others laughed.

"Not much!" Gui yawned, leaning his back against the shattered remains of the stern castle, while he watched the *Mary* pushing upriver. "I am just a simple knight! Old Father Gerome gave up on me years ago. Said I was borne to plague the life out of him, poor old boy. Alicia was the one with all the brains!" And thinking of her, he sighed...*and where are you now, my darling?*..."Still, my father taught me to fight, keep account of everything and the importance of planning, and mother taught me to care for people, so I didn't do too badly...which is why we came so well prepared. So money is not a problem, yet. The two strong boxes we brought with us are filled, and if we need more, we can seek out a Templar House as I said before we left Malwood. Sir Yvo made a big deposit in London and I have his mark with me against our needs."

"That little escapade with that bastard, El Nazir, has set us back weeks," Richard said. "Even if we get the horses we want, we'll now have to journey overland to Bordeaux, and by the time we get there de Brocas will be long gone."

"He's been gone weeks already," Gui replied, "So a few more won't make much difference."

"It's nearly two hundred miles to Bordeaux from Nantes," Matthew broke in. "I know, I did it with your father, years ago: pretty wild countryside, with lots of small villages along the way, very twisted trackways and several small rivers until Bordeaux...we should aim for forty miles a day, say five days."

"We'll bugger the horses at that rate," Sir Richard said, stretching his arms out languorously as he spoke. "So why not push 'em a bit harder and cut a

32

little more time off the journey. We're going to have to buy more at Bordeaux at that rate anyway. Four days."

"Because your way will bugger the men as well, My Lord!" de Beaune chipped in. "You've not travelled long distances in France before. I have, and as I said, it's not like England, soft and green even in summer. And with all due respect to Father Matthew, I bet when he travelled with Sir Yvo they had no wagons with them? Seven days...even ten!"...*And that might be pushing it!*

"Mmm, you're quite right, Jean. We didn't...just he and me and a sumpter apiece. Well noticed!"

"Thank you, Father. And we are going even further south, my Lord. It will be hard, hot, and very dusty, and water will be a problem. These lads are all we have, and they have already taken a beating. Of course, Sir Gui...Sir Richard, it's up to you, but allow a week to ten days and I'll guarantee we'll *all* get to Bordeaux in one piece...short of another fracas like this one today. There's no point in pushing everyone so hard that they're worth nothing when we get there."...*And I can't say fairer than that. Now I'll see what kind of a leader we really have!*

"That is good advice, Jean," Gui said after a moment's thought. "I can see why Mercardier recommended you to me." Then tapping Sir Richard's mailed feet with his toes, he added. "It would be wonderful to get there more quickly, Richard, but we have Beau and your Merlin to think of too, as well as the girls' mares and the men, and I don't want any charger but my own under me when I meet de Brocas!"

With a languid groan his tall guard commander got to his feet at last, and came to stand beside Gui, resting his arms on the *Mary's* scored rails, as they both looked at the distant banks of the Loire, leaving the others to talk amongst themselves.

*

By chance they had crossed the bar at the height of the tide, and with the wind still in their tails, and Thomas having set more sail as they entered the smooth waters of the great River Loire, as he'd said he would, they might even make Nantes before sunset.

He, too, wanted to get to Narbonne as soon as possible, and Merlin was his favourite, huge and strong, good natured but a terrific fighter when called upon, and not to be risked unwisely. He could see him now, ears pricked forward, huffing through his nose, looking for his master, and he turned towards Gui then, and smiled.

"You do know, Gui," he said seriously, with no affectation. "There is no way we could have left anywhere tonight. No matter how much you might have wanted to. We all need a proper rest after this morning…especially the wounded. It's not lack of courage, Gui, nor lack of desire. You know I will follow you anywhere, anytime. Just prudence and a simple question of basic logistics: we have lost most of our stores and equipment, have no carts and no horses either. And, as Jean said, these lads are all we've got right now, and we need to take a bit of care with them, or we'll never get to the Baron's bloody Château in one piece. You nearly pushed me in to a nasty corner, dear boy!"

"Yes, Richard. I know that," his friend said, turning to face him, placing a meaty hand on his shoulder. "I have *never* doubted you, Richard: your loyalty, nor your bravery and courage, for all your lazy ways, my friend, they don't fool me. I know how organised you are, how fierce you are in battle! When danger threatens, Richard, there is no man I would rather have to guard my back. And the lads look up to you and trust you, as I do. I just want to get there so badly that I am in danger of becoming reckless! So…you are *all* right. And in the end training will out. I could hear the Old Man's voice in my ear as clearly as you could. I know," he added with a rueful smile. "I saw you quirk your eyebrow at me. Sir Yvo was never wrong in his advice. And what he didn't hammer into me, Baron John de Methley did in Yorkshire, and up by the wall in Northumbria where we campaigned together. So, of course we must regroup, rest and get things properly sorted. I promised I wouldn't let you down, Richard. Nor the lads…nor their people at home, and nor will I.

"Nevertheless we'll still have to treat this whole journey as if we were in enemy territory with a bandit behind every tree or boulder that we pass. What about our wounded?" he asked, turning to their black-clad physician, just coming up to join them.

"They'll keep up," the tall monk said quietly. "Don't you worry, Gui. Trust me, they'll be fine. I've not lost a man yet whom I didn't expect to. They can always travel in a wagon if necessary. And well done for this morning, Gui, your father would have been proud. And even prouder for your decision to rest the men before pushing on."

"Well…the old buzzard was right, Father. He always held it was right to make sure of your ground before you jumped! *'Beware the tiger in the long grass'*, he used to say…'though where he ever saw one I've no idea. But the beast certainly impressed him because he never would set out for anywhere without first considering all the complications. And: *'never employ a dog and bark yourself!'* So little point in listening to the advice of my commanders and

34

then completely ignoring it…well, mostly anyway! He would have given me such a bollocking! I can hear him doing it too!" And they all laughed, remembering the Old Lord and his choleric outbursts with affection.

"However, gentlemen; when we do leave," he said tersely, "I will expect everyone to keep up. The wounded as well, Matthew," he added firmly to the dark-robed Benedictine. "Even if we have to tie them to their saddles, 'though I don't think anyone is that badly hurt. But it is going to be really hard on everyone. So remind the lads, Fitzurse," he said, turning back to his Master-at-Arms. "That they've all been hand-picked for this trip, and I don't expect them to go soft on us now. We have to get to Narbonne as soon as possible, and then on to the Château Grise to smoke that bloody fox from his lair. I tell you, I won't rest 'til I hold Alicia safely in my arms again if I have to wade through rivers of blood to do it!"

"What about that bit of extra for the men, Sir Gui?" Fitzurse reminded him, then. "Now with a bit of time to 'play' as it were, that would be good for all of them."

"Well thought of, John. And those flagons as well. So wine tonight and silver for the lads tomorrow out of the small strong box. How does that all sound?"

"Good to me, my Lord. Thank you. Now if Jean will come with me, we'll get those lists sorted out before we reach the port," and with a smile he and the tall Burgundian leader turned and walked away, the others crossing the *Mary* to watch their progress from the shattered forecastle, while Thomas and his crew worked her up the river, the *Pride* following.

Chapter 6...Sir Gui defies Sir Alan de Courcy and the Chef du Port.

Three hours later they reached Nantes safely at last, just as the sun slowly dipped below the hills and the trees around them were casting long purple shadows across the drowsing countryside; the air warm, filled with the scents of high summer and the sound of bells calling the faithful to Vespers.

Crammed with shipping of every sort, the houses crowding down to the edges of the great cobbled concourse that separated them from the quayside, the port of Nantes was still bustling with life despite the hour. Above them the sky had turned a liquid, shimmering gold streaked with broad scarlet rollers; great streamers of colour that flowed across the whole heavens as if they were on fire, the clouds limmed with orange and crimson flame, and tinged with amethyst. Deep indigo of the coming night above...blush pink and palest yellow streaks beneath.

Here also the river divided, narrower on the side facing the town, but both sides crowded with wharfs, stables and timber yards, forges - with smoke puffing from them even now- houses of every size, and shops and hostelries of every sort.

It was almost as busy as Brest had been, and it was here that Thomas finally brought the *Mary* hard up against the long wooden piles that lined the broad staithes, where they could disembark at last, and the horses could be led ashore to find fresh water and good stabling, and with the *Pride* following behind her both commands could be re-united again and their plans shared.

And with no curfew in place, as Father Matthew had said, there were people everywhere: merchants going from ship to wharf and back again, food sellers with trays hanging from narrow cords around their necks laden with pies and sweetmeats, fruit tarts, smoked meats and olives smeared with golden oil; pedlars with ribbons, bows and trinkets; apprentices calling their master's wares, amidst shop keepers, farriers and stable hands; ostlers from nearby taverns and serving girls in bright woollen dresses and pretty aprons; families out to see the ships and the bustle around the port...and whores, with bold, painted eyes and sly, winning ways...children, hounds and wandering pigs; drudges, beggars and thieves; slatterns, scrubbers and crones; old men and striplings, and sailors of every shape and hue. The noise, colour and swirling activity was vast!

With both ships clearly damaged, the *Mary* especially so, with her fothered hull, smashed fore and stern castles, blood-stained planking and still stuck full of arrows, they quickly became the focus of everyone's attention, so there were plenty of idlers willing to grab the hawsers the crew cast over to warp both ships tightly alongside the quays. And when Gui's men began to disembark, carrying their wounded with them, there was even more activity, so it was not long before officialdom duly appeared from within the town.

Large in importance, but small of stature, in a padded jacket of fine red wool, laced across the front over a white cotton shirt, a man came strutting plumply towards Gui in trousers of soft blue leather, feet in well soled boots of scarlet leather to match his jacket, and a red felt hat with two short green feathers sticking from its side on his head. His face was round, mouth prim, and nose pointed, and he had small eyes, black as currants, beneath narrow black eyebrows, and busily carried a sheaf of parchments in his hands to portray his massive self-importance....*Now who is this fat little peacock who this way comes so boldly strutting? And who is the gallows-bait in armour by his side? Complete with guard as well? My...we are popular! 'Ware hawk, Gui. 'Ware hawk!...*For beside him strode a much taller man in full chain mail over a padded gambeson, covered with a long cyclas in the simple colours, ermine, of the Duke of Brittany, held in with a wide sword belt from which hung both a long blade and a short tapered dagger, both in sheaths of fine scarlet leather. He was well muscled and looked both lean and hard, with sharp grey eyes and his mouth was grimly closed.

Accompanying him was another man, larger, with a neat red beard and a nasal helmet, grey eyes and a broken nose, wearing the same colours, ermine, on his surcoat over a tough mailed hauberk overlaid by a coif of thick mail, with mailed chausses and mittens. He alone was carrying a shield, a long, kite shaped Norman shield emblazoned with a dragon azure, armed and langued sable on a field gules...a blue dragon on a red background, with claws tongue and teeth all black as pitch.

With him was a small bodyguard of eight men in light mail byrnies over leather chausses, two carrying resin torches in iron holders, with chain coifs and round casques on their heads, the Count's simple colours on their chests and plain swords at their waists; the other six similarly armed, but carrying long spears over their shoulders, and from whom the crowd of cheerful onlookers quickly backed away in sudden silence to let them through.

All moved towards where Gui was standing with Sir Richard, idly watching their arrival, while their men began to unload both ships, their sides now broken open to allow the horses to be walked off and their other gear to be removed and stacked. So it was not long before the small man leading this command raised a plump beringed hand and brought his whole escort to a swift halt.

"I am Monsieur Roland du Clefs," he said sharply in Breton, rolling his 'R's, definitive with his name, and waving his papers at Gui. "The Chief Port Officer for Nantes, *Le chef du Port*," he suddenly added in bad Norman-French, tapping his chest. "And the Chief Revenue Collector. All arrivals must report to me at once, explain their business to me and pay their port tolls, or they cannot stay here. You have done none of those things, and you are late in. The sun has gone down. No-one can enter the port after the sun has gone down. *It is the law here!* This behaviour is unsupportable, and unless you warp your vessels below the port immediately, they and all their gear will be impounded, and you will be arrested!"

Gui and Sir Richard stood there while the man's Breton words rattled around them in complete incomprehension...*this idiot is clearly mad!*...so they shrugged their shoulders and smiled, both shaking his hand and patting his shoulders in warm friendship, as one would any mad foreigner whose words were beyond understanding, before turning to get on with their tasks, while the little man stood and gazed at them in outraged amazement.

But before the little man could speak with them again, his armoured companion in his knightly cyclas stepped in front of him. Hand on his sword hilt and in strongly accented Norman-English, indicating the man by his side, body now trembling with affronted dignity, he said sharply: "I don't think you understood Monsieur Roland! He is the *Chef du Port*...the Chief Port Officer for the Duke of Brittany, and that was not a welcome! That was an instruction!" he growled, thrusting his head forward aggressively. "You have broken Nantes regulations for landing here, and if you do not move your ships immediately everything will impounded until it can all be sorted out, and yourselves, and your men, will be arrested!"

"Arrested?" Gui said softly, in clear Norman-French, swinging towards him. "*Arrested*, and these ships impounded? Are you mad? This is an open port, there is no curfew here, and we are both belted knights of our realm, as you clearly know from our speech and our blazons. Men of personal coat armour," he said with icy calmness, indicating the long cyclases both he and Sir Richard were wearing. "How *dare* you address me in so coarse a manner, as if I were a common peasant. On whose orders are we so threatened?"

"By the orders of our Lord Duke, Prince Arthur of Brittany," the man answered sharply, again thrusting his head forward, tapping his own cyclas, bristling with annoyance. "If you do not comply, I will order you arrested."

"*Arrested?*" Gui asked again, his voice rising. "Do you have a brain in that bony lump on your shoulders, you fool? Look around you, man! Do you think my troopers will stand by while you and that rabble at your back, those apologies for soldiers, attempt to lay hands on us? Do you want a bloody skirmish in your town? To lie smashed down in your own blood and that of your men? And who are you to order my arrest?"

"I am Sir Alan de Courcy. This man," he said, indicating his companion, "is my Sergeant-at-Arms, Victor Jonelle. We are both of the Duke's personal forces, to assist the Chief Officer of this port in his duties. Who are you, to question my orders?"

"I don't care if you are Chancellor to the King of France!" Gui replied tersely, his voice cold and hard. "I do not answer to you, Sir Alan; nor to your men, and even less to the Duke of Brittany, who is a Prince anyway, and barely three years old, being Geoffrey of Brittany's son, the younger brother of King Richard of England who is my Liege Lord…and Count of Nantes! And Prince Arthur is in the care of his mother the Duchess Constance…and she, Sir Alan, would not give any such order to you, nor to anyone like you! I am part of our Lord King's Meisnie, by order of King Richard and by oath. So…Sir Alan…not now, nor at any time will I ever answer to you! And you are a fool to even think so. My men and I are duty bound for Narbonne, and on the very highest of authority.

"We were attacked by corsairs just off Belle Île this very morning. You can see the damage! Some of my men were killed and others injured, but we destroyed two of their galleys completely, killing everyone. And in three days' time we will leave here, together, as one command, unmolested and in one piece. Neither you, nor your men, nor Monsieur Roland du Clefs," he added rolling his own 'R's as he spoke, "will stop me. Do you understand me…Sir Alan?" And he leaned slightly towards him, like an armoured tower, and put his hand on his sword…*Dear God, who does this idiot think he is? Does he want to die?*

At the very mention of the attack, the words '*Les Corsairs!*' flew around the crowd in a gale of terrified whispering. All those around them visibly affected, many with their hands to their mouths in horror, others huddling together or moving swiftly away to put the town's walls between them and any possible attackers.

Up on the *Mary's* deck, Father Matthew and Jean de Beaune listened to the small contretemps with complete amazement, while their men stopped what they were doing and began to reach for their weapons, archers on the *Mary* for their crossbows; Allan-i-the-Wood's men on the *Pride* with Hordle John for their long bows. Beside him, de Beaune said softly to the dark cowled monk, "Father…I think I know those men."

"From where? Who are they?"

"From a sharp skirmish my lads and I had under Mercardier, against some of King Philip's troops in the Vexin. That tall bastard down there in the cyclas was their leader, Sir Alan de Courcy, and 'red beard' is his Sergeant-at-Arms, Victor Jonelle. A real bastard! I'd recognise that blue dragon on red anywhere. Those are de Courcy's personal arms and Jonelle always bears them. I took a chunk out of his shield, and broke his nose. His nasal piece saved his life, but he scrabbled away before I could finish him off. We trounced the lot of them! Alan de Courcy is a good fighter and leads men well. But he's no match for Sir Gui on his own, nor for Sir Richard…but together with Jonelle he's bloody dangerous, and not to be trusted. If Sir Gui turns his back, either one of them is quite capable of running him through from behind."

"So…they're two of King Philip's bully-boys, are they? I wonder what they're doing here in Brittany? The current Duke is only a boy, and very much under his mother's care. But his father, Duke Geoffrey, was King Richard's younger brother. In fact the boy, Arthur, is known as the 'Prince of Brittany' and his whole people are staunch supporters of Richard's, not least because their Prince only holds his lands through Richard's favour. Brittany is very much a part of the Angevin Empire he inherited from his father, and Richard guards it well. In fact the King was named Count of Nantes when his brother was killed, and Overlord of Brittany when he became King"

"Oh…that brother," Jean de Beaune growled softly. "The one killed in that Paris tournament four years ago. He was trampled to death after being un-horsed!"

"Yes, Jean. *That* brother! And I smell a rat! I had better get down there quickly before this gets any worse. I know Sir Gui well, and these men around us. If those idiots are not careful, and attack Gui and injure him, they will sweep them out of the way and probably sack the town, and that will ruin everything! Stay here, Jean. It might be well for them not to recognise you. Use your imagination and organise these men, while I get on!" And throwing his big leather scrip over his shoulders, and lifting the hem of his long black habit, he raced across the deck, down the dropped sides of the *Mary* and onto the quayside.

Meanwhile de Courcy, with Jonelle, had taken another step towards Gui, coming dangerously close, their men a few feet behind them. "I am no dog for you to address me so," de Courcy snarled, face red with anger, cocking his scabbard forward to draw his sword. "I am the Duke's leal man. And you *will* do as I say, or I will cut you down where you stand!"

"*Step back, de Courcy!*" Gui then roared at him. "Take your hand off your sword, unless you wish to die…and take that pompous, bloated popinjay away with you before you both regret it!"

Then, stabbing his hand towards the Chef du Port, terrified now rather than affronted, and taking a swift half stride towards them both he shouted: "Who is overlord of these lands you stand on, eh? Who gives orders to the Duke of Brittany, you *oaf*? And who is the Duke's Overlord in all matters?...And who is Count of Nantes as well anyway?" But before either man could answer, he added furiously: "And if that idiot Sergeant beside you shifts *one* more foot, or hitches his shield *once* more; or one of your pathetic excuses for a soldier so much as touches his weapon, *I will kill you all!*"

Behind him, even as they had watched the strutting figure of the Chef du Port and his bodyguard arriving, Sir Richard and Allan-i-the-Wood had swiftly organised their men: some running the horses out of immediate danger, the Verderers moving swiftly to the *Pride's* sterncastle to ready their long bows, Hordle John and his other Lions picking up their weapons, raising their shields and shaking themselves into good order.

Even Thomas Blackwood and the crews of both ships had armed themselves, as they had done against the corsairs, and were loosely forming up behind Gui's whole command, Sir Richard standing, arms crossed before them.

By then the town's people had swiftly retreated to the edge of the cobbled concourse, agog to see what would happen next, but equally ready to flee if necessary amongst the narrow twisted streets and ginnels of the town for safety, where somewhere a horn was blowing and a great bell tolling.

However, by then Monsieur Roland, Sir Alan and the red bearded Jonelle, were all in a frantic argument: Sir Alan and Jonelle wanting to draw their swords and order their men to the attack, du Clefs desperate to restrain them, and all waving their arms and shouting. If the situation had not been so serious it would have been funny. And it was at this point, in a rush of heavy sandals and flying robes, that Father Matthew arrived before them.

"Is there some trouble, my Lords?" he said moments later in his quiet, commanding voice, calmly looking around him despite his haste. "You all look very belligerent...and sound it too!" he exclaimed.

Then, motioning de Courcy and his big Sergeant to move back, he turned to the Chef du Port, and quietly said in Breton, with his soft Spanish lilt, "You, Monsieur Roland du Clefs, are being very officious. Unnecessarily rude and unpleasant to people who have just arrived in this port, which is an open port as well you know. Very unwise of you, Monsieur, *very!* No!" he said, holding up his hand. "*I heard you!* And if you wish to keep your position, let alone your head, I advise you to be eternally careful," he went on ignoring the pompous little man's open-mouthed shock.

"*Monsieur le Duc* is almost a babe, *Monsieur*...he does not rule Brittany. But his uncle does! King Richard of England, and both he and his appointed

41

Regent are known to me," he breathed at him, watching his face turn pasty-faced as the blood suddenly drained out of it. "Very well known to me indeed. It is *King Richard's* word that rules here, you foolish little mountebank!" he snarled, flicking the man's papers with contempt. "And *I* come with King Richard's personal seal, *on his Royal business*, as do the men with me, as Sir Gui has just said. And I also come with letters from Rome, from the Holy Father himself! If I were you," he hissed at him dangerously, tapping firmly on his plump. rounded chest with a hard finger: "I would start by begging this man's forgiveness, render him every service possible that you can think of and then pray to God that he does not report your conduct, personally, to the King himself! And take that madman, de Courcy, with you, and his Sergeant-at-Arms, before they get you all killed! Look around, you Monsieur Roland du Clefs, *now!*"

And stepping away from him he gestured towards both ships.

Du Clefs looked, saw, and finally dropped his papers in shaking terror. On the *Mary* a dozen crossbows were pointed at him and on the *Pride*, Allan's verderers were standing with their longbows stringed and armed, each clothyard shaft bodkin pointed, and ready to be raised and fired in a moment.

"*You, de Courcy!*" Father Matthew shouted out next, his voice every bit as tough and sharp as any Commander of a Royal Guard. "*Draw back with your men, now!* You and Sergeant Jonelle, both. Be advised that King Richard of England is Overlord of these lands, and these men are on the King's Royal business, *and under his Royal Warrant!*" And with a flourish he opened his scrip, pulled open the curled parchment with all its seals, and thrust it at him, the King's Seal, huge and beribboned, dangled prominently before his startled eyes, and was pleased to see the sudden shock that rippled through them all....the crowd included.

"These men do *not* pay tolls, do *not* pay duties and will *not* be hindered against the King's extreme displeasure, and you *will* assist them in every way while they are in Nantes." And in a ringing voice he shouted out to all around him: "*This is the Great Seal of King Richard of England...Count of Nantes, and your rightful overlord!*" holding the parchment up for them all to see as he did so. "Where that seal is, so is the King," he said with cutting definition, turning back to Sir Alan as he did so. "And you will kneel to it or be foresworn! *Do you understand me?*"

"Yes! Father!" de Courcy growled through gritted teeth as he dropped to one knee and bowed as he had been so ordered.

"All your men, de Courcy! Your Sergeant Jonelle as well, I will brook no mistakes in this matter! Do this or I will order your immediate arrest for treason against the King." And he held up the King's seal before Jonelle's shocked face as well, who also dropped to one knee and bowed his head, as did all his men.

"Good! Lastly, you du Clefs!"

"Yes! F-Father," and he, too, knelt and dipped his head, then stepped back, grovelled for his dropped papers on his hands and knees, now somewhat scattered by the breeze, then practically fled the quay, through the crowds who jeered him, followed by de Courcy, and Jonelle, their faces flushed with humiliation. Teeth clenched and bodies rigidly upright, they swiftly marched their men back towards the town, through jeering crowds and tribes of scampering boys who pelted their backs with straw and refuse off the street, while Gui and his men roared with laughter.

Behind them Father Matthew turned and held out his arms to Gui's whole command as their laughter finally died away and smiled. "There! That ought to sort things out for all of us. About time I did something to earn my keep. How was that?"

"Matthew!" Gui exclaimed for all of them, as they rushed to gather round him, swordsmen, archers, crews and hound. "I have seen and heard many things since you came among us, but that?...that was beyond simply amazing! That was spectacular...*outstanding!* See, Father, you have stunned us all. But where did you learn Breton? And how did you know those fools' names?

"Oh, I am lucky with languages," he said humorously, tilting his head. "I picked it up in my soldiering days from several Bretons in my Command...and as for those two idiots, De Beaune recognised them. And I know you, dear boy!" he laughed, patting his armoured back. "*I know you!* One more word from de Courcy and you would have been at him, and that other, and cut them both in pieces with that great big shaft of steel you so love to wield. Blood and slaughter all over the place! Yes?"

"Mmmm. Probably!"

"More than likely," Sir Richard added with a grin, coming up to him and banging him on his shoulders, while the men dispersed to get on with clearing both ships.

"See, Gui?" Father Matthew smiled. "And Richard knows you better than I. But justified or not...and I know things now about those two that they would not be pleased about, and which I will discuss with you later...they are both still Officers of the Prince of Brittany, whatever we may think of them. And they wear his colours. Richard is Prince Arthur's Overlord. An attack on those two could have been taken as an attack on the Prince, young as he is, and therefore upon King Richard himself, and where would that have left us all? Blood shed now would have been just awful!"

43

Gui smiled and shrugged his broad shoulders, bringing up his hands in a gesture of mock defeat, his eyes going up to heaven under raised eyebrows.

"I had not thought that far, Matthew," and he sighed...*Where would I be without him?*..."As it is, those two have had the biggest bollocking of their tiny lives. You have made clear from whom our orders come, and they must now help us to fulfil them or be in contempt of the King...which they will not dare to be! Truly, Father, you are brilliant and I'm a numpty! Now, let's get all this gear sorted and then find this Angel Inn that Tommy Blackwood has sworn by. It's been a long day!"

Chapter 7...Alicia and Agnes meet Soraya.

For the Lady Alicia de Burley and Agnes Fitzwalter, the nightmare seemed never ending!

From the moment Sheik El Nazir's great galley had swept up and hammered the *Pride of Beaulieu* with her artillery...each smashing blow shaking her from truck to keelson, as if she had struck a reef...they had not known a moment's peace or comfort.

Handed over to the Cousins, whom she believed were true and to be trusted...*and look how mistaken that had turned out to be?*...Alicia had only just stepped out of her cabin before she saw them first hack down the two men standing on either side of the Master, and then, even as she had stood there horrified, had watched Lucas Fabrizan slaughter Robert of Christchurch. One great, swingeing blow that had cleaved his head almost from his shoulders in a rushing, scarlet fountain of blood, making her scream in absolute terror...only to be smashed unconscious to the deck! And the next moment she had been swept up beneath Fabrizan's arm like a sack of meal, while the *Pride* had lost all control, flinging her head up into the wind, sails and loose sheets banging and clattering in wild confusion.

That had been the moment the dromond had grappled with them, and a flood of corsairs had leapt on board. And despite all that their men could do to reach them...with Agnes screaming, *"To me, Lions! To me!"* and kicking and struggling with all her strength, Bouncer leaping and savaging all he could sink his teeth into, and the dozens slain as their men had fought desperately to reach them...they had both been carried off.

They had been no match for the two renegade Frenchmen, Jules Lagrasse and Lucas Fabrizan, who had held on to them like grim death...and dragged them on board moments before the dromond had swiftly been cut loose and rowed away towards the *Mary*, leaving them both marooned on her deck surrounded by their enemies.

For Alicia, that had been the very worst moment of her life, worse even than being drugged and abducted from Castle Malwood!

Held out across the galley's rails, her arms pinioned behind her back and shaken like a fine sapling in a storm, with El Nazir telling Gui she was destined to be the Baron's bride, she had seen him looking at her. Horror stamped across his belovèd face, surrounded by those who cared for her most, as they had shouted and raged helplessly at their enemies. She had heard his anguished cries, shouting across to her with all his might, *"I love you!...I will come for you!"* And then, as the Cousins had dragged her and Agnes below, she had cried out her final words, holding her arms out to him in desperation, and screaming, "Remember me! *Remember meee!"*

Then, mercifully, even as the rowers had dug in their blades to the first thud of the hortator's drum, her emotions had got the better of her at last and she had felt as if her heart was breaking. As if everything she had ever lived for had been destroyed, and all the strength had rushed out of her...and she had collapsed in a small armoured heap onto the galley's deck and been swiftly carried away.

*

Hours later she awoke after an exhausted sleep, to find that she and Agnes had been stripped of their armour and their bodies cleansed. Both now in long, soft, loose-fitting gowns of white cotton, with wide sleeves embroidered with flowers in fine ivory thread, and both lying in a fine cabin at the rear of the ship below the sterncastle.

Beside them the sea rushed past their heads, making the whole ship quiver as if alive, the heavy clunk of the steer-boards as the steersmen fought to keep her on her course causing the two brass oil lamps on their gimbals above her head to twist and sway, filling the room with pale golden light and flickering shadows.

Here the ship's sides had been panelled with mellow pine, polished so that they shone golden in the soft lamp light, and on the decking was a huge, thick square rug, deep red with black patterns, fringed in the same colours. The bed was a box bed of dark wood, filled with a mattress of goose feathers on wide leather straps, covered with canvas and overlaid with soft Egyptian cotton sheeting. And there were a host of plump cushions in purple, blue and scarlet cotton, with silk and satin on the reverse side, scattered at its head. The whole bed overlaid with a cotton-stuffed coverlet, embroidered with great blue and purple fronds and flowers, on which they were lying.

Struggling awake, her eyes still sore from weeping, Alicia looked at herself and at Agnes, but could remember nothing. Then, pushing herself up against the mass of cushions, she looked around her cabin.

At the foot of the bed was a long padded chest, and against the side, just beyond the door, was a bench seat with a finely polished table surrounded by hardwood fiddles inlaid with coloured woods. On it, in deep wooden fretted holders, so they would not fall over, was a gilt-lined silver jug for wine and one for water, along with three red glass goblets set in chased silver holders.

Opposite, seated with calm elegance on a cushioned settle, was a tall, deeply tanned girl, looking steadily at her through huge, almond shaped green eyes with long curved lashes, whose beauty was enhanced by thick lines of kohl on her eyelids, across which she was wearing a yashmak of palest blue silk, tied with fine ribbons behind her head, that also covered her hair. Of the very finest material, it could neither hide the rich, glossy, chestnut waves, now piled up and held in place with ivory pins, nor disguise the fine lines of her nose, and of her warmly curved mouth.

She wore a padded silk jacket, beautifully embroidered with flowers and small birds in iridescent colours, wide open at the front and cut short above her waist, with sleeves to her elbows, beneath which was a white chemise of finest silk, almost transparent, that covered her full breasts, richly crowned with proud nipples set in neat areolas all touched with gold. The chemise too was short cut, leaving her slender waist bare, roped with a heavy gold chain studded with pearls, and over the swell of her hips and loins she wore long cotton pantaloons to match her jacket, with gold sandals of the softest leather on her feet, the tips curled up and held so by the finest gold chains around each ankle.

Her arms were smooth and silky, along which she wore heavy bracelets of red and yellow gold twisted together, studded with turquoise, and her shapely hands had long, tapered fingers, nails also tipped with gold paint. Quite simply she was the most lovely, and exotic, creature that Alicia had ever set eyes on and momentarily she was too stunned to speak.

"Where are we? And..and who are you?" Alicia asked at last, almost in a whisper, giving Agnes a sharp shake.

"You are on the *Morning Star...'Surah At-Tariq'*, and my name is...Soraya," the girl replied hesitantly in softly accented English. "Soraya Fermier." Her voice was rich and husky, and full of the warm south of the Languedoc, of Southern Aquitaine, of sunshine, red wine and olives, but which Alicia recognised immediately. "I have eighteen years...the same as you, my Lady Al-ic-ia," she said in her husky voice with the hint of a smile. I have served the Lady Rochine de Brocas for six years..and..and now I am yours," she hesitated prettily.

"You are from the Languedoc!" Alicia said suddenly.

"Yes, my Lady Ali-c-ia," she replied softly with surprise, her voice trembling around the syllables. "How did you know?"

"Because of Queen Eleanor of England," Alicia answered tersely, running her fingers through her tousled hair. "Our Lord King Richard's mother. The Languedoc was her home. She also speaks the language."

47

"Ah...Queen Eleanor of Aquitaine. You know this Queen?" Soraya asked, startled.

"Yes, of course! All who know Richard of England know his mother," Alicia shot back at her. "And the King is my guardian. How do you speak my language, and know my name? How is that?"

"*Monsieur le Baron*, ordered me to learn it, my lady. He was in-sis-tent that I should do so," she shrugged elegantly. "So I did. He also was telling me your name. The Lady Rochine, his daughter, told it to me also. El Nazir himself told it to me as well."

Alicia smiled briefly at her fractured speaking...*and does that make this girl one of that man's creatures?*... then seizing a cushion she violently threw it across the cabin. "Those *people!*" she, snarled, swinging her feet to the deck. "Those people, my girl, are murderers! They are my *enemies!*" she exclaimed again," hurling another cushion. "These are *all* my enemies," she added waving her arms around her. Then she snapped: "Why are you here, Mistress Fermier? Are you my enemy too? Who are you?"

"...And-and-what will happen to us?" Agnes broke in, having pulled herself awake and sitting up while Alicia had been talking.

"I am not your enemy, my Lady!" the lovely girl denied urgently, fear in her voice as her eyes suddenly dilated. "I am here to care for both of you. To see to your needs," Soraya said, collecting up the cushions and putting them beside her on the settle. "To help you...make sure you arrive before *Monsieur le Baron* safely at Narbonne. And my name is Soraya...Soraya Fermier, as I you told."

"Narbonne!" Alicia exclaimed blankly, slumping down on the edge of the bed. "*Narbonne?*"

"Yes. It is a Roman city, very old. The largest in the region, with a busy port. Much wine, much olive oil, many ships. *Monsieur le Baron's* Château is near there, at Gruissan. Right beside the Circle Sea...the Mediterranean. Very blue, very warm, beautiful...you will like it there. Both of you, I think?"

"Like it there, Soraya? *Like it there?*" Alicia growled, leaning forward, hands on knees. "Are you moon-mad girl? Do you think I am here because I want to be? *And who are you?*" she asked again, more sharply.

"I have been the handmaiden, personal, to the Lady Rochine de Brocas, as I said. Since fourteen, chosen especially by *Monsieur le Baron*, and now I am...I am to be yours," she ended simply, with another elegant shrug

"*Mine?*" Alicia replied, astonished. "How do you mean, 'mine?'"

"I am your gift from *Monsieur le Baron*," the girl replied softly, holding out her arms towards her, her eyes sparkling with unshed tears. "I am to care for you, dress you, chaperone you, Yes? Serve you in any way you order me to. *Monsieur le Baron* gave me to the Lady Rochine in my younger days, as I said. She has taught me many things in..in serving her," she added, giving a sudden shudder. "And now she has been ordered to give me to you. A be-tro-thal gift. To...to show the love for you," she ended with a brave smile. "It is why I was ordered to learn your language. I am good at it, no? And he has sent me with this letter for you," she said, holding out a sealed parchment she drew from within her jacket. He has signed it himself, see it is sealed with his special mark. Please, my Lady Al-ic-ia," she said in her broken English, tears welling out of her eyes as she spoke. "They will be so cross with me if I do not please you."

Alicia, astonished, took it and broke the Baron's seal, green wax with a great boar's head stamped into it, and flicked it open, her eyes widening as she cast them across the page.

"*Bah!*" She snorted a moment later, seething with disgust, holding it in her hands as if it were poison. "He writes...'*You have imprisoned my heart. Impaled it with darts of Cupid's love, such that I cannot live without you by my side!*" Is he mad that he thinks I should actually believe such appalling rubbish? Oh... '*And for love of you I send you, as a belovèd gift, my daughter's servant, Mistress Soraya Fermier, to care for you. Do with her as you will, she is wholly yours to command*'...and so on and so on!" And scrunching it up between her hands she hurled it across the cabin, and stamped her feet in fury on the deck.

"His love for me?" She cried out loudly. "That man is a double dyed, black-hearted, murderous devil in human form, Mistress Soraya Fermier," she swore through gritted teeth.

"I am ward to King Richard of England and already betrothed...before God and with the King's blessing...to Sir Gui de Malwood!" she raged, jumping up. "Now seized from his side, and against my will, by this bloody pirate, El Nazir, and carted off to serve the *so* dear Baron's will," she added with withering sarcasm, "by a pair of disgusting French traitors, as if I were of no more value than a piece of common baggage! 'His love for me?...*Arrrrgh!*' And her whole body shuddered. "That man utterly disgusts me!" she raged, and stamped her foot on the cabin floor again making Soraya, and even Agnes, flinch away from her.

After a moment's silence, while Alicia paced around the room in fury like a caged tigress, Soraya asked quietly: "Jules Lagrasse and Lucas Fabrizan?"

"*Ha!*" Alicia snorted. "You know them?"

"Yes, of course. They have been in *Monsieur le Baron's* pay at the Château for some years. They are not good men, I think."

"Not 'good men'? They are *dreadful* men, Soraya!" she shouted at her, turning to walk across the deck, swaying as she went. "And Lucas is worse than Jules, if that were possible, with a mouth like a rotting sewer! I hope *never* to be near them again without a sword in my hand!"

"You need have no fear of that, my lady. Sheik El Nazir will make sure of it…"

"*El Nazir?*" Alicia rasped, her face filled with anger, as she turned towards Soraya, now calmly seated again. "*Sheik El Nazir?* How dare that man seize us!" Alicia shouted, feet apart as the deck rolled beneath her. "How *dare* he! And as for that…that…*fiend* Roger de Brocas! I would rather *die* than be married to that…that murderous *butcher!*" she ended, spitting the words out in disgust.

Then, suddenly realising the implication behind the language issue, she whirled round at Soraya and demanded of her: "When did you begin your lessons in English, Soraya? When?"

"About a…a year ago, my Lady," she stammered, visibly distressed. "Why are you so cross with me?" she went on, her eyes filled again with tears. "I have tried so hard. Please, please do not beat me. Do not hurt me. Please, I beg of you, I will be better, I will be!" And she buried her head in her hands and wept, her whole body shaking.

Seeing the girl's obvious fear and now having her in floods of tears before her, Alicia was aghast…*Dear God, what have these people done to her?*…and immediately she rushed to Soraya's side and put her arms round her to comfort her: "Shh, shh. No-one's going to beat you, you foolish girl. I have never treated my servants so. Never, Soraya. Shout at them, maybe…but strike them? No!…I am not cross with you, Mistress Fermier, but I am furious with what that…that *bastard* has done!" she exclaimed, springing up with renewed rage. "He must have planned all this months ago, Agnes," she shouted then, swinging round to face her friend. "He planned this whole bloody charade, from forcing Soraya to learn English, to arriving at Malwood, just so that that…that dyed in the wool *bastard* could murder all those I most love in all the world and..and marry me! *Marry me?* Dear God, *how I hate him!*" she shouted, stamping her feet to the beat of her rage: "Hate him! *Hate him!*"

"Shh. Shh!" Soraya cried out desperately, hurrying across the cabin to where Alicia had now flung herself down again on the bed, Agnes's arms around her, her whole body trembling. "*Shh!* I beg you, my lady. I beg you, to be quiet…please do not be alarmed."

"Shh! Shh?" Alicia hissed at her fiercely. "Why should I '*Shh! Shh!?* Why should I not be 'alarmed'?"

50

"Please, my Lady. *Please!*" Soraya begged her again, falling to her knees at Alicia's feet. "There is an armed guard outside this door, one of El Nazir's most trusted men. If he comes in here I will be in dreadful trouble. The Sheik has his orders too, my lady. I may be your gift from *Monsieur le Baron*, but if I upset you, and that man has to come in here, then he will beat me and beat me. It will be terrible...not to mention what the Lady Rochine will do to me once I am met with her again!" and she visibly shuddered, the tears rolling down her face in black streaks. "She truly will hurt me...vraiment! *Vraiment!"*

"Alright, Soraya," Alicia said horrified. "Alright! I am sorry," she added, cradling the weeping girl in her arms. "I did not mean to alarm you so. I will calm down...but I am so *furious* about what has been done to me, so terrified for my life and for Agnes, and feeling so helpless to do anything about it, that shouting is my only release, apart from tears!"

"Soraya?" Agnes questioned her uncertainly. " Soraya. All this talk of you being a 'gift' for my Lady? I do not understand...are you not free to choose? To ask?" she added hesitantly. "To leave, if you want to? I mean...I have served my Lady, and Sir Gui's family, for years and years now, but I am still free to leave whenever I want to. I am not..."

"...Not a slave?" Soraya interrupted her softly, in her rich husky voice.

"Yes...I mean, No! Oh...I am confused."

"Well, Mistress Agnes," Soraya said then, kneeling up on the fringed rug at Alicia's feet, and wiping her face with the back of her hand, smearing her yashmak with kohl as she did so. "I am not a 'slave' as such; but I might just as well be one."

"Explain!" Alicia demanded, looking down at her, her face softening. "Agnes, dear, bring that water here, and let Soraya wash her face, and let us have some wine as well. A drink just now will do us all a power of good!"...*And give me a chance to understand better just what is going on here. Gui always says, 'that to know your enemy is to defeat him'. Well is this girl my enemy? She says not...but can I believe her?*

51

Chapter 8...Soraya Fermier becomes a friend.

Moments later, when the wine had been poured, and freely sampled, and Soraya had washed her face, replaced her yashmak and was redoing her eyes as best she could from a polished silver mirror in the mellow lamp light, she told them about herself.

"My father, Dumas Fermier, was born a Freeman on de Brocas's lands, my Lady Al-ic-ia, near Gruissan where is the Château of *Monsieur le Baron*."

"So, your father owned his own lands, Soraya?"

"That is so, my Lady. Olives as well as vineyards. But of the lands not all were his, some were of his grandpapa and had been of his family for many years. His papa also paid rent to *Monsieur le Baron* for some of them as well. But my papa was not always a farmer. Before he had been also a soldier in the King Louis's army, King Louis *Sept,* And went with the King, and the army of the German Emperor, Conrad, on the Second Crusade..."

"But that was a disaster, Soraya," Alicia interrupted her. "I remember Sir Yvo, Gui's father, talking about it. They all set out with great armies from Germany and France, and wasted everything! Queen Eleanor went too, King Richard's mother. She was married to Louis then. They got as far as Damascus, and after a three day siege the Crusaders gave up and they all came home. Tens of thousands died! The whole thing was an absolute disgrace."

"That is right, my Lady, *scandaleux!* He was of the few to survive, and return with in his pockets much gold, and more wonderful stories than you can imagine. I adored him. He took over from Grandpapa the family vineyard and the olives also, and with his money he bought some more land of the very best.

"And papa proved to be a farmer *très bon*, very good. After all it was of his blood. He was not Dumas Fermier for nothing!" and they both laughed. "His vineyards were successful for many years. His wine was known, far and wide, and so was the oil of his olives. *Un succès fou!*...a success of the most mad," she said turning to Agnes. "But, suddenly something happened to the springs he used, the water it dried up, and for two years the grapes did not do well and he fell on hard times. By then there were also many little ones at home to care for, and after a while papa could not pay his dues to the Baron. And..and then," she hesitated, looking suddenly haunted as if by some distant memory. "Then..there were other things for which he needed money, *beaucoup d'argent*...much money, that I may not speak of. No! Please...do not press me. It is too shameful for me! No matter, at first *Monsieur le Baron* was very understanding. He lent papa money and gave to him more time to pay...but unknown to papa, he added big interest on the payments every month making it impossible for him to clear his debts."

"But that is usury!" Alicia said shocked. "Forbidden by the Church. It has been considered a sin for many years. It is illegal and damnable. St Jerome declared it to be the same as murder!"

"Ah, that may be so, my Lady," she shrugged. "But my father would not know that, and he did not want to challenge *Monsieur le Baron. Moi?* I might have done. But papa? *Non!* He tried always his proper dues to pay. *Toujours*…always! And then there were the rents, which the Baron also increased until papa was grey with worry! He was of all men very good, my lovely papa …*très bon*," she added with tears in her eyes.

"How do you know all that, Alicia?" Agnes asked, astonished. "About the usury I mean?"

"Oh, Sir James told me, Agnes…my guardian's Seneschal," she added, turning towards Soraya. "He runs all my lands, and those of my fiancé, Sir Gui de Malwood. The Holy Father, Alexander III, also declared against usury a few years ago, just before he died. The Church condemns it."

"The Church condemns it? Ha! *Monsieur le Baron* is to the Church close, like this," she said bitterly, crooking her two forefingers together, tugging them as she did so. "The Archbishop of Narbonne is of his friends the dearest, I think. He gave the Lord Roger a special dis-pen-sation that allowed him to force papa to sign papers giving me into his hands in exchange for the debts of papa's, which he could never pay back. Faced with ruin, papa signed me to bondage."

"No!" Agnes gasped, putting her hand to her mouth

"*Mais oui!*… Mistress Agnes. *Yes!* It is not unknown in my country. By parting with me he thought the farm would be saved. But within months of papa signing, *Monsieur le Baron* demanded more payment, and all his rents also. Papa could give nothing. He asked for more time to pay, but *Monsieur le Baron dit Non!*…No!, and he threw my poor papa off his lands."

"All of them, Soraya?" Agnes asked, appalled.

"All of them!" she exclaimed bitterly…*Tous les terrains*…even those that he held as freehold, which were the very best of all, many, many vines and olives, and the wine? *Très, très bon*. Good, very, very. Of the best. All of which papa had bought and all that had been *en famille* for generations. Baron Roger took them as payment. Papa lost everything. All that papa had worked for all his life, and the lives of the family before him…all gone! Pouf!" and she clapped her hands. "*Dans un instant!* Then, *Monsieur le Baron* shared the lands with the Archbishop."

"*No!*" Alicia gasped.

53

"*Mais oui!*...That is what it was all about, Yes? They took all of them, *tous les terrains!*...It was of the most, most badness, *terrible!* But of the very worst was that once *Monsieur le Baron* and the Archbishop had the lands...the water that papa had so relied on all those years, and had disappeared? *Oui?* Well, it came back!"

"*No!*" Alicia gasped again. "Oh, Soraya...he had diverted the streams. How...how wicked!"

"*Oui, méchant!* All the water went. Though how such a thing could be done I do not know? But somehow the springs on papa's land dried up. So when the vines needed so badly the water...there was none. Then, after *Monsieur le Baron* and the Archbishop had shared it all out...*Pouf!* She snapped her fingers. "The springs, they flowed and bubbled again"

"Then they were in it together! What wickedness indeed! No!...not just wickedness, real evil!...*Dear God, how I hate that man!*" she shouted suddenly, stamping her feet on the deck again in anger and frustration, while Soraya desperately tried to shush her.

Then a moment later she said quietly: "But Alexander...the Holy Father, Soraya... declared that anything taken by a cleric through usury must be paid back! Sir James told me that also. Oh, Soraya. If God shines on us, we will gain your freedom and may yet restore *all* your lands. Both those stolen by de Brocas, *Monsieur le Baron*," she ended, giving the girl a brilliant smile, "and those by the Archbishop!"

"But what of your family?" Agnes asked, slipping her arm around Alicia's waist.

"Well, when all that happened the family was scattered completely," Soraya said very sadly, sitting back on her feet. "I had an elder brother...but..." and she hesitated, her huge eyes filling with tears.

"But?" Alicia prompted her. "What happened to your big brother, Soraya?"

The girl hesitated again then, and bowed her head briefly, and when she raised it again tears were just falling silently from her eyes: "I cannot talk of him, my Lady. He was the cause of much trouble. *Beaucoup de malheur!* Much of unhappiness, my Lady. *Beaucoup! Beaucoup!*" and she broke down then into a wild flood of tearful French: "*Non! Milady. Non! Je ne peux pas vous dire. La douleur c'est trop! Trop!*...'I cannot tell you. Too much pain! Too much!' her sobs shaking her to her foundations. "Please do not make me. He was as a brother, and as a man, the very worst. *Très méchant!* In very truth, My Lady Al-ic-ia...I do not know where any of my brothers are now, nor my little sister...and a year later my poor papa died. His heart it was broken."

"And your mother?" Agnes asked, quietly, deciding not to press her any further on her missing siblings. "What of your mother?"

For a few moments Soraya was silent, her thoughts as far away as her eyes, which seemed to stare into nothing, then she softly murmured: "*Ma belle mère, ma plus belle maman.*" Then with a great sigh she said: "It was autumn time. I would have been about twelve then; two years before Lord Roger took me. The trees were changing, very pretty, and mama was in the forests around us collecting herbs and mushrooms. *Monsieur Le Baron* was hunting *sanglier*...the wild boar?" she explained to Agnes, who was about to ask. "All the mountains and forests around us are for the *sanglier* most famous. Big and fierce," she said, using her hands to explain her words. "It was a hunting party, *très grand*...very big, *beaucoup de chevaux*...many horses, *beaucoup de chiens*...many hounds. *Le Sanglier*...the boar, was a great one. Old, ferocious, a male with tushes of the longest. Upon my mother with her basket it came suddenly from the forest, and gored her: then, '*Taroo! Taroo!*' the hunt rode right over her. She was very beautiful...*très, très belle*, my lovely mama," she went on, tears now starting from her eyes. "I am like her, very much, people say. She was Persian, slender like me...

"*Persian?*" Alicia broke in amazed. "From beyond the Circle Sea. I had thought her to be from around Gruissan, or Narbonne, like your father?"

"*Mais non*! My Lady. Mama was from Persia. Far, far away. From outside Damascus my Papa rescued her. She had been a slave to an Arab master killed in the fighting. Papa found her about to be raped by some German soldiers of Conrad's army. He killed them both and brought mama back with him to France. He adored her, and she him also. I have her eyes, and her body; but she came back to us on that day most dreadful completely broken, you could not know her. Torn open by the boar and trampled by the hunt. It was terrible!...*Terrible!*" She said, clutching her breast, as her tears streamed down her face. "Me...I could not speak, and my poor papa? He was of the heart most broken. Crushed. We both cried and cried. Never was he the same after maman was killed. For him the life just seemed to go out. It was after her death that everything became of the very worst. It still makes me weep."

"Oh, Soraya," Alicia said with a deep sigh. "Such sadness...such trials. And now you are in bondage until all the dues are paid. Such bondage deals were made like that at home once, many years ago. Oh dear, you are in as sad a case as we," she added giving Agnes a cuddle. "And with your father dead there is no way those debts can ever be paid and the papers redeemed, unless some other does it for you. Dear God, what an evil man he is. To all of us!"

"The Archbishop also, my lady," Soraya said, dropping her face. "I have shed many tears. Many. But what can I do? Except carry out my orders in the very best way I can, and hope, somehow, that things will change. I am well housed, and dressed," she added, sweeping her hands across her body. "And it is not all bad. But how can I ever find a man of my own to care for me? And love me, and with whom I can have a family, when I am trapped like this?...And as for the Lady Rochine..." her voice trailed away and she just shook her head, tears starting from her eyes again, making them glitter in the lamplight. "Sometimes she is truly *affreuse!* Dreadful!" she whispered.

"Oh, Soraya, how terrible for you," Alicia said gently, impulsively reaching her hands out to lift the girl's face, Soraya still meekly kneeling before her, and kissed her cheeks, still wet with tears. "Of course we will do our best not to get you into any trouble. We are both in dreadful circumstances, Agnes and I...and you," she went on.

"We know nothing of what is expected of us, except what El Nazir shouted across at Gui. And that I will resist in every way I can! The Baron, God Blast his wicked soul, may think he has won, but there are many ways they say of skinning a cat, and this 'cat' is not yet ready to be skinned. Not for a while that's for certain! So come, Soraya, be friends with me...with us, Agnes and me. Exchange the kiss-of-peace," she smiled warmly, pulling the lovely girl into her arms, "and we will do all we can to be good and cheerful partisans against the *so* kindly Baron's evil ways...and those of that scheming bitch, his daughter!"...*or By God and the Pheasant, I will want to know the reason why!*

56

Chapter 9...Sheik El Nazir on board the Morning Star.

Sheik El Nazir al-Jameel-Aziz-ibn Nidhaal's great cabin, that stretched almost the whole width of the dromond, was immediately above where the three girls were speaking, and was sumptuously appointed with thick Persian rugs both on the deck and hanging from the polished hardwood panels that lined the walls.

There were a number of beautiful silver lamps on brass gimbals above him, and horn windows around the stern in sliding casements, one of them pushed open, beneath which was a long padded seat of the finest green wool, with green and gold silk cushions embroidered with gold thread and great green and silver tassels on each corner.

Along either side were two beautiful, long chests in polished oak and cedar, together with a number of strong X-shaped chairs inlaid with ivory, with backs of scarlet leather and padded scarlet seating. There was also a large, octagonal walnut table inlaid with rosewood and ivory, its fiddles of polished cedar, the underside adorned with the most delicate fretwork.

It was here that El Nazir was seated, quill pen in hand, on a tall-backed armed chair to match the table, a beautiful porcelain bowl of honeyed almonds by his hand, and his Galley Commander, Raschid el Din, standing relaxed before him.

"I thought that all went well, my Lord, considering," Raschid said, taking off his helmet, before bowing briefly, his hand touching his lips and his forehead. "Exactly where the Baron said they would be, and his two lads on board couldn't have performed better."

"Yes! But it was clever of their leader to switch ships," El Nazir replied, beckoning him to a chair as he spoke, his voice rich and dark, with a hint of gravel. "Fooled that idiot son of mine, Siraj: cost him his life and his command," and he paused a moment in thought...*that fool, plenty of spirit and a good fighter, but no sense*...before continuing: "Those two, Jules and Lucas, used their heads well."

"Yes! That green silk was an unmistakeable marker," Raschid el Din replied, picking up a silver-gilt beaker of sherbet. "The rest was easy. They slaughtered the ship master and his guards and whisked both those girls away in a moment, for which they should be well rewarded. The infidels stood no chance. I thought all our lads did really well, considering."

"But at some cost, my friend," the Sheik cut in tersely, tapping his teeth with the stripped quill. "As you said, 'considering'! Those bastard Sons of the Devil fought like all the fiends from Tartarus. How do the Franks do it?" he queried, amazed, pushing the bowl of almonds towards his tall commander. "My son was a fool, for which someone at last has made him pay the price. Two galleys should have been ample to cripple that cog!" And turning to look out of the windows he smiled...*Allah Akhbar. That strutting ass has been a pain in my side for years. His mother will grieve, but not I. There will be many others also who will be pleased to see him gone, and I have many other sons to follow me!*...Then turning back a moment later, he asked: "You have no comment, my Raschid?"

"No...my Prince. Siraj was a great fighter, but lacked discipline and common sense. This time his rashness has cost us all dear. Two galleys destroyed, and nearly a hundred fighting men slain...not to mention the rowers! This is not the first time he has chanced his arm against the infidels."

"No, but to lose his whole command? May he burn in hell for it, *Insha'Allah!*" He exclaimed in disgust. "And all for one girl!..."

"But such a girl, my Prince. Have you seen her hair? Such a shining gold colour. So lustrous. Never have I seen the like...and her breasts!..."

"...like silver moons, I know. But even so, my Raschid. Breasts or no breasts...Hair or no hair. I have no sympathy for him. Pray *Allah* she does not fall into any other's hands. She would fetch a fortune in gold to match her hair...or her breasts!" And he laughed.

"And her companion!"

"*Shaitan* take the damned companion, Raschid! I hope Lord Roger knows what he is doing. For this morning's little escapade is going to cost him plenty. Whatever I may think of Siraj...*the stupid bastard!*...I lost a son out there today, *Allah* blast his soul. For which the good Baron will pay handsomely, I promise you. Enough, my friend!" he exclaimed, licking his fingers. "The subject of my son disgusts me. Now...where are those two bitches?" And he looked up at his tall commander and smiled.

"Below with the girl, Soraya, my Prince. The one brought on board by the Lady Rochine before we set out from Bayonne last week."

El Nazir stood up and moved to sit beneath the stern windows, slid open to let in the breeze and the morning sunshine, taking the bowl of almonds with him, rubbing his forehead where his turban had left a mark, his commander moving to sit in his tall backed chair. "That woman is full of more wiles than a *djinn*, and can burn just as fiercely," the Sheik said, resting his arm across the windowsill, his eyes following the gulls as they swooped and soared around the *Morning Star*. "I hear tales of her that make even my hair stand on end."

58

"Mmmm, you are right, my Lord Sheik," Raschid replied. "A true *djinn*...'The fire of a scorching wind,' according to the *Surat al-Djinn* in the Koran. I have seen that Lady both ways. Calm and dovelike, when she can almost coo with sweetness...and moments later a raging fury that would consume anything it touched. But she was most insistent about the care to be given to those two infidel bitches...who fought like cornered leopards I may add. Those two Frenchmen were scratched and bitten all over." And he popped an almond into his mouth with a smile.

"No matter, Raschid. We got the Baron's message before we left Bayonne, and now we have them safe, and will be back there in a few days. Next, you must get our temporary pigeon expert to send a fast bird off to Gaston de Vere in Bayonne at first light. He will urgently be waiting for it, but please, Raschid, make sure he chooses the right cage. No good sending a bloody bird to Lord Roger's man in Nantes!"

"This business with pigeons, my Lord? Seems...well madness. Why trust so vital a message to a witless bird?"

"Oh, my loyal, hard-hitting friend. These are no ordinary birds, I assure you. These come from a long line of racers and are bred for their speed and courage. People have been doing this for ages, my Raschid. I thought you would have known that? Started in India centuries ago, and the Romans used them as well, so the books say. They can cover hundreds miles in a single day...without stopping. Their only enemies are hawks and stooping falcons...oh and ignorant peasants with bows and arrows! We have been using them in the Holy Land for years against the Christians who only see a pigeon as food, truly they are ignorant fools! Each bird takes a great deal of training but once trained the really good ones are worth their weight in gold. Each one of those on board is worth a small ransom. So, Raschid, go carefully, yes?"

"Yes, O Mighty One!" He mocked his leader gently, touching his forehead. "I had no idea they were so special; we have not done this before."

"No, my friend, and neither have most foolish Christians! Lord Roger being an exception...and he learned from the Emirs amongst whom he and his daughter trade."

"But why at first light and not straightaway?"

"Raschid, am I supposed to know everything?" El Nazir snorted with a smile. "It is something to do with the sun, I think. But in very truth I don't know. It is just what I was told by the expert who came on board with The Lady. *Allah Be Praised!* Who would have thought those stupid barbarians would not have thought of this message system for themselves? Truly they are mad!"

59

"It seems a great system. We could do with something like that ourselves, both to warn us of trouble and advise us of good chances."

"Mmm. That is a worthy thought, my Raschid. Perhaps we can find an expert of our own to work with us? Train some of our men.

"I will speak with the man, Almahdi. He has come from the Emir of Damascus no less. He is bound to know someone, if you are serious. But what about the Lady Alicia de Burley, my Prince? Will there be trouble from her King?"

"From Richard of England or Philip of France? Take your pick, my friend. They are all infidels whom the Prophet, *Allah bless his name*, will curse from Paradise so we can destroy them once and for all, as Saladin did at the Horns of Hattin! They are of no consequence to me. I do not give a fig for either of them," he said snapping his fingers. "Not even the one known as 'The Lion Heart'. Saladin destroyed King Guy and the entire crusader army at Hattin, *Praise Allah*. He will do the same for this King Richard and that weak fool, Philip of France. None can stand against him. Trust me! *Allah Akbar!*...God is Great!"

"And her young man?"

"A strutting, dung heap cockerel!...*Pray Allah he is drowned and all his men with him*...Let him crow his heart out. In *Allah's* name, what can he do?"

"He sank two of our ships today and killed many of our men. Without him, that skirmish would have been easy."

"*Pish!*" El Nazir exclaimed dismissively, with a wave of his hand. "My son, the 'Great Siraj' was a monkey! A thrice damned baboon to let that Ship Master make such a..a *bonfire* of his whole command! But I have sorted it all properly. By this time that wretched scarlet ship of his will have sunk. Did you see what our artillery did to it? Huge chunks of timber everywhere, and a hole in her side you could drive a camel train through! And the yellow one likewise. Fahwaz and his crews did a great job, and will be well rewarded when we get to Bayonne. No, Raschid. They were sinking when we pulled away. They will surely all be fish food by now."

"And if not, my Lord?"

"*Sweet Allah*, my friend. What ails you? He is no better than any other metal-clad madman who comes out here waving a sword. Even if he managed to survive, do you seriously see him assaulting Château Grise with that rabble at his back? The Baron would make mincemeat of him. And anyway, even if he does make it that far, we will be long gone and he has no way of following us. No fat cog would ever be a match for the *Morning Star*...For my *Surah At-Tariq*...No, Raschid. I have no fear of such a one as he."

"So...to Bayonne."

60

"To Bayonne, indeed. And then round Spain and back to the Circle Sea. Lord Roger has paid me mightily to cage his precious pouting 'pigeon' for him...did you see her breasts? Magnificent! No wonder Lord Roger lusts after her! I tell you, Raschid, were she not an infidel, I would be tempted myself. And now it will cost him even more for I must replace those two lost galleys and their crews. All we have to do now is to deliver that infidel bitch, and her companion, in one piece to the *so* kind and caring Lady Rochine, and that sly bastard, de Vere. Collect our money and get back into the war, and some decent trading. *Insha'Allah!...*God willing" And he touched his forehead with his fingers.

"Will you entertain them here, my Lord?"

"Who?"

"The girls below us. We were specially asked to take 'royal' care of them."

"What? In my cabin, along with that...that painted Jezebel whom The Lady has placed here to watch over them? Are you mad, Raschid! Just listen to them," he said, cocking his head to where they could both hear sharply raised voices. "Shouting viragos, dressed as men! Did you ever see anything more ghastly, or dishonourable? By God, Raschid," he went on, as the shouting below suddenly increased. "If that stupid French bitch doesn't quell them I'll have that great Syrian bastard, Abdul Aziz, whom you have placed outside their door, drag her up here and flog the back off her!"

"That would not please The Lady, I think, my Lord."

"No...but it might please me!" he snarled. "Take 'royal' care of them indeed! That woman takes too much upon herself. I owe her *nothing*, Raschid. I have risked the *Morning Star*, my lovely '*Surah At-Tariq*' in these dangerous waters because I owed her father a huge favour, and for the money, which is truly considerable! Not because I am beholden to that raven-haired witch. And anyway, they *are* being 'royally' cared for: finest clothes, lovely cabin and people to wait on them almost hand and foot."

"So, my Prince. No pretty dining companions."

"I will not sully my soul with even the *sight* of them until I have to. The one dressed like a Houri may be enough to enflame any man...*how strange that in the Koran all Houris are always white? There are no black Houris in paradise...* but she is just another infidel with no shame. God alone knows why the Lady Rochine has dressed her so? To tempt all of us I suppose? But at least the girl is clean. The others stink! Why do these western infidels not wash themselves? Can you imagine sleeping with one of them? Breath like a wet fart and stinking of stale sweat and sewage. Disgusting!" And both men laughed.

"They think washing too often is bad for their health," His Galley Commander said, standing up. "Some only wash three times in their lives, I am told: once when they are born, once when they marry and once when they die!"

"*Sweet Allah!* They are all mad. No wonder so many die in the Holy Land."

"So, Lord. What do you want me to do with them?"

"They can eat in their cabin. Abdul guards their door; Najid can cook for them and bring them their food; that fool, Zafir, can remove the slop bucket, it's about all he's good for, and the infidel bitch, Soraya, can serve them."

"Fine, my Lord. But they cannot stay below the whole time. That would not be good."

"No...we need to keep them healthy, I suppose," he paused then to eat some more honeyed almonds. "They can come on deck before dawn and at sunset, and properly covered, that way their presence will not inflame the men. And they can use the facilities in the bows at the same time. Otherwise they can have a bucket in their cabin. The *Morning Star* is a fighting ship, Raschid, not a fat, lazy, passenger-carrying merchant.

"Now, my friend, get off and speak with Almahdi about pigeons and tomorrow's release, we'll be losing him at Bayonne to return to the Château Grise, and then come back here and dine with me. In the meantime tell that lazy bastard, Yussuf, to bring me some coffee before I see his backbone. *Allah Akbar!...*God is Great!"

Chapter 10...The Lord Baron awaits his messages in the Château Grise.

Away in Gruissan, in his fine suite of apartments at the top of the great Donjon, known to all as the *'Tour Barberousse'*, the 'Redbeard tower', because he'd had the plaster that covered it painted crimson, the Lord Baron, Sir Roger de Brocas of Narbonne and Gruissan waited. Anxious to hear how well his scheme for seizing Alicia de Burley had worked...and whether Sir Gui had been slain along with his whole command as he had planned for, the Baron was impatient for news.

Seated at the great table in his solar, drenched in sunshine, his crystal on its beautiful cedar stand before him in all its pure beauty, he waited for the news to come in, a full silver-gilt goblet of the finest Bordeaux to his hand, alongside silver dishes of dates and delicate sweetmeats.

That they had all set out, he knew. For with Rochine still with him, his crystal had told him so: the ring he had given Gui the night of the fire, and the bracelet Rochine had given to Alicia, making perfect conduits for his mind. And he knew also that the message sent to El Nazir by those two men whom he had placed in Castle Malwood after Alicia's escape, the young man from Oxford and the older man, Henri Duchesne whom he'd sent out there as a guard, had arrived safely because his pigeon relays told him so.

He chuckled at the memory.

Those simple fools thought they had escaped his vengeance!...*Bah! I will show them what the Lord of Narbonne and Gruissan can do when he puts his mind to it...I am better than all of them!*...Better than the Lord of Toulouse under whom he held Narbonne, better than that fool, Philip Valois, King of France, and his ridiculous crusade. Better than anyone!

He sighed with quiet pleasure....*The pigeons have been a brilliant decision. And so easy once you know how to do it...and they fly swifter than even my Charlemagne could ever manage, no matter how fast his four hoofs could carry him...*A true racer could fly fifty miles in an hour, in as straight a line as possible, and cover hundreds miles in a day without stopping. Wonderful! And all his idea...gained from talking with the Emirs that he traded with across the Circle Sea, who had been using pigeons for carrying messages for generations.

But...you needed experts to do it, and they were not easy to find, because mostly they were Muslims. And he smiled at the ignorance of so many Crusaders...*Pigeons carrying messages? What madness! Pigeons are for*

63

eating, dear boy!...And he threw back his head and laughed, his harsh voice echoing round his room....*What fools some people are!*

No...my pigeons are for messages: from home to Narbonne, twelve miles by road, less than half an hour's flying; and to Bordeaux, two hundred and forty miles by road, days on horseback, but by pigeon, without the delays and all the twists and turns, only a few hours!

He could know which ships were going where almost as quickly as their captains did, and plan accordingly. Or to where troops were being sent, or...where an ambush could be set up! And once a bird had been properly trained it would fly to its particular loft from wherever it was released...even from a ship at sea, provided it was not too far from land.

And he never overtaxed his birds. While knowing they could fly great distances, he preferred them doing shorter hops when there was less danger of their getting lost, or of stopping, when he might never get them back. Not always of course, but often, so he had set up relays. Town to town and port to port, and where they might be flying over hawk-infested forests more than one bird would be released. And God help any peasant who shot one down, or any petty lordling whose falcon might stoop on one of them for sport!

He sat back with his goblet in his hand and looked around his room, and out across to where the huge étang, that almost surrounded Gruissan, stretched out to meld with the great Circle Sea beyond.

It had been a hard journey after his family had been kicked off their lands around Toulouse and Cahors, following his father, Lord Thibault's, hopeless rebellion against King Henry of England. A rebellion in which his father had been slain, and the family had been effectively banished to Gruissan.

He growled at that, and drank deeply from the goblet, still full of rage and injustice.

Picking up the dish of sweetmeats beside him, swiftly rising as he did so, he walked across the room to the nearest window and looked across the wide bailey at the great pigeon loft he'd had built inside one of the corner towers. There, around the walls inside it, were myriad square spaces for the birds to nest in, and wooden galleries so that his Pigeon Masters could care for the birds in every way possible.

Even as he watched, there was a great wheeling swirl of them even now, white, grey and mottled black and white, sweeping and twisting around the far side of the castle. And he lifted his goblet as he watched them swooping and tumbling, flashing out around the towers and battlements and then winging away in great circles across the vast étang that almost ringed the castle, their wings flickering in the sunlight as they banked and swirled over the sparkling blue water before racing back again.

He loved to watch them. So harmless to look at...so deadly in effect, and he smiled and grunted in quiet satisfaction, relishing the rushing *swoosh* of their wings when they whistled close past him overhead.

Those pigeons had been his salvation.

The foundation of his success.

He had brought experts back from Syria and the Lebanon, and they had shared their knowledge with those he had carefully chosen as Pigeon Masters. He'd paid out handfuls of silver for the birds themselves, and then he had set up a series of lofts in those towns with which he most wanted to trade along the coast and inland, and, of course, in various ports along the shores of the Holy Land.

And the money had rolled in.

He was always a jump ahead of other traders, and as long as one was not too particular with whom you traded and what that trade was...then there was money to be made. And by fair means, as well as foul, he had built up his vineyards and bought, or acquired, olive groves as well: setting up presses for both, so his wine and oil was now shipped everywhere and he was able to indulge himself in every sort of joy that came to mind.

He smiled, thinking first of Constancia, whom he had loved above all others...and then of Rochine and the deep sensuous pleasure she gave him, and the power she brought to the great crystal he had left on its delicate carved stand, and he pressed his hand into his loins, wanting her. Then he thought of Alicia, and the pleasure that possessing, and schooling her, would give him, for she would be no easy catch and Rochine might well resent her... and he felt the blood rush through him in a sudden burst of fierce excitement.

He drank again, and bit another sweetmeat, while he looked out beyond the great castle and its powerful defences, beyond the town that huddled all around its walls, across the étang that almost surrounded the Château Grise, to the wide, blue, shimmering expanses of the Circle Sea, the beautiful Mediterranean.

...No...it is not just because she is such a challenge that I want the English girl, nor because of her beauty, which is ravishing, nor even for the children I will spring from her womb...nor because it was her father, Sir Henry de Burley, who slew mine at Cahors all those years ago, before my very eyes! No...it is for the Crystal!...

But then it had been Sir Yvo de Malwood, this Gui's father, who had fought Sir Thibault first. Like Tigers they had been until Sir Yvo had fallen. Then, just as his father had stepped up to kill his hated enemy, Sir Henry had attacked him. If he closed his eyes he could see the blows slamming home and

65

hear his father's desperate cry of shock and horror, see his head fly from his body and still feel his hot blood falling all over his face.

Possessing Alicia will wipe that whole slate clean, not least because they are the very last of their lines. With Gui dead she will inherit everything, and by marrying her I will get all the Malwood and Burley lands together...and in so doing I will avenge my father's death, and my vow will be fulfilled... And he ground his teeth with barely suppressed rage.

Well, Sir Yvo and that fucking bitch to whom he had been married were both dead. He had seen to that...and Gui, too, should have been killed...burned to death in the fire he had started. He must have a powerful angel indeed to watch over him, he seethed. He had left him with an arrow piercing his shoulder, pinned by a great timber, and almost surrounded by flames...and the Malwood Emerald about to be completely destroyed for ever!...*And how he got out I still do not know?*...But he and Rochine had taken the girl with them anyway, drugged her and ridden off into the night, while castle Malwood had gone up in flames.

He stalked back to the table and banged his fists on it in rage.

But the bloody girl had somehow slipped Rochine and escaped them...and he, The Lord Baron, Sir Roger de Brocas, had been forced to flee the Old Conqueror's great forest like a common criminal, like a whipped cur, and take to his ship without her...*Yet, God's Wounds, I need the little bitch...she is of the blood!*...The fact that she was already betrothed, with King Richard's agreement and with God's blessing was of no importance...*I have Archbishop Berenguer of Narbonne in my pocket. There is no way that old pederast and whoremonger will dare to deny me...*He would have the good Archbishop dissolve that bitch's betrothal, and then he would order him to marry them out of hand.

As for King Richard, the so called 'Lion heart'...he surely would not make any kind of fuss about one stupid girl and her affairs at this time, no matter how fond of her he might be. No! High politics would take preference! Richard was far too wrapped up in the total madness of his crusade, for which he desperately needed the King of France by his side. And he, de Brocas, had paid Philip plenty for him *not* to be beside him at Vézalay when he and Richard had set out...*And anyway Philip is as involved with John's plan for Richard's murder by the Assassins as I am myself! Sweet Jesus. The Assassins! We must all be mad!...And who had arranged the money to change hands? He had! King Philip Valois of France owed him...and one foolish girl was a small price to pay!*

He snorted with derision.

Quite apart from revenge for past misdeeds, he needed the girl for a wife. That would give him *all* their combined lands, and with Richard killed and John on the throne, with Philip's help of course, and the French army under his own leadership, he would be the most powerful man in the Kingdom, next to John: and with John being the kind of useless little *shit* he truly was, then he could be guaranteed to wreck everything; leaving him, Lord Roger de Brocas, free to seize the crown of England for himself...*and the Devil take the hindmost!*

He grinned then, hugely, and sat down again in front of the great glass orb that was the real seat of his power. Placing his large hands on both sides of it he looked into its crystal depths, wishing Rochine was near him, beneath him, above him, to make the damned thing work!

He gritted his teeth. Alicia-Rochine! Rochine-Alicia! Damn it. He wanted them both! But he needed the girl, first! And that fucking bastard, Sir Gui de Malwood, dead, second! Mother of God!...*Where was that bloody message?*

He looked across his room at the sun now slipping down the heavens, the light changing from harsh to soft gold tinged with pink, and sighed. He would have to wait for the morrow now. Almahdi would not make a release until sunrise, then he would fly off the bird to Bayonne first, and from there the message would be relayed to Narbonne and so to the great loft in the far corner tower.

Then he would know!

Rochine had left several days ago for Bayonne with de Vere and a strong escort, and without her he could not work the Crystal. He writhed his loins at the thought of her, the blood rushing through him again. He knew he wanted her.

But he also wanted Alicia...*Because, above all, I need an heir!*

Someone to carry on his bloodline, something Rochine could never do, even if she had wanted to. What they were to each other was forbidden enough anyway. But a child of such a union? Impossible. Even for him. No! Any child of his had to be born in wedlock and out of a known and accepted lady of virtue and honour. And Alicia de Burley, from one of the oldest families in England, was the perfect chalice for his seed...And always I come back to the Crystal...*It is the blood that makes the Crystal work...and she is of the blood! Her grandmother was my grandfather's sister, and that is how the whole thing works...through the blood. I know that now because of Rochine...because it would not work with my belovèd Constancia! So, with Alicia by my side...anything is possible!*

With Gui and King Richard dead, John on the throne and himself in control of the royal army…she would have no-one else to turn to but him, and he would have the heir he so desperately needed.

He grunted again, with satisfaction. This time it would work, he *knew* it!

In the meantime, he would prepare a message for his people in Bordeaux, and in Nantes, just in case that fucking bastard, de Malwood, survived El Nazir and his *Morning Star*. Either way there were excellent places for an ambush between Nantes and Bordeaux. That was the longest, wildest stretch of their journey…over two hundred miles. Of course, it would need to be carefully arranged, and the troops chosen must be proven fighters and led by men who knew what they were doing. There was now a loft at Nantes; just set up, true, but the men there were keen. De Vere had chosen them himself, and he had arranged for them to be placed in The Duke of Brittany's castle. Port Enforcers in the little Duke's colours…Alan de Courcy and Victor Jonelle. It was just a pity that the Cousins were on the *Morning Star,* this would have been perfect for their skills. No matter. De Courcy was a Knight and Jonelle his right hand man. Both had fought in numerous skirmishes and escalades together and would know exactly whom to engage to join them.

He would send a message out first thing in the morning, and alert them, and Bernard de Vernaille in Bordeaux, whether he had heard from de Vere by then or not…*If that bastard has drowned off Belle Île, with his whole command, so much the better. I will be shot of him at last!* But if, by some miracle, he has survived…then de Courcy and his men down from Nantes, with de Vernaille's help up from Bordeaux, will sort them out once and for all…*Then, by God's Blood, I will finally be finished with him!*…And he chuckled then, thinking of the great emerald ring that the wretched bastard still wore. What an irony! That it should have survived the fire, where it should have been destroyed, only to trap its wearer even more perfectly than even he had planned for; for once Rochine was back with him at the Château, they would then know his every move.

And he chuckled again, not least because he still had his greatest plan yet to look forward to. No fox was ever more cunning! And with that certain smile on his face that all men knew meant trouble for someone, the Lord Baron, Sir Roger de Brocas, tipped the last of his wine down his throat and threw back his head and laughed. Then rising he went out of his room to find his Pigeon Master, Raheel al Moukhtara, the Lebanese founder of his feathered fortunes, and arrange with him two urgent releases for the next morning.

This time there would be no mistake!

Chapter 11...Sir Gui leaves Nantes for Bordeaux.

Three days later, at cock-crow, in the cool, grey half-light of the early morning, Sir Gui de Malwood and his command left Nantes while the mists were still writhing like thin smoke on the river, veiling the fields and the trees all around them in their opaque whiteness, everything fresh and touched with summer magic.

A long line of armoured men in pairs, Gui and Sir Richard in front, Father Matthew on Jupiter behind them and then their squires, followed by all their own Lions. All were freshly mounted, and with all else following: sumpters with their panniers re-packed, some half dozen more than before, and three big tilt carts rather than wagons, they kicked-off from The Angel. Two horses to each cart, and each with large spoked wheels making them lighter and faster on the road. At their trail, trotting on long leading reins, were the girls' mares, Sunburst and Gillygate, and behind them, as a rear guard, rode Allan-i-the Wood on Caesar, de Beaune beside him on a tough, long-legged courser, followed by all their men, and Bouncer running free.

With four scouts ahead and four following behind the last man, each alert to any possible danger, and each regularly replaced with another from the main column so no-one would get bored and careless, they were a formidable force, and Gui was immensely proud of them.

*

Days of furious activity had followed their arrival at the port.

The Angel, as promised by Thomas Blackwood, the *Mary's* enormous Shipmaster, had proven to be a well set-up hostelry indeed: a long two storey building with a large hall, and a staircase along one long wall that led to a handful of rooms above. Each with a simple pallet bed, and fleece-filled mattress in canvas, wrapped round with coarse linen sheeting, a long bolster and a plain stuffed linen coverlet of blue serge. There was a covered slop bucket in one corner, jug of water and basin on a wooden stand in another and each small room had a shuttered window.

Downstairs, tall wooden posts held up the floor above on wide crutches, with pine tables scattered about, some separated from others by simple wooden partitions, like booths, with benches and plenty of stools to sit on, and even a handful of carved straight-backed chairs with greasy cushions. Candles of local beeswax from the Abbey hives, and a large number of simple oil lamps lit the room, casting strange flickering shadows, and there was a wide empty fireplace along the middle of one side of the building.

The whole was presided over by a tall, stooped *aubergiste*, Charles du Vin, scarred from the wars, who was helped by a handful of busy serving men and a bevy of cheerful, wide-eyed tavern girls in blue cotehardies over white kirtles, with red pocketed aprons tied around their waists.

Tommy Blackwood had been right. It was a good and friendly place to be!

With du Vin's help Gui had found good stabling for their destriers and for Sunburst and Gillygate off the *Mary* and for Caesar, Jupiter and the sumpters off the *Pride*; reputable shipwrights and chandlers for Thomas, and an excellent farrier who would sort out all their metal problems. Sir Richard had found a great wharf nearby where the stores from both ships could be kept safe and guarded, and where the men could bed down the following night. It had been a truly welcome start.

That first evening, with Tommy Blackwood and the crews of both cogs, they had packed The Angel to the rafters, devouring with gusto the thick meat pottage for which the *auberge* was well known, with cheese, olives and fresh bread, and drinking toast after toast in wine and Breton cider, for which The Angel was famous throughout the area. The following morning both ships were to be warped down river; wholly emptied and repaired, then keeled over so their fat bottoms could be scraped of all weeds and barnacles, and re-sheathed with tar, pitch and brimstone. There would be no time in the morning for farewells.

So it had been their last night all together, and it had been memorable: John Fitzurse, Gui's huge Master-at-Arms and Tommy Blackwood, their great rolling bear of a shipmaster, having a rowdy drinking match, with both sides roaring on their chosen champions. Each man vowing to drink the other under the table! So it was as well that Gui had spoken with Thomas earlier and secured his willingness to risk the long, dangerous sail south around Spain to meet with them again beyond the Château Grise. There, across the vast étang that almost surrounded Gruissan, they would now meet again; below La Robine, the great canal built by Caesar's Legions that had made Narbonne a famous port, and for which the Château Grise had first been built to guard against *Les Corsairs*.

God willing, in a few weeks' time, their ship repairs would be done...*or by my finger bones there'll be a few broken heads!*... and they would be free to journey on to Gruissan, below Narbonne, and from there to Messina...*where* *the girls are bonny, but their men have heads full of fire and hands full of steel!...*with my Lord Sir Gui, and all his men, to join King Richard's army which by then should safely have arrived there.

"*Christos,* Thomas!" Gui had exclaimed then before the drinking had started, completely astonished. "Will you really? Pick us all up at Gruissan and ship us to Messina?...*If God has helped us to victory and we are all still alive!...*It is a damned long way to go and could be dangerous with known pirates about, and you'll not have us with you round Spain if things get difficult: but to know you will be there for us would truly be outstanding! And be certain, Thomas, I will pay you well."

"*God's Bones, my Lord Baron!*" the big man had roared out, giving Gui such a buffet he had almost fallen over. "I thought you were never going to ask! My lads would not miss such an adventure for all the world. And with good cargo space now you idle buggers have cleared my ship...and after we are seaworthy again...we'll breeze down to Bordeaux, pick up a good load of whatever's going, and sail round to Narbonne.

"It is a famous port, my Lord, and we can unload there, at the deep water quays below the canal they call La Robine, and then just sit tight and wait for you to find us. Narbonne is a lively city, handsome in places: the wine is good and the whores are pretty...an excellent place for tired old sailor-men like me to take some rest!" And he had grinned broadly. "By these finger-bones," he had then added, cracking them enough to make Sir Gui wince, "it will be a pleasure."

"Have you been there before, Thomas?"

"Yes, Lord. Many times on your father's business. Wine here and there, bales of wool and olive oil elsewhere. You father had many interests, Sir Gui."

"So I keep finding out, Thomas," he had said with a wry smile: "In death my father has surprised me more than he ever did in life! I am sure Sir James would have told me all...but we left in such a harum-scarum manner he never had the chance. Tell me Thomas," he had then asked earnestly. "As you seem to know that area well...is there anywhere near Narbonne we could lie up? Someone you could recommend who might help us?"

For a moment, the huge man had looked blank, and Gui's heart dropped. Then with a vast smile he had turned with a great roar of laughter and smitten him on the back to almost send him flying.

"By all the saints, my Lord, there *is* such a place!" he had boomed, with another great shout of laughter. "I am just amazed not to have thought to say so before. One really good place, and a really good man who owns it too. A man I would trust my life to. Armand Chulot of *The Golden Cockerel* at Les Monges. It is a small hamlet about six miles out of Narbonne; noted for its

71

food and its comfort. His wife, Claudine, sees to all that and rules her large husband with a rod of iron. And Armand is a big man, Sir Gui. He and I could be brothers. Get there and he will see you right. He has no love for the Baron, any more than you do. My word on it! Give him my name and he will help you."

"Thomas…You're a saint! Thank you, for that and we will look for you, and *The Pride,* in a month's time…about the turn of August I expect."

"*Ha!* A saint, am I?" and he had thrown back his head with another great shout of laughter. "I don't think even my dear mother would have thought that!" and he had laughed again hugely. "My Lord, I'll not let you down. My lads and I will be there, I wouldn't want to miss such an adventure with you for a whole hogshead of Burgundy! You're as fine a man as ever your father was, my Lord. I would be proud to serve you as I did himself, and that's no error!" And reaching out his enormous, calloused hand he clasped Gui's in a hard, dry grip that had made his eyes water.

"And there's my hand on it! Now, my Lord, I'm off to drink that soft-skinned, feeble-minded bastard of a Master-at-Arms under the table. God be with you Sir Gui, for we must be warped from here tomorrow, so I'll not see you again for a while. But my thoughts and prayers will be with you, and your lads too. Just you get that beauty of yours back, and sort out that fucking bastard who's got her. Look for me in August below the Château Grise. I'll not let you down!" And with a last solid buffet, he had rolled away with a final great shout of defiance to join Fitzurse and all their supporters.

*

And now, before cockcrow, they were leaving.

Crossing the wide river on the old cable ferry in the early morning mist, just busy grey shadows with the water sliding by, tall rushes at the edges full of pink and white milkweed, amongst which brown water voles scurried. The splash of a fish, the flash of an otter, the ripples spreading outwards; the quack and flurry of wings as a duck sat up in the water, startled by the sudden appearance of the old ferry in the strange misty light that covered the river…then rushing silence and the heavy, dank smell of fresh water and river weed as they hauled their way across.

The ferry's cable was cold and slimy; the old boat of long planks and dark timbers, with stout rails on either side was wide and slow…as backwards and forwards they hauled the boat until all were across. And then away towards

Vertou and distant Bordeaux. Tilt carts, horses and men, swallowed up by the early morning river mists, just turning from grey to opaque white and softest pink, then golden as the sun finally lifted up behind them to herald the new born day with fresh warmth and colour.

Chapter 12...How many plans were laid at The Angel.

That first day in Nantes, and the two days following, had been filled with unrelenting activity, from paying courtesy visits to the Castle, and the absent Duke's Seneschal under de Courcy's bitter glare, impotent to do Sir Gui any scathe; to spending time with Abbot Hugo Gravier at the great Benedictine Abbey at Vertou, just beyond the town.

A thin, ascetic man, with high cheekbones and piercing grey eyes that missed nothing...the Father Abbot, together with Father Matthew, pleaded their cause throughout the town. And the Chef du Port, still shivering in his boots at the sight of the tall Spanish Benedictine, pledged his continued assistance to Thomas Blackwood and his damaged ships.

Fresh horses had been bought and bargained for, and fresh stores found to replace those lost in the attack; armour had been checked and dents hammered out; horseshoes looked over, and replacements for Beau and Merlin created by the farrier recommended by du Vin. And everywhere they went they found people friendly and willing to assist them, as much because of the silver they had to spend as the sharp manner in which de Courcy and the Chef du Port had been so firmly dealt with, and their defeat of the corsairs that frightful morning.

A whole day of fierce bargaining had secured the horses, with the help of the good Abbot Hugo who, with his own expert knowledge of sound horse flesh, sharp eyes and closeness to Holy Church, no-one wanted to fall foul of! And everywhere the old Abbot went, Paul of Bartley and William Fisher went with him, lifting feet, tapping frogs, peering at teeth and running expert hands down hocks and over withers to make sure that every beast bought was as good as could be found. Each horse was then run up and down to check its action before being led to a wide corral behind the inn...where every soldier was given his choice of mount to care for.

And it was the Abbey itself that had provided them with the three big tilt carts and the bags of meal, oats and huge nets of hay with which to fill them, along with earthenware pots of honey, wonderful fat candles from their bees, three large kegs of cider, for which the area was famous, and the inevitable skeins of smoked sausages, nets of hams and fresh baked loaves Truly the Abbey did them proud.

As Abbot Hugo had said to Father Matthew when he moved to thank him, "Those carts are of little value to me, Matthew, compared to where you are going. Bring me back a Holy Relict from Jerusalem as just repayment and take it off your mind...and when next I write to the Holy Father, I shall tell him of your need, and our loss, and I am sure his treasury will replace them twofold!" And they had chuckled at the Abbot's scheme for fooling the Curia.

As for the men?...They had rollicked and strutted round the town like the bold cockerels they were, a girl under every arm, jolly bully-boys out for a good time. Their pockets full of silver and their hearts full of lust, and none of them had hung onto their money for long, as Sir Richard had forecast. They drank it, ate it, gambled it or cheerfully lusted it away, leaving the girls and the merchants of Nantes better off, their carpenters with plenty to do, and themselves with thick or broken heads and empty purses! *And the girls with bigger bellies come Christmas!*

Sir Richard had his three nights between clean cotton sheets; de Beaune his hot meals and a pretty girl or two to warm his pallet; Allan spent time with his verderers...and Gui, Richard and Father Matthew gained a breathing space to talk over the next stage of their journey.

Then, on their last night, Gui had called all his commanders together in The Angel.

*

And on that night the place was heaving, the *aubergiste* and his serving hands dispensing leather jacks of local wine and cider as fast as they could go...as well as trays of local cheese and olives, fresh bread and smoked meats, or rough glazed bowls of pottage, thick with herbs and onions and flavoured with garlic.

Gui and his men had sat in a far corner in deep shadow...*don't worry m'Lord, you'll be private there for certain*...their table shielded with high wooden partitions, as were some others. With knives and spoons in hand, and their table softly lit with small oil lamps, they had cheerfully enjoyed the wine, pottage, cheese and cider that had been brought to them and placed around a great wooden platter of fresh baked bread. All around them the room was packed and filled with loud noise and bustle: shouts for wine or food, along with cheerful shrieks from the serving girls and bursts of raucous male laughter.

"So..." Gui said, wiping his mouth with the back of his hand, as he finished eating, and looked round the table. "We leave tomorrow at first light, before the sun is up. Is everything done?"

"Yes, my Lord," Fitzurse replied through a mouthful of pottage, putting his spoon down. "Panniers packed and ready to load; carts checked over...we had to replace a cracked axle, harnesses too...and all loaded with stores: smoked meats from the town, and some great hams, with barrels of wine from The Angel, and cider from the Abbot; oil for cooking and freshly filled water bags. They also gave us some spare hides for repairs. You did fine work with that Abbot, Father; saved us time and money, loads of it!"

"Abbot Hugo has been very good to us, that's for certain," Father Matthew replied. "For all that Vertou is a brother House, sight of the Holy Father's letters helped hugely. And he *does* know a good horse when he sees one! With his sharp eyes around the horse market," he smiled broadly, "no one dared to try and over-charge us. We are almost as well provided now as when we set out from Malwood."

"Just a shame we had to ditch so much of our armour and spare weaponry, my Lord," Fitzurse said ruefully. "Where we are going I think we could do with them. Thank God, we hung onto our clothyard shafts. Arrows for longbows cannot be bought in Brittany, that's for certain!"

"Oh...I wouldn't worry too much about that, Master-at-Arms," Sir Richard said lazily. "If our sunshine cruise was anything to go by, we're likely to pick up all we need along the way!" and there was a ripple of laughter around the table.

Then turning to Gui and pointing to Allan-i-the-Wood, he added in his laconic fashion. "Talking of which, this lad's been a tower of strength, Gui. Got that young farrier who made those shoes for Beau and Merlin to knock up a great pile of spare arrow heads, both shaped bodkins and broad heads. He and his assistant have been hard at it the past two days. There are two good bags of goose fletchings we rescued off the *Mary*, and we can cut fresh shafts along the way...so the arrows John was concerned about should now be less of a problem. Allan also found a tanner to make a load of extra water skins, remembering what Jean had said earlier about needing plenty of water. He's done well." And there was a general growl of pleasure from them all.

"And what about the lads?" Gui asked, after giving Jean a smile and a further nod of thanks. "There are none in here that I can see. But I expect they're about somewhere?"

"Spoke with Sir Richard, My Lord," Jean de Beaune said firmly, "and they're under curfew tonight. Hordle John has them well organised; he and young Thomas Ringwood, along with two of mine. Want them fresh and bright tomorrow...not rat-arsed like they were two nights past! Those two Bashleys could drink the Loire dry, let alone half a hogshead of Chouchen cider!"

"Good Lord!" Father Matthew exclaimed, laughing. "Chouchen cider? That stuff is made with bee stings and honey...strong enough to knock over a horse; I am surprised they got up at all!"

"Bee stings?"

"Yes, Gui. Bee stings, traditional in Brittany," he added, laughing at Gui's grimacing look of horror. "Added during fermentation, gives it extra kick, dear boy!" And there was a further ripple of laughter.

"Anyway, my Lord," de Beaune persisted. "Fitzurse and I will check on 'em later; so they should be fine for early tomorrow.

"Good, well done. Now people," Gui said, with a nod of his head toward the tall Benedictine by his side, dropping his voice as he did so. "Gather in, here's the plan."

And pulling a curled piece of parchment from his scrip, Father Matthew had unrolled a small crude map across the table, weighting it with a small oil lamp on each corner, and using the point of his knife to show them what he and Gui, with Sir Richard, had decided, they all bent forward to see and hear more clearly what there was to say.

"Here are we in Nantes," Matthew said dropping his voice, "and we need to get here, to Bordeaux. There is no old Roman highway from here to there, more's the pity. The old Via Aquitaine that will take us to Narbonne starts at Bordeaux. But there is a reasonable route that will get us there starting at Vertou.

"I had several hours with Abbot Hugo and he knows it well, as his monks journey from here to Bordeaux about four times a year to sell wine and buy wool. The Abbot's advice is to go from Vertou to Chantonnay, through Clisson, and then to Niort. King Henry has built a great castle there, which Richard is strengthening with a huge Donjon, so we can be sure of a warm welcome. From there we go through Saint-Jean-d'Angély, to Saintes, Pons and finally to Bordeaux.

"Over two hundred miles of difficult country; but at this time of year it should be dry enough not to slow us down too much. Saint Jean should be a good place for us, Gui. There is another Benedictine Abbey there, said to house the Head of John the Baptist."

"Hence the name of the town."

"Yes."

"Wasn't there some trouble there, Father? Years ago?" Sir Richard asked. "Over Henry's marriage to Queen Eleanor?"

"Yes. The town objected to their becoming part of the King's lands. But Henry besieged the place, smashed a hole through their walls, burst in...and, um, the good town worthies of Saint Jean d'Angély rather swiftly decided that perhaps Henry wasn't such a bad fellow after all!" And they all laughed.

"Nevertheless, Father," Allan-i-the-Wood said slowly. "That is still a long journey through what is to us unknown country. What do we know of it?"

"A broad mixture, Allan: small villages and little towns scattered amongst vast woods and forests; wide areas of wasteland and busy cultivation, the soil is good here...much like the Forest at home but on a huge scale, with vineyards, orchards and olive groves. And wild game of course: much boar, '*sanglier*' they call it here, deer, partridge, pheasant. You may feel more comfortable in it than I would. And I have been through it before."

"And bandits and outlaws, beggars, muggers and thieves...and somewhere de Brocas!" Sir Richard snorted.

"Yes," Gui said grimly, looking round the table, dropping his voice. "Sir Richard is right. Somewhere de Brocas! And maybe closer than you think," he added quietly, leaning back against a wooden partition. "Remember de Courcy? That idiot who nearly got himself killed when we arrived, and the other big man with him, Victor Jonelle? Well, they are more than just in the Duke of Brittany's pay. They are both in Philip's pay as well."

"The King of France, Sir Gui?" Fitzurse asked him startled.

"The very same, John. De Beaune here recognised them. Fought against them in the Vexin a year back...only they don't know they've been recognised...that's why I wouldn't take Jean with me to the castle yesterday. And we know what Philip has planned for King Richard...and what part de Brocas hopes to play in that. I think, now, that he engineered that whole confrontation just in order to have a crack at me!"

"Didn't realise what they was taking on, my Lord," Fitzurse said, with a chuckle. "You'd've made mincemeat of them!"

"Maybe, John. But even the best can make mistakes. They only needed to get lucky once, and then de Brocas would have won everything!"

"No matter, Gui. It didn't happen," Sir Richard said smoothly, leaning across the table, this time with no casual affectation. "And I know you're the best blade in the King's army! However, forewarned is forearmed! So the sooner we slip out of here tomorrow the better."

"I agree," Gui said quietly, rolling up the map and handing it to the tall Benedictine by his side. "I want us to be up and away before sparrow-fart tomorrow. No fuss and no farewells, do them tonight. A Roman breakfast to start with, and then off up-river to the ferry, and across to Vertou. And don't worry," he added with a grin, full of mischief, seeing their faces drop. "Father Matthew has arranged a proper meal break there to see us on our way, so don't let anyone be dismayed by a drink of water and a hunk of bread first thing!

Now, my friends, no getting up, but a quick toast…" and he hesitated…*be safe, my darling. Wherever you are, be safe!*…Then looking round at them he said quietly: "To 'good fortune and absent friends!' And with that they raised their jacks and beakers, clacking them together with a quiet burst of noise, and broad smiles of satisfaction.

"Right, gentlemen," Gui said, wiping his mouth. "I've paid our shot with Charles, with a bit extra, as he's been mighty good to us too. So…off with you all, and get what rest you can, for we have an early start tomorrow and a long way to go!" And with muttered conversation and muted laughter, they had all stood and left. Gui, Sir Richard and Father Matthew up the stairs to their pallet beds…the rest, arms across each other's shoulders, and rocking slightly as they walked, to join their men and bed down for as much rest as they could get.

*

And with their leaving, The Angel also seemed to empty.

The men streaming out into the soft warm darkness of that moonlit July night, talking, laughing, staggering, in groups and in ones and twos, into the streets and alleyways, with the houses leaning into one another full of whispers. And so away to their homes, while inside Charles and his people tidied around the inn.

But amidst all that earnest talk, no-one saw the small, motionless figure slouched in the darkest shadows of the booth beside that from which Gui and his Commanders had just left; nor noticed the sharp eyes glinting, nor heard the soft shuffle of movement drawing closer. Nor had anyone any occasion to hinder the slim figure, deeply hooded, of Peter Le Croix, the 'Ferret', who slipped out amidst the cheerful farewell bustle of everyone just then leaving, pausing to look up to the shuttered windows above him, before turning up the nearest dark alley.

Quick and nimble as a dockside rat, hugging the noisome darkness. Furtive, scuttling from ginnel to ginnel and crabbing round corners, a long cloak hanging from his shoulders, the little man set off to find the Chef du Port, Monsieur Roland, and the lean, hard authority of Sir Alan de Courcy and Victor Jonelle.

The 'Ferret', ostler at The Angel by day and petty thief at night, had been used by them before. Promised a handful of silver for information about the English soldiers, the Ferret had rubbed his gritty hands together and smiled.

But just a handful now for what he had heard? *Non!* He had really good stuff to give them. Red hot from the fire…and this time he wanted more!

*

An hour after the sun had risen the Lord Baron's pigeon relays fluttered into life:

From Sheik El Nazir at sea to de Vere and the Lady Rochine at Bayonne: 'I have the girls. I left him sinking. Two days.'

From Bayonne onward to Narbonne and to the great pigeon loft at The Château Grise: 'He has the girls. Red cog sinking. Bayonne in two days.'

From Château Grise to de Vere at Bayonne: 'Good news. Bring them to me swiftly as arranged. Unmarked. Undamaged. One week. Be wise!'

*

Backwards and forwards de Brocas's winged Mercuries flew with their tiny cylinders, each one closely sealed and colour-marked to avoid loss of time at each transfer: high and fast and without pause. No hawk or stooping falcon with hungry eyes stopped them; the bells in each loft signalling their arrival, as crooning and bobbing their heads, their messages were taken, replaced or simply transferred to the next carrier. Each pigeon master holding his bird with care and gentleness; each feathered Mercury worth its pigeon-weight in gold.

From Nantes to Bordeaux to Narbonne and to Grise: 'He survived and has left. Seventy men and three carts. Nantes-Niort-Saintes, via Saint Jean d'Angély, then Pons - Bordeaux. Suggest the stream this side Saint Jean!'

From Grise to Bordeaux to de Courcy at Nantes: 'Agree! Liaise with de Vernaille at Bordeaux.'

From Grise to Bertrand de Vernaille at Bordeaux: 'It will be at the stream the other side of Saint Jean d'Angély! Liaise with de Courcy at Nantes.'

Lord Roger de Brocas drank his wine and rubbed his hands…*So, the bastard escaped El Nazir! He must have the luck of the Devil…But at least I have the girl…now I will kill her man!*…The trap would be set, and he like the great black spider he was, would now wait for his fly to become helplessly

80

entangled in the web of his careful planning, and suck his victim dry of every hope and dream.

Throwing back his head, he held up his goblet to the sun and smiled.

*

Later the same day, the notice of the Chef du Port, Monsieur Roland du Clefs, was brought to a body found in the stables that morning, where the two stranger knights had left their horses. A small man, three fingers of his right hand hacked off and stuffed in his mouth, his green woollen cotehardie torn around his shoulders and filled with vomit, the body hidden beneath a great pile of hay...its throat cut to the bone. An obscene, yawning smile in a vast pool of blood. An ostler from The Angel, Peter Le Croix, 'The Ferret'. And the Hue and Cry was raised!

Chapter 13...On board the Morning Star.

A licia and Agnes were standing near their cabin door waiting to go up on deck at sunset, as they'd been instructed would then be allowed...*and not before time too!*

Both now finely dressed in beautifully embroidered bliauts with wide sleeves of finest blue and crimson cotton, belted at the waist with the softest suede dyed to match and studded with small pearls, they were astonished by the sheer quality of their clothes. Each lovely dress moulded to their breasts and flowing over their hips to the floor in long pleats, with soft leather shoes to match.

Agnes, looking down at herself and running her hands over her hips, had never experienced such luxury, and was amazed by it: "Oh, my Lady...Alicia," she gasped, spinning round making her skirts swirl out. "This is just beautiful!" And she twirled again out of sheer pleasure, her mind completely lost to their situation.

Alicia, very aware of the cost of all they had been given, and the trouble taken to provide them, was anxious...and full of the fear of the unknown: of how long it was going to take to get to their final destination; about Gui...*and how, in God's name, am I to cope with de Brocas?*...Concerned also with what might be expected of them in return for such expensive finery...*For surely this will be no free gift!*

"Agnes, you..you look just splendid, sweetheart," she responded, her mind not fully engaged. "We both do. This material is truly delicious," she added, running the fine cotton through her fingers. "Light and soft. And these belts must have cost a great deal too."

Soraya smiled then. "I am so pleased you like them. I chose the material, and *Monsieur le Baron* had them specially made. He said he knew what fitting to give you both. I don't know how? Do... do you like them, my Lady?" she asked hesitantly.

"Oh, Soraya, very much," Alicia said then with her brilliant smile. "Though I hate the giver! Nevertheless we cannot wear rags...and these are surely better than that. And, please, when we are together like this, please call me 'Alicia'. In public, of course, we must observe all the niceties, but not when we are alone. I could not bear that. Truly, these clothes are very costly. I only hope they do not cost us all as well!"

"Money?" Agnes asked puzzled.

"No, not money," Alicia replied softly. "In other ways that I can only guess at!" And she shrugged eloquently at Soraya, and turned away.

"What do you mean, 'not money', Alicia?" Agnes questioned her innocently.

"Oh, nothing, Honeyone," she replied with a smile. "Just a stray thought; don't let it bother you." and she looked at Soraya again with slightly raised eyebrows. "Things are not always quite what they seem, are they?" Then noting Soraya's slight grimace, and sideways look, she said: "Greeks bearing gifts don't you think?" and there was a pause then, until she realised her allusion to the wars of Troy had been lost on both of them, adding with another shrug: "Oh, don't worry about me; I'm just feeling sad, not bad...or mad. Just fed-up not *knowing* anything!" And she turned then and went and sat down on the edge of the bed.

Fed and watered in fine style they might be, but cut off from any normal contact with the outside world, and not knowing what was happening to them, or those they most loved and cared for most, was very frightening.

After their sudden arrival, El Nazir had never called to see his two captives, leaving it wholly to others to do so, treating them as if they carried the plague, concerned that his crew might be infected by the very sight of two such lovely Christian girls. They were only to be allowed on deck at dawn and sunset, and even then only if covered with a chador, which having tried on they both hated. *It isn't just the feel of the things, all enveloping and stifling, it is their unrelieved blackness!* Used to fresh air, openness and colour, both English girls felt oppressed. Soraya, who had travelled with the Lady Rochine and her father across the Circle Sea to Syria and beyond, was not so affected.

And they were tightly guarded.

Outside their door stood a huge Syrian warrior, Abdul Aziz, one of El Nazir's most trusted men, with pointed black beard and black sloe eyes; Christian mail on thick leather strengthened with extra iron plates across his chest, and polished steel from wrist to elbow. He wore heavy mail on black leather chausses, a mailed coif and a polished nasal helmet topped with a gilded point behind which was a silver plume holder, and on his feet black thigh boots with toes and greaves of shining steel.

Across his arms he carried a great scimitar, which he sometimes rested, point down on the deck. Its broad curved blade, forty inches long and six inches wide at the bottom, was a shimmering terror of sharpened steel, a truly wicked looking weapon that could cut a man in two, and which he hefted as if it were matchwood every time they went on deck, or when he barred the door with his great body should anyone need to leave or enter the cabin. From his shoulders hung a long cloak of the finest white silk embroidered with a great golden scimitar, the symbol of his master, and his voice was dark and full of stones...*in very truth he terrifies me!*

So apart from Najid their cook, *who is really kindly despite I cannot understand a word he says*, and Zafir their chamber servant, and of course Soraya herself, *whom I love more and more each day*, and who was with them almost all the time, they saw no other members of the *Morning Star's* crew. The exception being El Nazir's Guard Commander, Raschid al Din, who had given the orders about their topside visits, and came down twice a day to look them over and ask Soraya if there was anything she needed for her two charges.

And each time he looked at them almost with disgust, as if they were something unspeakable: as if even to touch them would soil him in some way. While very different from what, in all abject terror, they had been half expecting, he never touched them, and each time he came, he only spoke Arabic.

Alicia, watching him watching her, was certain he could have spoken in Frankish if he had wanted to, and she felt subtly humiliated, which was presumably his intention. The second time he came she just shrugged it off...*If he wants to behave in such an ignorant, boorish manner that is his problem not mine. The man is no better than a common peasant!*...And she determined that every time he came to their cabin she would make a practice of smiling at him. And every time she did so he grimaced and almost visibly shuddered, until she felt like sticking her tongue out at him, like the hoyden she used to be!

"What on earth is the matter with that man, Soraya?" Alicia asked after his second visit. "He looks at us as if we are unclean in both body and soul. He behaves like an ignorant peasant!"

Soraya laughed. "*Au contraire*, my Lady...Al-ic-ia," she said with a smile, her husky voice tripping prettily over the syllables. "He is of the Arab class most high. And you are both Christians, therefore infidels, and women," she added sweeping her hands over her figure. "And in his eyes 'uncovered', and, so...so you are...*sans honneur*...without honour...*effrontée*..shameless," she added triumphantly, struggling for the right word. "He also regards you as *putains*..whores, because you are showing your arms, and your hair and faces, uncovered. I always wear a yashmak, sheer silk though it may be, and my huque, when I go from here, that long dark blue cloak with a hood? So I don't have to wear a chador. It is the Lord Baron's orders, and I am properly covered, so the man has to accept me. And-and...then," she hesitated again, blushing prettily. "Then, you do not wash as often as they do...and..and as I do. So he thinks you..you *empester*," she said shaking her hands in frustration. "That you stink, and are...unclean, and therefore unworthy!"

84

Alicia shrugged her shoulders and shook her head. "I have noticed that you wash yourself often, or at least try to do. At home we are told too much bathing will make us ill. Gui and I bathe at least once a week, and that is considered dangerous by many. But I do my best with a hazel twig to keep my teeth clean at least."

"You are travelling to a hot country, Al-ic-ia. At the Château, *Monsieur Le Baron* insists that everyone must bathe *every* day! Not only that but that every girl must be shaven smooth...in all places!"

"*No!*" Both girls exclaimed, absolutely shocked.

"I know about the Lady Rochine," Alicia said, ignoring Agnes's open mouth and stunned eyes. "She showed me the night of the fire, before we went to bed. I thought it was just her. The sort of thing she might do to shock; and I was shocked. Well, stunned to be honest, never having seen such a thing before. But you say every girl in the Château? Every girl?" she asked again. "*Completely?*" Looking at Agnes' horror struck face, and trying not to giggle

"Yes, Al-ic-ia," Soraya said, smiling at Agnes' reaction. "*Completely!* Underarms and...and secret places, *both!* But not every girl. Only those amongst us who serve his guests the most. *Monsieur Le Baron* insists, and in truth there is less sickness in the Château than anywhere else I know. We use special balms to make our skin soft and silky, and perfume to enhance our beauty...not to hide the stink of a dirty body as most women do. And with no hair on us, except on our heads of course, it is much more comfortable in the hot weather. We do not get so sticky...nor so itchy in...in...our secret places," she ended in a rush, blushing again. "No horrid spots or rashes." Then, taking hold of the rim of her pantaloons, and looking wickedly sideways, she added, "Shall I show you?"

"*No!*" Agnes said, surprised at Soraya's easy acceptance of something so intimate and shocking. Something she was not used to from someone she hardly knew.

"No, not tonight, Soraya," Alicia said with a chuckle. "I don't think Agnes is ready for that yet, are you, sweetheart? But we'll get there. I can't imagine what Maude and Judith would say at home!" And they both giggled and then laughed.

A little bashfully Alicia said, "I have my..my 'fur' clipped, as Agnes knows, because she does it. But never shaved. I had never even heard of such a thing until the Baron came to Malwood. Is it difficult? Painful?"

"No - and one day I will show you how, and shave you. Both of you!" she said with a huge grin at Agnes's appalled face. "You will see then how free you feel and how smooth and fresh. Truly," she added, with her husky laugh, "you will both be amazed! Now come on," she beckoned, handing them their chadors, and helping them put them on as the sound of heavy feet came to their ears: "It is time for us to go on deck, and I can't wait to use the 'facilities'. That ghastly bucket? Urrrgh!"

*

From where they were, two short flights of steps took them past the upper deck of rowers, the stench of them strong on the evening air, past the Hortator's great drum and his fleece lined seat, through a small arched doorway, and onto the top deck at last, right beside the sterncastle on which was mounted the Scorpion that had so smashed the *Mary's* fo'c'stle to pieces.

Beside them were Sheik El Nazir's suite of rooms, lamps being lit inside just as the sun was almost touching the sea in a blaze of yellow and orange glory, the whole sky seeming lit by scarlet and crimson flames, the clouds of night coming down upon them, tinged with purple and midnight blue.

"Thank God, this day is over at last," Alicia said when they had finally reached the bows, where the *Morning Star's* Roman-style ballista stood unmanned on its turntable atop her forecastle. Without doubt this has been the worst time of my life so far! Just so dreadful! I still can't wholly believe it! Only this morning we were happily on the *Pride*, bumbling along towards Bordeaux, Gui just over there," she pointed to where the *Mary* might have been. "Now," she said getting angry, "we've been stolen onto a foreign vessel filled with our enemies - and I am on my way, like some sort of Christmas present, to be placed in the power of the very worst, and most wicked of men I have ever met. Even worse, a man who is intending to force marriage on me! The very thought of which is more hateful than anything I can ever imagine! Oh...oh, *Christos!*" And she stamped her foot on the deck. Then with a sigh, "Where are those 'facilities' that idiot Zafir mentioned to you, Soraya? I need them almost as much as you do...*to be sick in!*"

Soraya, who'd been listening to Alicia's rising voice with great concern, was swift to answer her. "They are close here, near the anchors, Alic-ia," she said. "Low down near the water, behind that wooden screen. When there is a sea running it can be very dangerous. There is a sort of closed-in box you sit on, holding onto some ropes on either side..and..and, that's what you do!" she stammered, suddenly embarrassed. Anxious not to offend the English milady whom she had been so strongly ordered to care for.

"You mean we stick our bums over the edge of this ship, holding onto ropes, and hope we don't get washed overboard?" Agnes asked horrified.

"Yes, Mistress Agnes. And no rags, the sea will clean you!" Soraya replied with a laugh, as if it was the most natural thing in the world. "Look, I will go first and you can see what I do. I'm bursting, and I *hate* using a bucket! You will see, this is not so bad...not so difficult as it seems. Just don't get caught short in the middle of the night when it's pouring with rain and the sea is running high!"

And with amazed looks on both their faces they watched while Soraya almost disappeared from view down a few steps, lifted up all her garments and squatted on the wooden box provided, hanging onto two thick rope handles that hung from either side over the gunnels of the *Morning Star*, while the sea playfully smacked her naked buttocks.

Agnes followed very nervously, and there were plenty of shrieks which made them all laugh. And then finally Alicia, no less anxious but absolutely refusing to show it to either of her companions...*if Agnes can do this so can I!*...and actually relishing the sudden cold freshness of the sea as it rose up and suddenly sloshed over her exposed tail, and between her legs, making her shriek almost as much as Agnes had done!

By then they were all giggling, and moving away to the port rails pointing out across the port bows to where the distant shore appeared to be floating past them, a long, dark undulating line of land, the black shadows of woods and forests, the twinkling of distant lamp light in the warm darkness where there were houses, farms and villages. But the sight of the shore so visible, yet so far way, flattened Alicia's spirits and she walked away to lean across the rail on her own.

Where are they now? she thought, the wind from their passage and off the sea fluttering her hair as she looked past the distant shore line, and beyond into the far blue yonder with unseeing eyes as the sun slowly disappeared behind her, the gold and crimson afterglow a vast sheet of colour across the sky...*Where were they? Gui, Richard and Father Matthew...and all the others?*...Had they really got away safe from the Mary? That dreadfully smashed up wreck?...*Surely I would know if anything really bad has happened...Surely, if Gui were dead I would know?*

But her very soul shuddered at that, refusing even to contemplate it, and she hugged herself fiercely. How she loved him...and missed him! Not just for the loving...but for himself: his humour, the sound of his voice, the crunch of his tread, the feel of his hands when he hugged her, the touch of his lips: the strong, musky very *maleness* of him!

That smell of leather, armour and stables...*He makes me feel so safe...and special. Oh Mary, Mother of God, keep him safe!*...And she felt the prickle of tears behind her eyes, and her heart shouted....*Where are you? I* *love you so much it hurts. I need you so: don't forget me, my darling! Don't forget me!...*A cry from the very depths of her soul, as lonely and forlorn as that of the passing gulls, planing and turning so closely above the waves.

"Are you alright, my Lady..my Alic-ia?" Agnes asked softly, coming up beside her with Soraya.

"No...not really," she said with a great sigh, turning her face towards her and back again. "I was just wondering where they all are," she added, putting her arm around Agnes. "Gui, Sir Richard and all the others. Your Allan, too, Sweetheart," she said to Agnes, giving her a swift cuddle. And she dashed her hand across her face with a soft sob, as the tears fell from her eyes. "And what will happen to us? How am I to confront that...that *bastard*, and his witch of a daughter? *How?* When he has been responsible for so much wickedness and misery to those whom I love most! I don't know. *I don't know!*" And she wept as though her heart was breaking, burying her face in her hands, while the others moved swiftly to put their arms around her and comfort her.

For a moment, as they clung together, they were all silent. Then, taking a deep breath, Alicia stood back, wiping her eyes with the back of her hands to brush away her tears and gaze out across the railings at the darkening sea.

"How silly of me," she sniffled briefly, giving them a watery smile. "This will never do! Lady Margaret would be brisk and cheerful about something like this, wouldn't she?" she said turning towards Agnes.

"Yes, my love, she would," Agnes replied, brushing her tears from her cheeks with her hand. "Sir Gui's lovely mother," she added turning towards a puzzled looking Soraya. "A wonderful Lady loved by all....murdered by the Baron. 'No point in crying over spilt milk, young Agnes,' she would have said with a smile and a swift pat on the back...and then got on with sorting things out. That's what she was like when things went wrong!"

"And so must we be!" Alicia said, taking another deep breath. "Gui would expect it of us...of me; no matter how much he might sympathise with our situation, or hate what has happened. All we can do is the best we can. And that does not mean dissolving into a hopeless puddle of salty water when things go bad. 'Things' just happen sometimes...and we'll just have to make the best of everything. Gui is coming for us, I am sure of it!"

She turned away for a moment then, listening to the sea hissing down the ship's sides, the calls of the crew at the stern, the creak of her timbers, the groans of her slave rowers below decks and the muted rattle of their chains...and then she looked up and around her.

At the *Morning Star,* oars drawn in, flying free with the wind behind her whistling across her deck, and through her rigging, as she barrelled into the warm July darkness. Ploughing through the short rollers, each topped with foamy white, she swooped down the darkly blue and green troughs, then up again. And as the *Morning Star* rose up, so Alicia's eyes were drawn the whole length of her tilted deck to the very sterncastle where El Nazir's great cabin, right above theirs, was filled with golden light and sudden laughter.

And to the steersmen by their great steer boards, one either side of the ship, lit by two huge lanterns at her stern, with other crewmen around them. Then up to the masts themselves, soaring up into the midnight-blue darkness, their great lateen sails let out as far as they would go, powering the *Morning Star* forward, two crewmen just glimpsed at the base nearest the stern, behind some great coils of rope, waiting for further orders…and all beautifully backlit by the last dying light of that awful day, as the western horizon finally faded to a long, broad band of palest crimson and gold, beneath the gathering velvet of the night, where the first stars were just blinking into life high above her.

Turning then, she opened her arms to Agnes and Soraya, so needing the touch and feel of human love and kindness.

"Oh, my Lady," Agnes said in a whisper, burying her head into Alicia's shoulder, as Soraya moved to put her arms around them both. "I think of them all too: my Allan and his gurt hound, that Bouncer, and the lovely burr in his voice, and his kindness and his kisses. Makes me go hot just thinking of them," she smiled. "Then - then I think of that poor busted up ship, with a hole in her you could drive a tilt cart through…and then I'm not sure of anything anymore. If they survived…or what?"

"Don't you dare think otherwise, Agnes Fitzwalter!" Alicia said firmly, turning the girl and giving her a shake. "I won't even let you think it. They were still afloat when those two bastards took us off the *Pride*. And the *Mary* couldn't have a better Master or crew. If something awful has happened I would know it. *I just know I would!* Nor will I believe otherwise until I am told so by someone I know and trust. So, my girl, cheer up. No megrims from any of us! Remember, all is not over, 'til the minstrel's last song, or the jester's tumble! Dear God," she added, pulling at her chador. "What I wouldn't do to take this beastly thing off!"

She turned then as they were hailed by Abdul Aziz, their huge Syrian guard, and ordered below. So, with a sigh all round, Soraya led them back down to their cabin, where Najid was waiting with their evening meal, and a great carafe of fresh orange sherbet, only missing the ice to make it a perfect drink. So she did not spare a single glance to the two figures that had just flitted away from up forward, where she had noticed them earlier behind the mast nearest the steersman, as they swiftly disappeared down a nearby hatchway.

Chapter 14...*The Cousins discuss the virtues of Alicia and her friends.*

Jules Lagrasse and Lucas Fabrizan, knowing that the girls would all be on deck, had come up after them, and now watched them from behind the mast nearest the starboard steersman.

Concealed as much by the falling darkness as by the heavy coils of sheets and halliards that hung from all the cleats around it, they watched them walk along towards the bows, back-lit by the glowing sunset. And as they ducked down behind the partitions that concealed the ship-board garderobe, they both grinned.

"Just think, Jules, of those lovely smooth arses hanging off the sides of this fucking tub!" Lucas grunted, his eyes leering sideways at his cousin. "Like soft, ripe peaches," he added, squeezing his fingers into his hands, as if there was a juicy half in each. "What I wouldn't give to get my hands into any one of 'em!"

"You're always such a crude bugger, Lucas. Is there no refinement in you?"

"What, you sod? Crude bugger, am I? I suppose you've never rolled a hot bitch in a hedge and fucked the arse off her then? What about that Cristobel outside Narbonne? Didn't see *you* being bloody refined then, you idle bastard. Nor with her Ma! At them both like a fucking fiddler's elbow!" And they laughed.

"Listen Cousin! You stand as much chance of laying a hand on any one of those beauties as you do of becoming King of Jerusalem...especially after what happened on board that ship! Shame about those chadors though. Was hoping I might get a glimpse. No bloody chance!"

"Did you see that Lady Alicia's fucking tits when we flung her on the bed? Gorgeous! And that Sheik El Nazir, bloody infidel, gawping at 'em, miserable sod. His eyes were falling out of his fucking face! On bloody stalks they were! Mind, he's not been anywhere near 'em since. And that other bitch of the Lady Rochine's? That Soraya...whom we've seen around the castle? She is a prize piece too...would love to stuff her one I can tell you, coz. She's ripe for anything from what I hear. She and that bloody bitch, Lady Rochine. Right sodding goings on! And there's that other silly cow, that Agnes, whom you was sweet on talking with at Malwood. She's full of luscious firmness too, that's bloody certain, I had my hands all over 'em when I was carrying her on board. Fucking lovely!"

90

"Proper dished her up, poor little filly! 'I'm saving myself for the King of France' indeed! Stupid bitch! Are all English girls so bloody useless? Still, she gave us what we wanted. Frankly that Under Sheriff's welcome to her. She's tighter than a Jew's arse. He'll get nowhere with her!"

"Don't you believe it, Jules! Give her to me for half an hour and I'll have her suck all the sweetness out of me, before I give her the solid sorting she deserves," and he gave a coarse, grunting laugh, pumping his fist up and down. "A shame for her not to have the sodding joy of being fucked by me from all angles! A proper sin that'd be."

"Well, we might just get lucky there, as long as you keep that great prick of yours under control between here and the castle! That Rochine…and she's a fine piece too I might add!...She has a plan for forcing that stuck-up tart, Lady Al-ic-ia de Bur-ley," he mocked, "to give herself to Baron bloody Roger, and no questions asked, that might be good for us yet."

"So he can give her a proper 'Rogering' eh?" And Lucas guffawed at his own crude humour, grunting like a boar rooting for acorns in the forest.

"Oh…very witty, you bloody moron," his cousin replied with a wry grin. "How you have survived all these years, Lucas, without my aunt throttling you, I'll never know!"

"That's because I'm her proper little soldier, with angel's wings!"

"Dear God, aid me!" he muttered, casting his eyes up, adding: "Anyway, this plan's not about Lord Roger, 'Rogering' you ignorant peasant! It's a quite different plan."

"What plan's that then, you tight arse?"

"Tell you, Lucas? Are you crazy? Three good clacks of wine in your belly and you'd spill bloody everything! No, you stupid bastard, I'll tell you when it's necessary, and not before. In the meantime keep that fat prod of yours buttoned up, or you'll ruin everything and I'll be forced to cut it off myself! Now, come on, coz, those girls are moving this way, time to leave. I'm ready for our scoff too anyway, so let's get about it. I could eat a horse!"

"And knowing this fucking country," Lucas growled, spitting over the side as they turned away, his arm on his cousin's shoulder, "that's just what we will bloody get, fucking horse! What I wouldn't give for a great, oozing chunk of roast pig and crackling!"

Chapter 15...How Sheik El Nazir created the Company of the White Rose.

Three mornings later, as the *Morning Star* turned in towards the Adour Estuary at last, they were finally summoned by Raschid al Din to go to El Nazir's great cabin beneath the sterncastle.

Accompanied by Soraya, and escorted as always by Abdul Aziz, they went to receive their instructions: knowing from the previous evening that they were now approaching Bayonne at last.

With their hearts somewhat in their mouths to say the least, and covered with their black chadors, Soraya by her dark blue huque, so that only their eyes showed, all three women came and stood before the Dromond's great Master and owner, Sheik El Nazir al Jameel-Aziz-ibn Nidhaal, famous across the whole Circle Sea. He, in complete contempt of them both, remained seated, leaving them uncomfortably standing before him while he ate soft dates and honeyed almonds and drank freshly squeezed orange sherbet from a beautiful tall goblet of green and blue blown glass on a fine twisted stem.

"I have brought you here as we shall shortly be entering the River Adour that leads to Bayonne," he said in Frankish, in his usual dark voice. "Soon we will furl our sails and my rowers will take over. *Allah be Praised*, we have made a swift passage, and I shall soon be finished with you. It was not my desire to make this journey, and it has cost me the loss of two fine ships, the deaths of many of my men...and of my son, Siraj."

"That was no fault...." Alicia started to say, stepping forward.

"*Be silent, you Infidel bitch!*" El Nazir suddenly roared at her, rising to his full height and making all three women flinch, and Agnes cower. "*No-one speaks when I do!*...least of all a Christian houri. Next time I will have that strumpet whom the Lady Rochine put on board my *Morning Star* stripped and flogged for not educating you better!" And he sat down again, fanning himself with a huge whisk of stiff peacock feathers lying on the great octagonal table before him.

After a pause to collect himself, and staring into Alicia's blue eyes, more outraged than frightened, he said: "You might not personally have been at fault, My La-dy Al-ic-ia de Bur-ley,"...he said, emphasising the syllables of her complete name to Alicia's surprise..."Nevertheless your capture has been very costly, and handing you over will be a total pleasure, if not one of great enjoyment to The Lady into whose charge I will shortly be placing you, along with the two Frenchmen who brought you on board! For certain she will have to pay me greatly more to do so!"

"*No!...Please...*"

"*Silence, you Nasraani whore!*" he bellowed again, making the whole cabin quiver. "*Take that one,*" he shouted at Abdul Aziz, stabbing his hand towards Soraya. "Strip her now and beat her with this," he ordered handing over a pliable rod of thick cane, "*until I tell you to stop!*"

Instantly Alicia fell on her knees, pulling Agnes down beside her as Matthew had once long ago advised, heads bowed and her hands thrust out through her chador in desperate, silent supplication, even as the giant Syrian seized Soraya to tear off her huque.

Without speaking, El Nazir threw up his hand like a knife blade, stalling the man completely. And coming to stand over Alicia as she strove not to tremble he snarled: "One more word from you, Infidel! *Sahera!*...Witch! Just one more of any sort, and not only will I have this pathetic creature flogged, but your friend, Mistress Agnes, will be given to Jules Lagrasse and his cousin for their amusement. Do you understand me?" he snarled at her. "And this time you may speak."

"Yes! I understand you, my Lord," she replied as calmly as possible. Then, raising her violet-blue eyes to his hot, black ones, she said quietly. "Please do not give my friend to those...those *animals!* And do not raise your hand to Mistress Soraya. We will do as you ask," and she bowed her head. Then looking up again, she added: "My Lord Sheik El Nazir ibn Nidhaal, I have been in the presence of many great men. Men greater than you, my Lord Prince. There is no need to shout at your humble servant." And she dropped her eyes and bowed her head again, hiding her smile at his astonishment for knowing how properly to address him, and for her courageous defiance.

Following her spoken words there was a deathly silence, as no woman had spoken so to the Sheik before, least of all a Christian woman. So they waited, breath held, for the sky to fall in on her as he scowled down at her, head bowed as Soraya had also taught them the day before, and still meekly kneeling at his feet.

Although he knew of her exploits during the fire, and how she had escaped from the Baron and his daughter, he was still stunned by the reality of this *Nasraani* woman the Baron had decided on for his bride...*Amazing! I have seen no fear in her eyes...only courage and defiance. No Muslim girl would have dared to face me in so...so bold, if shameless, a manner. This Nasraani is truly special. I have not seen her like before...*Nor had he seen one so lovely either, for in all truth, *By the Beard of the Prophet,* she was very beautiful, her deep blue eyes piercing, penetrating, her body lusciously curved as he had seen when she had been dragged on board…such magnificent breasts, and so richly crowned!…*No wonder the Baron has been so determined to seize her. She is a true rarity. As I said to Raschid, had she been Muslim, I would have desired her for myself!*…And throwing his head back he laughed, as much at her demure boldness as his own unbidden lustful thoughts that had suddenly coursed through him like fire, and on an impulse he reached down for her hand and raised her up, Agnes following her.

Such an action startled everyone, apparently even El Nazir himself who, after a moment's stricken pause, conducted her to the long stern window seat, motioning the other two girls to join her there, as he moved to his high backed chair, ordering Jussuf to adjust it to face them. At the same time Abdul Aziz moved to stand across the closed door, while Al Raschid strode behind the Sheik, sending two of his men to stand guard outside, while El Nazir ordered Jussuf to bring more goblets and more fresh orange sherbet.

For a moment there was silence in the great room, broken only by the shipboard noises beyond and below them, and the distant cries of gulls above the estuary, as everyone mentally shook themselves over what had just happened.

Then, to the absolute astonishment of Alicia, and others around him, his rich voice switched seamlessly from Frankish to lightly accented English: "You are a very remarkable woman, My Lady Al-ic-ia. You fear me, I can 'feel' it. …yet you do not show it. There is only courage in your defiance and purity in your answers, and you are very beautiful…*Jameel.* You also have knowledge and wisdom which, in a woman, is rare. I can see why men can desire you, even love you. Why the Lord Baron, Sir Roger, has set his heart on seizing you, and why his daughter fears you! You may speak, my Lady," he said, seeing her sudden astonishment, and he deferred to her with the very slightest of head movements.

"You-you speak English, my Lord Prince!" she stammered, amazed at his grasp of her own native language which even the King could not speak.

"Yes, my Lady Al-ic-ia," he said with a smile. "Your people are being found everywhere. Your language is useful in trading as well as in warfare, as is Arabic and Frankish. In my trade you need clearly to be understood," and he gestured towards her, and to all the others around him.

"You do me great honour to reveal so 'secret' a skill. I am astonished."

"So am I, my Lady," he replied with a rueful smile, surprise in his voice, again slightly inclining his head towards her. "It is your eyes, I think. They are…very compelling," and he smiled broadly, his hard face lighting up with sudden, unexpected humour.

94

"Why, Sheik El Nazir ibn Nidhaal," she said then, reverting to formality, "do you say the Lady Rochine fears me? I am amazed. It is I who fear her."

"Not so! She sees in you a deadly rival for her father's affection. Be warned, my Lady, she is not what she seems!"

"I know what nature of woman that *witch* is, my Lord Prince, She has had me in her power before."

"After the fire, you mean."

"You know about that?" she replied, startled.

"Of course. Why else have I had to seize you so violently? *Monsieur le Baron* failed. I have not. And remember, when you escaped from the forest the Lord Roger was still with The Lady. He would not have allowed her to destroy something he so desired!"

"Is my life in danger then, my Lord Sheik?" she questioned him urgently, adopting a more Frankish approach to his name.

"Only if the Baron is not immediately present."

"But will he not be here to view his 'captive' personally?" she asked with a flash of disgust, gesturing towards the port they were approaching. "Here in Bayonne?"

"No, my Lady Alicia. He has sent his daughter, The Lady Rochine de Brocas, to do his greeting for him; along with an escort led by his own Guard Commander, Gaston de Vere. I am also required to add to his command the two men who brought you on board my ship...Jules Lagrasse and Lucas Fabrizan. Together they will conduct you, and your companions, to the Lord Baron at Gruissan."

"*No!* my Lord Sheik!" she almost cried out in shock. "Not those two French *animals!* Not them along with just the Lady de Brocas and her men as my escort. My Lord Prince, I implore you. Do not send me from you so unprotected. They are not to be trusted, *any* of them. Least of all de Vere whom I believe rests in her pocket, not the Baron's as he might choose to believe. I had thought the Baron, himself, would be here to view me...us," she added, pointing to Agnes beside her, "and gloat over his success. If what you say is true, that we will be under The Lady's 'protection', and those of her men, and surely she will slay us all. Please, is there nothing you can do?"

He paused then, considering her, and sipped his drink, turning his eyes away to look through the open windows and beyond...to the furthest distance of his mind: to the time Lord Roger had saved his life from the rocks that had ripped his boat in pieces, slaughtered the men trying to kill him, soothed and healed his wounds and introduced him to his beloved, beautiful Constance. And to thoughts of the Lady Rochine, his daughter...*whom I am now certain poisoned her mother to acquire her father's love. She is truly a djinn, and*

*Roger is a fool who will not be warned. As far as his daughter is concerned she is an angel! In very truth she is a shaitan!...*And then there was the continued use of the Crystal with her father, which he knew she relished hugely; her plotting; her murdered lovers; her obsession with his friend, the Lord Roger de Brocas...and her truly deadly jealousy wherever her father was concerned! And finally to what the Baron had persuaded him to do...*By Allah and the Prophets, left to herself that shaitan could yet destroy everything!...*and with a sudden grunt his mind snapped back to the present, to the Lady Al-ic-ia de Bur-ley seated before him, and turning towards her he smiled:

"Of Course...my Lady Al-ic-ia! I am not Sheik El Nazir al Jameel-Aziz-ibn Nidhaal for nothing. Before this morning I would not have cared. But now I have met you, and for the love *I* have for the Lord Bar-on Roger, I will send you under an escort of my own."

"*You?*" She exclaimed, startled. "You have a care for the Baron Roger? *An infidel Lord?*"

"As a brother, my Lady. For no-one else would I risk my ships on so dangerous a mission. Especially not my '*Surah At-Tariq'*...my *Morning Star*...The Baron once saved my life in exceptional circumstances when others were trying to destroy me. And he cared for me, introduced me to his wife, the Lady Constance, trusted me, and took me safely back to my family. We have been close friends now for many years."

"And his daughter, my Lord Prince?" she said reverting to her earlier use of his title. "The Lady Rochine de Brocas, those whom men call 'The Lady'?"

"No...my Lady de Burley!" he honoured her with her proper title. "I do not care for his daughter. His wife, the Lady Constance, was a true beauty, exotic and amazing....and faithful in all things. All men admired the Lady Constance de Brocas, and loved her too. Not so her daughter, who has since taken her place, and in ways I can neither condone nor approve. She has become a blasphemy before *Allah!* And, I believe her passions are turning her mind. Men respect the Lady Rochine out of fear...but her father will hear no ill of her...even from those who care for him most."

"Like you, my Lord Prince?" Alicia asked him quietly, looking up at him.

"Yes...like me," El Nazir replied, eyes of liquid brown looking into eyes of sparkling blue.

"My Lord Prince," Alicia implored him again. "Will, you help us, please? At least to get safely to Gruissan."

"To the Château Grise, my Lady? To the Baron himself?"

"Even so, My Lord Prince. To the Château Grise at least. After that..."

"After that, my Lady, *Insha'Allah!*"

96

"*Insha'Allah*! my Lord Prince El Nazir al Jameel-Aziz-ibn Nidhaal," she replied, putting her hands together and bowing her head towards him.

"My Lady Al-ic-ia de Bur-ley, "he said looking down at her with a surprised smile. "You never fail to amaze me. Who taught you that?"

"A Benedictine monk from Spain who has travelled even to India, a Black Monk. He is a very wise man, quite unlike any churchman I have ever met. His name is 'Father Matthew'. He has travelled widely amongst your people, has their language, and advised me of many things before we all set out to join King Richard's army. Like your al Zahrawi of Andalusia, he too is a great surgeon."

"I am impressed, my Lady," El Nazir replied, astonished. "You have more learning in you than I have ever before discovered in a woman. This Father Matthew is man with whom I would like to meet. I am delighted that even among the Black Monks, who are amongst our greatest enemies, there are cultured Nasraani Churchmen who speak the language of *Allah*. I have never met such a man, though I have heard of him, a Black monk who has the language of 'The Book.'

"Of 'The Book', my Lord Prince?"

"Our Holy Book, The Koran. He was a friend of one of our Emirs, I believe? A shame he is not with you now. His teaching makes me even more willing to help you."

"At least to Gruissan, my Lord Prince."

"My Lady Alicia, I was engaged to carry out your capture by The Lady Rochine's father, The Lord Baron, Sir Roger de Brocas of Narbonne and Gruissan, to whom I am deeply indebted, as I said. Not by his daughter whom all men call 'The Lady'. She is nothing to me. I am *not* one of her creatures, though she would dearly like me to be so. Indeed I almost fear for her father at her hands. He seeks absolute power through her…and absolute power can turn even good men into monsters! My promise was to my friend…*not* to his daughter!" and turning he called out, "Abdul Aziz, come here!" Then, turning to Al Raschid, with a nod of his head and raised eyebrow, he said. "Send for Mhaktoun Aquib to come here to me also, my friend. Do not be so astonished," he said to the sudden concern that flashed across his Galley Commander's face. "I have not gone moon-mad. All will be well. Now, Abdul Aziz," he said as Al Raschid went out. "Come to me. I have a special task for you."

"Yes, my Prince," the huge Syrian replied in Arabic, coming to kneel before the Sheik, touching his forehead with his fingers and then his lips as he did so.

"Abdul Aziz aal Suriyyan," El Nazir said in his accented Frankish. "You see these three ladies whom you have been guarding these past few days?"

"Yes, my Lord Prince," he replied similarly, to Alicia's immense surprise.

"You are to guard them as if they were myself, and I am sending Mhaktoun Aquib with you to ensure that all goes well. I know he is your friend, so I will expect you to work together at all times to keep these *Gamila Nasraani*...these beautiful Christians, safe and in your sight whenever possible. At night you and Mhaktoun will stand guard over them, turn and turnabout. And Najid will feed you all. No-one else must prepare your food. Even after you have handed them to the Lord Baron de Brocas of Narbonne, at his great castle in Gruissan, your duties will not end. They will not end until I come for you in the *Morning Star*. I will write to the Lord Baron today to say so, Abdul, and this Lady will give it to him. Do you understand?"

"Yes, my Prince. These are good ladies," he said rising and turning to the three women on the long window seat, sitting stunned at all that was now taking place before them, his voice strong and light, his black eyes steady, with a glint of humour Alicia had not seen before.

"I and Aquib will care for you. By the *Beard of the Prophet* we will make sure you are safe," then he put his hands together and bowed to them and to Sheik El Nazir: "*Salaam Alaikum!*"... 'Peace be unto you'... And he stepped back towards the door, moving swiftly to one side as it opened to allow Al Raschid to enter, followed by another soldier, who walked soft-footed to where the Sheik was sitting and knelt down before him touching his forehead and his lips also.

"You called for me, my Prince" he said, also in Frankish.

Soraya, who knew the man, just smiled, but Alicia and Agnes had actively gasped because, quite simply, while Aziz was big...this man was massive!

Taller than either Gui or Abdul Aziz, and perhaps twice their bulk. With arms like knotted tree trunks, thighs sculpted pillars of hardened muscle and a chest like that of the Colossus itself, he towered over everyone. But like many very big men he was surprisingly light on his feet, carried his chainmail armour as if it were tin, and in his hands his sword, even larger than Aziz's was more like a bodkin than the sixty inches of clouded steel it truly was. He had a strong face, with a square chin and deep nose, and very dark brown eyes that also hid a certain twinkle. Alicia liked him at once, not just because he was so large but because he had about him an air of trust and dependability.

"Yes, Mhaktoun Aquib," El Nazir said switching effortlessly to English. "I have a task for you to share with Abdul Aziz, but under your command."

"Yes, my Prince. It will be as you say," he replied in like manner, in English, to Alicia's complete astonishment, and that of her companions.

"Very well. That is good. I want you to go with these three ladies, and Abdul and Najid, to the castle of the Baron, my friend as you know, the Lord Roger de Brocas of Narbonne, to the Château Grise, and make sure they are safe and well at all times. You will take your orders from Lady Ali-ic-ia de Burley, and use your common sense. Do you understand? Good! But you are in command, my Aquib, and all must do your bidding or be lost."

"Yes, my Prince," he replied in his dark gravelly voice. "They will be safe. *By the Beard of the Prophet,* I promise this!" he said, raising El Nazir's hand to his forehead in ritual acceptance of the man's authority.

"So! That is excellent," the Sheik said with quiet pleasure in his own deep voice. Then, turning to Alicia he smiled. "I understand that some people call you 'the White Rose of Malwood', My Lady? That white roses are your favourite flower, both for their pure beauty and for their scent...as are they mine also, when I am not on board the *Morning Star.*"

"It has been said, my Lord Prince," Alicia replied bowing her head towards him, surprise writ large across her face. "But it is a private name between me and my family. In jest and not generally known. I am astonished you should know of this."

"There are many things I know of you, my Lady," the sheik replied with a smile. "You would be surprised! But no matter. Today you leave the *Star* together as one company. You three," he said gesturing to her, Agnes and Soraya. "With Aquib, Aziz and Nijad to guard and guide you. All for the one purpose of getting you, the 'White Rose of Malwood', safely to Gruissan and to my friend The Lord Baron, Sir Roger de Brocas. And, knowing The Lady, it may not be a safe journey. That is why I am sending my two most trusted, fiercest warriors with you. So...you will be one Company together, I think. Yes?" he asked then, the word shooting out of him tersely.

"Yes!" my Prince," Aquib replied swiftly.

"So, with what you are all doing," he said then, with another smile at Alicia and a subtle tilt of his head towards her. "You shall be the 'Company of the White Rose'!" And he raised his glass of sherbet to her as those around him gasped and suddenly clapped their approval.

"If that is your wish, my Prince?" Aquib said then, bowing his head.

"It is!" Sheik El Nazir said, standing, his eyes bright and glittering in the sunlight off the water. "It is what I wish...and so it will be. And with a good name like that to believe in, you will all be the stronger for it, and will bind together better when you most may need to do so!"

"It is a good name, my Lord Prince El Nazir," Alicia said smiling, bowing her head towards him again. "I wish I had thought of it myself!" And they all laughed, a light ripple of sound that ran round the great State Cabin, and startled the guards standing outside the door.

*

All this time Soraya had been sitting, utterly astonished, to one side of the long settle. In all the times she had known the Sheik, *never* had she witnessed such kindness or generosity. And not just because he had chosen to be wooed by Alicia's beauty and spirit...but because of his close affection for the Baron.

Lord Roger wanted Alicia. And badly enough to risk everything, that much was plain. And Sheik El Nazir had equally risked everything to deliver her to him, even to the point of sacrificing one of his sons. Now, clearly he believed that Alicia's life was threatened by the Lady Rochine...as well he might for The Lady could, indeed, be maniacally jealous, beyond all reason. So, by assigning two of his most trusted soldiers, and a much valued cook to support them, he truly was nailing his colours to the mast for all to see. And the name he had so suddenly assigned to them simply bore that all out. And she was just amazed by it.

Aquib and Aziz, and little Najid, were all men whom Rochine would not dare to assault; but The Lady was so uncertain a quantity that Soraya felt she must do something more to help her new friends survive the coming journey. So, dropping to her knees before Sheik El Nazir, head bowed and hands held out, she begged leave from him to speak.

Chapter 16...More plans are made...and others secretly revealed!

Turning his sharp, black eyes towards her, Sheik El Nazir paused and studied the lovely girl kneeling silently in front of him, head down and hands out in supplication...before ordering her to raise her head.

And looking into her green eyes with the penetrating stare of a falcon, he gave a slow gesture of his right hand for her to rise: "What is it you want of me, Mistress Fermier?"

"Please, my Lord Prince," Soraya said humbly in the warm voice of the Languedoc. "Before we all leave, may I speak?"

For a moment longer El Nazir looked at her steadily again through hooded eyes, before saying: "Yes, Mistress Soraya. You may speak."

"My Lord Prince," she said quietly, raising her face to his. "For your men to carry out the orders you have given them, the new 'Company of the White Rose,' I believe it is imperative that they do not speak anything but Arabic *at all times!* Neither The Lady, nor any of her people...especially not her Guard Commander, Gaston de Vere... must know that either Abdul Aziz or Mhaktoun Aquib can speak different languages. My Lord Prince," she said, hesitating, "will you ask them if they speak Farsi?"

"*Farsi?*" he said astonished. "*Persian?*"

"Yes, my Lord. It was my mother's tongue. I learned from her and have never forgotten it. None of The Lady's people speak it. Indeed very few do anyway around the Circle Sea, but both the men you have chosen have travelled widely before entering your service, and may just do so."

"How do you know this?" he asked her severely.

"I am an expert, silent listener, my Lord Prince. Those who serve The Lady, as I do, have learned to be! Amongst The Lady's guard, and she always travels with the same men, some speak Arabic, all know some English and of course all speak Frankish. But none speak Farsi...neither dies The Lady. If either of your men can speak it, then we can converse in a manner that no-one else can understand. And if they only ever speak Arabic around her guards, and no other language, then anything that may be planned against us in ignorance of their skills...may be revealed."

Leaning back in his tall chair he studied her in silence...*now why didn't I think of that? This girl, also, is remarkable...* his great peacock fan moving gently from side to side as he did so. "I am impressed, Mistress Soraya," he replied at last. "You have thought of something both Al Raschid and I have missed. I will ask them," he said, turning to where both of his chosen men were standing. "Abdul?...Mhaktoun? You heard this lady. Do either of you speak Farsi?"

"A few words only, my Lord," Abdul said, with a wry smile. "But none that a lady would want to know!"

"Mmmm, guardroom language!" He grunted. "You are right, my Abdul...not helpful for us now. Mhaktoun?"

"Yes, my Lord Prince. I do speak Farsi...not fluently perhaps, but enough to be useful and more I will catch onto quickly, I am certain."

"How do you know Farsi, Mhaktoun Aquib?" El Nazir asked, fascinated at finding so unlikely a skill amongst his fighting men.

"In my younger days, as Mistress Soraya says, I travelled a great deal. I wanted to be the greatest wrestler of all time. They have many cunning wrestlers in Persia, so I travelled there...and then...and then...

"...There was a girl!" El Nazir interrupted with a deep laugh at his enormous guard's embarrassment. "Be not ashamed, my Mhaktoun. *By the Beard of the Prophet*, when was there *not* a girl about you somewhere? You are so huge I sometimes think you hide them about your person!" And he smiled.

"Even so, my Prince. Being so large seems to encourage them to come to me," he added with a twinkly grin. "But this one was very special to me. Leila, a true believer and the guardian of my heart," he said simply. "So I was as keen to learn her language as she was to learn mine," and to much laughter he added. "I found I learned quickly!

"And the girl, Mhaktoun? Your Leila?" Al Raschid asked him, still grinning.

"Sadly, my Lord, she was bitten by a black scorpion in the desert lands near Tabriz, as we were travelling home, and died. In truth I loved her greatly. Her name means, 'Beautiful with dark hair', and so she was...and she was with child...so I lost them both. *Insh'a Allah.* But I could have wished it otherwise."

"I am sorry for that, my Mhaktoun," Al Raschid said, briefly laying his hand on the man's massive shoulders. "I had no idea any girl had ever come so close to your soul."

Sheik El Nazir watched the confusion on his giant guard's face and was moved by it. Then he looked at them both and smiled. "Very well, you two. You have heard all that Mistress Soraya has had to say, and I believe it to be both wise and sensible. Do not speak any language other than Arabic while you are away from the *Morning Star* unless you may be certain of being neither observed nor overheard. Najid can only speak Arabic anyway, so he is not a problem. If anything else needs to be discussed, then speak in Farsi with Mistress Soraya, except in private when you are sure no-one else is near to hear you. I put her and her companions in your charge, both of you. But it is to be Mhaktoun's responsibility to ensure their ultimate safety. Your balls on a plate before me if any harm comes to them! Understand?"

"Yes, my Prince!" they both replied, bowing before him, touching their fingers to their foreheads and to their lips as they stood up again.

"I will speak with you all again, before you leave the *Morning Star*, my new 'Company of the White Rose.' You may both go. *Salaam Alaikum!*"

"*Salaam Alaikum*, my Lord Prince!"

El Nazir watched the men leave, and turned to the two English girls and smiled, pleased with their astonishment at his munificence and at the new name he had given them all...as much as the wide-eyed surprise on the faces of all those around him. He liked to do the unexpected; it kept everyone on their toes!

"Mhaktoun Aquib is a good man, My Lady Alicia," Sheik El Nazir said turning to her. "The name 'Aquib' means '*Protector*'...in fact he is a great wrestler as you may have gathered, as well as an amazing swordsman. 'Abdul Aziz' means '*Servant of the Powerful One*'...and so he is," he added with a grin. "He serves me...and has been with me for many years, and has never been beaten in a fight. They will care for you, these two men of mine...and they will obey you. They will keep you safe. And Najid will ensure that only the best, and safest, food is served to you. And be warned, you must eat only what he has prepared!" he added, with a hard stare and a sudden quirked eyebrow. "Even so, my Lady! Even so!" he ended, looking into Alicia's eyes, as the import of what he had said sank home. "You cannot trust anything that may come from The Lady's table. She is a woman of great resource, the Lady Rochine de Brocas, and, I am afraid, of great evil also!"

Surprised at his final words, Alicia then rose from the long settle, with Agnes and Soraya beside her, and while Soraya bowed deeply to the Sheik, Alicia and Agnes, encumbered as they were by their chadors, still managed to give him a truly royal curtsey.

Alicia, stepping forward slightly, her blue eyes glittering behind her chador, said: "My Lord Sheik, when we were so violently seized off my ship three mornings ago I hated you with great bitterness and anger. I feared for my honour and that of my companion. Yet you and your people have treated us with great generosity and care on your *Surah At-Tariq*...your *Morning Star*. She is a fine vessel and I can see why you are so proud of her. There are many Christians who would not have been so generous, nor so caring, were we to have foundered in a like manner.

103

"I thank you also for the great kindness in providing us with such unexpected protection in the face of one whom I now know to be an even more dangerous enemy than I had expected. And for the lovely name you have chosen for our little Company. I have no wish to be allied to the Baron in any way, and while deploring him as a murderer and a man of evil deeds, I respect your friendship for him and hope that if I was faced with the same situation, I would behave towards my enemies in the same manner in which you have behaved towards me and my companions.

"We may be of different religions, my Lord Prince. But we both honour the same God. We are also 'People of the Book'...*Ahlul Kitaab*...as I learned from the Black Monk who is my fiancé's friend, and has journeyed as far as Persia and the Arabian Sea in his travels, and has taught me many things as you know. May *Allah* protect you, *El Nazir-al Jameel-Aziz ibn Nidhaal*, as I pray for God to protect me, and I thank you, from the bottom of my heart." And she rose and, bowing deeply, said. "*Salaam Alaikum!*" Before stepping back beside her friends, everyone astonished by all she had said.

Standing, Sheik El Nazir looked directly into Alicia's violet-blue eyes, and once more gave her the slightest inclination of his head, touching first his forehead and then his lips with his fingers as he did so. "*Insh'a Allah*, my Lady," he said in his dark, rich voice, before gesturing for her and her companions to leave his great cabin, along with everyone else, except his cabin servant, Jussuf.

To him he gave a written order for Almahdi aal Suriyyan, his Pigeon Master, to send a bird to the Baron immediately informing him that Alicia had arrived at Bayonne and his secret plan was now in operation, before waving Jussuf away about his master's business.

*

No sooner had the door softly closed behind him, than Sheik El Nazir leaned back against it with a sigh of relief and breathed out deeply. So, that was that, the Baron's careful plan was now in motion and he could move forward at last, master of his own destiny again. No longer in Baron Roger's coils. All he needed to do now was collect his men from the Château Grise in due course, and get back in the war!

And moving towards the wide stern seating, collecting his glass of orange sherbet from the table as he passed, he paused first to listen to all the shipboard sounds going on around him, before bending to slide the oak panels that held the horn windows in place to one side. Then, sitting down, he turned to look at the blue sparkling waters of the great Bay behind him as he drank, and giving a another huge sigh of relief, he smiled.

Above him, with a sudden bang and clatter he heard the great double banks of oars lifted up and outboard on either side of the ship; the first deep, reverberating *thudd!* of the Hortator's drum...and the great shout of the rowers, all two hundred and fifty of them, as they made that first deep pull into the sea. On deck, he knew that the sails would soon be tightly furled, their halliards coiled and sorted and the two anchors readied to drop if necessary, while his two 'captives' and all their gear, and that of Soraya and the men he was sending with them, would soon be gathered together and taken up there also. The 'Company of the White Rose'. He liked it. It pleased him, and he smiled at the shock his words had caused that morning.

Her oars beating together as one...*like gulls' wings*...he always thought, the *Morning Star* would make a powerful sight as she swept from the estuary into the River Adour itself, passing all the many smaller ships like a great shark amongst a shoal of simple herrings.

It could not be often that a great fighting dromond from the Mediterranean ever came into a Christian port like Bayonne on the Atlantic Coast. Frightening for some...even terrifying...*What a panic we would cause if we entered with our artillery manned, our great siphon in place and Raschid's marines all armoured-up on deck!:...'Les Corsairs! Les Corsairs!'*...he could almost hear the screams. And he grinned mischievously at the thought of it, then laughed. But he had a special pass for this visit. From the Lord Baron, his friend, signed by King Philip of France himself no less. And he had ordered the white flags of peace to be flown from both mastheads and from her stern. So...no panics today! He sighed, and sipped again from his glass.

How the Baron had managed such a thing was beyond him. But he had it, and it was real! And he laughed again, gazing without processed thought, to the far, far distant horizon where the azure sky and the deeper blue of the Atlantic finally met in one long, dark line.

It had been an extraordinary time...and what an extraordinary woman, the White Rose of Malwood.

A battle as fierce and bloody as any he had witnessed, or fought in. By *Allah*, but those Franks could fight! And their women too! And what a girl?...no, a 'Lady'...that one had proven to be! He was astonished. Both at her boldness under pressure, and at her courage, and pride...and her learning, extraordinary! Who would have thought any woman could read, let alone use Arabic at him?...*No wonder Roger had been so impressed.*

105

He drank again, watching the local shipping bobbing in the *Morning Star's* wake. He had started this expedition with a profound contempt for all Christian Franks, especially their women. And all just to serve his friend, The Lord Baron, Roger de Brocas! He had ended not just touching one, but offering her hospitality and the services of two of the most trusted and ferocious warriors in his command…and that not just because he had already agreed to do so with Lord Roger…but because he actually wanted to! And he suddenly rocked with laughter.

It was such a cunning plan that the Baron had devised…and he had *loved* the role of bestial, roaring, infidel Pirate…after all that's what he was! And then, next moment, to show himself to be suddenly caring and understanding, and so friendly. It had all been masterly, and he chuckled again, pleased with himself…*especially as none of the men leaving me know a thing. Not even Al Raschid knows the truth of why I changed my mind about the two Nasraani women*…And poor Lady Alicia?…He smiled. The White Rose…she had been properly fooled, and no mistake.

But the Lord Roger needed a wife. His friend needed an heir, he understood that, and Rochine knew that too, and had planned and schemed with her father to seize hold of the girl he wanted, no matter what the cost, expecting to control everything as she was used to doing. She had thought she would be grabbing hold of a silly pigeon ripe for plucking…but she had found instead a wild, bating goshawk, with a wicked beak to tear and the sharpest of talons with which to pierce and bind on! And their plan in England had been foiled, *Insha'Allah*, and so Lord Roger had turned to him for help.

Well…he, Sheik El Nazir, had now done his part for his friend…and more! Not only had he succeeded where Lord Roger had failed. But he had made sure the girl had the support she would need when the time came for her to flee from The Lady again. And two of his best men too! And little Najid. Such planning had gone into all of this that surely, *by Allah's Mercy*, it must succeed?

And if Roger's Guard Commander, Gaston de Vere, played his part too, *and* did the right thing with what he'd told him about Najid's pretty sister, Faridah, and the powdered roots he would be bringing from Gruissan; then The Baron's plan might work really well…*For if they all flee from Rochine's men, as Roger has planned for…and he then rescues her from de Vere and The Lady in hot pursuit of them; then surely she will see him in the light of blessed rescuer and not of hated jailor and enforcer*…He grinned again. It was masterly.

And the Baron could be so very charming when he wished to be…and so dissembling! Now was the time to see if his friend could hold on to what he

106

had stolen. He couldn't wait to see Rochine's face when they docked, and her 'pigeon' walked off the *Morning Star* with her own little coterie of servants and her two giant bodyguards. The Company of the White Rose!

And he smiled and raised his glass to the morning. *Allah Akbar!...God is Great!'*

Chapter 17...The White Rose and The Lady meet again.

On the upper deck, as the *Morning Star* swept up the broad Adour towards the long quays that marked the port city of Bayonne, all was tremendous bustle and noise. Stretching away on either side of the main river the wide staithes that lined the quayside lay beneath the town's battlemented walls and towers, and along its main tributary, the River Nive.

Everywhere there were ships of every size loading and unloading: cogs, galleys and hulks, with carts and wagons arriving and leaving all the time; strings of pack horses and braying mules, laden donkeys, porters and dockers carrying loads on their backs, and busy cranes, their huge wooden tread wheels in constant motion as they dipped their hooks deep into the bellies of a number of great cogs that had recently arrived, laden with huge hogsheads of wine and casks of oil.

And there were people thronging everywhere.

Even with her white flags streaming from masts and stern, so that all could see she came in peace, the *Morning Star's* sudden appearance had brought wild consternation to almost the whole waterfront, and in the town the bells were tolling. Had she arrived with her vicious artillery fully manned, her marines armoured-up and crowded on her deck and castles, and her siphon for spewing out Greek Fire properly mounted, the terror and confusion could not have been any greater.

So no-one noticed Almahdi carefully choosing a bird from one of the two wicker cages that had been brought up onto the high sterncastle, playing with her legs briefly before throwing her up into the air, where she circled the *Morning Star* briefly before flying off like a feathered arrow to the south. Nor did they see him dipping in again amongst his crooning, fluttering charges to choose a second message carrier, and releasing that one too. And no-one heard him say: "'Ware hawk, my lovely! 'Ware hawk!" as he threw them both upwards.

Up on the deck Alicia, Agnes and Soraya, with their baggage and new belongings beside them, stood watching in amazement at the sight of so much pandemonium along the dockside: people running in all directions, many screaming; bundles dropped, donkeys kicking and braying, packhorse trains being run up the streets of the town, the iron rattle of cart wheels, horns blowing, dogs barking...even some ships desperately trying to cast off before they could be seized and boarded. All expecting '*Les Corsairs*' to pour out

108

amongst them, with all the terror and violence for which they were so well known.

With their two huge warrior guards behind them, fully armoured, with all their baggage beside them, and Najid and his collection of pans, ladles, baskets of spices and special provisions close by his side, the three girls laughed and pointed out to one another all the chaos going on as their ship made her dramatic approach, drums and oars beating in quick time, a great froth of white water beneath her ram, cymbals clashing and trumpets blowing from her raised sterncastle.

But it was not a universal panic.

Others stood in fascinated groups as they watched *'Surah At-Tariq'*, Sheik El Nazir's *Morning Star,* swooping down towards them…great white silken flags of peace fluttering gaily from every masthead. Spray flying from the great iron ram at her beak, and water running in sparkling rivulets from her oar blades as they flashed in the bright sunlight, moving all together in spectacular rhythm as the great infidel warship swept towards the town. And as she came she churned the river into a maelstrom of white water, into beautiful rows of fierce whirlpools every time her oars thrashed up and down into the blue water. No-one who was stood on the quayside that morning, and who saw her come, and heard the rapid deep *thudding!* of the Hortator's drum and the rushing bang and groan of a hundred rowlocks, like a stampede of wild horses, as she swept past them all less than half a cable from the quayside, could have failed to be moved. For with her size and her speed, her great ram thrusting out before her, her artillery fore and aft and the fierce thunder of kettle-drums, cymbals and great blasts of wild, brazen music as she came, the *Morning Star* was a thrilling and terrifying sight.

Suddenly, as if by magic, the noise stopped and the oars suddenly rose up as one, level with the river…but for one moment only before both sets dropped down again with a mighty splash and held water, forcing the *Morning Star* to lose way rapidly. Then, with a fresh great *thudd!* on the Hortator's huge kettle-drum deep within her, while one bank of oars dipped down again and rowed forward…the other held and backed water so that the whole vessel spun around as if on some amazing hidden turntable, all one hundred and thirty quivering feet of her.

And losing all speed as she did so, she glided almost silently, until with another *thudd!* from within her gracious hull her oars flowed into motion once more and she began to paddle quietly towards the quays, both sets of oars just dipping and rising to hold her steady till the way came off her completely, till with a bang her oars lifted out and upwards, like the wings of some giant bird, the lower set to disappear within her hull, the upper set to catch onto her gunnels so she could sidle gently with the current against the great sprung timber piles that were waiting for her.

Truly it was a bravura performance and many actually cheered and clapped wildly as the spin stopped and the *Morning Star* came to rest.

But clearly someone had been watching for her, for even as she had appeared, and the bells had tolled out, a whole company of soldiers in immaculate mail had trotted out of the town gates and formed up around what was clearly an agreed space for her to moor up to. And in moments they had created a human barrier between the dromond now being tied firmly to the quay with great ropes fore and aft, and the town itself. Flags of peace there might well be flying from her mastheads...and her artillery might well be covered, but this was a great fighting dromond from the Circle Sea...and no-one was taking any chances!

With the ship finally at rest, a long ribbed gang way, with rope sides on spaced stanchions, was rushed forward by four of the soldiers who made up the sudden dockside guard, while from behind where Alicia was standing two trumpets sharply blew, and two dozen of Sheik El Nazir's men ran out, down the gangway and formed up on either side of it.

Each wore pantaloons of white silk, with a quilted jacket of white serge, sleeves embroidered with gold thread, under a short breastplate of polished steel; and each also carried the curved scimitar for which the Corsairs were famed, wore a white tarboosh with a great gold tassel on its crown, white cloaks from their armoured shoulders with the golden scimitar of their Prince's House, and looked both magnificent...and clearly ceremonial.

Behind them came Al Raschid, the *Morning Star's* Galley Commander, in glittering Christian mail that fell below his waist over mailed chausses on black leather. He wore a gold chased pointed helmet, a host of green feathers fluttering from its plume holder, over a shining chain coif. A long jewelled sword, of Christian pattern, hung off a glittering belt of scarlet leather, studded with disks of pure gold, and a long cloak of green satin shimmered from his armoured shoulders, his master's scimitar, in threads of pure gold, deeply embroidered in the centre of it.

And behind him strode *Sheik El Nazir-al Jameel-Aziz ibn Nidhaal*, in white and gold like his guard, only all of purest silk, with a long cloak of cloth-of-gold hanging in glittering magnificence from his shoulders in the sunshine, and a white satin turban with a huge emerald in its centre on his head. Around his waist, from a gold leather belt studded with emeralds and rubies, hung a jewelled scimitar on one side and across his chest a great *khanjar*, the curved dagger for which his people were famous, its hilt encrusted with jewels, its scabbard of gold chased with silver and rimmed with emeralds, the colour of

Islam.   Quite simply he looked every inch the prince he was. Gleaming…outstanding…dazzling! No-one in Bayonne had ever seen anything like him before in their lives.

At a sign from the crew manning the deck, Alicia and her small party quietly made their way to the head of the gangway and stopped.

Below them the Sheik's personal honour guard were still drawn up in two lines either side of it, he not yet having actually stepped onto the quayside. Before them, well-spaced out, stood the soldiers who had trotted from the town at the *Morning Star's* arrival, equally still and silent; the crowd behind them murmuring, gabbling, pointing and jostling; pushing amongst themselves for the best view of all that was happening.   Then came a sudden, almost unnatural, stillness.

The only sound was that of the gulls as they swooped and wheeled, filling the sky with their mewling cries, while the sun blazed down, its summer heat making the roof tops shimmer, and the sweat flow.   It was but a momentary frozen tableau: the wind fluttering tassels, feathers and silk alike as it whispered amongst them, flacking loose halliards against the *Morning Star's* tall masts, scuttering small fragments of hay and straw across the cobbled ground. An unreal silence that was as swiftly broken by the sudden clatter of shod hooves, the scrunch of wheels and the snort of horses…and the scramble of booted feet as a whole section of soldiers around the dockside swung open like a gate.   Through that a small party of nine men on horseback, fully armoured, weapons at their side…four with crossbows on their backs, and one woman, accompanied by two large tilt carts, two horses to each cart and a number of horses on leading reins, slowly made their way.

At the foot of the gangway, in all his magnificence, El Nazir stood with his guard around him. At the top, still in her chador, stood Alicia, with her new household around her, her Company of the White Rose, her blue eyes chips of ice.

Below, on her white mare, having stayed in a local auberge since arriving in Bayonne a few days before, sat the Lady Rochine de Brocas. Upright in her saddle, she was dressed in a scarlet bliaut of stiff damask, embroidered with swirling patterns of gold and silver thread over a white silk chemise edged with pearls, and around her narrow waist was a broad belt of blue suede enriched with enamelled panels of scarlet and blue edged with gold. Her black hair was covered by a white satin caul, threaded with gold and studded with rubies, which she wore above a brilliant scarlet silk coif that flared from her neck like flames, and overall a long scarlet mantle that flowed off her slim shoulders right over her horse's back; even her feet were clad in scarlet leather. She looked imperious…untouchable.

111

Alicia thought...*Sweet Jesus, she is dressed in blood*...and shuddered, her heart fluttering, suddenly glad of the black chador that covered her.

Kicking her horse forward, her Guard Commander by her side, her personal guard fanning out in a semicircle around her, the Lady Rochine's emerald eyes were as hard as jade, her mouth a scarlet slash. She had come to collect her father's bride-to-be...*A week's journey if all goes well*...She grunted, looking up at the women standing above the gangway, and her eyes glittered. She *knew* which one was the Lady Al-ic-ia de Bur-ley!...*Not even that ridiculous chador thing can hide you from me, you foolish girl!*...And she swayed delicately in her saddle, her thoughts venomous, her stomach suddenly griped with bile, and she turned to look up river.

Nearly two hundred and fifty miles lay between Bayonne and Gruissan. By river first to Peyrehorade, then all the rest by road and trackway: mountains, forests, wilderness and streams; deep valleys, small villages, little towns and rough tracks; bandits, murderers and thieves. Nothing civilised until Carcassonne. She had just travelled it, the last miles by stately barge.

She kicked-on some more and smiled...*A lot can happen over two hundred miles!*...and she smiled again.

Chapter 18...Gui leads his men on the long road to Niort.

They broke fast at Prime, at the great Benedictine Abbey at Vertou, with the mists burning off the land as the sun rose gloriously into a powder-blue sky filled with great streamers of pink and gold, just as the lay brothers were setting out for the fields, their tools across their shoulders...and the monks for the cloisters, pens, parchment and trays of delicate paints and brushes in their hands.

As they approached the great Abbey gates, the ground still wet with dew, the air clear, Abbot Hugo Gravier came out to greet them, his arms open wide, first to clasp Father Matthew, and then Gui, while their men flung themselves off their horses to make their way to the trestle tables that the Abbot had ordered prepared against their coming. Bread still fresh and warm from the Abbey's ovens in baskets; cold meats, cheese and olives all on polished wooden platters; crocks of butter, and golden honey from the Abbey's hives...and wine, French ale and cider. And while they ate and drank in the Great Courtyard before the gates, some standing some sitting on the verges nearby, the horses were watered by the lay brothers, and those men off the *Mary* and the *Pride,* still too wounded to ride, were comforted and had their dressings changed.

"Where to next, my son?" Abbot Hugo asked of Sir Gui, as he stood with his Commanders, drinking from a horn beaker.

"Bordeaux, as you know, Father; but we'll go there the way you have suggested: Clisson, Chantonnay, Niort and Saint Jean d'Angély. The same route your monks take with their wagons. Then Saintes, Pons and Bordeaux at last. One week!"

"That will be very hard going, Sir Gui. The road is not smooth and there are many streams and fords. You may need more than a week...but there are some small towns along the way, and castles, which will always take you in of course, especially at Niort, where King Richard is building a massive donjon, and has re-arranged the castle his father first commissioned."

"Who holds there, Father?" Sir Richard asked.

"Count William de Forz holds for the King and is very much Richard's leal man; and a man who has made his pilgrimage to St James of Compostella. So a man of Godly virtue as well...which, sadly, cannot be said of all the Poitevin Barons. He and I have known each other of old, and I have a parchment for him that might be of help," he said, handing Gui a short scroll tied with blue ribbon, secured with blue wax and stamped with the abbey's Great Seal.

"Thank you, Father. Is there anything else you can add?"

"Not more really than I told Father Matthew yesterday. There are a few inns where you might get shelter," he added. "Not perhaps of The Angel's calibre...but good enough," he smiled. "And once you reach Saint Jean d'Angély you are nearly there. It is a cheerful place and will serve you well. They are good people there, and another brother house, famous for having the head of John the Baptist...well so they say! The town has good walls and a tall tower the merchants there are very proud of."

"Thank you, Father, for this parchment," Gui said smiling, shaking it at him briefly before tucking it into his saddle-bag. "And for all your kindness...and for your advice," he added sweeping his arms around him. "God willing, we will come back through here and bring you the treasures you seek from Jerusalem."

"A blessing, Father," Sir Richard drawled, dipping his fingers in a bowl of warm water. "And then, Gui, we must leave. We have stayed overlong as it is, and have plenty more miles to cover today before we can stop. I don't trust de Courcy, and we are still too close to Nantes for comfort!"

"I agree, Richard!" then calling to his men: "*Fitzurse, Jean, Allan-i-the-Wood*, mount-up, we are leaving. Change the scouts around, Master-at-Arms. Father Hugo, my warmest thanks," Gui bowed to the Abbot, who briefly laid a cool hand on his forehead in silent blessing, before he swung himself back onto Beau, as with a clatter and grind of wheels, they all began to leave. What the men couldn't eat they took with them, stuffing it into the small leather bag that each man had hanging off the back of his saddle, together with a small flask of watered wine for each man that Abbot Hugo had also provided.

Then, while the old Abbot stood in his long black gown, with its cowl down, and his arms up and open wide to give them all the blessing Sir Richard had asked for, with a scrape and a *clip-clop* of iron hooves they pulled off all around him and were gone, the last scouts behind the column turning in their saddles to wave a final goodbye to Abbot Hugo and his brothers, all clustered around him like a small parliament of rooks.

*

114

Throughout that remaining day they travelled south hard, the track they were on busy with travellers in some places, and barren and empty in others. Sometimes, on the edge of far clearings, deer could be seen at gaze from amongst the trees, or leaping across the track as they approached, only to vanish amongst the trees as swiftly as they had been seen. And there were those amongst them who twitched to draw a bow at venture and shoot one down, all eyeing Bouncer to see if he would give chase. But Allan was not a King's verderers for nothing, and he had trained him well, and the great hound stayed close to Caesar when called to heel.

There were pedlars with heavy packs on their backs, bulging with trinkets; farmers with solid wheeled carts laden with vegetables, chickens and piglets in wooden crates; a farmer with a calf on a rope bawling for its mother; a tilt cart with tall spoked wheels like their own and packed with family belongings, father leading a horse, mother and children piled amongst the furniture; a boy with a dog, his bait over his shoulders, a set of pipes in his hand and a small flock of sheep; players and musicians, tumblers and groups of sturdy peasants trudging between fields, tools across their shoulders; a wandering grey friar; a Palmer in his wide brimmed hat, his scrip full of relicts, fragments of the True Cross...*no doubt culled from a local carpenter*, Father Matthew thought...*or the 'nails' from Christ's hands and feet stolen from a nearby blacksmith. Some good Christians would believe anything!*...And the tall Benedictine shook his head and smiled. And there was a lady in a covered horse litter, an armed guard at her head and two at her side who pushed back the embroidered curtains from her litter and smiled at Gui and Sir Richard with ruby lips and arched eyebrows. But they pushed past them all in a jingle of spurs and bridle irons and a thunder of wheels and flashing feet, and with such determined faces no-one chose to try and stop them.

The trackway, hot and dry under the relentless sun, and deeply rutted in places, was hard under their hooves, as they barrelled on their way. And the dust of their passage floated like pale smoke above them, whitening their faces and their armour, making those at the very end of the column spit and choke, tying masks across their faces, and cursing their Commanders for not allowing them to stop, for the July heat bore down on them without pity.

Walk, trot, canter! Walk, trot, canter! Walk, trot, canter!

Everyone joggling in their saddles, or swaying from side to side: those leading the sumpters straining with their long reins; those driving the tilt carts watching the traces and head collars for any signs of breakage, and doing their best to keep up the pace. Hard on the men...but even more so on the horses, both those ridden and those pulling the heavy carts in all the cloying heat and dust of that first long day.

115

At noon Gui flung up his hand and they bounced wearily to a stop beside a small stream, pulling off the road under the shade of some trees to refresh the horses, which stood heads down in the crystal running water, as much to cool their feet as to drink their fill. All around them the men sat or lay flopped with tiredness, eating from their packs that which they had saved from the morning, and drinking from their flagons, before going upstream to re-fill them. Many relieved themselves amongst the trees...all grateful for the rest in the sweltering noon-day heat.

"You were right, Jean," Gui said ruefully to de Beaune a while later with a grimace. "It *is* different in France from at home. Greater empty distances and much harder and drier...and hotter," he finished, wiping his face with a cool linen cloth wrung out from the stream.

"You think this is hot?" Father Matthew chuckled, flapping the loose neck of his woollen habit as he joined them. "You wait 'til you get to Grise...or even more, to the Holy Land! Now...that really *is* what one might call *hot!*"

"'Redders!' As the men would say." Richard chipped in with a grin.

"God willing we will be more hardened to it by then," Gui grunted. "How are the lads doing?"

"Oh...fine. Hot, bothered and dusty. Especially those at the rear of the column. We ought to change them round more often. And the horses are suffering a bit."

"Yes, my Lord," de Beaune nodded. "Especially those pulling the carts. They need more care or they'll not make it. Trying to get them to drink from a waterskin wastes too much...and a helmet isn't big enough."

"And we have no buckets from which they can drink!" Gui groaned, levering himself off the ground. "Bloody silly of us not to have thought about that sooner. So simple really! We must try and buy some on our way through the next town, or market we come to. Come on, O my noble Guard Commander, it's time to move."

"Can't think of everything, dear boy," Richard said with his lazy grin, as he gathered his things around him. "Must have something to moan about, don't you know, or where's the fun in life?" Then, standing up he shouted: "Master-at-Arms! Get the lads moving. We can't stay here all day...*Mount up!*"

And banging the dust from his cyclas and off his steel chausses, Sir Richard pulled his squire, Philip, to his feet and went to inspect Merlin, lifting each enormous foreleg in turn, checking the frogs on each hoof for stones or damage, and testing his shoes for movement. Then with a swift ruffle, a pat on his withers, and a foot-up from his squire, he was back on Merlin again and together with Gui, their scouts already ahead of them, he led the column back onto the road and away again.

*

Fording streams and wending down steep valleys cloaked with trees, helping with the tilt carts where it was most needed, the ruts deepest from the winter or where the trackway was badly broken up, they pushed forward until the sun was beginning to fall.

Through sleepy hamlets and small villages strung out along the highway they rumbled and clattered their way, a wave and a smile from many of those they passed, scowls and shaken fists from others; the men and horses bothered by clouds of flies, and by the heat and dust of the beaten road until they came at last to the Sèvres River, from where the battlements of Clisson Castle could be seen poking up above the trees ahead.

Standing up in his stirrups Gui groaned and stretched himself, swinging his body from side to side in his saddle, before leaning forward on its high pommel to look about him...*Twenty miles a day a Roman army could cover, according to Father Matthew last night. And we have done almost thirty since leaving Nantes...and that includes the long river crossing before Vertou.*

He looked up at the sky, still blue and clear, the occasional bird passing high, high overhead like an arrow...*A pigeon probably from the way it's flying, wings beating fast and continuously. It will take a rare hawk to catch that one!..*And watching it speed away he suddenly thought of de Brocas, and looked again at the bird, now fast disappearing...and, for a moment, he wondered, his face creased with a frown...*I shall never see one of those flying like that and not think 'de Brocas'! God's Blood, where is that bastard now...and where is Alicia?* And he leaned back down against the high cantle of his saddle with a sigh.

All around him, as well as great acres of vineyards, were vast open fields filled with wheat and barley, some with a mass of scarlet poppies amongst them and tall, ox eye daisies. purple vetch and meadow sweet thrust out from the verges, along with toad flax and pink valerian, and the hedgerows were thick with old man's beard, goldenrod and red and white campion. And seeing so much calm beauty he breathed deeply and relaxed.

But even as Beau pushed forwards the big horse disturbed a great covey of partridge that leapt up with a frantic whirr of wings, almost from the feathers around his clomping feet, making him snort and toss his head as they rocketed away into the nearest wheat field. As they disappeared amongst the swaying

117

golden heads, so a startled flock of sparrows and goldfinches suddenly rose up, tiny wings blurred with speed, and flashed in brilliant colours across his path to settle in the hedgerows, swinging and chattering fiercely from the bushes as he and Beau ambled past, making him smile.

Drawing another deep breath he turned round, his eyes flicking past Sir Richard on Merlin just behind him, and studied his long column of men and horses, sumpters, carts and all.

Tired faces, plodding beasts, dust covered and weary. They could keep going 'til almost dark, find a bivouac and hunker down...or they could call a stop here. Cross the river by its bridge and beg a bed for the night from the castle. Then they could check again for loose horseshoes, stable the destriers properly, hobble the rest, and start again fresh in the morning. Not so early as today...but early enough to get to Chantonnay tomorrow night; and that was much closer to forty miles than they had covered that day.

Stop now...or press on?

He reached down and patted Beauregard on his neck and pulled his long flicky ears, soft as silk, gently through his hands, making the big horse shake his head and hurrumph through his nostrils. "So...that's it is it, old chap?" he said as he reached forward and patted his withers. "Had enough for today then?"...and Beau tossed his head and hurrumphed again.

"Talking to that great lump of horseflesh are you, dear boy?" Richard drawled at him, with a grin. "At least it's y'r horse and not y'r sword! That really would worry me!"

"Don't you insult Beauregard, like that, you affected apology for a Christian Knight! He's very sensitive. See," he added, "as Beau tossed his head again. "Much more of that and we'll push on till dark!"

Richard laughed, and bent his head forward. "O, great and worthy horse," he intoned solemnly. "O great wise one! What is your wish today? Go on...or stop?"

At which question, without further ado, Beau halted and thrust his head forward into the nearest bush, pulled out a great mouthful of long grasses and nodded his head again, and they both laughed. "Well. I think that settles it," Gui said. "We stop here for the night and move on tomorrow."

And turning to his own Squire he said, "Simon, ride back up the column and tell Fitzurse and the other commanders we will be stopping here at Clisson. Then go with Philip, unfurl our colours, and ride on to the castle and call for aid for tonight. Father Matthew is with the wounded on the carts, so make sure he knows too. Now...I wonder what kind of reception we'll get. I don't know who holds here, but he is on King Richard's lands, so we ought to be alright!"

118

And with every anticipation of a pleasant evening they both kicked on, their column following, their two squires with the colours of Malwood and L'Eveque bravely streaming from their standards as they galloped ahead of them towards the castle, from which brazen trumpets were already calling.

*

Four days later they reached Niort.
Four days of hard travelling and frustration, for despite their care at Clisson, Merlin cast a shoe half way after leaving, as had two of their sumpters. A truly maddening delay, while they paused at the tiny village of Saint Fulgent to get them fixed, dealing with the dumbest farrier it was possible to imagine, whose speech was almost unintelligible and who had to be dragged out of the nearest alehouse and threatened with castration before he would pick up his tools!

Even then he had been too drunk to do the job, falling all over the place like a witless clown, until Fitzurse had hurled him into the village pond in disgust, to the huge amusement of his men and half the village, while Hordle John pumped up the forge, and Pierre Léclosse, one of de Beaune's Burgundians, sorted out Merlin's shoe and hammered out two more for the sumpters.

A job well done…but it had all taken time, so they had bivouacked for the night alongside a small stream they'd come to, and then started out again at first light to reach Chantonnay early enough to push on to Niort, still hoping to reach there two days after leaving Nantes. But, two miles out of the town, while negotiating some vile ruts on the trackway, itself littered with jagged stones, the wheel on one of the tilt carts cracked, the whole iron rim spun off amidst a medley of fierce curses, the heavily laden cart collapsed on its side…and they'd lost a whole day!

But Chantonnay was a market town, and having unloaded the cart, gathered up the shattered wheel and its truant rim, trailed back in and found a wheelwright who could do the job properly…who was neither one of 'God's Children' nor drunk…Gui decided that they would stay there properly, and leave the following morning. A handful of weary troopers, left by the broken-down cart as a guard against theft.

"God's Blood, Matthew!" he cursed, tearing off his helmet and throwing it down onto one of the packs. "What a damned mess of pottage this is. First

119

Merlin, and now a bloody cart's wheel. I thought we'd fixed all that up before leaving Nantes?"

"Remember what I said, my Lord?" Jean de Beaune said in passing, with a grin. "France is not England! Hotter, drier and harder. The more we try to hurry, the more likely it is we'll break something."

Gui laughed ruefully. "More haste less speed, you mean?"

"Something like that, Sir Gui. But I tend to look at things in the light of 'things happen when they're meant to'! In this way, as it's market day here," de Beaune added, "we ought to find those buckets we need for the horses, and some fresh eggs as well," he added with a hungry look. "Fresh bread would be good as well. The horses need the buckets...and I like a hard-boiled egg, and my smoked meat in a warm bun..."

"And a flagon of cider with which to wash it down," Sir Richard interrupted, with his lazy voice. "Father Matthew's chasing up some milfoil and vervain he saw some on one of those stalls in the market, and he's collared the local priest about some shrine or other we passed earlier. Gui, dear boy, just bend to it. We can't move on without the damned cart, so you might as well take it off your back and enjoy it!"

"Well that's for certain. Life's just a real sod sometimes!" he groaned ruefully. "Never mind, we will just have to make the best of it. And, Richard, make sure you change the guard on that cart out there, otherwise we'll have problems with the men!"

"Already thought of, dear boy," his tall Guard Commander smiled. "Fitzurse has that all in hand. Those lads will not miss out on all the fun of the fair...and neither will we!"

And nor did they, for the market was a joy, and so were the people. They found the buckets they needed, the fresh eggs, fresh bread and fresh vegetables...and lots of local red wine!

The arrival of so many strangers, with money to spend, and some time to spend it was good for everyone, and before long the men had dispersed amongst the market stalls, and the houses, shops and bothies that made up Chantonnay. Arm in arm with a cloud of girls who had suddenly appeared amongst them, gaily dressed as for a festival, Gui's command was determined to enjoy itself to the full!

The horses were hobbled by the stream that ran along the edge of the little town where they would bivouac for the night. The local inn was thronged, and the townsfolk produced the best they could, especially fresh bread from the town ovens...and the men drank, spent their silver, squabbled and boasted cheerfully amongst themselves...and fought the local lads over the local girls, who shrieked and laughed and fled amongst the barns and bushes in the warm night like so many fireflies hotly pursued by Gui's cheerful, lusting troopers.

*

In the morning they left again at first light, with the sky streaked with white streamers, and soon after the sun had risen in a blush of crimson and gold it began to cloud up from the north west before a blustering breeze, the clouds casting great drifting shadows across the long ridge of hills that ran along the horizon on their right.

And as the day progressed, the cloud cover grew denser, the sun disappeared and rain threatened, the wind now scurrying amongst them, and Gui pulled the column over so that the men could dig their hooded cloaks out of the packs they had rolled up against the high cantles of their saddles.

"Rain...and soon, I think." Father Matthew said, looking up into the darkening sky. "Those clouds are getting lower. I've lost sight of that long ridge over there already."

"That'll cool everyone down," L'Eveque drawled. "Especially all those with a thick head this morning. By God, that local wine was rough! Certainly left my mouth full of moths this morning!" he ended with a wry grin.

"I expect there'll be a few blue-eyed strangers amongst that lot, too, come the Spring," Fitzurse laughed, pointing back along the way they'd come. "Some of our lads were in amongst those girls like rats up a pipe. A fair number of Hail Mary's in Chantonnay today I'll warrant!"

Richard laughed too and Gui grunted, shifting in his saddle. "All the more reason to press on now!" And standing up in his stirrups he waved his hands in a circle around his head, calling them all forward again and kicked Beau back onto the road, while his Master-at-Arms waited to let the column leaders go past, before spurring back to his chosen scouts at the rear.

Ten minutes later the rain started in earnest, a fine driving mizzle that soon became a steady fall, first laying the dust and then pooling in the ruts that scored the track. All around them the trees shook their heads in the wind, rattling more drops over them as they passed, and the birds flocked from the fields to shelter in the woods and hedgerows.

And so it was all that long day.

In dark, sweeping veils the rain was driven across the countryside. Sometimes in heavy bursts that hammered down 'til the trackway was almost flooded...and sometimes it lifted until the distant hills showed through the

121

murk like the shrouded backs of whales. And worst when the trackway wound amongst the vineyards and the great open fields where there was no cover at all, the wind-driven rain making the men hunch their shoulders in under their cloaks and drop their heads, pulling their hoods further forward as they did so. Their horses, too, tucked in their tails whenever the wind squalled across their rumps with a sudden extra blast of rain, and plodded forward, heads down and miserable. Nor was it much better amongst the woods where wet branches, in full summer leaf, smacked them as they went by, each time giving them all an extra soaking. And as the day progressed, so their passage slowed as the carts got into trouble amongst the deeper ruts and the trackway turned from hard passage to sticky mud.

Twice they stopped briefly to change scouts around and rest the horses, but Gui was determined that they would reach Niort that day, no matter what, and so it was a very weary, rain-sodden Command, that crested the road that led down to the bridge, and so across the Sèvres again at last.

Chapter 19... The Lord Baron makes his plans with care.

In Nantes the Baron's pigeon message arrived safely at midday. The bell that Sir Alan de Courcy had arranged in the tower loft the Baron had set up two years before, when he had bought the manor in which Sir Alan was now living, rang sharply to tell him so, and it was only a few minutes later that his Pigeon Master brought the tiny cylinder through to him.

Freed from castle duties as he was, he and Victor Jonelle, his right-hand man, were together in the house's modest Great Hall when they received it.

"So...Lord Roger wants us to set things running with Bernard de Vernaille in Bordeaux. That's good. I expect we'll get a message from him too shortly. But I do not intend for us to miss out on all the fun, Victor. What did you do with that little rat who came sneaking to us last night?"

"After I cut off his fingers, and threatened to cut his throat?"

"No...after that. After he told us all he knew."

"I dragged him down to where those two bastards had stabled their horses and cut his throat, of course! Lovely mess. Blood everywhere! Covered him with hay and straw and left him for someone to find. He has no family, so next stop the river!"

"Good! I'll arrange for that idiot du Clefs to find the body...and then we'll both shout Blue Murder and rouse the Hue and Cry against those bastards."

"But we have no warrant to arrest them, my Lord, nor ever likely to get one...not least because they didn't do anything! And you know as well as I do that the Hue and Cry is only strictly local."

"Are you going soft on me, Jonelle?" de Courcy rasped.

"No, Sir Alan!" the big man replied tersely, straightening his shoulders. "I want those bastards as much as you do! They shamed me as well as you, and our men. But we swore on King Richard's Seal...and I like my job here and value a whole skin. A shame we couldn't have done for that fat fool Roland, that really would have given us a lever against them."

"No matter! King Richard is on his way to Marseilles, and we are Arthur of Brittany's 'leal' men, or so his mother believes, and the Hue and Cry will enable us to mount a strong party at the Duke's expense. His Seneschal is down with the bloody flux, and can do nothing to stop us. Be bold, Victor. We have done this before...there is no reason it won't work just as well again now! So...how many men do we take?"

"Thirty, I think. And if Sir Bernard brings swordsmen and archers, we'll bring lancers with reinforced chest pieces, shields on their backs and long swords. We can draw rations for five days, and be on our way before Vespers."

"We need to fix the ferry for our use. So send half a dozen of your lads to seize it now. And if that stupid bastard who runs it complains, break his fucking head for him! A little blood spilled now will save us hours later."

"What about Roland?"

"Leave him to me! He's in as deep as we are. If he knows what's good for him he'll keep his trap good and firmly shut. He has made a mint out of working with us over the port tolls and revenues, and I have kept a record of *every* penny he's taken out of the Count's proper dues. He'll be no problem; values his fat skin far too much for that. Any real nonsense and he can join the 'Ferret' in the bloody river...and so I'll tell him!"

"Right, my Lord. I'll get on and sort out the men I want with us. No new ones. Just the right hard bastards who know what cut and thrust is really all about. What will you do?"

"Send a message to the Lord Baron at Gruissan, and another to Bernard in Bordeaux. He'll need eighty men at least...and he'll have to be careful where he gets them from and how he musters them. That bastard Sir Hugh Willoughby is the High Constable of all Aquitaine, *and* Guard Commander at Bordeaux. He *is* a truly leal man to King Richard, and as hard as bloody nails. If he gets even a whiff of what we are planning, there will be a dreadful reckoning to pay. He can cut de Vernaille, and any command he has, in bits before he's even gone a mile!"

"Let's hope Sir Bernard has as much sense as we do, then?"

"Victor...I hope so too! Now, those fuckers left at first light this morning, and they have carts with them which will slow them down. We don't, and can travel fast and light. In five days at most they should be at Saint Jean d'Angély. Plenty of time for de Vernaille to close in on them from the south, and for us to catch up with them from the north. Then, between us, we'll take them to pieces and feed their bits to the bloody crows! We leave in four hours!"

*

Just before Vespers the bell in Bernard de Vernaille's pigeon loft on the southern edge of Bordeaux also rang, and moments later he held de Courcy's message in his hand, having already received an earlier one from the Baron in Gruissan, and sent one on to Nantes as well.

A tall rangy man, with a loping stride and narrow shoulders, his face was smooth, with dark eyes to match his hair and eyebrows, and a mouth made more for smiles than frowns. But his soul was bitter, and his humour sour, not matching the smiling face he showed to strangers; and his prowess was with ill-tutored townsmen, loose women and the wine for which Bordeaux was famous.

His father, Sir Rupert de Vernaille, had been a famous warrior. A man of steel whom all men could trust. It was his trebuchets that had battered a way into Cahors in the Old King's war against Toulouse in 1159. But his sons seemed not to be of their father's making, and the old Lord had turned them both off his lands, not given them any authority over his estates in his lifetime.

So both men had come to the Baron's notice, and had joined his faction; and Lord Roger had fed their esteem, Bernard de Vernaille in particular as the eldest son, and had given him money and built up his meinie with soldiers of his own. And now the old Lord was dead at last, he had inherited all that his father had so carefully built up; had thrown out all those who had worked for Lord Rupert without a penny, and installed his own people in their place. He was a mean master and a perfect fool, and good men would not work for him.

Now, waving the tiny message in his hand, he fancied himself a warrior in his father's mould. A cunning fighter; a man for tomorrow whom men would follow into Hell's mouth itself and he viewed the coming skirmish with relish....*An ambush, near Saint Jean d'Angély? Good thinking*...He knew that area. There was thick forest all round there, apart from the great fields that edged the town...and nothing much in between beside several fordable streams, and a river with a proper bridge just this side of the town where they would be sure to draw up for the night. From Saint Jean to Niort was the best part of forty miles. So they would not push beyond the town...If they could get moving as soon as they could muster our men, they would have time to do some useful scouting...*Pin things down properly, as father would have done, the old bastard!*

They should get there with a day to spare, maybe more...But eighty men would not be easy...especially as they had to be certain that Sir Hugh Willoughby didn't get wind of anything!...*For he's a cunning bastard and no mistake!*...The man had eyes and ears everywhere, especially just now with the English King about to set off for the Holy Land, everyone a bit uncertain about what might happen behind his royal back once he'd gone....*And not all his*

*Barons can be trusted…*he thought with a sardonic smile for his own treachery…. *So…it will be difficult, but not impossible!*

"Geoffrey, you idle bugger," he shouted over his shoulder. "Get yourself here straightaway! We have had our orders from the Baron at Gruisssan…and advice from de Courcy at Nantes. He's setting out with thirty lancers today…and advises us we'll need eighty men from here. Come on dear brother; we need to put our heads together, and send for that Master Sergeant of ours to join us!"

Moments later both men were seated at the long table in Sir Bernard's hall, wine to hand in tall silver gilt goblets, both elegantly dressed in long gowns with wide sleeves, coloured hose, and suede half boots on their feet. Sir Geoffrey de Vernaille, square where his brother was lean, and more broad shouldered, but with the same dark hair and eyebrows, and the same smiling face with the evil intent hidden behind it.

Shortly after that, with a brief bow, their Master-at-Arms, Martin Riberac, joined them, a tough, burly man with a weathered face like tooled leather, piercing grey eyes, and great butcher's hands that could wield an axe as if it were of wood, not hardened steel. In tough, riveted mail and leather chausses, plain sword and dagger at his waist he looked what he was, a hardened, professional soldier.

"Wine, Riberac?"

"Thank you, my Lord."

"We have had the message we have been waiting for, Martin. We need eighty men, horsed, fully armoured-up and ready to leave by tomorrow. No fuss, no arguments…and no boasting!"

"Where for, my Lord?"

"Saint Jean d'Angély in four days' time. Mixed forces, Sergeant. Half archers, half swordsmen. No spears. They are coming from elsewhere."

"We have half of those already under arms several miles outside the city walls, at Saint Savin, my Lord," the tough soldier replied quietly. "Your father held land there in the days of the old King, Henry Plantagenet. It was a kind of training camp for the old King's wars. We just kept it going."

"The Sergeant's right, Bernard," his brother said swiftly, putting his drink down in surprise. "I had forgotten that. And it's been a while since we rode out there and gave the old man's lands the once over. That bastard, Willoughby, would never question us doing so now we have inherited…nor taking a guard along with us."

"What, Geoffrey? Twenty men apiece? He would have to be both blind and stupid not to question such a large bodyguard. And while Sir Hugh Willoughby may be many things we both deplore…blind and stupid he is not!"

126

"You are forgetting that Richard of England is gathering an army to fight the Saracens in the Holy Land, Bernard," his brother sneered. "Troops are moving around all over the place just now, leaving many manors vulnerable...and we do hold much land hereabouts, as Sir Hugh knows."

"True, dear brother. True...and not all the Poitevin barons are as secure as our noble King would like," he added, looking sideways at his brother with a sly grin. "So taking a good guard, with what men we can muster, to visit our newly gained lands in Saint Savin...since that miserable old bastard, our late and unlamented dear Papa is now finally dead and buried thank God!...Willoughby will not think that surprising."

Geoffrey de Vernaille looked at his brother and grinned. "A particularly useful idea, Bernard, as Saint Savin just happens to be towards Saint Jean!"

"And if I set out with half now, my Lords," Riberac interjected. "And you two follow tomorrow individually with the rest, but from different gates and at different times, I doubt anyone will be any the wiser. Not least because you have lands in both directions! It might mean a slight detour to join up together, but that would be a small price to pay, my Lords. Don't you think?"

Bernard de Vernaille looked at his brother across his wine goblet, and then up to his powerful Sergeant-at-Arms, standing with his hands on his hips. "Yes, Geoffrey. That could work. How would you sort it, Riberac?"

"Well, my Lord. If the men play their part, and ride out with plenty of jokes and laughter, all light-hearted like, and full of bounce, saying they're on a training exercise, who would question that?"

Sir Geoffrey stood up: "Martin Riberac!" He laughed. "There are as many rogues in this city as there are fleas on a dog's back, but you surpass them all! We, on the other hand are both belted knights about our lawful business, with no-one to say us nay! You are right...no-one will suspect a thing!"

"I agree, brother. We'll do it. I'll go and see Sir Hugh about the necessary passes; you, Geoffrey, get a message off to the Château to tell Lord Roger what we're doing. And you, Martin, get the lads organised. We travel light, understand? Rations for five days, and weapons only.

"We'll take four sumpters with us to carry our armour, and for spare strings, bolts, extra food and sundries, and we'll leave by stages as discussed and all meet up at Saint Savin. Just pray the weather doesn't turn really foul. Meet me back here in four hours," he ended briskly, banging his hands together, "and we can sort out all the finer details.

"You, Riberac, will leave with a third of the men as soon as you can. Night bivouac exercise is what I'll tell Sir Hugh. You and I, Geoffrey, will leave at first light," adding with a laugh, "So no staying with your favourite doxy tonight, brother. If I must do without the so luscious Miranda...you can do without your vulpine Leonora! Up at dawn, and away the moment the gates are opened...and the Devil take the hindmost!"...*Father, you old sod, wherever you are, we will make you proud of us at last!*

Chapter 20...Sir Gui arrives at Niort.

After such a long, bruising day in the saddle, by the end of which there was scarcely a dry bit of flesh on anyone, the welcome they received at Niort was every bit as warm as the absent sun.
And draggled as they were, the flags that Gui ordered Simon and Philip to unfurl as they approached the long stone bridge over the River Sèvres, just as they had done at Clisson, snapped and fluttered in the gusting wind as bravely as any could have wished.

The Scarlet Lion Rampant of Malwood, and the Sable Lion Rampant-Gardant of L'Eveque both snarled and swiped with their great clawed feet as their two young squires carried them forward with as much pride as if they were bearing the King's own colours on their standards. Over the bridge they clattered, forcing all others to the sides as the long column of mounted men, carts and sumpters entered the town and rode up to the castle gatehouse, all taking note of the long crenellated walls and the twelve well-spaced towers that reared up out of them.

The moat, fed by the river, separated the walls from the rest of the town, a serious barrier in itself, but completely dwarfed by the truly massive donjon that King Richard had ordered to be built. One part was already at its full height of nearly a hundred feet, the other still only half built, the whole further protected by a ferocious dry ditch, twenty six feet deep, and nearly as broad, that separated the donjon from the castle bailey and the walls around it.

Gui and Richard halted their column before the gatehouse, its heavy drawbridge open, its portcullis raised, and just stared up at its immensity, the very fighting tops almost lost in the low misty clouds that had bedevilled them all day, the standards flacking wetly in the rain-laden wind, and trumpets blowing.

"Well, this was worth the bloody journey just to see it!" Gui said almost breathlessly. "That thing is simply stupendous! Those walls must be twelve feet thick at least...probably twenty at the base, and I hear the ditch is just a nightmare. God help anyone trying to batter their way into that...let alone try and scale it! Amazing!"

"You like my castle, then?" a soft voice broke in unexpectedly. "Sir Gui de Malwood..and..and Sir Richard L'Eveque? By your colours and your blazon?"

Gui, completely taken aback, looked down astonished at the slight figure before him, who must have walked out from the Gatehouse and across the drawbridge to greet them while they had been talking, and was reaching his hand up in welcome even as he spoke.

The man was immaculately dressed in a long flowing, pleated bliaut of finest green cloth, with narrow sleeves down to his elbows; and on his chest, in beautiful silver thread on a scarlet background, his own blazon of three Escalopes Argent on a field Gules, to show his pilgrimage to Santiago of Compostella, over a blue chemise with more silver sea shells all down the long sleeves. He was open faced under a green chaperon, with a long liripipe wrapped round his neck beneath it and a sweeping cloak of red wool around his shoulders, lined with blue sendal, and held by two great ouches of worked gold, his blazon in beautiful silver orphrey all across the back of it. His face and style were those of a man very much of Sir Yvo's age, with bright blue eyes that twinkled even in the rain, a short pointed beard and a wide smile; his Chaperon held in place with the staring eyes of three enormous peacock feathers. He looked magnificent.

My Lord Count - William - de Forz?" Gui asked hesitantly, clasping the man's outstretched hand.

"Yes, Sir Gui; the very same. I am the constable of this castle and have been watching your approach for some time. You are welcome indeed, but please kick-on out of this rain. You look soaked!"

Gui laughed. "Soaked indeed…since eight this morning when we set out from Chantonnay," he said, shaking the rain off his helmet. You are most generous, my Lord Count," and swinging off Beauregard's broad back he clasped the Count's hand again, leading Beau forward as he did so, while Sir Richard came down off Merlin as well and also took the Count's outstretched hand.

"In truth we have all been looking forward to getting here since leaving at dawn. It has been a long, bitter day and we must leave tomorrow again at first light, for we have a long way still to go. But, my Lord, you speak as though you know our colours with more than passing interest?"

"I am King Richard's leal man here in Poitou, Sir Gui, and there are not many knights who can knock the King out of his saddle without their names becoming known…and that of his closest friend," he added with a friendly nod towards Sir Richard. "Quite David and Jonathan, I understand."

"Oh!" Gui exclaimed surprised. "Yes. I suppose so. Or even Roland and Oliver?" he added with a laugh. "Sir Richard and I have rubbed along together well for some years now. He's an idle hound, but has a sound head on his broad shoulders," he added with a grin. "And I am impulsive…so we rather complement one another. As for the other, the Christmas Tournament in London? I am surprised you heard about that."

"Indeed?" The Count smiled, his eyes fairly sparkling. "And who has not heard how the young Sir Gui de Malwood of the King's Guard, with the scarlet lion rampant on his chest, dumped the mighty Lionheart on his royal armoured bottom in front of all London! Your fame goes before you."

"A lucky strike, my Lord Count, I assure you," Gui answered with a laugh. "The King was not trying!"

Count William chuckled: "Wisely said, young man. Kings can be of a very uncertain temper...and Richard is famous for being less...shall we say 'temperate' than some others I can think of?"

Gui looked into Count William's eyes, saw the twinkle and smiled. "Mmmm, some might say so, my Lord...but *very* quietly!" And a further ripple of laughter ran around them.

"In fact, Lord William," Sir Richard said in his usual laconic style. "Our Lord King roared his head off, as only he can, and rewarded this miserably bedraggled fellow with a ring off his own finger." Then, pausing to give Gui an arch look with a raised eyebrow, he added: "Mind you, next moment he gave him a thumping royal buffet between his shoulders that almost sent him sprawling, just to remind this young sprig of fancy here that he was no weakling!" And they all chortled at Gui's embarrassment, swiftly at ease with one another, even though they had only just met, all knowing *exactly* what it was like to be dumped off one's horse at a tournament...but better there than on the field of battle!

By then they had walked through the long gatehouse passage, under its hidden meurtrières and iron plated portcullises and were paused, out of the wet, just at the end of it before a huge open bailey. Smirred with rain, the King's new donjon sprang up from the far side of it in all its power and strength, and the enormous ditch that went all round it was every bit as frightening an obstacle as Gui had been told. There were also a large number of additional buildings within the bailey: a long row of stables and a large corral with a handful of loose horses; storage barns and slate roofed lean-tos; a large, busy forge and sleeping quarters for the garrison, some with families; chapel, kitchens, castle well, and an elegant Great Hall for visitors; even an inn, with its own stables and hay barn, as well as numerous other outbuildings.

"As you can see, Sir Gui," Count William said expansively. "We have plenty of space for all your men, and your horses. King Richard did not stint anything in the re-building of this fortress, and the kitchens will supply you with plenty of hot water for a bath for you and your principal officers if you so wish. Frankly you look as if you could do with a long soak and a large goblet of Burgundy! I bring it in especially as it is a true king among wines." Adding softly with a wry grin: "We have nothing so noble here in the Vendée."

131

"My Lord Count, a king among wines indeed; you never spoke a truer word," Sir Gui replied, shaking the water off his mailed hands. "A good soak, a goblet of your finest and a chance to get out of this damned armour and into real clothes for all of us would be just wonderful."

"That is all as good as done, Sir Gui," Count William said cheerfully. "My steward will see to all those details, show you to your rooms and ensure your squires know where to find you. He will also send some pages to help with hot water and things, so you can be comfortable. My Master-at-Arms, and yours, can direct the men. I see you have a Benedictine with you?" he added, as Father Matthew rode through beside one of the tilt carts.

"Yes, Lord William. That is Father Matthew, on special assignment from the Holy Father himself. He is both friend and confessor, as well as a brilliant doctor. We would all be lost without him. His skills saved my life!"

"On assignment from the Holy Father?" Count William queried astonished. "From the supreme Pontiff himself? He must be a rare man indeed. My chaplain will be delighted to find another of his calling in the castle tonight. I will make certain he is both properly housed and seated at the High Table tonight. I cannot promise you a feast, Sir Gui," he said warmly. "But I can promise you an evening of cheerful friendliness and good food, for your whole command, with which my Lady Hawise will be certain to provide us. She is my heart's ease...but frightens the life out of me," he said with a certain smile, as a bell began to toll across the bailey, "so do not be late! That is the Vespers bell. We shall eat in two hours in the great hall."

Just as he finished speaking a number of castle varlets, all in the de Forz livery of silver sea shells on a scarlet background, came running up, accompanied by a tall man in hauberk and cross-gartered leather chausses, followed by a small retinue of servants, chattering like magpies, led by Count William's Steward, himself in a long red gown, split to the waist, and blue hose in long red leather boots, silver scallops on each shoulder, and carrying the long black polished rod of his office.

"Here are my people now, Sir Gui," Count William said, clapping his hands for immediate silence. "They will care for you, and later will show you where to go. So, I will see you then." But, just as he moved to leave, he stopped and turned back towards them again.

"Forgive me, gentlemen," he said, quietly, looking at them steadily. "But I feel there is a tale yet to be told, as to what two belted knights, one clearly of the King's personal retinue, are doing in the Vendée, fully armoured-up and with so professional, and powerful, a body of men...and in the company of a Benedictine under the auspices of the Holy Father himself no less? Moreover, a clearly tired command, who must all leave again tomorrow at first light? As

Constable of this royal castle I am intrigued, my Lords. I am sure it will be a most illuminating tale," he added with a firm glance up into Gui's face, in which there was no sign of a twinkle. "I shall look forward to it!"...*and it had better be a good tale, my good Lord Baron of Malwood, or my dungeons may yet find themselves overcrowded!*...And with a bow from his guests, and a tilt of the head from himself, he was gone.

Chapter 21...Count William de Forz agrees to help the 'Lion' of Malwood.

Later, when all the food had been cleared away by Count William's varlets, the Great Hall had mostly emptied, and the long tables that everyone below the dais had been seated on removed and replaced with wool stuffed pallets for sleeping; Gui, Sir Richard, Father Matthew and Count William remained seated at the huge table of polished oak planks at which they had eaten.

Lady Hawise, a lady as large and bountiful as her husband was small and lean, with irrepressible humour and sound common sense, had left her husband with their guests to retire to her own private solar, taking her two daughters with her, and her tire-women. Count William's eldest son was away learning his Squire's duties with a neighbouring baron, as Gui had done in Yorkshire, and his younger son, James, had gone with Simon and Philip to clean armour and help prepare them for tomorrow's journey.

With the summer darkness now upon them, the huge hall, lit by flickering oil lamps and flaring flambeaux in iron holders on the walls, was a mass of dancing shadows warmed by the great fire the Count had ordered against the unexpected chill of that wet, summer evening, the clouds still low overhead dampening the natural light.

With a wave of his hands, and a quiet word with his steward, Count William dismissed all the servants, preferring to care for his guest's needs himself, rather than have even a single page left standing nearby to serve them....*no little pitchers with long handles*...So after filling their glass beakers in their silver holders from a beautifully chased silver-gilt carafe, he first moved a huge multi-branched candelabra closer for better light, then sat down in his great armed chair and looked at them, their faces half in shadow and half lit by the fire and the candles.

"So, my Lords," Count William said firmly after a while, with a gesture. "As you see, I have dismissed all my servants and my pages, and there are armed guards at every door, inside and out as you can see. My Steward has seen to that," he added pointing to two armed men standing before the doorways. "We will not be disturbed, I assure you. Now...I think you have a tale to tell me?"

Gui, looking at his host's face, fully lit by the candles, was under no illusions. This was a man, chosen by his King, to guard this whole area of the Vendée against attack. Mild as he might seem, he had a core of steel...and this great castle could as easily become a daunting prison as it was a pleasing place of rest and friendship….*But how much can I trust this man whom I hardly know? How much should I say of all that I have learned? And how much help might I get for this quest?*…All questions that he, Richard and Matthew had asked themselves before entering that great keep for dinner. With those thoughts still tumbling over themselves in his mind Gui looked briefly into the flickering shadows all around him, at the flames in the massive grate leaping and twisting, at the flaring flambeaux now beginning to die down…and back again into the sharp, concentrated gaze of those two bright blue eyes looking at him so shrewdly…*Trust…or secret? Honesty or betrayal?*…And he smiled: "Indeed I do my Lord Count…"

And Count William de Forz relaxed, and smiled in turn, his eyes losing their hardness. "Mmmm, my Lord Baron, a good choice," he interjected, banging his hand on the broad table top. "A good choice! Now…Please, Sir Gui," he continued, reaching for his wine beaker. "There is not the need now for such formality. Not now you have made your choice, yes?" he added with a tilt of his head and a flick of his left eyebrow.

"Yes, my Lord Count…and I will tell you all I can. Meanwhile please be advised that I and my whole command are the King's leal men too…as you are."

And first looking into the hard, tense faces of those around him, Count William paused to study the young man before him, and smiled.

"I never doubted it," he continued tersely, looking straight into Gui's eyes as he spoke. "As I said, you have made a wise choice. Just as our King has made a wise choice in you! And I would rather, by far, have you all as my guests than as my prisoners, for we live in unquiet times. The Vendée is not the safe haven for our King Richard as he would wish it to be. I am charged by the King with keeping his peace. But peace is fragile, and needs great strength to maintain it…hence this castle's new defences, and it is good for a wise man to be prudent! I thank you for your trust…please call me, 'William' and I will use your given name as well. And you, Sir Richard, if that is agreeable? At times like these I feel titles are not helpful."

Gui looked at him and nodded his head. "Very well..William..I thank you for that, and thank you and the Lady Hawise for your enormous kindness and generosity this evening, and at such short notice…"

"Gui. Please," the Count said a firmly. "Keep your many 'kindnesses' for tomorrow. It is your 'tale' I wish to hear…and to learn how your sudden presence in Niort may affect me here in Poitou, given the King's absence from his lands at this time. So…how may I help you?"

135

Gui smiled and bowed his head towards his host, then turning to his black robed confessor and friend, he said quietly: "Matthew, show Count William the Holy Father's Commission and Writ of Passage…and the King's Warrant for de Brocas, and we'll take it all from there." Noting as he spoke how the mention of Lord Roger's name had brought a sharply indrawn breath from de Forz, and a very fierce look indeed from those blue eyes, now shorn of any hint of amusement, but only piercing interest.

"You have the King's Seal, Gui?" he asked, completely astonished. "Here in my castle?"…*Dear Lord, how powerful are these men I have under my roof tonight?*

"Yes, William. Along with other…very special papers, some of which Father Matthew will show you. Others we cannot."

"I understand, Gui," he said leaning forward into the light. "I *am* the King's leal man in Poitou, as I told you. Now, I am agog to hear your tale…and will render all assistance where I can!"

And so Gui, and Sir Richard, with Father Matthew's help, told Count William of all they knew, and of all that had happened to them since the terrible night of the fire at Castle Malwood…while the candles burned down in their sockets, the carafe was emptied twice over and owls were calling beyond the castle garth.

They told of the foul murders of Gui's parents to Greek Fire; the deaths, the treachery and the plots against themselves and against their King by both Philip of France…*God help him if any of this ever gets out!*…and Prince John…*What a little shit he truly is!*…Of the desperate battle against the Corsairs, their efforts to save the *Mary*…and finally of the dreadful loss of Alicia to de Brocas after all through his corsair ally, Sheik El Nazir.

And they shocked the Lord Count William de Forz to his very core.

"My God!" He exclaimed at the end of it. "And you have the proof of your claims against Philip Valois…against the French King? And against Prince John?"

"Yes, William. Father Matthew has them. If you like…?"

"No! No! I have no wish to see them," he exclaimed fervently, holding up his hand as if to shield his eyes, almost in fear…*Even to know of such things is bad enough. To know actually where they are…or to see them without the King's permission to do so is almost terrifying*…."I only wished to know you had them.

"This is a very bad business. Roger de Brocas is a most dangerous enemy, Gui. He has the French King's protection anyway, as all men know; and is allied to Count Raymond V of Toulouse who is Richard's sworn enemy at this time. But I did not realise de Brocas was so thick with Prince John as

136

well?...*Sweet wine of Christ that man is a monster!*...That is not good! And with Richard going to be away in the Holy Land on his damned Crusade...Yes! Yes!..." He said, waving his hands as Gui broke in to defend Richard's decision. "...I know it is all very honourable, and re-claiming Jerusalem is every Christian knight's true ideal. We all know that, but Richard is just two years a King, and the land is unquiet. John and Philip plot against him, and we, Richard's loyal men, cannot be everywhere."

"Are you in danger here, my Lord?" Father Matthew asked, intrigued, leaning forward across the table.

"From those petty Lordlings who hold around here? *Pish!*" And he snapped his fingers in dismissal. "They are nothing, Father. But from greater Lords further afield who have greedy eyes for chunks of Poitou, if they join together? Maybe.

"Niort is wealthy, and important...that is why Richard has commissioned such a powerful new Donjon...and it controls the river Sèvres for miles. I can hold Castle Niort, and the town, in the teeth of Richard's enemies for as long as it takes, have no fear of that. But if the King is absent for too long or, God help us, he should be killed, then there are those who may change sides sooner rather later. But de Brocas? That is another matter altogether. He is as bad a man as ever spoke our language. He certainly needs to be taken down, as the King's Warrant declares. What do you have in mind?"

And for some time they discussed all their options, but came back again and again to their one real difficulty.

"The simple thing is, Gui, you need more men!" the Count said, leaning back. "I agree," he said, gesturing with his hands, "that a sudden assault is the only way you can get into that Château. I have been there and can assure you it is a most powerful castle. No siege will work. You have neither the machinery nor the time to build it either. Slam, bang and in y' go, is the way to do it!...But you need three times the men you have as a hard core no matter what, and you can expect high casualties."

"I am hoping that when we arrive we will find those who will join our standards against the Baron. There must be many who want him dead...but lack the leadership, or fighting skills to give that bastard a real run for his money!"

"You may be right, Gui. But you need more good fighters to make an impression!" And standing up, the Count called two of his men over. "Philip, Stephen. Go now and find de Fontenay. Tell him I want him here immediately. Go now, quickly!" And seizing a nearby torch from its iron sconce they trotted off across the darkened hall.

"De Fontenay is my Guard Commander, Gui," he said, adding with a twist of his head towards L'Eveque. "As Sir Richard is to you, so Rousseau de Fontenay is to me. Charles Fouissy!" He called to another of his men, "Bring us another carafe from the Buttery, and another silver glass beaker. If that fat fool Gisgard wants to know who, tell him your Lord commands it!"

Moments later there was a bang and a clatter and a rather square man of medium height, with a strong face under a shock of black hair strode into the room dressed in a long pleated bliaut of red wool over an amber chemise, the Count's blazon of silver shells all down his sleeves, the whole belted in with a long sword hanging off a stout blue leather belt and blue leather half boots on his feet.

"Ah, Rousseau. Thank you, for coming so quickly. I am sorry you could not have joined us earlier. I hope all is well?"

"Yes, William. A fine foal, sturdy like his father," he said, excited. "Dark with a white blaze like his sire, and four white socks like his dam. A real beauty, already finding his milk. He and his mama are doing well. I am sorry, gentlemen. But this a most favoured mare, and it is her first foaling...I always like to be there if I can. I sent my Sergeant-at-Arms to meet your men when you arrived, I hope that was satisfactory? Robert Bourchier is a good man. I hear he and your John Fitzurse are getting on well!"...*But what does the old buzzard want with me at this hour? And what is going on here?*

"A first foaling!" Gui exclaimed with a broad grin as the burly knight came to sit down beside him. "That is always an occasion. Practically the whole castle turned out when my Beau was dropped, all wobbly legs and his dam snuffling him all over with many blowings and licks. Just beautiful! 'Gui de Malwood'," he said extending his hand. "And this is Father Matthew, our Benedictine Saving Grace. Stitches our wounds, absolves our sins, and generally keeps up our spirits. He also stops me from being impulsive," Gui added with a laugh. "I would be lost without him! Meet your opposite number."

"'Richard L'Eveque'" his own Guard commander responded, with a smile, thrusting out his hand as well. "Yes, I heard that Fitzurse and your man, Bourchier? were as thick as thieves," he said in his lazy drawl. "Had a run in with the same gal in Normandy some years ago so I understood when I went to check on them all before dinner. They were knocking it back heartily. Have some of this wine," he said filling a glass beaker. "It is excellent!"

"Rousseau," the Count chipped in. "We have a problem that I think we might be able to help solve for our friends. Come, snatch a bite of these," he added, pushing a plate of cherries and an empty bowl towards him. "And let us see what we can do to help."

138

And without further ado, while the long, wet, summer night settled around the castle like a large towel dunked in a pond…filling the water butts, pouring out of the lead shutes all around the towers and soaking the men on guard along the battlements…Count William, Gui, and all those gathered around the long table on the top dais wrestled with the problem of more men.

*

"How many do you think they need, William?" Rousseau de Fontenay asked after everything necessary had been explained to him…*and keep your sticky hands off my crossbows!*

"How long is a piece of string?" the Count replied with a shrug. "And is it a question of numbers, or quality? Numbers we have…there are always plenty of farm boys who want to go for a soldier! The money is better, the need is constant and there's always the chance of a bit extra if things get interesting. But quality? That is much harder to find so quickly."…*And you're not going to get all my best men!*

"Fifty, William?" Gui asked, raising his eyebrows. "Sixty? Enough to replace those who've been killed and a good handful more."

"Half and halfers will do fine," Sir Richard drawled, as if he could read the Count's mind. "Half, good, hardened fighters who know the difference between a sword and a falchion, and which way to stick the damned thing…and half green 'uns. Those who aren't sure but are damned willing to give it a bloody good try…with a smile!"

They all laughed at that, and then settled back on the benches, while Count William, in his great armed chair, idly rolled his silver drinking beaker between his hands.

"Can we find sixty, Rousseau?" he asked his Guard Commander a moment later.

"Fwoough! Sixty?" his Guard Commander queried, the breath hissing out of his mouth as the Count's sudden request rattled round his head…*where the hell do I find sixty men?*… Then he smiled…*oh, I don't know though…* "Yes, William," he said after a further moment's thought…*Bergerac will just love me for this!*…and a long look at Gui and Sir Richard. "Yes! I think I can find them sixty."

"And have them ready to leave straight after Lauds?"…*Lauds? First cockcrow? Is the man mad?*

"Not Lauds, Count William," Father Matthew said quickly, seeing the shock flit across de Fontenay's face, tugging his cowl further back off his neck as he spoke. "I know Gui would like to be off at daybreak...but no-one will be ready by then. It must be getting on for Matins now, and none of us is abed yet. But if we all rise at Prime, Gui," he said, turning towards him with a quirk of his left eye. "About 6.00am...and leave three hours later, at Terce, that should do us all well. That way we should reach Saint Jean about Vespers, at sunset, with plenty of time to bivouac before a proper daybreak start in two mornings' time."

"Thank you, Father, Terce will do nicely," de Fontenay said...*all blessings on your head Sir Monk*...and he smiled towards the tall Benedictine and tilted his head. "Nine o'clock will be good. Give the sun a chance to get going, Sir Gui. Nothing like a bright start to lift the spirits."

"Good suggestion, Matthew," Gui replied swiftly to the Benedictine's lifted eyebrow. "That sounds good to me too. But can you really spare sixty 'half and halfers', William?"

"Oh, no problem...Sir Gui," de Fontenay cut in with a smile, hesitating slightly over the name. "I'm sure I can find sixty 'half and halfers' for you. But they may not all be the easiest men to handle!" he added with a grin and a studied look of innocence.

Sir Richard guffawed quietly. "Mmmm, know what you mean, you hound!" he drawled, with his lazy grin. "I saw that sudden smile too! Bloody good fighters all the way round! Fighting their bloody selves, and their officers, as well as the bloody enemy you mean!"

"Mmmm, probably," de Fontenay, replied with another sideways grin...*well what did you expect?*

"'Probably', you shameless rogue?" L'Eveque laughed, banging him on the arm. "*Most likely* you mean! A handful of good'uns...and then all those useless buggers and malcontents whom their sergeants have been wanting rid of for years!" And both men laughed. "Well, as long as they can fight when they most need to, then I'll not be complaining. Do you want 'em back, Count?"

"Only the 'good'uns' if they're all in one piece," de Fontenay grinned. "I can't do much with bits and pieces!"

"And I'm left with the rotten eggs, the useless buggers and mother's boys! Well, those whom de Brocas and his merry men haven't managed to kill off in the meantime. Still...you never know, they might all turn out to be wolves in sheeps' clothing. Achilles, Hector and Odysseus all rolled into one!" And there was a sudden burst of laughter.

140

"You know your Homer, then Sir Richard?" Count William asked with a smile.

"Brought up on him, Count. Positively brought up on him. Anyway, better for them to be like Hercules than King Eurystheus…"

"…Who hid in a bronze jar out of sheer terror every time the great hero returned from a labour," Father Matthew chipped in with a smile, his rich Spanish lilt warm in the cool depths of the Great Hall despite the fire. "That would prove a problem…where would they put them while on the march?"

"Oh, very droll, Father," Sir Richard drawled sardonically. "Ho! Ho! Ho! Very droll!" And the laughter rippled amongst them again.

"Well, bronze jars or not, 'good'uns or hell raisers, I'll pay the ferryman, William," Gui chipped in. "I won't be rubbing any salt into anyone's injury, that's for certain."

"Lancers, or just plain fighters with sword, shield and gisarme?" de Fontenay then asked, after drinking deep from his beaker.

"Half and half again…Rousseau?" Sir Richard queried. "We have excellent bowmen and swordsmen…but no lancers, and no specialist spearmen either, and that gisarme your fellows like to use seems to me to be a wicked weapon. Wish we had them ourselves. Long as a spear, but on a thicker shaft; with a goodly billhook at the top, one side for hooking and an axe blade on the other for chopping down. Lovely!"

"Can we do that, Rousseau?" Count William queried, looking at his Guard Commander with concern. "Lancers? They would certainly balance Sir Gui's command nicely. And we are definitely not short of horses."

"Yes, William we can do that, and I know just who should go as their commander."…*Poor bastard!*

"Who is that?"

"William of Bergerac," de Fontenay said immediately. "He truly is a first class soldier, and as hard as bloody nails when he needs to be. He has hands like a side of beef, rides a horse as if he were moulded to it…and he is worthy of promotion. Put him up to 'Sergeant', and the men will be as delighted for him as we are…as well as not wanting to get the wrong side of him. He will sort out all your malcontents in short order. He has a voice to shame the abbey bells, and a boot like a thunderbolt! Him I *do* want back in one piece if possible!"

"His old mother, too," the Count added. "She dotes on him…and young Gislaine."

"Gislaine?"

"Gislaine Routier, his much adored girlfriend, Sir Gui," de Rousseau replied with a tight look across his face. "A real beauty whom he will not want

141

to leave behind!...*well I certainly wouldn't, knowing this lot!*...They are hand-fast already and due to marry as soon as he can rise above being plain 'Trooper Bergerac'. She will miss him sorely, poor bastard!"

"And he her, I know," the little Count replied with a rueful smile. "But that's life...*C'est la vie*...but needs must when the Devil drives, and de Brocas must be brought to heel before he can do any more damage. Anyway, Bergerac deserves the promotion, and he certainly needs it for he can't marry the girl without it. But I am certain he will jump at the chance anyway; will be thrilled by it. But tell him that when he gets back I'll give the bride away myself, with a parcel of land, a fine ram from my own flocks and a shoeful of silver."

"Shoeful of silver?" Father Matthew asked, puzzled.

"Don't ask, Father," de Fontenay said with a laugh, holding up his hands. "Ancient Vendée custom."

"Well, he sounds just John Fitzurse's kind of man," Sir Richard grinned. "'Like a thunderbolt,' eh? That I must see! And 'Sergeant' is good. Outranks all his troopers...but of lower rank than Fitzurse, so he'll have no problem with taking orders. Are you happy with that, Rousseau? There can only be one leader of any armed expedition...and that is Sir Gui. We follow him...and your men must follow us."

"Quite right, Richard. I would expect no less myself. There will be no problems, I assure you," the burly Poitevin knight said, getting up. "William of Bergerac is a good soldier, and I will miss him. He won't let you down. And thank you, My Lord Baron, for your generosity over their pay."

"Excellent!" Gui said, and standing he clasped de Fontenay's arm in a Roman salute, before turning to the Count.

"William, for a man whom I had never met until today, you have proven to be the most amazing host and companion-in-arms. I bet when I knocked the King out of his saddle that afternoon in London, he could never have guessed what a spectacular result his gifted ring would bring him! Thank you, so much! And please thank the Lady Hawise for her kindness around this table tonight, and your Steward for all he has done for my men."

And stifling a yawn, he added: "Please, if it does not seem too churlish to you, I crave your indulgence for me and my fellows to leave and get what sleep we can before cockcrow. As I said this afternoon when we arrived, we need to be on our way at first light as we have a long way to go."

And bowing to their host, Count William de Forz, and to his tall Guard Commander, Sir Rousseau de Fontenay, Gui and his fellow leaders stepped down from the dais, and with two of the Count's soldiers to lead them with flaring torches, they made their way back to their quarters and so to bed at last.

142

Chapter 22...The road to Saint Jean d'Angély.

They left the next morning, the far hills still shrouded, the horizon grey and drear, but at least the rain had cleared.

Driven south before a stiff breeze that fluttered the standards Gui had ordered to be unfurled and carried again by the two squires, the heavy rain clouds had lifted and the sun now faintly promised, an opaque golden disc just palely shivering behind the thick veils of grey that still drifted overhead.

All had broken fast with chill water from the castle spring and fresh bread, warm from the ovens, a drizzle of spiced oil and a handful of olives. More than a Roman breakfast of just bread and water, but still strange to the English troops who found the olives bitter, and moaned for the hard cheese and bacon they were more used to at home. But with cold meats cut and packed for them in panniers slung across some of the sumpters, along with a score of fresh loaves, wheels of soft cheese and fresh picked peaches and cherries...each man with a flask of watered wine to carry with him, they were all well enough prepared.

True to his word, and much to Gui and his commanders' delight, Count William and de Fontenay had found the sixty 'half and halfers' they had discussed the previous night, and they halted to watch them coming up from the stables: first William of Bergerac, with his new sergeant's colours stitched on his right shoulder, and a new standard carrying the de Forz blazon of three Escalopes Argent on a field Gules bravely carried beside him...followed by a long double line of troopers, the lancers and spearmen they had hoped for, together with a pair of their own tilt carts for all their spare equipment, their spears and their bivouac material, and pulled by two horses each.

Every man was clad in stout ringed mail, over a red padded leather jacket with steel bracers around each wrist, and a polished nasal helmet. They also carried the traditional kite shaped shields across their backs over long cloaks, and a plain sword, or mace in a shaped leather bucket, at each man's side.

Behind the flag rode the lancers, with their nine foot shafts tipped with long, lethal diamond-shaped pointed heads, flanged for extra weight and penetration, each butt-end carried in a toe bucket at the right stirrup edge. They were true specialist forces trained in the use of the lance in battle, whose impact could be decisive if wisely used. And each lance carried a fluttering pennon bearing the de Forz blazon. Following, behind their carts, their long gisarmes upright in long racks all round their sides, came the spearmen, shields on their backs also, personal weapons by their sides.

And they were all proud.

Despite having been roused at Lauds, just as daylight was pushing out the night, and then being buzzed about furiously by Bourchier and others, like bluebottles in a privy, they had been chosen, sorted, fed, horsed and armed... and were now leaving. Standing upright in their high saddles, straight-backed and heads held high, booted feet thrust into their long stirrups, they felt like the best of the best and looked it, despite the fact that many would be going into action for the first time...and many might not return.

They represented their castle, their friends and their families, who had flooded out across the bailey to watch them go with cheers and much weeping from those whose loved ones had been torn from their arms when called to muster before dawn that very morning...and were now leaving under a leaden sky. Beside de Bergerac, her hand on his stirrup iron, strode a lovely young woman with rich chestnut hair and blue eyes red from weeping, Gislaine Routier. Head held high, her body swaying as she walked, a smile on her face determined to let her man know how proud she was of him, her woven scarf of red wool and silver shells tied to his stirrup leather as his guerdon.

By the castle's great open gateway, before the first portcullis, she stepped aside to join an older woman who was waving and crying out: "Be safe, my darling boy! Be safe!" and who flung herself into Gislaine's arms as her son, William of Bergerac, his back straight as a steel blade, his gaze unwavering, his mouth a firm line in his lean face, led his men past her.

From above the tall gatehouse great double trumpet blasts peeled out, joined by others from the thick battlements of King Richard's mighty donjon even higher above them. It was a wild, brazen farewell for the Silver Shells from Niort, and the Scarlet Lions from England, as they clattered and rumbled over the drawbridge and away down the long road south to Bordeaux and distant Gruissan beside the Circle Sea.

*

All day Gui and his command pushed south towards Saint Jean d'Angély, the weather steadily clearing from the north west as the brisk wind of the morning finally drove the clouds away at last.

By late afternoon the sun finally broke through, melting the last vestige of grey from a burgeoning azure sky, and throwing dappled shadows through the leafy branches of the trees hanging over the trackway. The light danced and sparkled off every hedgerow, each rain drop turned into a dazzling array of

144

crystal teardrops that dangled from every leaf and bush like glittering earrings, just waiting to be caught, as they plunged once more into dense woodland, leaving a vast span of open fields behind them.

And as the sun's warmth caught up with them, so the trees and bushes steamed, like pans held over a fire to boil, and coming to a sudden clearing, Gui halted the column so that the men could take off their cloaks and roll them up again behind their saddles, take a short breather to relieve themselves, and check hooves and harness, bridles, bits and leathers before kicking on again.

*

Once more they stopped to water the horses beside a small stream, now rushing wildly along the edge of the woods from which they had just cleared, gurgling and leaping as it sped amongst the ferns and rushes, lilac water mint and yellow loosestrife growing strong amongst them, and as the men dismounted and clustered round one another, a laugh here a joke there, so all the leaders came together as well.

"God's Blood, but yesterday I thought it was never going to stop!" Sir Richard swore, shaking out his cloak. "I really thought we'd be bivvying in the rain again tonight! This is the first time I've felt warm in two days! Much more of this and my armour will rust solid!"

"I'm more worried about our lads' bowstrings than about your rusting armour," Gui said with a frown. "I hope they've kept 'em well-greased, John," he said turning to his huge Master-at-Arms. "There are few sorrier sights than an archer with a limp bowstring!" and he waggled a limp hand as everyone laughed.

"No, Sir Gui. All strings will be as tight as bow strings should be when the need comes, and every man's blade is sharp and rust free. De Beaune and I made sure of that this morning!"

"How about your men, Allan?" he asked, turning to the young Under Sheriff. "How are things with them?"

"They are fine, My Lord. Of course longbow men carry their bows in leather cases, and their strings in their hats to keep them greased. So they are fine. But something has come up, my Lord, that I think you should know about. I haven't spoken before because I have only just found out...*and a mighty buffet I gave them both too, the fucking idiots!*...but two of my lads think we may have been followed yesterday."

"Followed, Allan?" Father Matthew broke in puzzled. "When?"

"Yesterday afternoon...just after it had really started to throw it down. They weren't back- scouting, some of Bergerac's men were on that duty. But my lads were just forward of them, when a flurry of pheasants came bursting out of the murk straight over them, cock-cock-cockling their heads off as only pheasants can, and then swung into heavy cover on their right. Not long after that, the same sort of thing happened, only it was young boar that time, shoats apparently, still in their creamy stripes, a dozen running close behind two old sows that broke cover behind them fast, Sir Gui...and I mean fast. Now you saw them, now you didn't!...they were gone in a moment. But the lads were so busy being excited about seeing game they know so well at home..."

"...That they didn't think of the implications!" Gui finished for him, with a real frown of concentration across his forehead. "I heard the pheasants...I mean, who wouldn't? They make such a bloody cackle when they take off. But I thought it was just one of us had disturbed them. Like those partridge Beau almost stepped on at Clisson. A pity we didn't know about it sooner?"

"I am sorry, my Lord," Allan-i-the-Wood replied with a grimace. "The boys have been admonished in no short order, I assure you. They should have known better."

"Why is that such a concern, Gui?" Father Matthew asked.

"Because, Father," the young Lord Baron of Malwood said, reaching for a peach out of a nearby pannier. "Pheasants aren't as stupid as some might like to think. No pheasant will fly unless it has to...especially in foul weather like this. They really don't like the wet, and they won't easily be startled by a fox or a weasel. They'll run first and fly later if they have to...and they won't scream about it. But if a man steps on them, then they *will* take off! Straight up into the air like an arrow from a bow...and you really *will* hear them go too, as Allan's men did yesterday"

"The same with wild boar, Father," the Under-Sheriff said, leaning back against Caesar, Bouncer by his side. "Boar lie up during the day and those old sows with their little ones wouldn't go anywhere near humans if they could avoid them, know they mean trouble! Least of all a great long column like ours. They are very protective mothers, wild boar sows are, and lie up close with their shoats, often in sounders...several sows in a group...and will not let them move into danger unless forced to do so. And boar have no natural enemies in the forests, save us!"

"So...if they shot across our paths yesterday," Sir Richard said, picking up Allan's words, "With their little ones close beside them, then someone scared them. Not something, Father. *Someone!*"

146

"Hmmm," Gui muttered. "So that was twice that game was startled in what…half an hour?"

"Yes, about that, Sir Gui. Do you want to check with the lads?"

"No, Allan. I don't doubt them for one moment. And don't be too hard on them. They are far from home and doing their best."

"If you say so, my Lord. But had it been me…"

"Well it wasn't, dear boy," Sir Richard drawled at him easily. "And at least your lads told you what they had seen. I've known many who would have left you to carry the whole can of worms: 'Bloody officers. Let's see them in the shite for a change!' Yes?"

"Yes, Sir Richard," he said with a lopsided grin. I've known it," and he nodded his head in wry acknowledgment.

"That's better. Now, come on, man, take it off your back. Worse things happen at sea!" And they all laughed, their experiences off the Belle Île still fresh in their minds. "Anyway, at least we know now that there may be trouble afoot."

"I told you you'd find yourself at home in these forest lands," the tall Benedictine said to Allan, shaking his long habit as he spoke. "And by Saint George you have, too. The thing is…what does it really mean?"

"Do you think someone's following us, Sir Gui?" Fitzurse asked him, crossing his massive arms across his chest.

"Well, it would have to be a bloody desperate poacher to be out after game in weather like that yesterday," he replied with a chuckle. "It would all have been closely laid up in the dry as we should have been if we'd had any sense!"

"Has anyone reported seeing anything on our tail?" Sir Richard asked, picking at a roll he had taken from his bag. "We've kept changing the scouts about so no-one gets bored with looking…but the weather has been truly foul. So they may have missed something that otherwise they might not have done."

"Well who would? Follow us I mean?" de Beaune asked just then, having listened to the conversation. "We are still hundreds of miles from Gruissan…so it can't be the Baron."

"But not so far that a pigeon might not have been sent somewhere with a message to intercept us," Father Matthew said quietly. "Remember what I said about pigeon carriers? Flight times and distances? And who do we know to be a likely traitor whom we've already met along our trail?"

"Alan de Courcy!" De Beaune exclaimed. "And that bastard Victor Jonelle, both of whom I fought against in the Vexin when they were in Valois colours; fighting for King Philip against Mercardier, Richard's Master of Mercenaries!"

147

"Well," Gui said, shaking his shoulders to settle his armour more comfortably. "There's nothing we can do about that now, gentlemen. But forewarned is definitely forearmed, so very well done, Allan, and tell your two lads I will see them to thank them properly later...even if you do think that's more than they deserve," he added, clapping the Under-Sheriff on his shoulder. "Meanwhile we must move on, but keep alert. Another hour, maybe two, will see us at Saint Jean. Fitzurse," he said briskly to his Master-at-Arms, "go forward now and have a word with your scouts. Yes?"

"Yes, Sir Gui. Extra vigilant, and report immediately if they see, or hear, anything wrong." And he left at once.

"Allan, I would like to put four of your best men forward towards Saint Jean. They may even need to dismount and screen the town on foot when they get there. And we won't enter until they have safely reported back. Now...*Mount up!...*" he shouted, waving his hand twice around his head...and swinging himself back onto Beau's solid back he led them all off again and back onto the trackway.

Chapter 23...De Courcy comes down like a Wolf on the fold.

(Apologies to Lord Byron)

Seven miles away, that very daybreak, as Sir Gui and his men were leaving Niort, Sir Alan de Courcy and Sergeant Victor Jonelle sat their horses at a small crossroads that would lead them either to the village of Benet on their right, or straight to Niort.

Their command, clustered in behind them, were wet, weary and stiff from bivouacking in the barns and sheds of Oulmes, a few miles behind them, and beneath the trees and hedges around it, wrapped in their cloaks, their saddles at their heads. Now up, fed and watered, they awaited their orders, their horses stamping their iron shod feet and shaking their heads in the grey morning light.

They had arrived there the evening before, almost at last light, having pushed hard all day to be within easy thrust of their quarry's route the next morning. And having hobbled the horses on a long line beyond the village, bought food from the people for their men, not wanting to cause any trouble so close to Niort, they had themselves slept in a rude inn just off the roadside.

The men, in small groups around a handful of smoky fires, pickets out against any unwanted surprises, their rations heated in small billies, had sheltered where they could. For Sir Alan, and his Sergeant-at-Arms, in the tiny inn, the food might have been a simple pottage with bread and wine, and the two small rooms kept for the purpose meanly furnished, but at least they were dry, and though the wide grate smoked foully it was warm enough on that suddenly chill, wet summer's night, and together they had laid their plans.

*

All that day they had tracked Gui and his men, having caught up with them just as they were leaving Chantonnay the day before. Not in close company of course, but from a distance with a pair of cunning trackers, who had kept Gui's own scouts, themselves riding some way behind their main body, just in sight. And that had been enough. They knew the make-up of the English knight's command from seeing them at Nantes. The only thing that mattered was where they were!

And all day it had rained steadily, the wind gusting and sighing, filling the eyes with water, chilling the hands, and stopping any dust from rising to give their movements away...as well as preventing Gui's men from keeping the sharpest look-out, deterring them from riding back across their line of march which otherwise they would have done. So, as Gui and his command had left Chantonnay, so Sir Alan had skirted it with his lancers sufficiently far off for them not to be seen, but close enough not to lose touch with their quarry either.

By dusk they had reached Oulmes and bivouacked in the rain, their men huddled in their cloaks wherever they could find shelter, making desultory fires as far out of the wind as possible for warmth and mulling wine in deep billies, with a handful of spices brought with them from the Duke of Brittany's own table. And having seen their men settled they had then retired to the ancient inn for the night.

"Well, Victor," de Courcy said, as he wiped his rough glazed bowl of pottage with a piece of bread. "At least we know where those bastards are...*and* where they are going. The lads have done really well, those brothers, Marcel and Antoine Renard, particularly."

"Fox by name and fox by nature," he answered with a grin. "But poachers or not, there were one or two times I thought they'd gone too near and were bound to be spotted...but it seems the luck was with them and they managed to get away with it."

"When those pheasants leapt out from underneath their feet and went off like shooting stars right over those bastards, cock-cock-cock-cockling their heads off ?"

"You saw them?"

"No...heard them! And Dan Massif told me the rest. Those English scouts must have been dreaming!"

"Marcel said they'd been lucky!" he replied, getting up to kick the fire into life.

"Mmmm...I hope so. Well, one more good day and we can lie up and wait for them at Saint Jean."

"Do you know this bit of country then, my Lord?"

"Enough to know that we can avoid Niort completely by taking a faster route to Saint Jean d'Angély through Benet; a small village just off this main trackway, a few miles from here. Cuts off a good dog's leg round Niort, and will lead us straight to Saint Jean. Niort is one place we do not want to go near if we can possibly avoid it!"

"Count William de Forz!" the big sergeant said tersely.

"Just so, Victor. He holds Niort for King Richard, may the Devil take him! He has very sharp eyes and a heavy hand, the good Count…and he may remember us from our time in the Vexin? I do not intend to put us anywhere near his executioner's grasp. Let's just leave it at that!"

"Right, my Lord," the tall soldier grunted, sitting down again. "So…How long to get there do you think…to Saint Jean?"

"At the rate we have been travelling? About half a day! We have no carts to slow us down, remember. So even if we have to walk the horses a while, we'll still get there long before those bloody English."

"It'll mean another early start, my Lord. We need to be away from here at first light in order to rest up before we have to go into action. And we will need to be careful not to alarm the people at Saint Jean," he added, pausing to drain his horn beaker. "We don't want them to alert those fucking bastards coming through the town later, that there might be trouble. How do you want to work this?"

"Well, firstly we can skirt the town completely, and cut back in towards it from the west. The place is well protected, and has a famous abbey, so there will be people about…but they will not bother us. The main trackway leads through the town towards Bordeaux through quite thick woods and then a huge open space of common land before the main river, many hectares, where there is a strong stone bridge. Before that there are a couple of streams with fords. From the bridge the track goes through more woodland until it meets up with wide open fields and vineyards, and so on until Saintes."

"You know it well!"

"Went on escort with those bloody monks and their wine to Bordeaux a few times…while you were off with that busted arm a while ago. So, yes, I do know it. And the best place to hit them will be just after they've have bivouacked for the night. The river is about half a mile from the centre of the town, and the land is quite flat right across the clearing, with a few dips and hillocks, before dropping down to the river.

"If Bernard can block off their route across the bridge with his spears, and pour in concentrated fire from the surrounding woods, he'll have them in bloody chaos in no time. Then we'll hit them with our lancers from behind, and push them onto Bernard's spears at the bridge. We'll make mincemeat out of them. It'll be the fastest action in living memory! There are only seventy of them anyway, and some of those are too wounded to fight. It'll be a piece of apple pie!"

Now, in the chill dampness of the early morning, the clouds still low overhead but moving with a brisk north-westerly behind them, de Courcy and Jonelle took the right turn off the main trackway and spurred their mounts away across the countryside, empty of travellers at that time, though they passed many small bivouacs as they rode. Clods of wet earth flew up from their hooves, spattering both horse and rider as they pounded at an easy canter towards Saint Jean d'Angély, and there was no-one to say them, 'Nay!'

Chapter 24...De Vernaille comes also in Azure and Gold,
And the sheen of their spears was like stars on the sea... (Apologies: The Destruction of Sennacherib: Lord Byron)

Away to the south, travelling steadily up from Bordeaux, Sir Bernard and Geoffrey de Vernaille led their men up the main roadway to Pons and then Saintes as swiftly as their horses would safely carry them, having been delayed by over a day in setting out from Saint Savin.

Getting the necessary passes out of the city from Sir Hugh Willoughby had not be so difficult, though he had asked some penetrating questions that had left Bernard sweating as he felt Sir Hugh's fierce grey eyes on him every time he lied. Nevertheless, even though he had still looked askance at him, Sir Hugh had granted him the passes he had asked for, so all his men had left the city as they had planned. And despite having to detour a long way round to meet up again, they had managed to do so without a problem, and had arrived at Saint Savin as expected.

But once there things had not gone so well!

The man whom Martin Riberac had placed in charge was sick of a sudden fever, and the men were out of control. Their equipment dirty and ill cared for, several of their horses in urgent need of shoeing; many out at grass, eating their heads off, and had to be rounded up and sorted before anyone could do anything; and the panniers for the sumpters could not be found!

In short, since the old Lord de Vernaille had died, and his two sons had stayed amongst the wine booths and doxies of Bordeaux, the estate at Savin had been allowed to drift and the place was a shambles. No proper organisation and no good leader to follow, so far from a disciplined, well-practised command, the men of Savin were an ill-disciplined rabble, and it took several immediate hangings and the ample application of Riberac's boot and fists to sort things out, so it was a sullen and thoroughly chastened command that had finally set out on the long road for Saint Jean d'Angély.

At first, with the sun on their backs and the men in better heart having had the worst of the Savin Command weeded out from amongst them, they made good passage and a brave sight as they trotted or cantered along the dusty high road. The Vernaille blazon of a Lion Passant d'Or on a field Azure with Etoiles d'Or was sufficiently bright and gay to bring people to the roadside to watch them ride by, a long column of armoured men relaxed enough to wave

153

back and catch the fruit and rolls that many threw up to them as they passed by with smiles and laughter.

The golden lion the men wore on their surcoats, with his one great paw raised, on his azure background dotted with golden stars was very eye-catching, and they had no difficulty in finding lively girls to keep them company at Pons when they got there, the inn keepers only too willing to have so many cheerful spenders come suddenly amongst them.

But after Pons the weather changed. Clouds came up, with a chill wind behind them from the north-west, hustling round the backs and rumps of their horses, and by afternoon on the third day the rain came. A steady drizzle at first that found its way into everything, followed by a thunderous downpour that turned the hard roadway into a foul muddy soup, splashed everyone and filled the ruts and potholes so they had to slowdown rather than risk losing a horse to a bruised fetlock, or worse, a broken leg.

By the time they reached Saintes, sodden wet and swearing, the men sullen and complaining, the horses with their heads down and plodding, they were nearly a day behind their expected arrival at St Jean still many miles ahead. So instead of stopping in Saintes as all had hoped to do, with its two spacious inns and good stabling for men and horses alike, Sir Bernard had led them forward a further ten miles until the wet summer darkness was almost upon them, arriving at the tiny hamlet of Saint Hilaire de Villefranche with little light left to see by.

Almost everyone in the brothers' command was weary and saddle sore, cursing the weather, cursing the lack of comforts and cursing their leaders, as they swung off their horses at last to find what shelter they could from the weather. And in truth it was a mean place. A handful of hovels and bothies, no manor house as such, just a huddled collection of larger cruck houses with a small collection of barns clustered around them. Nearby was an ancient smithy and a broken wine press in a large thatched building with rough stone walls and an open front, the whole roof space now a great hay loft, with a rickety wooden ladder leading up to it.

With two of their men carrying their saddles, the Vernaille brothers climbed into the loft space and spread themselves around, while below them others tended their horses, or struck a fire in the round space where the pressing stone should have been, and began to heat up some wine in a deep pan.

"What a completely vile day, Geoffrey," his elder brother growled later, holding a large horn beaker between his hands. "I had forgotten what real campaigning was all about! If it hadn't been for those fucking morons at Saint Savin we could have reached Saintes yesterday, and covered the last bit to Saint Jean in a single easy stage with almost a day in hand!"

154

"As it is we shall have to be up with the bloody larks in order to cover the distance and still have the time to seek out the best places to mount this ambush. God's Bones, Bernard, I could have slaughtered the lot of them! Stupid ignorant *bastards!* That idiot, Georges Le Breton, is lucky to be alive. Fever or not, I'd have hung him along with the rest! Dear God, I *hate* the rain!"

"Yes," his brother said getting up and looking out into the pattering darkness, leaning against a great roof truss as he did so. "That damned stuff gets into everything, and ploughing through all those muddy ruts and ditches has left my boots saturated....*I'd forgotten how much I hate campaigning!*... If I take them off now, I might not get them on again. Come on, Geoffrey, we can't stay up here like this. That old bastard was right..."

"Which old bastard?" His brother queried him at once.

"The Old Lord...our bastard of a father! Who else...Moses?"

"Might just as well be, given all this bloody rain just now!"

"That was Noah, idiot! Moses was the Red Sea and the damned Egyptians!"

"Well...let those bastard English whom de Brocas wants so badly killed *be* the thrice damned Egyptians, and by the time we get to Saint Jean let's hope the stream we want to pin them against is so bloody swollen that the whole bloody lot of them will bloody well drown, like Pharaoh's lot in the Red Sea! Then we can bloody well go home and get bloody dry!"...*Holy Jesus! What am I doing here? I must have been bloody mad to agree to all this.*

His brother laughed. "Don't be such a misery! As I was saying...it was always the Old Man's contention that men won't fight well if their leaders don't show they care...So, come on, let's go find our noble Sergeant-at-Arms out there somewhere in that wretched, soaking darkness and show our lads, who have had just as bad a day us, that we are all in this together. Then he can come back and join us for another beaker of hot wine, and we can decide who is to do what tomorrow!"

"Do you have a plan?" his brother asked, getting up with a groan, as Bernard began to go backwards down the ladder...*because I am damned if I do.*

"Yes. Of course," he said, looking up into his brother's pinched face. "A combination attack using our bowmen from concealed positions and our spearmen to hold the ford, while de Courcy's lancers drive that fucking English rabble onto our spears...and if that stream *has* swollen into a rushing torrent so much the better. We can then hold it from this side so they can't get away...and then they really might all bloody well drown! What do you think?"

"Sounds good to me," he said starting down the ladder himself. "Have you discussed it with Riberac?"

155

"No…not yet. I thought we could do that over some more hot wine…as I suggested. Then it's heads down as best we can, for we must be away as early as possible. *Sweet Jesus!* But this is a miserable place," he exclaimed bitterly, throwing his wet cloak over his shoulders. "At least we will be dry tonight in this hayloft…those poor bastards we are leading are mostly out there under the hedges, poor sods. So let's see what we can do to cheer them up, eh? And pray for better weather tomorrow!"

Chapter 25... *Now entertain conjecture of a time, when creeping murmur and the poring dark fills the wide vessel of the universe...(Henry Vth: Act IV)*

After a long day in the saddle, with men and beasts bone weary, Gui and his command came within sight of Saint Jean d'Angély at last; just as the sun was beginning to slip away to the west, firing up the clouds left behind from yesterday's rain with gold and crimson streamers, and the night-time shadows grew thicker all around them

A small walled town athwart the road that led from Niort to Bordeaux, St Jean nestled against the right bank of the River Boutonne, from which two small streams flowed around the west side of the town, both crossed by fords masked by heavy woodland. The main roadway however, ran straight to the bridge that spanned the river itself, before stretching out across more great open fields carved out of the wild that reached out all around them, now heavy with wheat and barley, peas and beans.

Thrusting up above the main entrance to the town was the great tower the merchants of Saint Jean had built to show off their success, and beyond that was the abbey that gave its name to the place. All round were the walls that protected those who lived there, and which the Old King, Henry Plantagenet, had assaulted with such overwhelming vigour forty years before.

Just off the trackway, carefully hobbled and picketed, were the four horses of the men whom Gui and Allan-i-the-Wood had sent forward to scout the whole area. Quietly cropping their way around their pickets, they were calm and settled, but of their riders there was no sign at all.

Throwing his hand up, Gui brought the whole long column to a bouncing halt, horses and men blowing as they halted, and called his commanders forward to join him. With night drawing on this was no place to linger. They needed to get the horses watered and settled, and the men fed and bedded down also. Above all, they needed to be sure of their safety...yet the very men sent ahead to ensure that were nowhere to be seen.

"Well, gentlemen," Gui said tersely, gesturing to the horses nearby. "Here we are...and no sign of the men whom Allan and I sent forward. The sun has not yet set, so the town gates will still be open to us, but I am loath to enter without being sure we will not be set upon. I know these men of mine well. If something goes badly wrong, and we are attacked, they will not hesitate to take this town by fire and storm...and that would be a disaster!"

"I agree, Gui," Father Matthew said quietly. "If Allan's men do not appear soon, I will ride on in to the Abbey and see what I can find out. After all it is a Brother House, and I hold the Holy Father's Commission, which will give us the most powerful aid. The Abbot would not dare to refuse us. But the Abbey is not large, and could not take in so great a force as we now have with us...nor do I think it wise to advertise our strength. But knowledge is power, and if there is anything untoward within his bailiwick, the Abbot will be sure to know of it!"

"That is a good plan, Matthew," Sir Richard cut in. "But even you cannot go in alone. Take the cart with our wounded with you and two of my troopers as escort. They can take off their surcoats so as not to be of much notice, and that way you will gain ready access to both town and abbey, and few questions asked by the town guard that is sure to be beside the gates."

But before any such move could happen, and with little more than a rustle, Allan's four verderers appeared before them, eeling out from amongst the trees that crowded over the trackway, their faces streaked with black, ferns and twigs tied around their helmets with bow cord, and their clothes grass stained and muddied....and they were breathless with excitement.

"Report!" Gui exclaimed swiftly, as he swung off his horse, the others following; Fitzurse, de Beaune and William Bergerac pushing theirs closer, eager to hear the news.

"Peter of Minstead...my Lord," the first scout said breathlessly. "Be warned! It is an ambush! The river is alive with men. Spearmen and archers, mostly, but some with sword and shield, dozens and dozens of 'em; led by two belted knights and all wearing the same colours: big golden lions with one foot raised, on a blue background covered with golden stars. Most are mingled in the woods between two small streams and the river itself. There's quite a lot of water, my Lord. Soft going after all that rain; not good for horses."

"Mostly between the streams and the river?" Sir Richard interrupted.

"Yes, my Lord. There are two streams, all swollen and running fast...and then there's the river itself. None of the streams are very wide, but too much for a horse to jump, so they have to be forded. The river is different, wide and deep, but there is a good stone bridge over it, more than a big wagon's width, across stone piers. Beyond the town gates, and before the first of the streams, there is a huge area of common grazing land, more than six furlongs, across which the trackway runs, with thick woodland around its edges."

"My Lord?" another scout intervened. "Roger Fox, came with the Sheriff," he said, saluting with his fist to his forehead as Gui turned to face him. "It looks as if they plan to hold the bridge with their spears! They were moving those men back across the river as we slipped away, must be thirty or forty of 'em at least. But grumpy they were, Sir Richard," he said, as Gui's tall Guard Commander came up to him. "Slumped like, spears at the trail. And wet, too. Not much like the golden lions they're wearing! Not up to much if you ask me."

"Do you know that blazon, Gui?" Matthew asked, urgently. "You've been to more tournaments than I have...though there is something about that golden lion on a blue field that tugs at my memory," he added thoughtfully.

"No, Father!...Richard?" But his tall Guard Commander said nothing, just shook his head, his mind busy with the logistics of fighting a swift, brutal action in poor light.

"Those are the colours of the de Vernaille family, my Lord," William of Bergerac rasped suddenly, nudging his horse forward: "I'd know them anywhere. They hold lands all around Bordeaux, and beyond. Their father, the old Lord, Rupert de Vernaille, died not two months back. Count William went to his funeral; I was in his honour guard. He was a fierce old bugger, the Old Lord, but straight. Knew whose side he was on. Supported the Old King all his life: swore allegiance to King Richard without a question. Those must be his two sons, Bernard and Geoffrey."

"Rupert de Vernaille!" Father Matthew suddenly chipped in excitedly, to everyone's surprise for so controlled a man. "But of course I know him! Well I did, if it is the same man. I knew I had seen that blazon somewhere. It was de Vernaille's trebuchets that smashed the way into Cahors for us in the Old King's first war. In '59. Henry's Toulouse war. Your father and I fought there together, Gui, with Henry de Burley...Alicia's father. That's where he cut Thibault de Brocas down!"

"No! Really? De Vernaille got you all in?" Gui asked, somewhat amazed.

"Yes. In the end. I thought you knew all that by now? Sweet Lord...that was thirty years ago!" And he sighed with sudden regret. "So long ago now... No matter," he continued briskly, taking a deep breath. "So, these are Rupert de Vernaille's sons. Are they any good? Their father was a doughty fighter. Better certainly than he was an engineer!" And he snorted at the remembrance.

"Up to much then, Sergeant? These de Vernailles?" Sir Richard drawled. "The sons I mean," he added with a grin at Matthew's *moue* of exasperation. "Not their dear Papa."

"Don't know, my Lord," the big soldier replied. "Had more of a reputation for wine and tavern wenches than hard campaigning and cold steel; though the older one is supposed to be a fighter. The old Lord wouldn't have them near 'im! Kicked 'em off his lands: didn't trust 'em his own self! The

159

Count held their fealty to be more likely towards Philip of France than Richard of England. He didn't trust 'em neither."

"Easy prey for de Brocas!" Gui said bitterly. "Just the kind of weak, greedy men he would choose to use against an enemy he needed slain!"

"My Lord," another of Allan's scouts said urgently. "They have also been joined by a strong body of lancers…this side of the river and the streams.

"*Lancers?*" Gui exclaimed. "Where the devil did they come from?"

"They are from Nantes, Sir Gui!" A third scout added swiftly. "Robert Bowyer, joined at Malwood. They are led by those two you met with just as we landed, about thirty of them. Riveted mail, and long shields. They look weary, but seem keen enough. Kit in proper order, and they are sharp. That other lot? Rubbish, my Lord."

"De Courcy!" Sir Richard exclaimed. "And his man, Victor Jonelle."

"I bet it was his scouts who startled that game yesterday," Allan said, reaching down to fondle Bouncer's head. "Takes a rare forest ranger to move across wooded ground without startling the quarry off in all directions!"

"If they are de Courcy's men, they'll fight, and fight hard," de Beaune said firmly, banging his fist into his open hand. "He only ever leads the best he can find."

"How many, Master Bowyer? Altogether?"

"Thirty lancers and about four score of the others, My Lord. Couldn't tell you exactly how many bowmen or how many spears…but certainly no heavy foot."

"Bows?"

"All cross bows, my Lord," Peter of Minstead replied. "You'll not find a longbow archer this side of the channel. Those Frenchies don't know 'em… can't use 'em. And have no idea what they can do!"

"Anything else lads?" The Under Sheriff asked, urgently. "Anything else Sir Gui ought to know that might help?"

"Well, Master Sheriff. As Foxy said, I don't think those lads with the golden lions on 'em are that keen…Ben Tiley, joined at Malwood, Sir Gui," the man said in explanation. "They looked pretty beat up to me. Lots of grumbling, and bad feeling. O'course, I don't know what they was saying, like. But definitely not happy…and their gear wasn't in good order. Bow strings wet, winders not working properly, quivers not filled. Bloody mess, my Lord. Their sergeant was going berserk with 'em! Those lancers though? They looked as if they were proper up for it, as Robby just said. Good equipment and well organised. But that other lot? Nahh!" he said with disgust. "One real taste of steel and they'll be off like rabbits from a fox!"

"However did you get so close?" Sir Richard asked, amazed.

160

"Practice, my Lord," Robert Bowyer said proudly, with a sly grin. "If you want to catch a Hampshire poacher in the great forest, you have to be as quiet as fox and swift as a weasel, or you don't get bugger all! That lot! They wouldn't have seen anything even if we'd danced in front of 'em! And that Foxy pretty near did on one occasion. Stupid bastards...we ran rings round 'em, my Lord."

"Well done, all of you!" Gui said with abroad smile. "Your information is really worthy. When this is over come and find me and I will make sure you are all properly rewarded. Now, off with you and find your mates."

"Well gentlemen," he said, leaning back against Beau as he looked around him. "Now we know...thing is, what do we do about it? Those bowmen will not be easy, and I could have done without a squadron of lancers on our tails, that's for sure."

"Nevertheless we do have the element of surprise," Matthew said, throwing back his cowl. "Firstly, they don't know we know about them. Second, they don't know we've got more men, *nor* that we have any lancers at all! Remember, de Courcy saw us in Nantes. He *knows* we don't have any, and they never saw beyond our rear scouts anyway...and, thirdly, they don't know how lethal the longbow is in expert hands!"

"Yes, Gui, those are excellent points that Matthew's just made," Sir Richard said, as if he had no care in the world. "Those longbows really are an ace up our sleeves! I've seen those men of Allan's at work, and those we brought with us with Dickon Fletcher. Twelve arrows a minute they can fire...and at two hundred and fifty paces too. We may only have twenty five of 'em, but they can lay down nearly three hundred shafts a minute on those boys out there...that's why we brought so many more clothyard shafts than bolts with us. If we can get those lads properly placed, and well balanced, they will slaughter those bastards before they can strike a single blow!"

Gui paused then and looked up at the sky, the sun now sinking behind a high bank of cloud that had wandered up across the horizon, the edges rimmed with purple against a crimson background shot with golden fire; listened to the birds beginning to fly home to roost in the gathering dusk; crows carking and squabbling high in the tree tops, the clap of a wood pigeon as it swooped into a nearby beech, the screech of a questing owl quartering for voles across a distant field.

"Well...gentlemen, here's what I would like to do. It's risky...but if we can make it work we'll win the day. William, I want your gisarmiers to lend their surcoats to twenty five of my crossbows. They will stay behind with my archers. Then, with all the courage you can muster, and as much noise as you like, I'll give you one of my trumpeters, I want you to take the whole lot of

161

them…your lancers and my crossbows…and walk-march through the town and out the other side as if you didn't have a care in the world! Straight up the main track, through de Vernaille's men, over the bridge and away as if you're off to Saintes!"

"Then what, my Lord?" the big man asked, appalled, looking as if he'd been asked to march them off a cliff….*this is one mad bugger that's for certain!*

"Spears are good against horses…but hopeless against bows. Sir Richard and I will assault those men amongst the trees with all the lads we have, making as much noise as we can. Trumpets, shouts, everyything. When you hear that, you come back and attack those spears like fury with my crossbows! And when my lads shoot…they don't miss. But hold your lancers back until you hear three clear blast of our trumpets: '*Tan-tan-tara-tantaraaa!*' repeated three times. You won't miss them, I assure you. Then come like all the devils of Hell were after you!

"You're mad, my Lord!" the big Niortian sergeant said grimly. "We'll be cut to pieces before we've gone a hundred yards, let alone cross that bloody bridge. We'll be shot down like rabbits!"

"Well…of course that is possible," Gui said, holding his heavy helmet in his left hand and fratching his head with the palm of his other. "But I don't think so. Firstly, they don't know you are with us, their scouts never got close enough to see. And, secondly, as Father Matthew said, de Courcy will be bound to tell 'em it's not us…because *he* knows we don't have any lancers! Furthermore, Vernaille will recognise the de Forz colours…and he won't want to make a terrible enemy out of the Lord Count of Niort' King Richard's most powerful ally in all the Vendée. If you are bold enough, you will bluff your way past them. They will see what they might expect to see…a tight body of men, in the colours of one of the most powerful Poitevin Barons in the Vendée, marching through the sunny evening countryside without a care in the world, looking as cool as a maiden's kiss!"

"God's Bones, Sir Gui, but you're taking an awful risk!" de Beaune said, his horse skittering beneath him. "That's almost a third of our whole force!"

"Well, Master Jean," Sir Richard drawled up at him with his lazy grin, his hand on his bridle: "'Faint Heart ne'er won Fair Lady!'" Then, turning towards the horrified Sergeant Bergerac, he added: "Everything forward and trust in the Lord, Sergeant, and the Devil take the hindmost. Don't fear so, man, and it will turn out better than you think. Trust the Lord Baron of Malwood…he has done this sort of thing before against the wild Northumbrians and the Scots, and they don't come much tougher than that! Now, Gui. What about the rest of us?"

162

"Well, Richard, remember, they don't know that *we* know both where they are, and what they are. So…Allan, take your bowmen, with Dickon Fletcher and his men, he's the finest shot in the Forest, and make your way round the town. And they are to take *off* their surcoats! Bergerac's gisarmiers will go with you. In fact," he added swiftly, looking round him, "We'll *all* fight in plain armour tonight, no colours for any of us. Far too easy a target in the coming dusk!

"Anyway, Allan, eel your way round the outside of the town to this side of that clearing, find a good place and lie-up and wait. When the time comes, I want you to stand up and be ready to drench their lancers with arrows, because attack us they will…and anyone else you see who is not one of us! Put the Niort spears in front of you with their big shields and wicked gisarmes. Horse won't charge home against a line of pointed steel…and their long shields will help protect all of you. Will your men stand, Sergeant Bergerac?" he asked suddenly, turning towards the gnarled sergeant. "Have they practised to do this?"

"Yes, My Lord. We have practised, but not for a while. But they'll stand, Sir Gui! Never fear. *My lads'll stand!* I'll put Robert de Fer in charge of them. He'd stand against a charging bull, that one. And the men will follow his lead."

"Good man," Gui said, with a warm smile, and a pat on his stirruped boot. "I never doubted you!"

Then turning back to L'Eveque: "As for you and me, Richard…Fitzurse, de Beaune and Hordle John…we'll attack on foot. I'm not risking Beau and Merlin, nor any of our horses, to flights of crossbow bolts across a darkening field. We can picket them here, along with these others, and the tilt carts.

"If Sergeant Bergerac does his stuff, and our lads shoot the living daylights out of those spears across the bridge, then when he charges with his lancers, they must drop their bows and pile into those bastards potting at us from behind the trees and cut them to ribbons. Give them the whacking they deserve. If all that Allan's men have said about Vernaille's troops is true…then they'll run for their lives, rather than be hacked in pieces by our Lions on the rampage: and my guess is they'll bolt right into Allan and Dickon Fletcher's sights. They will be beautifully back-lit by the sunset's afterglow …and they *will* fall like bloody rabbits!"

"And me, Gui?" the tall Benedictine asked, his head tilted slightly, with his deep Spanish lilt.

"Do almost what we suggested before Allan's lads came back, Matthew. Take the cart with the wounded, and go to the abbey…but get two of those who are on their feet to act as an escort. This will not be an easy fight, Matthew,"

163

he said, turning to face him closely, "despite all our courage and a good plan. We are going to need your skills this night for certain, and the abbey is perfectly placed to be our headquarters. Remember, we still have to reach Bordeaux, let alone Gruissan. So be ready with your salves and your bandages, and your needle and thread...and God be with us. Right, let's get to it before it's too dark to do anything," and he strode off with his huge Master-at-Arms, his other commanders following, to get their men ready for battle.

Chapter 26....*"I see you stand like greyhounds in the slips straining upon the start. The game's afoot; follow your spirit...* (Henry Vth: Act III)

What followed next was an intense period of re-arrangement!

All the men from Malwood took off their distinctive white surcoats with the scarlet lion rampant all over them, those with crossbows put on the de Forz colours that Count William's spearmen had taken off, while all the rest were bundled into the spare tilt cart from which sheaves of extra clothyard arrows were taken and handed out to Allan's men, and those under Dickon Fletcher, Malwood's famous Master Bowman. Then, while Gui and all those going with him picketed their horses by the stream, Allan's verderers filled their quivers, taking one extra sheaf per man on their backs. And with personal weapons at their waists, and de Forz's spearmen with their long shields and wicked gisarmes beside them, they slipped off into the trees and disappeared.

On the track, Father Matthew climbed up onto the other tilt cart, with two of their walking wounded by his side, and prepared to follow Sergeant Bergerac and his standard bearer, one of Gui's trumpeters blowing mightily at his side.

With the great house flag of the Lord Count de Forz of Castle Niort floating above his head, Gui's mounted archers all boldly wearing de Forz's blazon as they walk-marched towards the town, and his lancers, with forked pennons fluttering from below every shining steel tip, it looked, and sounded, very much as if a travelling fair was come to visit. And before long people began to cluster round the town gates to see what all the fuss was about, running out of their houses or thrusting their heads out of their windows and all to shout and wave at the brave parade now just entering Saint Jean d'Angély.

All the time that Bergerac and the tilt cart were cheerfully distracting the townsfolk and the town's guard, Gui, Sir Richard and all the remaining Lions were swiftly making their way around the eastern walls of Saint Jean, weapons free and shields now firmly on their left arms.

In ones and twos and little groups, they slipped from corner to corner along the base of the walls, hidden by the long shadows they cast across the many tracks and pathways that criss-crossed the ground beneath them. And all the time they could hear the braying trumpet and the shouts of the townsfolk as William of Bergerac led his men through the narrow streets of the little town.

With no moat, or town ditch, to be bothered with, and pressed against the mortared stones of the walls, Gui and his men were hidden in the deep shadows cast by the sun, now setting behind the trees at the far side of the clearing...all of half a mile away, and quite beyond the sight of anyone looking out for them. Especially as anyone looking would be seeking white surcoats with leaping scarlet lions across them...not men flitting amidst the deep shadows in plain armour and dark brigandines, their shapes lost in the dusky background.

*

Overhead the sky was awash with colour, the air warm and lazy with high summer, the wind light and playful, the scent of late mown hay heavy on the senses. Bees wandered busily from flower to flower and the two de Vernailles, and their whole command, lazily dozed in the late evening sunshine.

All day they had been stood to arms waiting, their horses picketed to a strong rope line along the river side, while the sun had risen over their heads getting hotter and hotter.

Waiting for de Courcy and his lancers; waiting for their scoff; waiting for the bloody English...Just waiting for *something* to happen! They were hungry, fed-up and wanted to get back to the wine booths and taverns of Bordeaux, to their doxies and their gambling. Not stuck out in the middle of nowhere playing soldiers for the two armoured-up fancy boys who'd brought them here! Sod the lot of 'em! And they lounged at their posts...and waited.

Those by the river looking for fish in the deep clear waters, still rushing past full of the recent rainfall; those amongst the trees and bushes that ringed the great clearing, leaning back half asleep, relishing the cool shadows out of a sun that had been getting hotter all day and was now, at last, sinking to its rest. Four days they had been on the road, and they were weary, bored and sleepy in the late summer sunshine, cooled by the breeze and lulled by the scents of mown hay and wayside flowers.

Across from where Bernard de Vernaille and his brother were lounging, sharing a flask of burgundy, De Courcy sat with his lancers and fretted. Pulled right back under the overhanging trees of the thick woodland to the left of the rutted roadway that led to the town, and mounted on his favourite bay, he could see that de Vernaille's command was dozing on their feet.

"Victor," he said fiercely, pointing across the clearing. "Those fucking bastards over there are practically asleep. Look at them!"

166

"Yes, my Lord," the big sergeant grunted sourly. "Just inviting a swarm of hornets to fly straight down their bloody throats!"

"Send Valentine across with a message from me to Sir Bernard to get his men to wake up before they get their fucking throats cut! The English fight like tigers. Tell him if he's not careful he will get well and truly mauled!" *Sweet wine of Christ, but I hope de Brocas knows what he is doing with this lot? They are a fucking shambles!* And he jagged his horse's mouth in frustration, making it twitch sideways and skitter its hooves.

"God's bloody Bones!" he exclaimed sharply a moment later, as the sound of cheering and trumpet calls came faintly to him from the town, getting louder by the moment. "What is that hellish noise?"

"I don't know, Sir Allan. It's coming from the town. Sounds like..like a fair, or wandering players. Shall I move out a little and see?"

"Yes, Victor. Just you. A single horse will not cause any alarm. Leave me your lance and shield, but take your sword of course."

And gently twitching his reins, Victor Jonelle kicked his horse forward and onto the track. Geoffrey de Vernaille, who had also heard the commotion coming from Saint Jean, was similarly sent forward by his brother, so both men broke cover together, too busy to notice the sudden movement of men falling flat, far away to their left as they rode forward...and de Courcy who was also mounted was too busy watching Geoffrey de Vernaille, and cursing him for a fool, to notice either.

*

A llan-i-the-Wood, who had eyes like a hawk, had missed neither of them, and hissed through his teeth to drop his men the moment that Jonelle had kicked out of the woodside, almost disbelieving his luck when the other man joined him...*Got you, you bastards!*...Now he knew exactly where the ambush was laid, and where he should best place his men to support Sir Gui's attack without endangering his Lions with their arrows.

With the long shadows as they were, and being over two hundred paces from the trackway, it was not difficult for them to eel their way backwards into the wooded verges of the clearing and move stealthily towards a small area of raised ground he had spotted earlier where he could make his stand when the time came. And once in the deeper evening shadows of the trees he quickly called the leader of his spears together and with simple signs and gestures, and broken French, he told him what he wanted.

167

"John-Paul, when Sir Gui begins his attack...*Quant Sir Gui commencer l'attack*...I want you and your men to run out and make a line around the edge of that little hillock," he mimed with arms pumping and pretending to run. *"Pres cet petit mons... la bas!"*...'There!'...He said jabbing with his finger until he was certain the big Niortian sergeant knew what he was on about. *"Et puis*... 'and then'...I want your men kneeling, with their gisarmes pointed up and out and your big shields across your bodies!" He urgently mimed again. "My archers," gesturing shooting arrows frantically with his hands, "will stand in a block...*un carré*...behind you...*vous derrière*...and you will see such shooting as will astound you...*c'est sera encroyable, mon vieux!* Now, *vitesse de dieu*...and down all of you," he said gesturing fiercely with his hands as he spoke. "Down and wait...*Attendez vous, mes braves!"*

*

I n the town, the streets were narrow and twisted, the houses timber framed and leaning towards each other so closely as to make any light struggle to break through, but the way forward was quite clear and before long William of Bergerac's men were passing the Benedictine Abbey of Saint John that gave the town its name on their right, and before him a deep stone archway bathed in light showed the other gateway leading directly to the streams and the River Boutonne beyond.

Here, giving them the sign of the cross and a silent blessing, Father Matthew left the column to seek aid from the Father Abbot, leaving the big sergeant to make his way out of the town, pursued by a crowd of shouting people, barking dogs and running children, with the trumpeter by his side red in the face and still blowing fit to bust.

Next moment they were passing out of the shaded streets, through the shadow of the gateway entrance and into the rosy glare of the setting sun...with Geoffrey de Vernaille in his golden lion and stars on their blue 'field,' and another armoured man in the ermine colours of the Prince of Brittany, coming slowly up towards them from the far side of the clearing.

Behind him, scampering from cover to cover as best they could find it, Gui, Sir Richard and the rest of his English command were just breaking away from the town walls, their movements masked by all the furore going on: the trotting hooves of William's men as they sallied out from the gateway causing swirls and eddies of dust; the hooves of his own horse that he sent curvetting prettily sideways down the track; not to mention all the townspeople who had flocked around the gateway to see them all ride by….running children, dogs rushing and barking everywhere, sheep, goats and even a few pigs from the town midden. It was all a cheerful chaos, as de Bergerac calmly led his men towards the River Boutonne and beyond.

De Courcy and de Vernaille were mesmerised by it all and only saw what Gui had hoped they would. Meanwhile, of Allan-i-the-Wood, his archers and their spear men, there was no sign at all. For all Gui could tell they might as well be in Bordeaux as anywhere near Saint Jean d'Angély…*All I can do now is pray they will turn up when I need them!*

*

With their hands on their swords Victor Jonelle and Sir Geoffrey de Vernaille, having forded the first stream, now reined in across the track at the head of the second. Amazed at the sight of William de Bergerac, with the great house standard of de Forz waving over his head, the de Forz blazon fluttering around the points of the lancers behind him trotting unconcernedly along the track towards the second ford, and even more mounted troops behind, all in de Forz colours, both men were confused. Even more so by the wild cacophony that had run through Saint Jean, and by the rollicking chaos by the gated entrance to the town…*What, in God's Holy name, is going on here?*

And seeing the long column of armoured men coming on relentlessly, Jonelle went to draw his sword, but de Vernaille pulled him back: "Hold back, man! *Hold back, I say!*" he shouted as Jonelle struggled to draw his sword. "These men are known to me. Their leader is one of the Lord Count of Niort's men. I know him, William of Bergerac. He came to my father's funeral, in the Count's Honour Guard. Put up your sword, you fool! Count William is one of the most powerful Barons in all Poitou. Let them by…these men are not English!"

"Sir Allan said *no-one* was to be allowed past, my Lord!" Jonelle raged, kicking his horse round in a circle. "*No-one* is to pass without challenge, Sir Geoffrey!"

"Allan de Courcy does not rule here, Jonelle. I am a belted Knight, and you *will* do as I say…*these men may pass!*" And he swung his horse off the track to let the riders go by, his men amongst the-tree line behind him standing up to watch what was going on, while Jonelle rode back to de Courcy, furious with Sir Geoffrey's decision.

Meanwhile Bergerac kept his whole column moving steadily forward, his heart in his mouth...*Jesus Christ, but I did not join up for this! Nevertheless, Sir Gui was right. God save me, but it seems to be working!*...and enough sense to signal his gratitude to de Vernaille with a simple nod of his head and a terse, "Thank you, my Lord," as his men clattered by, all sixty of them. Lancers first, crossbowmen behind, each horse's hooves making small swirls of dust in the dried up trackway. Hearts pitter-pattering like mad in every breast, all trying not to look sideways at the other horseman now cantering away from them, they crossed the ford and rode on towards the bridge, just less than two furlongs further on; every moment expecting to get an arrow in the back.

*

At the bridge, the spears holding it had also heard the trumpet, but no sounds of fighting or yelling, and many of those there also recognised the de Forz blazon, and knowing the Vernaille brothers were both ahead of them, they made no challenge, but opened their ranks and let Bergerac's men through with a few shouts and gestures of friendship as they did so, before returning to the boring duty of waiting for something to happen. And many propped their spears against the stone walls that ran either side of the bridge, nudging each other and laughing, while they watched the long column of riders bounce and joggle out of sight.

*

Gui, watching them go past Jonelle and de Vernaille, saw the row of heads and bodies raise themselves above the bushes, and where Jonelle was making for, and wormed his way further forward, sliding his shield across the warm, tawny grass and slithering behind it until he dropped down into a slight dip in the ground he had been making for. This was a sort of long fold that ran across the huge clearing, into which he could gather his men before launching his attack...which must be soon as by now the light was definitely fading...and without light his archers would be useless. But he still couldn't see where Allan and Dickon Fletcher were, and he raised his head in desperation.

170

*

De Courcy, joined by Jonelle, was seething at Geoffrey de Vernaille for allowing the column of men to pass without challenge...if only because they shouldn't be there!...*What are sixty armed men doing riding out of a town just before sunset when the gates are about to close? Why be out so late, when they should be settling in there for the night? That leader was no belted knight...his kit's not good enough! What is going on?*...And it was as he turned to rage again at Jonelle about de Vernaille's decision, that he caught a flicker of light and movement ahead of him and he stiffened in his saddle, like a hound at quest, standing up in it to look out across the whole area, now heavy with shadows...*Now, what was that?*

"What is it, Sir Allan?" Jonelle asked urgently as de Courcy's voice died and he stood up to shade his eyes.

"I saw something, Victor. Out there in the middle. A flash of light, a waving hand...something!"

"An animal, my Lord?

"*No, Victor. An enemy!*" he shouted, pointing fiercely where Gui's head had briefly shown itself, settling himself firmly into his saddle. "A fucking English enemy. Look, man! *Look!*" he shouted, gripping Victor's arm. "We've been fooled. Those bastards are out there! *Look!*" He pointed furiously again, as a long line of soldiers leapt to their feet, almost as if they were bursting out of the ground. "There they go! The bastards! *There they go!*" And as the leaping, thrilling sound of an English trumpet shattered the evening, he turned to his own command and roared, "*Attack! Attack!*"

Chapter 27...Alarums and Excursions in Saint Jean d'Angély.

Gui, hearing De Courcy's wild shout, realised he had been seen and knew it was now or never, so trusting Allan's men would be there, he grabbed his trumpeter by the arm and they both leapt up. Gui raised his sword and roared, William Bell put his trumpet to his mouth...and all hell broke loose around them!

"*Tan!-Tan!-Tara!-Tan-Taraaaa!*" Three times William Bell blew his heart out as Gui had promised Bergerac he would do, the bright, shining notes shrieking out their desperate call: "*Come to me! Come to me! Come to meee!*" until the whole clearing seemed to be filled with its wild brazen screams. Until William slung it across his back, picked up his shield and raced to join his Lord in their sudden ferocious attack.

And as the trumpet blew, so Allan-i-the-Wood, Dickon Fletcher and their men rushed out from the tree line and covered the small hillock he had spotted earlier in a crescent shaped formation, thrusting a dozen arrows each into the soft ground around them, each man with enough space to draw and loose. Some standing half way up the slope, some across the top so they could shoot over the heads of their friends below, and all round the base facing their enemies, the spearmen from Niort crouched behind their big shields with their gisarmes thrust out before them, butts to the ground, with every man's heel behind them. A ring of pointed steel no horse would choose to challenge.

And not a moment too soon, because by the time Gui's trumpeter blew the second ringing blast, de Courcy and his lancers were already on the move, sweeping forward in a thunder of flying hooves, their nine foot, steel-tipped shafts already couched beneath their arms as they dropped them towards their running enemies.

"*Loose! Loose!*" Allan shouted as de Courcy's lancers swept down towards Gui's running men. "*Loose!*" And in seconds the air was filled with the deep *twang!* of strings and the soft swooshing whistle of dozens of shafts, as the first flight leaped into the sky, springing off the bows in a constant bright stream that flickered in the sun's fiery light as they soared up and turned, followed by another and another and another, as the bowmen got into their stride; bending and loosing, and bending and loosing with seemingly effortless ease until all the arrows they had laid out for their first strike had been fired.

They didn't look to see where their shafts were going, they didn't need to, they knew by instinct and fierce, constant practice exactly where they would land; and in one minute three hundred arrows shot up into the glowing back-lit sky of pink, orange and gold…and fell on de Courcy's lancers like a sleet of death, horses and men riddled with shafts, the first line of men going down like ninepins, the rest floundering into, around and over them, the screams and howls of the wounded and the groans of the dying filling that great clearing with agony and death.

In one minute of concentrated effort a proud squadron of well mounted and armoured lancers had been turned into a bloody shambles of smashed men and horses, broken legs and shattered bodies. Those not killed outright staggered and crawled around in mindless pain and fear, arrows sticking in them like cloves in a Christmas orange. Some horses stumbled with broken fetlocks, others screamed and trampled in searing pain and terror, and some ran free, arrows sticking in their flanks and rumps, the blood running down them in thick, dark streams. It was a terrifying scene, made all the worse by the deep shouted *'He! He! He!'* of the longbow archer's traditional cry of success, for in one minute of concentrated firepower de Courcy's whole command had simply ceased to exist!

Nor did the horror cease, for a minute later a further violent douche of steel sleet fell upon them as Gui's archers loosed a second deadly flight that skewered to the ground any who might have survived their first assault. And once more their devastating attack was followed by another fierce shout of *'He! He! He!'* that rang out across the bloody skirmish field.

Only a few lancers right at the very front were spared, and recognising the English knight from Nantes by his size, his great fighting helm and his long coat of mail, de Courcy hurled his horse towards him. Lance lowered, feet thrust downwards into his stirrups and leaning back in his high saddle ready for the strike he rode at him like a steel thunderbolt, roaring in anger as he came.

Hearing the thunder of hooves and the bellow of hatred, Gui turned and stood foursquare, shield held high and sword held in front of him across his body, left to right, as de Courcy hurtled down on him, his eyes fixed on the gap between Gui's shield and his neck….*right there I will take you, you English bastard, and you will go down!*...He could imagine his lance tip bursting through that guard, the great spout of blood as his lance tore open the throat, and the scream as his enemy fell beneath his hooves. He was exultant, and as he rushed upon Gui still standing there, apparently paralysed with fear, he tightened his grasp on his lance and thrust down for the kill.

It didn't happen!

Gui waited for that final thrust, parried the lance point away from him on his shield, turning as he did so underneath its point and smashed his sword back-handed across the horse's back legs as it rushed by and with a scream the bay fell, catapulting its rider onto the ground in a tangle of legs, lance, helmet and flying equipment. But de Courcy rolled as he fell and came up onto his feet, dazed but fighting-fit, and drew his sword...and Gui was on him like a tiger, while crossbow bolts flickered around them and Fitzurse led his men into the attack, bellowing like the great bull he was.

Crash! Crash! Crash! Gui mercilessly hammered de Courcy, still reeling from his fall, with his long blade across his shield and his sword arm, driving him backwards with every blow, his eyes glittering through the deep eye-slit in his great helm with all the joy of battle, concentrated, deadly, marking his prey, striking at him until the man was almost on his knees.

But de Courcy was no mean opponent and despite the force with which Gui attacked him he fought back strongly, rising to his feet as he caught the Baron Malwood's blows on his shield and with his sword, turning the English knight's blade over his own with a shriek of steel, his sword a flickering dart in the dying light of the sun, thrusting with foot and hand as he fought to protect himself and to gain an advantage.

Stab! Stab! with the point, and *cut!* with the hard edge of his blade, forcing Gui to cover himself with his shield and sword, the sharpened steels slithering and screeching together in a welter of sparks as Gui parried every stroke with expert skill.

Like a rock of armoured granite, the big English knight stood and soaked up the fierce vigour of his enemy, while all around them the wild mayhem of battle went on unabated as Fitzurse led the Lions onwards, his men shouting and roaring as they dashed forwards, hacking the life out of de Vernaille's men in a spray of blood and shorn limbs. Slaying and being slain; delivering death and shocking mutilation to those upon whom they fell, a howling maelstrom of blood and steel that continued with visceral violence until the remnants rushed screaming with terror from the field of battle.

As those few of de Courcy's command who had survived the early arrow strikes were finally cut down without pity or remorse, so Gui stepped up his assault on their leader as with a great shout and shower of blows he now stalked forward relentlessly. Side to side and overhead, as well as with the point, as Sir Richard had said so many times, he drove forward with the point of his blade at every joint in de Courcy's armour: *Stab! Stab! Hack!* thrusting and slicing at his legs and shoulders until the renegade knight's mail was shredded and he was pouring blood. So Gui de Malwood prosecuted his enemy with unforgiving power, until every parry was weaker, every blow more feeble and the man could barely stand.

And so Gui finished him off at last; seizing his sword arm in a grip of steel so that he could not move, he bent de Courcy backwards and thrust him

174

through the belly with a great spray of blood, and as the man fell forward with a howl of agony Gui delivered a final massive overhead blow that burst his skull in a violent spray of blood and brains and clove him through his back and shoulders, hewing through his armour as if it were paper, splitting his body open as a cook would cleave a lobster, lungs, heart and entrails falling out onto the torn ground as he did so.

As de Beaune had said to Father Matthew at Nantes, de Courcy was good…but no match for the Lord Baron, Sir Gui de Malwood. And as for Victor Jonelle, de Courcy's right hand man? Dickon Fletcher shot him through the neck, his blood fountaining out of his wounds like a gargoyle spewing water in a violent storm.

*

Down by the river, de Vernaille's men heard the shining notes of the trumpet and were electrified, fizzing with sudden life as they rushed to grab their spears, galvanised by the desperate screams and yells coming from the other side, grinning and nudging each other in their eagerness for the hunted rabble they could hear being massacred to come running down towards them. Relishing the prospect of hurling them backwards over the stone balustrade and into the swollen waters rushing by below them, they stood with their spears thrust out and waited.

Nor were they dismayed when they saw marching back towards them, now on foot, their crossbows in the crook of their arms, the same men that had passed through their ranks not half an hour earlier, all wearing the de Forz colours as before, and behind them the lancers, who halted to address their lines, while the crossbows continued towards them. It wasn't until the marching men stopped, shook themselves into two loose lines and raised their bows that anyone realised that something was wrong…and by then it was too late.

Twang! Swoosh! Thunk! An immediate and terrifying plethora of sounds. Like a horde of wild butchers hacking into great sides of raw beef, the bolts flashed across the distance and hammered Vernaille's spearmen into a terrified rabble. Blood and brains splattered the stonework, muscles ripped and tore, bodies punctured to the very hilt of the fletching…and de Vernaille's men fell about like shot rabbits.

Within seconds over half were killed, others wounded, the rest too shocked to do more than stand with their mouths open. But not for long,

175

because having fired their one volley, with a fierce, triumphant '*Tan!-Tan!-Tara!-Tan-Taraaaa!*' from Sir Gui's trumpeter, the Lancers drawn up behind the crossbows thrust their rowels into their horses' flanks and charged into the attack.

And de Vernaille's men did not stand...they took one look at death on the hoof thundering towards them, dropped their spears and fled. But no running man is any match for a lancer! William Bergerac's men hurtled over the bridge with wild shouts and cries and hunted their quarry to destruction, thrusting their lances into backs, sides and chests without mercy, their hardened steel points ripping and tearing the lives out of their enemies. Like hunting the wild boar they ran each man down, thrusting their lances into them with controlled fury, then riding by to let the horse pull the lance free before driving on to stick the next one and the next one, shouting exultantly with every kill.

Behind them, the Malwood Lions dropped their bows, rushed over the bridge and plunged into the woodlands beyond with drawn swords to hunt down the enemy crossbows lurking there, striking down the men they found without pity, flaying their bodies with sharpened steel, thrusting into their bellies and flensing their flesh away in gouts of blood and brawn; shoulders, heads and arms cleaved through until their armour ran red and their blades were thick with it.

*

In the great clearing the fighting was over.

With the death of de Courcy and the stamping arrival of William Bergerac and his lancers, the fight went out of their enemies, and with desperate cries for mercy those still standing fell on their knees and begged for their lives. And while Gui looked around at the carnage his men had wrought, at the piles of bodies of both men and horses where Allan and Dickon Fletcher's archers had mown down de Courcy's lancers, Jean de Beaune and his men were already tidying up.

Sorting the living from the dead, horses and men both, Jean's men worked hard and swiftly, helped by Allan's verderers and the men from Niort, as some poor beasts were still struggling and heaving for life, while others staggered, heads down, their flanks pierced with arrows, or stumbled hamstrung or with broken limbs, and were swiftly put out of their misery and pain.

Everywhere that Gui looked there were bodies, and strewn body-parts in bloody confusion, many those of his own Lions who had lost their lives in the swift and brutal attack.

He looked and felt very grim indeed.

And it was in this spirit that the two Vernaille brothers were dragged before him, caught trying to flee the stricken field by two of de Bergerac's lancers; their bridles seized in an iron grasp, themselves heaved from their saddles and now hauled before Sir Gui to face his fury, their standard in de Beaune's tough grasp.

"These are the two Vernaille brothers, my Lord," he said, casting their standard at Gui's feet, disgust in every word he spoke. "Two of William's lads caught them trying to flee. This one," he said, shaking one by the shoulder like a terrier with a rat, "is Sir Bernard   I found this in his saddle bag, Sir Gui!" And with a grim face he handed Gui a tiny roll of parchment.

Gui took it carefully from his hand and read it, before handing it wordlessly on to Sir Richard, who hold it up to the light, the better to see the tiny writing more clearly.

"Bones of Christ, Gui. De Brocas! Another of his messages. Sent five days ago, the day after we landed at Nantes. That means de Courcy..."

"...Also had a message to come here," Gui interrupted him savagely, and as he looked at both men with such anger, their faces visibly paled, turned to parchment, while he was seized with an almost uncontrollable urge to kill them where they stood so arrogantly before him.

Meanwhile Gui's command gathered around him, their dead scattered round the clearing, many wounded, several badly so and leaning on their friends, their wounds roughly bound with blood-soaked rags, their faces dark and bitter as they looked at the handful of survivors thrown at Sir Gui's feet where they cowered on the bloodied grass, hands tied behind their backs with the spare bowstring every archer carried. All waiting to hear what their Lord would say to the men who had led the attack against them.

"You two miserable wretches deserve to die, for what you have done today," he growled at the brothers, through gritted teeth. *"And, by God's Bones I have a mind to slay you both!"* he suddenly roared, his bloodied sword whirling over their heads, making them flinch and step away from his anger.

"How *dare* you stand there before me, with your heads in the air you...pathetic *cowards!* You...*Nithings!* Men of no honour and no courage. At least that bastard over there," he shouted, pointing to where de Courcy's shattered body still lay amidst its burst offal and bloodied entrails, "had the courage to fight. He led his man bravely and bears his wounds to the front. You...you brought your men to the ring, and left them to hop! Abandoned

177

them. No wonder your father detested you both so greatly!" And he glared at their shocked faces, as his words struck home.

"And for what?" he derided them. "To curry favour with King Philip? To please Roger de Brocas?" And snatching the message from Richard's hands he seized Sir Bernard's face, squeezed his mouth open and forced the crumpled parchment into his mouth, stuffing it in to the back of his throat, the man's eyes goggling at him in terror as he gagged and choked on it, falling to his knees and scrabbling desperately to pull it out with trembling fingers, his brother hiding his face in his hands unable to watch.

"So...de Brocas put you up to this! You are in his pay, you miserable worms. You are both no better than dog-shit! Belted knights? Yes and so you should be, stripped and flogged through Saint Jean d'Angély at the cart's tails with stirrup leathers, like the common felons and murderers you are, until your backs are bloody while everyone pelts you with rubbish...because that's all you are!!"

And stepping towards them he ripped their surcoats off them and trampled them under his feet, tore their standard apart at the seams, stamping on it, and heeling it into the ground until it was indelibly soiled, while his command looked on with fierce faces in full agreement with their young Lord Baron's actions.

"*You are not worthy of the colours you bear!*" he roared into two faces white with shock and fear. "I hold you both responsible for this...this carnage scattered around us. You will come with me to Bordeaux, in chains if necessary, where I will hand you over to Sir Hugh Willoughby, the Guardian of the King's Peace, the Seneschal of Aquitaine, where you hold your lands, for him to do with you as he sees fit. But be certain that when I meet with King Richard of England...which I will do, I will seek to have you banished from all Aquitaine, and *all* your lands held forfeit to the crown."

Then dropping his voice completely, he walked right up to them and almost whispered in quiet, seething rage: "I assure you, *both*, that you will rue this evening's filthy work, and any allegiance you might have had with that Man-of-Blood, till your dying days. Now take them out of my sight and feed them. Any attempt to escape...cut them down without mercy!"

Then turning to Sir Richard beside him, he pointed to the handful of men still crouching on their knees: "Release those men, Richard. Give them five silver pieces each and send them home. There has been enough killing today. There is no need for more!" And ignoring the pardoned men's cries of gratitude and prayers for God's Grace upon him, he walked away to meet Father Matthew now coming towards him from the town with his tilt cart, a large

178

group of monks and assorted town's people in his company, all bringing help and succour for any who had survived the battle.

*

Far away in the Château Grise the Baron waited to hear that Gui was dead and his command scattered…and how his other plan for Alicia's 'rescue' from his daughter was working. He knew that El Nazir had seized her, and that she had arrived at Narbonne. Now it was up to de Vere to play his part…*The man has all he needs…he just has to set the ball rolling.*

The Lord Baron rubbed his hands together fiercely with sudden pleasure, and grinned. Good so far. Excellent!…*But where is my message from Bertrand de Vernaille, or de Courcy? What has happened at Saint Jean d'Angély?*

Chapter 28...Alicia begins her journey to the Château Grise.

The Lady Alicia de Burley had never taken twelve more difficult steps in her life than the ones she took that morning at Bayonne, when she, with her small household behind her, stepped onto the gangway that led to the quayside...and the Lady Rochine de Brocas waiting beyond!

Her enemy, and the daughter of her enemy, now down from her horse and standing tall, her long, scarlet silk coif swirling in the breeze, her red cloak covering her right down to her scarlet booted feet, her face smiling a welcome, her eyes bleak as midwinter.

Alicia looked at her and stretched her shoulders, her own eyes sharp with fierce determination...*Two can play that game, cousin. I am not my father's daughter for nothing!*...and unlike The Lady, Alicia's face was masked. Rochine might see her eyes, but she could not see her face!

Coming across the quayside Alicia greeted her French cousin with a smile, holding her hand out through her black chador as she did so, such that Rochine could do nothing except receive it.

"Welcome, cousin," Alicia said, her eyes a-glitter from between the black material that covered her head and the lower part of her face. "I had expected the Great Baron himself to be here to greet me...after taking such trouble to 'collect' me," she added gesturing towards the *Morning Star* and El Nazir, standing not twenty paces away from them. "No matter, I suppose if the blade himself cannot come, my dear Rochine...I must make do with the oil that keeps it bright!"...*Now see how you like that, you bitch!*

Rochine's green eyes stabbed at her with fury, and gripping Alicia's arm above her elbow she hissed viciously: "How *dare* you! How *dare* you insult me! Had I had my way you would have been delivered to me in chains!"

"But I *am* in chains...cousin!" Alicia bit back at her sharply, her eyes like sapphires, hard, unblinking. "Bound by them, *cousin*! Chains of truth and honour and everlasting love that you and your father will *never* break. Even if he drags me up the aisle and nails me to the altar, he will *never* possess me. All he will ever have of me is my carcase...my heart and my spirit will always lie elsewhere. Now...unhand me!" she snarled, tearing her arm out of Rochine's grasp. "If you have not noticed, I am not alone!" she said, directing Rochine's furious gaze to her two enormous guards, and to Najid standing near them. "See those men there? They are my Household and my guardians, and the smaller one is our personal cook. They are on loan to me from the Sheik,

Prince Nazir, your so dear father's dearest friend. And will travel with me to the Château Grise. *All the way!...*" she hissed at her fiercely. "For my added safety, and yours too, dear coz," she added then sweetly. "To ensure that nothing surprising happens to prevent our safe arrival beneath your father's walls. Yes? Just so that no sudden accidents happen between here and Gruissan...and no-one would want that, would they, sweet coz?" she ended with a lift of her eyebrows. And she gave her cousin a swift bob, and turning her back, she walked back to where Aziz, Aquib and all the others were standing with stately grace...*Never will she have me in her power again as she did that night in the Forest. Never!*

The Lady Rochine de Brocas stood rooted to the spot, almost shaking with rage...*How dare she speak to me in such..such cheap terms! And with such contempt!...*And she stared with naked venom at Alicia as she walked back towards her 'Household' and snarled. Her '*Household*' indeed! Two great lumps of humanity, one small cook, whom she knew all about, and two stupid girls...one of whom she had personally trained in her ways!...*Just wait 'til I get Soraya Fermier under my hand again. Then we shall see whose 'Household' siezes the best cards?...*The thought almost made her purr.

De Vere would deal with them in short order. Once they were clear of the quay, and on board the barge her father had commissioned for the river journey to Peyrehorade, she would see about her pathetic 'Household.' No-one...but *no-one* could be allowed to treat her like that...*that English putain! That whore whom my father so desires. Sweet Jesus, I have given him everything...heart and body! What need does he have for une salope, une trui!...une conne anglaise!...*And in her inner fury she almost stamped her foot and spat she was so angry, panting with suppressed rage.

But swirling her long scarlet cloak around her she turned away, almost pop-eyed with fury, steadied her breathing, and then stalked slowly back towards the Sheik El Nazir, striving to calm herself when she almost wanted to run, surprised at how easily the wretched girl had disturbed her. She smiled...*just give me half an hour alone with that..that English whore in my private chamber and I will soon make her sing a different tune!*

El Nazir, who had watched the little scene with hawk-like eyes, grinned quietly to himself...*The little one has shown too much spirit too soon!...*She should have played The Lady on a string for much longer; not have declared herself so soon in the game. Dissembled more. He grinned to himself then...*Instead she has done exactly what I hoped she would do. Stuck the knife into The Lady and then twisted it hard!...*And his eyes crinkled with another quiet smile of satisfaction.

He had seen how rigid Rochine had gone while they had been talking, and that look on her face would turn milk sour and stop hens from laying! The rest he could guess, and looking across at Abdul Aziz and Mhaktoun Aquib, he shrugged. He had done his bit for the Lord Roger, as he had been asked to do, and she'd had first throw of the dice. Now she and The Lady would have to sort it out between them, with de Vere to help things along if he could. *'Insh'a Allah!'* And he turned and walked towards The Lady Rochine de Brocas with his hands held out to her, a welcome smile on his sun-hardened features.

Alicia watched them greet, and then grimaced as she walked back to Soraya and the others, while some of Rochine's guard swung off their horses and ran out to load their things onto the tilt carts: chests of clothes for the girls and all their essential belongings, bundles for the men, and baskets of tools and spare armour, grinding stones and oil, along with all Najid's pans and ladles; fresh eggs, smoked meats of fish and pork, bags filled with fresh lemons and oranges, and his precious boxes of rare spices. Sugar from Cyprus, peppercorns and turmeric from India and even cinnamon and nutmeg from the magical Spice Islands of the distant East, brought by caravan to Damascus and Egypt from across the top of the world...many were beyond simple price... along with rice from the Jordan river, bundles of dried herbs and a great box of salt crystals. And last of all, accompanied by their Master, Almahdi aal Suriyyan, came the Baron's precious pigeons in their large wicker cage.

"I think I overplayed my hand," she growled to Agnes and Soraya, when she reached them. "I was too cross for my own good. Thought I'd give as good as I might receive." Then she chuckled, and pulled a wry face. "I don't think my French cousin likes me very much...and with two hundred miles to go, I'm not sure that was too clever!"

Soraya sighed, and put her arms around both girls. "She *hates* to be crossed, Alicia. She always has to be right! When things go well she can be as warm as the sun itself, both loving and generous. You would be surprised. But there is a vicious twist in her...almost evil, that she cannot control, and her moods can change like lightning; cooing like a turtle dove one moment and a spitting virago the next...then she can be *truly* dangerous! And she has great power over her father.

"I have heard of terrible things they have done together, and when she is jealous her temper can be horrifying. Yet she has a way with her even I have found hard to resist, and have done things with her that I could never have dreamed of!" she said, her face ashamed, suddenly pale in the sunshine. "I told you...on the *Morning Star*? She can be a monster...and she loves her silken lash!" she added with a shudder.

182

"Right now, she is in a fury! I can tell. By tomorrow, after proper food and rest, she could be your best friend for life. Thank God, we are not reliant on her for protection, or for our food, and can avoid her completely. Thank God for the Sheik. He has proven to be a greater friend than I could ever have imagined."

"She will not be pleased about that, I think." Agnes said quietly.

"No…I told you, she likes to control things. But she will not go against Prince El Nazir. She would not dare. He is her father's greatest friend, as he said, and for many years. Before her mother died. And she is afraid of him. Afraid he knows a terrible secret about her, that she dare not risk her father *ever* finding out."

"What secret is that?"

"I do not know. But I am certain she had two girls murdered who tried to find out!"

"*Murdered?*" Alicia and Agnes whispered, aghast.

"*Yes!* Of it I am sure. But I have no proof. One moment they were around her chambers and with her father close…the next moment they had disappeared…*disparu! Pouf!* Gone…and their bodies were found two days later almost eaten by the castle swine. Who knows how they were killed?…But The Lady's hand was in it, of that I am certain!'"

Agnes shuddered. "Pigs will eat anything! They're almost as bad as goats."

"But not flesh, sweetheart. Clothes and such…but not bodies," Alicia added. "Sweet Jesus, Soraya. But you have served a dreadful mistress…just be careful I don't turn out to be like her," and leaping round in her chador, making sudden claws of her hands, she growled like a tiger… "*GRRRRRR!*"…so that everyone laughed.

"Right, that's enough doom and gloom for a while. As long as we stick together, and have Abdul and Aquib to watch over us," she said, looking up at them both with a smile, "and Najid to cook for us…and I don't irritate her any more, then we ought to get by. Oh, Soraya, Agnes, how I *wish* Gui were here. I do miss him *so* very much!" And her eyes suddenly flooded with tears.

"I know, *ma pauvre petite choute*," Soraya said softly as she would to a child, drawing her into her arms and kissing her cheek. "*My poor little darling,* he will come for you, your so brave Sir Gui, on his great charger. *Moi,* I am certain of it. We must just hang on until he does, and do all we can to keep things smooth in the meantime. Now…no more tears. They will make your eyes red," and she laughed. "Right now I can't wait to take off my huque…and you your chadors. They are impossible to ride in!

183

Chapter 29...The White Rose twists The Lady's tail.

Four hours later and they were all on the great barge that Lord Roger had commissioned for the first part of their long journey to Gruissan, and well on their way up-river to Peyrehorade.

From there they would strike across country towards Carcassonne and the Via Aquitania, the great Roman road that still linked Bordeaux with Narbonne. Once it had carried the eagles swinging through Gaul at the head of the legions at twenty miles a day, meeting the Via Domitia coming up from Rome, having crossed the Alps where Hannibal had once driven his elephants a thousand years before.

They were the two great high roads that joined Italy to Spain and to the Atlantic coast through Narbonne, over the long Roman bridge with its five great arches that still stood over La Robine, the great canal that the veterans of Caesar's Xth Legion had dug to join up with the river Aude. It was what had made Narbonne a great port, ships sailing all over the Old Empire with oil and wine in great amphoras...now in great casks and hogsheads to all parts of King Richard's Plantagenet Empire, including Toulouse...an Empire put together by his father, King Henry II, and was so important a source of the money Richard needed to fight the Saracens in the Holy Land.

And the mighty County of Toulouse, the greatest single county in all France, whose ruler Raymond V was a mortal enemy of King Richard Lionheart, included Narbonne and Gruissan ruled by the Lord Baron, Sir Roger de Brocas who was his closest ally!

Sweet Wine of Christ!...Alicia thought, as she looked along the great barge they were in, at the rowers on long sweeps either side, now resting, and at the great square sail spread above them, its broad, brown belly filled with the brisk north-westerly that had carried the *Morning Star* down from Nantes...*What a dreadful tangle to be caught up in. And it's to Narbonne we are going now*...Narbonne first, then Gruissan.

Twenty miles of gentle sailing against the current, always pushing east, saw the river curving and bending through the warm, sun-drenched countryside, past great open fields of wheat and barley, busy with groups of hoers. Past long rows of vines, that stretched in all directions, bright green lines against the darker woodlands, the rich red earth lightly dug around them, thick with grapes hanging from them in a welter of great fruity clusters...and past the silver-grey leaved olive groves, the trunks and branches gnarled and twisted with age, heavy with green and black fruit, the wind making the leaves turn and flicker silver bright in the brilliant sunshine.

Dressed in the blue pleated bliaut she had worn three days ago, her hair brushed out and piled beneath a snood of golden thread, with matching blue leather half-boots on her feet, Alicia felt elegant and comfortable, delighted to be free of the hated chador, and she looked at Soraya, now similarly dressed, but in deep green to match her eyes, no longer like a Houri from an Eastern harem, and smiled...reaching out to tap the girl's hand gently and draw her attention away from the drowsing countryside.

"You look lovely like that," she said, taking her hand with a wide smile and giving it a shake. "You could not go across half of France in the way Rochine had dressed you, Soraya. You are a part of my Household now, Honeyone...not hers. She cannot control you any longer, no matter how much she may wish to. Her father ordered you to serve me...gave you to me as a gift of 'love'," she added dryly. "So I will have you dressed as it suits me, not her...as I told her. Do you not like the clothes I have chosen?"

"Oh, yes, my Lady...Alic-ia," Soraya replied instantly, with her stunning smile. "They are lovely. Not as free to wear as my yashmak and half jacket...and my breasts feel squashed," she said giving her body a shake, "and no-one can see my golden tips, which I quite liked," she added with a shrug and a swift grin. "But they give me an elegance, and...and...so-ph-ist-ic-ation," she said stumbling over the word, "that I have not enjoyed before. They make me feel...to you special," she added softly looking down.

"But was it worth that awful, awful row, Alicia?" Agnes asked quietly. "I thought she was going to kill you where you stood. And those two cousins? Did you see their faces afterward? Maybe you are pushing your cousin too hard, my pet," adding with a wry smile: "I thought you were going to try *not* to irritate her so much?"

*

They had arrived at the barge earlier, having waited for the *Morning Star* to sail, de Vere chivvying his men to get every last thing loaded on the carts as swiftly as possible...especially the large wicker cages of pigeons, the special responsibility of their Syrian Pigeon Master who was also coming with them off the ship.

And finally Jules Lagrasse and Lucas Fabrizan, who'd come last off the *Morning Star*, and were by his side to assist with the pigeons, and then help the

Lady Rochine up the rough gangplank and off the stout wooden pier against which the barge was moored: Alicia and her Household bringing up the rear, not wanting to be any nearer to any of them than was necessary.

The boat itself was large, with long sweeps on both sides and a single tall mainmast that carried a great square sail of brown canvas. Half decked, with a number of cabins at bow and stern, and a huge long empty belly for cargo, the space was now only partly filled by their many packs and saddles and the contents of both tilt carts, so the barge was quite spacious, horses and tilt carts having been left behind ready for the next travellers to come that way.

At first all had been well, with both parties settling into their little cabins at either end of the boat, prior to sailing, until Rochine, with a mouth pinched as if she'd been sucking lemons, and a face to match, had sharply ordered Soraya to come to her quarters. Soraya, used to such peremptory handling, and knowing what would happen when she got there had looked terrified, but was still about to do as instructed when Alicia had stopped her.

"Where are you going, Soraya?"

"The Lady Rochine has ordered me to go to her. But I am afraid!"

"Of course you are afraid, Soraya. But I am not...and you are in my Household now, and she cannot order you about any longer without my say so. And I don't say so! Tell Aquib what we are about and ask him to speak with Aziz and then both must come and join us. Agnes, we will be back shortly....ask Najid to prepare some orange sherbet for later. Now, you two, come on," and Soraya, having spoken briefly to Aquib, then said in Farsi, '*Ba man bia*'...'come with me'...and had moved to join Alicia.

Aquib, after first speaking with Aziz had padded along behind them like the great soft-footed bear he was, and together they had gone up to speak with Rochine.

"I understand you have ordered Mistress Soraya to come to your quarters, cousin," Alicia had said quietly. "Why is that? She is not your servant to give orders to any longer. Not without my say so. Please," she had added, the sweetness flowing off her like acid drops. "If you need any of my Household for something, I would be grateful if you were to ask me first!"

Rochine, who'd been momentarily speechless at her presumption, had then lost her temper completely and shouted: "*How dare you interfere!* Soraya Fermier is *nothing* to do with you...*cousin!*" She said bitingly. "She is mine to control. *Mine!* You understand? And has been since she was given to me by my father six years ago..."

"But that was six years ago, Rochine," Alicia had interrupted sweetly, smiling into her cousin's raging face. "As I understand it she has been given into my sole care, by your father, as my 'Betrothal Gift'...because he 'loves'

186

me. I have it here in a letter Soraya gave me when I was brought on board the *Morning Star*," she added, waving the crumpled piece of parchment in her face. "So please do not interfere with my Household again!" And thrusting her father's letter into Rochine's hands, she had turned her back and walked away, saying sharply over her shoulder: "Soraya. Come with me...*now!*"

"*NO!*" Rochine had almost screamed, hurling the letter tempestuously onto the deck and stamping on it in her fury. "*NO!* I say. That girl shall stay here, as *I* have ordered. Jules, Lucas...take her to my cabin now and strip her! De Vere, remove this...*this person*," she had raged, stabbing her finger at Alicia. "And have her conveyed to her quarters and keep her there. Kicking and screaming...*I don't care!* And you! You great *lumpen oaf!*" she had snarled up at Aquib, standing before her, his arms crossed, while she had gestured at him violently. "*Get out of my way!*"

But Aquib had not moved.

His face impassive, his body enormous and seemingly immoveable, he had just stood there, completely calm in the face of her unbridled fury, while he had waited for Soraya to tell him what to do...all the time watching the two Frenchmen as they had rushed to carry out Rochine's orders, and de Vere as he had stolen up behind Alicia to seize her and carry her away.

But the moment Soraya had felt the Cousins' hands on her she had shouted in Farsi: "Aquib! *Ahay anha!*...'Stop them!'...and absolute mayhem had followed.

With two great strides Aquib had seized both Frenchmen by their arms and simply hurled them overboard behind him as effortlessly as if they had been sacks of feathers, sending them soaring over his head, in a wild cartwheel of arms and legs, their cries of shocked alarm brutally cut off as they had hit the river bank with a terrific *thump,* landing amongst the reeds and rushes, half in and half out of the water, all the stuffing knocked out of them, unable to breathe, let alone move.

De Vere, seeing them spin through the air, had stopped dead in his tracks, awed by the ease with which the huge Arab had hurled two fully grown men, armour, weapons and all, straight over his head...and had backed away immediately to give himself space to draw his sword.

But Aquib, who had been expecting it, did not give him the chance to do so.

Moving more swiftly than de Vere could possibly have imagined, the giant Arab had pounced on him, clamped the big man's sword arm in his enormous hand and then shaken it till de Vere's teeth had almost rattled and, willy nilly, he had been forced to drop his sword with a clatter on the deck. And before he could speak another word, Aquib had seized his head in such a fierce grip under his arm, with his other hand twisting the far side of it, that de Vere had stopped struggling immediately for fear his head would simply have been torn from his shoulders…as he felt was surely about to happen.

With the two Frenchmen still flat on their backs just shuddering back to life like a pair of ancient cripples, her Guard Commander completely immobilised and his horrified soldiers, with no bows to hand, now threatened by Aziz and too scared even to move, there was nothing else that Rochine could have done save to accept defeat with as much grace as possible…which was not much!

"*Very well!*" she had almost spat at her cousin, her fists clenched in humiliated fury. "Very well! Soraya Fermier stays with you as my father seems to have ordered."…his very tattered letter now clutched in her hands…"At least until we reach Gruissan, then we shall see, *cousin!*" she had snarled viciously, poison in every word. "He needs me in ways you cannot even begin to guess at…ways that may bring *us* together sooner than you think, you foolish girl! And you are not even married yet, my *so* dear Alicia…nor have we reached home. You have drawn the lines, coz. Pray God *I* do not have to cross them to find you!

Now, take that *putain* with you! That cheap whore…that *conne francaise*," she had railed obscenely. "And dress her how you wish. They say that revenge is a tree that bears sour fruit," and she had thrown back her head and laughed. "But I do not have a sweet tooth in my entire body, *ma petite choute*," she had hissed venomously, chucking Soraya under her chin. "I prefer my food to have lots of lovely, salty savour…*ma pet-ite lap-ine…*" she had snarled, bitter sarcasm dripping from every syllable. "*My lit-tle bun-ny rabbit…*as you know *so* well. And savour you I will, *ma mie…to the very last, precious, .tasty., drop!*" And pausing to plant a soft kiss on Soraya's cheek with her sweetest smile, the girl's face wet with the tears now coursing down her face as she cowered away from Rochine's bitterness into Alicia's arms, The Lady had turned away to rescue de Vere. Gesturing fiercely to Aquib as she did so, she snapped: "Now, you big *lump!* Put my man down and get about your business…your mistress has more need of you than I do! And you may be certain that my father shall know what has happened here," she snarled at Aquib as he released de Vere from his stranglehold, the big Frenchman scarlet in the face and puffing hard; rubbing his neck where the giant Arab had so firmly gripped him.

"It may be you will not find so warm a welcome when next you step back onto the *Morning Star*. Follow me to my quarters, de Vere," she had then added imperiously, "and we will see what can be done!"…And with her head held high, and her thoughts in a rage…*That little bitch will not do that to one of* *my men ever again! A lot can happen before we reach Gruissan. And maybe she never will!...*The Lady Rochine de Brocas stalked back to her own quarters to plot her revenge.

So everyone had parted, and while the dust settled, the boat was quanted from its moorings, and the captain had seized the heavy tiller as the rowers heaved on the long sweeps against the current, backwards and forwards in stirring rhythm until the great sail had been raised and their journey east to Narbonne had got under way at last.

Chapter 30...And the Morning and the Evening were the First Day!...(Genesis 1:5).

"So...was that awful row worth it, Agnes?" Alicia asked her, sitting on one of their long clothes' chests with a padded top. "For that- that wicked Harpy, that shocking Medusa, to know how I feel? That she is my enemy...and the daughter of my enemy? Father Matthew always says that *'knowledge is power'*...and that *'to know something is better than to know nothing.'* He also says that *'to enjoy ignorance is the opinion of fools!'* And, before God, Agnes, while I may be many things, my love...I am no fool. So, *yes!* sweetheart, it *was* worth it...if only to force that bitch, that *'salope'* to show her true colours."

"The colours you saw the night of the fire?" Agnes said coming to join her on the long chest, putting her arm around her waist. "When her father killed Gui's parents and she drugged you and helped him steal you away?"

"Yes, Agnes! Oh, I heard what you said, Soraya," she added turning towards the lovely girl with a smile, "about her being warm and generous and loving. I experienced that also after the banquet, when we shared a room together...and before it...when I am sure she tried to make love to me. Wanted me to play her games...only I would not...could not, even though I was tempted. She seemed so sophisticated, so much a 'woman of the world', and I a simple country bunny! But country bunnies have claws, Soraya, and teeth...and know when to run and hide from the fox...and I escaped her."

"And today, *ma mie?*" Soraya asked, reaching out for her hand. "When she threatened you...screamed at you, weren't you afraid?"

"Yes. Of course I was afraid. Only fools have no fear, sweetheart. And no...I was *not* looking forward to meeting with her again. Walking down that gangway off the *Morning Star* today was one of the most difficult things I have ever had to do. But I was far more afraid of showing it, of letting her know such a thing of me. Of giving her that kind of power over me. So, yes, I taunted her a little," she said with a grin. "After all she is my cousin, we share a certain blood. Grandmother Philippa was her great aunt remember...and I know first-hand what a murderous creature she is...and how her father so wants me in his bed!...Not as his *salope,* his 'bitch' - his piece of *conne anglaise*, his 'English cunt!'" she said, shocking them both, Agnes putting her hand to her mouth with a sudden squeak, Soraya's eyes popping out of their sockets. *"But as his legal wife!* To bear his heir, as he hopes. Sweet Jesus what a ghastly prospect! The man must be mad even to think of such a thing.

So El Nazir was right - she is far more afraid of me than ever I will be of her. For that is the one thing she can *never* do for him, give him a child, and I can guess the rest...and dreadful that is too. So, yes, I believe she fears me."

"Thank God for Mhaktoun and Abdul," Soraya said breathlessly.

"And little Najid, with his pans and baskets and spices," Agnes added with her gentle smile. "He will need caring for, too; it would be dreadful if anything happened to him because of us."

"And thank God for the Prince...for Sheik El Nazir," Alicia said, standing up, and leaning against the smooth gunnels of the barge, as Najid bustled about with the orange sherbet behind her, while Mhaktoun Aquib, her '*Protector*' and Abdul Aziz aal Suriyyan, her '*Servant of the Powerful One*', stood nearby, their hands on their huge swords, their eyes looking everywhere.

"Before today perhaps we could have dissembled. Played The Lady on a long line with a mask of sweetness and light...and watched our backs: pretended respectability, while harbouring rebellion. But we have over two hundred miles to go, and I would rather *know* of her personal hatred and her anger...of her jealousy and spite, and mine for her, and for her to know that I will not be suborned nor trifled with...nor have my people ordered about without my say so, than play her game with lies and deceit and dishonour, and in the end be no better than she is!

"After today's experience she will know not to interfere with our arrangements...and that Aquib is more than a match, single handed, for *any* of the men she has with her. And of Aziz's true abilities she still knows nothing...but she will secretly fear him, for what she doesn't know! As I said, '*Knowledge is power*'. We have it; she does not. Anyway, we are safe enough on this barge, with us here and she over there," she added pointing across to Rochine's cabin at the other end of the long barge. "Good arrangement!"

Then, turning to look out across the countryside, she added: "The real trouble will start when we reach Peyrehorade, and start across country. That's when we will need to start watching our backs with a vengeance. Until then, let's just enjoy ourselves. Oh, look!" she called out, pointing; we're mooring up for the night. Well done the captain, we might get a hot meal after all...how lovely! Soraya, call the 'boys' and let's see what they can get for us from the so dear Lady Rochine's people for our food tonight. You'll have to go with them...they can't speak the language, remember? Agnes, my love, pass that sherbet, I am thirsty!"

*

191

L ater, after de Vere had done his rounds and all had settled for the night, seated on sacks and woolfells beneath where The Lady was lying amongst the cushions his men had brought on board for her, Gaston de Vere, Jules Lagrasse and Lucas Fabrizan plotted their revenge...and the relief of all The Lady's troubles, with a couple of wineskins and two small brass oil lamps, while they chewed on the remainder of their dinner.

"That fucking bastard will pay for what he bloody did to me and Jules," Lucas swore, as he rubbed more ointment into the massive bruises that were now blackening his back and shoulders. "Tossed us overboard as if we were a pair of bloody maidens! And as for that sodding piece of English shit, if I don't stuff my fat prick up her fucking arse, my name's not Lucas Fabrizan!"

"You're welcome, coz," Jules snarled, tearing a piece of bread between his hands. "I want the other one. That Soraya. Dark meat is always delicious, especially after a good smacking! Tenderises it like prime beef...makes it even more juicy. You can have that other English bitch, de Vere. That fucking Agnes. I swear she's dying for it! And she's whole...untouched by human hand. A virgin hole is always tighter, more springy," he leered. Then chuckling hoarsely he added: "And there's *nothing* like popping a fresh, young cherry...always that lovely sweet burst of bloody flavour!" And they both laughed, a vicious gasping sound that made their bellies shake.

"It's not the fucking girls I want, lads," de Vere growled, drinking from an almost flaccid wineskin, the red wine splashing over his face, before tearing at a piece of smoked meat with his teeth. "It's that sodding great lump of infidel muscle pretending to be human...that Aquib. *No-one* does that to Gaston de Vere. He may be big, and quick...*Jesus was he quick!*...but cold steel, or a well-heated iron from the fire, in the right place will quell any fighter faster than a bucket of water on hot coals!"

"Just shoot the fuckers," Lucas swore. "Him and that bloody Aziz. You brought some sodding bowmen with you in your guard...I saw the buggers."

"Yes!" Jules agreed, reaching for the wine skin to fill his beaker. "Wait until we get off this damned barge. There'll have to be some hunting if these people are all to be fed...then wait until we are all away up-country, or somewhere lonely, and shoot some bolts hard into 'em! Nice, barbed, broad-head hunting quarrels, and they'll go down like shot rabbits. *Shhiew!...Thump!*" And he banged his right fist into his hand. "The bigger they are, the harder they'll fall!"

"No...can't do that," de Vere growled again, looking at them both sideways. "Though that would work a treat, for sure. But they are off the *Morning Star.* Two of that fucking Sheik's best men, I have met with them before; they are never far from his side. We do for them out here and the Baron will hand us over to Monsieur Gullet for that bastard's amusement soon as look at us. No…it has to be cunning! So no-one can blame either us…or The Lady."

"Well how the bloody fuck do we do that?" Lucas sneered. "With fucking magic?"

"The man's a bloody mountain!" Jules cursed bitterly, pouring the wine down his throat. "None of our lads want to get near him. "They both are. Whole ranges of bloody mountains the pair of 'em! If the lads can't shoot the buggers from behind a rock, they're sure not going to stick bloody cold steel in 'em!"

De Vere smiled and leaned forward, his voice dropping to a husky whisper as he sneered: "Don't you worry, lads. I know something about that little cook, that stupid bloody 'Najid' that will put him right in our frame!"

"*What?*" both men exclaimed sharply, leaning towards him.

"*Shhh!*" He hissed at them urgently. "Softly! Keep your voices down. Do you want the whole bloody world to know what we are about? Especially as it's something The Lady doesn't know," he husked, leering at them. "Remember, we have travelled on that sodding *Morning Star* before, she and I…and with the Lord Baron, several times. And I happen to know that Najid has a sister he's devoted to; got the word secretly from a friend," and he tapped his nose and winked. "'Faridah' she's called…means '*Precious Pearl*'," and he snorted in derision. "Pretty as a picture she is, all sloe-eyed and slender; only twelve, with a beautifully ripening body, and that stupid, fucking little cook dotes on her!" And he paused to take another swig from the wineskin.

"Well, go on!" Jules urged, drinking from his beaker and wiping his mouth with the back of his hand.

"So…their parents are dead," de Vere continued, turning his head one to the other, his eyes glittering in the lamp light, sly, full of secrets. "And that Najid is her only real protector. She lives with an aunt, his Papa's elder sister, a real miserable, sodding bitch of a woman. Bitter as stale piss in a bucket: she'd sell her grandmother if she could find a buyer…and Najid knows it! It's only his money that keeps the old bat caring for the child at all, or she'd be out on the street…and she's *just* the sort of young meat that The Lady so likes to trade with!"

"So?" Lucas, sneered, and spat across the deck. "He is also part of that bloody Sheik's crew. We're no further forward"

"Does this stupid sod have any brains at all?" de Vere snarled at Jules. "Or are they all in that fucking prick he carries dangling between his legs?"

"Coz?" Jules asked with a sigh. "Do you suppose that Najid knows what The Lady is really like?"

193

"Yes!" he said quietly, after a moment's thought, his brow creased. "Yes…he must do."

"Well suppose, then, that our beloved mistress learned…somehow, Yes?…that Najid had a problem about his darling little sister, and she suggested to El Nazir that she should care for the child herself? Yes? Well, Nazir knows what a vicious old hag the aunt is, that she doesn't want the silly little bitch…and that Najid can't take her with him on the *Morning Star*…so, suppose Najid found out about it? Suppose that someone told him of The Lady Rochine de Brocas's interest in his baby sister, and that she'd spoken with El Nazir about her?…Well, Najid might easily think the Sheik would agree, seeing as he and The Lady are always as thick as bloody thieves, and gave the girl to her…or sold her…then Najid's '*Precious Pearl*' would be well and truly stuffed. Literally, knowing The Lady's tastes! Yes?"

"Yes! So?"

"Dear God, it's like wading through bloody treacle with you sometimes, Lucas. You tell him, Gaston!"

"So…if Najid thought that The Lady might *really* get her hot little hands on his sister, with El Nazir's blessing…what might he *not* refuse to do to prevent it…eh??"

"And he does *all* their cooking, coz!" Jules added, looking at his cousin with his head on one side, finally sitting back and smiling as the lights came on at last behind his cousin's eyes.

"So…So…the stupid bastard could slip something into their fucking scoff to prevent that happening, and..and then, when they all bloody died…or…or something… *he'd* fucking get the blame and not one of us!" And he looked so pleased with himself the others laughed.

"Brilliant, Lucas!" And Jules gave his cousin a cheerful thump on his shoulders. "I knew you'd get there in the end! What will you tell him?"

"He's only a dumb fucking Arab," Lucas sneered. "Tell him it's a fucking powder to make that stupid bitch forget her boyfriend; that sodding Gui! He's fucking stupid enough to believe anything, that fucking cook!"

"My God, Lucas!" de Vere exclaimed, astonished. "Now that *is* a good idea…I didn't know you had in you! That is just the sort of thing he might well believe, the silly bugger. A 'forgetting potion,' something real 'special' from distant lands. Good plan! Good plan! And if The Lady had any sense," he added, shaking the wineskin hopefully, peering down its open end, "which she has plenty of, she would then kill off the little shit as well - have us stick a knife in him, or garrotte him, saying it was done in passionate grief for her father's *so* sad and unexpected loss!"

194

"That would solve everything neatly," Jules said quietly, passing him another wineskin. "No witnesses! So, Gaston. You'll speak with the Lady in the morning?"

"No!" he exclaimed softly, looking at them from the corners of his eyes, half closed. "No, I don't think so, lads," he murmured, drawing them closer. "I think this is something we must do ourselves. Leave The Lady out of it until it's all fixed. One whiff of her personal involvement at this stage will frighten him off. He'd have to get permission to speak with her, and that fucking English bitch will smell a rat straightaway. No, I have enough Arabic to speak with him myself. Remember, the stupid little bastard doesn't *know* that I know about Faridah. One hint from me that The Lady would just love to help his *'Precious Pearl'*," he drawled suggestively, "...and had spoken with Sheik El Nazir about her, will be enough to make him shit his pants!" And they all guffawed, eyes bright as berries at Christmas time.

"What will you give him to use on those fucking buggers then?" Lucas asked.

"This!" Gaston whispered, his voice slow, deep; and reaching behind him he pulled out a handful of twisted roots, dried black and dark brown, with a faint tangy odour to them. "This is what they're going to get."

"What's in the devil's name are they?" Jules asked in a hushed voice, while Lucas just gaped, his eyes narrow slits.

"*Black hellebore* and *Belladonna*...deadly nightshade." de Vere murmured darkly, holding them up in the faint lamp light for the others to sniff at and touch. "Gathered at dead of night, and dried over a slow fire...real witches' brew stuff, got them from that old Greek perfume seller in Gruissan whom The Lady uses from time to time."

"Stanisopoulos," Jules said softly. "He's a bad one."

"What the fuck do you do with them?" Lucas asked slowly, awed by the sight and feel of the hard, blackly twisted roots.

"You grind them to a powder and mix it in with food," de Vere grunted. "In very small amounts either of these can be used in all sorts of good ways. But in quantity, it is the most deadly powerful stuff!"

"So, what does it do?" Jules whispered. "If you give too much?" And he reached out to touch it.

"*No! Don't!*" de Vere hissed fiercely, knocking Jules' hand away. "Not even the tip of your finger. The stuff's bloody lethal. It will gripe your belly horribly; make you vomit blood and squit yourself like pissing shit, and you'll foam at the mouth and go mad before it paralyses you and you die.

"*Fucking Hell!*" Lucas exclaimed softly, with a wide grin on his face. "So, if that fucking Najid mixes that stuff in with their sodding scoff, they'll

195

get fierce griping bellies, go bloody green and purple in the face, froth at the mouth, roll about like lunatics and fucking shit themselves to death. Lovely!"

"Yes!" de Vere said grimly, shaking the small box at them both, and then closing it. "And after what those bastards did to us, that's just about how it should be for those fucking shits! Can't wait to see Najid's little face when I tell him about his sister, poor little sod. It'll ruin his day, that's for certain!" And he laughed, grunting like a hog. "Now, bugger off you two," he added, thrusting the remains of the wineskin at them. "Piss off. I need my beauty sleep. We've a lot to do in the morning…and I need to be fresh for it!"

Chapter 31...Sleep that knits up
the ravelled sleeve of care...(Macbeth II:II)

Gaston de Vere watched through slitted eyes as the two Frenchmen left for their own sleeping pits, their arms over each other's shoulders, and he held up the box of powdered roots in the flickering lamplight and laughed...*Stupid buggers, the lot of 'em!! What they have all forgotten is that I am not The Lady's Guard Commander...I am the Lord Baron, Sir Roger de Brocas of Narbonne and Gruissan's Guard Commander!...*

And as such he was as close to his Lord, as any man of his rank could be. And it was Lord Roger who had sent him to Stanisopoulos for the roots, planned with him to have the two Frenchmen placed first in Castle Malwood and then on the barge...and had told him what he had already asked the Sheik El Nazir to do.

The Baron knew how ferociously jealous Rochine could be when pushed to it, and how unstable her temper was. And he had also known about the little cook, that fucking Najid, and his pretty sister. And he grinned...*The moment that poor little sod knows that I know about her, he will be terrified...fucking gold bricks everywhere!...*The Lady's trading tastes were well known. Once let her get her hands on the girl, and Najid would never see her again!...*He will surely promise anything on earth to prevent that...and then he'll blab! Even if he really thinks this stuff is only a 'forgetting powder' he'll still blab! No fucking oyster that one; known for it...*Heart like melting butter, he'd no more poison that lot than fly. He would be in despair, sick with the very knowledge of it...*and those three girls will get it all out of him. Be sure to!*

De Vere tossed the box of ground powder between his hands and grinned. Powdered Hellebore and Belladonna root indeed...more like powdered toast crumbs! And he chuckled...*As if I'd let the silly sod really poison them. Oh...the roots are real enough, bloody frightening too, but the powder? Twice toasted breadcrumbs ground up fine, with a little ground rice to keep it dry...*And he grinned to himself once more in the darkness. He'd done it all himself with a pestle and mortar. Got the bloody stuff everywhere! But only he and the Baron knew that. And he chuckled to himself again, pushing the box carefully under his cloak as he did so.

Sort that lot out, get the girl away from The Lady as the Baron had planned, and into his waiting arms, letting her see him as a saviour, not an abductor...and who knows what might happen? Women are funny things, and 'love' can strike unbidden at any time...and the Baron can be truly charming!

197

Then, if all goes well, maybe he would give him Soraya for himself? That would be good, he'd always fancied her. Gorgeous body, lovely smile...*That'd be good on my pillow every morning!*

He lay back on the great bolster of woolfells that he had provided for himself and blew out the lamps, looking up at the stars, the sky full of them, a million, million lights blinking down at him from the soft, velvet darkness of the warm summer's night. And laying there, as he thought of Soraya beside him, he listened to the creak of the barge as she pulled at her moorings and the soft rushing of the river as it passed them by, the croak of a frog, the sudden quacking of a startled duck, the splash of a leaping fish in the river, a dog barking far away across the sleeping countryside, and he smiled.

Tomorrow they would reach Peyrehorade, then off the barge and onto horses again for the long haul to Carcassonne and home.

He thought of Najid and of Alicia...and The Lady's fury when, one day, she found them gone...*And get away they will; Lord Roger has charged me with fixing it! After Foix probably*...And he thought of the Baron's face when he'd get the pigeon message that they were on their way for him to 'rescue' her, and he laughed...*Now that would be worth seeing!*...and with that thought in his head he turned on his side and fell asleep.

*

And as the moon finally rose in all her silver splendour, The Lady Rochine de Brocas lay back in her cabin above him on a long quilted mattress of soft cotton, bolstered by the great pile of satin cushions she'd brought with her, dressed only in a short chemise of cream embroidered silk.

With her raven hair unbound around her head, and sipping a deep red Burgundy from a great silver-gilt goblet, she delicately picked honeyed dates out of a silver dish, unable to sleep, still seething with inward rage as she planned the death of the two women who had opposed her will that day: the Lady Alicia de Burley...and that *conne française*, Soraya Fermier, whom her father had given to her after he and the Archbishop had stolen all her family's lands...and she clenched her hands until they were white with suppressed fury!...*Those two I will have begging for mercy*....And that they surely would do before she was finished with them! As for that silly bitch, Agnes Fitzwalter?...*The Cousins can have her for their amusement!*...And as she dipped her long fingers in the wine to suck the honey off them, she smiled.

198

...Papa is such a fool at times!... He had planned the thing so carefully, but she had heard and seen almost everything! He had forgotten about the many secret spy holes around the Château from where she could watch him. She'd been doing it for years. First, goggle-eyed, when she had been a just a little girl, watching him making love with her mother...and then with the various whores who had gone to his bed...*until mother died and I finally took her place!*...and she giggled at how shocked her mother had looked when she had finally realised what she had done to her.

Killing her had been so simple!

And she wriggled her body sensuously, feeling fresh warmth flooding through her, making her whole body tingle...*And of course Stanisopoulos, the little Greek perfumier in Gruissan, is my creature of the night...That's what makes this all so delicious!*...And she laughed at her father's naivety, who should have known better. That's where everything had come from!...*So I knew all about the roots Papa gave de Vere, and how they had both set out to fool the little cook...*And she laughed again. Twice toasted bread crumbs ground up and put in a box indeed. *Bah!* They might trick a stupid Arab...but not her! And, of course she knew about 'Faridah'...his *'Precious Pearl'*...too. And she giggled softly...*I know everything...*But that particular beauty could wait. That would be a pleasure yet to come...*It is that conne anglaise I am really after!* And she snorted in disgust.

So she had bided her time and then, at the right moment, she had changed the stupid powdered crumbs for the real thing, that when sprinkled on their food would give them all a horrible death: a wicked combination of violent emetic, madness and paralysis! And she chuckled at her cleverness and her father's simplicity.

She sighed and gently caressed her breasts, flicking at her nipples beneath the sheer silk that covered them...*Mmmm, Such a shame they both have to die so soon. I would so like to 'play' with them first. Have some fun. Twist their flesh, pour hot wax on their breasts, shave them, thrash them, cut them 'til the blood flowed as much as their tears...*Anything to hurt them, make them cry out, beg for mercy as those two wretched sluts had done at Grise, trying to find out her secret, until she had slit their throats in a violent spray of blood that had spattered all over her naked body...and de Vere had later thrown them to the pigs!

She shivered at the delicious memory: at the horror on the girls' stricken faces, at the *feel* of her knife slicing into each neck so deeply, cutting right to the bone, the flesh springing open beneath her blade in a great bloodied yawn, their cries becoming helpless gurgles as the hot blood fountained over them

199

both…and the rough grating of her blade against their neck bones…and she giggled again, her eyes wide and staring, her thoughts running wild.

She smiled and sighed, and stroked her breasts more firmly, and then between her thighs, feeling her lips grow plump and wet…as she 'saw' in her mind the Frenchmen rape Alicia, while the other two *salopes* were forced to watch, their voices joining with her cousin's frantic screams. Before they also were seized, one after the other, held down on their hands and knees and well and truly *dog-fucked* like the stupid bitches they were!…*Oh…that would be so good!*…And she thrust her hands between her legs, curling up over them as they pierced her loins. Those two cousins on her cousin together?…and she laughed..*Yes!*

Then she shook her head. *"No!"* Not because she did not want them dead…but because she had not sampled the bitch herself while her father watched. He always liked that, to watch her fuck one of his whores with her favourite Roman harness before plunging into her himself…and she almost purred, rubbing her breasts with her hands at the thought of such fun together, feeling her nipples stiff beneath her silk shirt, peaking against the palms of her hands, before she stroked the lips of her wet loins with her long fingers…*Mmmmm…the girl has such a luscious body*…as she'd seen the night of the fire…*My Lord father will love it. Will love to thrust his strength into her again and again…as he does to me!*…and she moaned, feeling her body quiver at the very thought of him doing so…of them both together…of her and Alicia!…*Such magnificent breasts - better even than Soraya's, fuller, heavier…but so proud, so upstanding and thicker teats, longer!*…

And she squirmed amongst the satin cushions, feeling her loins open, her own breasts tighten under her questing hands, her dark nipples standing out like stiff soldiers on parade until every movement of her silk chemise was such a sharp agony that she had to tear it off. Tossing her head from side to side she moulded her breasts with her hands, squeezing them, milking them, grasping her swollen teats with her fingers and twisting them fiercely, drawing her breath in with a gasp as the pain lanced into her loins, pulling her breasts into tortured cones 'til the blood pounded and her nipples were almost swollen black with pressure…*And then…and then…I will sell her! For the price I have already agreed with Wazzim: six thousand bezants!*…And she cried out at the thought of it. Of all that money, and of how shocked Alicia would be to be sold! To be examined and tested. Her naked body abused by de Rombeau, her Enforcer, so that it would be in the very peak of condition before Wazzim…and she moaned at the delicious thought of it, of Alicia in such utter torment. And all the while she caressed her loins fiercely, pressing her hands into them until they were on fire yet soaking, as the fierce, rampant desire she so longed for rushed through her whole body.

And seizing her hard nipples between her thumb and forefinger, she rolled and crushed them even more fiercely, pulling her breasts upwards again into taut, swollen cones, shaking them as she did so, spiralling her emotions upwards as she moaned and tossed amongst the cushions, her whole body ragingly flushed with heat until suddenly her loins flooded at last.

Like a salmon leaping and twisting on a gaff, she jerked and spasmed violently, her whole body liquidising in violent heaves, gushing like a warm torrent, as with a great cry... muffled by the cushions she pressed against her face...the Lady Rochine de Brocas flew up amongst the stars, to float down softly into exhausted oblivion, as with a sigh her whole body relaxed and sleep finally claimed her, a sweet smile of satisfaction on her lovely face

Chapter 32…Najid's terrors break The Lady's spell.

La Bastide de Serou.
A tiny settlement of hardy folk, warm hearted and well satisfied with their lives under the Count of Foix, perched high on a long ridge with the Arize River foaming at its feet, that would lead them down at length to the walled town of Foix itself.

It was there by the river, way below the tiny village, that Soraya found Najid weeping. Sitting with his back to a rock overlooking the rushing water as it bustled under the old stone bridge, fast and clear this high in the hills, a plain wooden box in his hands, and his whole body shuddering with his sobs, as if his heart were breaking.

Soraya was appalled, and plumping herself down beside him she put her arms around him, speaking soft Arabic in her husky voice: "Najid! Whatever is the matter? Come tell me, I am your friend. You know, you can tell me anything," and she rocked him in her arms as she would a child. "Come. Sah! Sah! Little One. Nothing can be as bad as that, surely?"

"Oh, Mistress Soraya!" He stammered, his words broken by his sobs. "I-I can-not tell you. My sister…my p-poor little Fa-Faridah. S-She is all I have le-left. I cannot tell you. I-I can-not! They will…they will ki-kill me! They will take my-my Far-Faridah…and then I am sure they will ki-ll you…*all!* Oh-Oh *Allah!* H-help y-your so h-humble Servant!" And he turned and buried his head in her shoulder, his distress just too much even for words.

Holding the little man in her arms as she comforted him, Soraya looked out across the countryside, at the great hills all around them, and the thick forests…and away in the distance the high, snow-capped mountains of the Pyrenees that marked the boundary of Spain…and then back up towards La Bastide de Serou where they were bivouacked for the night; and she sighed.

*

They had left the little town of Saint Girons early in the morning two days before, all looking forward to journeying on to Foix, with its great castle on a huge knotty crag and a whole busy town to enjoy below its lofty battlements. Now, with a long day's journey still to go, they were encamped at La Bastide, the place being too small for any wayside inn worthy of the name.

But while setting up camp, Najid had slipped away without a word, and Alicia had sent her off to find him. For days he had seemed low about something, refusing to say what, even to Aquib and Aziz, his two giant companions. Next moment, while all had been busy, instead of preparing their evening meal he had disappeared, and while Alicia and the others had gone to search through La Bastide, Soraya, with her warm heart and her soft Arabic, had set off down a steep track to the river far below…and so she had found him at last.

Now here she was with him in her arms, rocking him like a baby as he wept into her shoulder. Najid, their dear little Arabic cook: small, slender with a shock of black curls, large brown doe-like eyes and a mouth made for smiles and laughter, but who had been like a stranger ever since they had stopped at the market in Saint Girons two days before. From light-hearted happiness and silly jokes to an almost silent figure, stark in his unhappiness and yet refusing to talk.

And now this!

Giving him a final hug, she pulled him to his feet and said briskly: "Najid. You are a very silly fellow. We have all seen how unhappy you have been these past few days, and now you talk about death! I have had enough of such nonsense. You are coming with me to the Lady Alicia now, and you will tell her everything!" She said firmly, giving him a shake. "*Everything!*"

"We all love you…and we love your cooking, and there is nothing that cannot be put right if we try. But no-one can help unless you tell us what the trouble is. I have had enough of rotten meals from you these past two days…so come on," she added, taking him by the hand and tugging him almost bodily up the hill. "This time you will tell us all!"

So, with the sun tilting down into the west, and the sky filled with gold and crimson bars, up the hill to the village they had gone, Najid snuffling miserably at her side, Soraya wondering what on earth had gone wrong this time?

*

*A*nd it was all so…wretched…so frustrating!
Since that awful struggle on the barge on the first day of their journey east towards Carcassonne and Gruissan, everything had actually settled down into a real spell of smooth travel and a fair truce between Alicia and her French cousin.

They had got off the river at Peyrehorade, with de Vere's men helping where they could, but after the brouhaha of the first day, giving quite a wide berth to Alicia and her small Household – her 'Company of the White Rose' - which seemed to please everyone.   Even The Lady Rochine had seemed delighted with their progress, though they were obviously slowed by the two large tilt carts they had found waiting for them, each pulled by two horses either side of a central yoke and loaded with all their goods, the wicker cages that held the Baron's pigeons right on the top of all so that the birds had plenty of air.

Every night their pigeon master, Almahdi the Syrian, would take each bird and examine it closely, holding it in the palm of his hand with firm gentleness, while he stretched out its wings, one by one, to test the muscles and check its flight feathers, feeling each bird's breast to be sure it was in perfect flying shape and weight…just as one would a hawk or falcon.

As a falconer would check his birds of prey's long legs and pounces - its sharp talons - so Almahdi checked each pigeon's legs for strength and fitness. For while it was the beautiful sickle shaped wings that gave each bird its speed, it was the legs that usually carried the vital messages.   And every bird was different: some for long haul, some for short; some for carrying weight more slowly…others ideal for the tiny, light brass message capsules and for enormous speed.   He also looked each bird in the eye to check for brightness and colour and to ensure there was no damage or scratch on each brilliant lens. And all the time he crooned to them and murmured soft words, just as they crooned and bobbed their heads back to him.

And they were all different colours: beautiful soft grey and white, slate grey all over with white wing feathers, white and a kind of ruddy orange…even almost dark blue with black wingtips, and some were white all over.

The girls were fascinated, and clustered round him to watch and gently stroke the beautiful breast feathers with their fingertips, and feel the taut strength in the wings as Almahdi stretched them out and showed what he was looking for in each of his winged Mercuries, while Soraya chattered to him in Arabic and they all laughed and giggled light-heartedly together.

Most days they had pushed on hard, adopting the long haul tactics of the military…Walk, trot, canter! Walk, trot, canter! Half of de Vere's men riding far ahead to check the way, the other half hanging behind to make sure no-one tried to make a break for it and so escape.   And where the roadway divided, or others joined it, two of his men, with their bows armed and ready, would dismount and watch them all go by before re-mounting and cantering forward to the next point along their way and the next beyond that.

Then there were lazy days when the men had gone hunting up into the hills for small game. Pheasants and rabbits, shoats still in their stripes...even two brace of geese on one occasion, bought from a smallholder up in the wilds somewhere. And on those days the girls had gone wandering themselves, sometimes to find mushrooms, sometimes to walk into the nearest village for fresh bread, or fresh fruit and vegetables, sometimes just to dangle their hot feet in a cool, rushing stream and watch the fish flashing by amongst the reeds and rushes. And always with either Aquib or Aziz in company to watch and guard their backs.

Then there were gold and azure days, when the sun shone bright from a cerulean sky and the air was as fresh and cool as chilled wine, as it so often is in the high lands close to great mountains that rear their snow-capped heights into the heavens. Brilliant days when eagles would sometimes soar out high, above them, or a more homely buzzard, twisting and turning in great up-draughts of hot air, their sharp screeing cries unmistakeable in the clear air of the high hills. Then the only thing to do was clap heels and gallop away up the track with shouts and laughter, giving de Vere's men nightmares of escaping prisoners as they chased after them, hurtling along at breakneck speed, only to find them all waiting by some vantage-point drinking in the view, chuckling and smiling at the men's fears and mocking their taut, sour faces when they caught up with them, as only girls can.

Even Rochine had joined them on two occasions, and for a moment both she and Alicia had laughed together at the sheer exhilaration of being young and beautiful and *alive* on a wonderful, fresh summer morning in the high foothills of the Pyrenees. Up here the streams cascaded off the hills in all directions, running fast and white, the water cold and fresh on their flushed faces when they stopped to water their horses, and delicious to drink from cupped hands, themselves cooled beneath the rushing flow, with the sun warm on their backs and the larks singing high up in the sky above them.

And all around was bursting with life: the green of wood and forest; or the distant patchwork quilt of strip fields heavy with wheat and barley; orchards of quince, rosy apples and apricots; peaches, plums and damsons...and small silver-grey groves of olives, black and green; and the dark twisted branches of cork oak that sometimes lined the trackway, their dark leaves hanging over them; small fields of purple lavender beyond. And dotted about up on the high pastures the white and mottled forms of sheep and goats with their clonking bells, and cattle too lower down, sometime bulling in the evenings when they were called in for milking, their deep cries echoing around the valleys.

The first time Rochine had joined them, Alicia had been quite startled, had even been about to speak when Rochine had suddenly realised what she was doing, her face had fallen and she had swiftly turned and walked away, head down, clambered into her high saddle and ridden back down the track.

Alicia had watched her go and sighed...*Now, that is the real sadness. It would be so easy to like her!...*The Lady was quick-witted and had a bright, gay spirit...*and I can see how she could be both loving and generous...just as Soraya said on the Morning Star...*And she was as well read as she was herself, with a wealth of experience that it would have been such fun to have shared...*And we are cousins...the only real family I have left since my parents died so many years ago. Even more so since Sir Yvo and lady Margaret were murdered...*And her eyes filled with sudden tears....*Bastards! Bastards!*

In different circumstances she was sure they would have been friends. But after what had happened at Malwood: that dreadful fire, the awful murder of Gui's parents by The Lady's father, his attempts to kill Gui, and her own actions that night towards her...such friendship was just impossible...*Bastards! How could they? That changed everything forever. Never can I forgive that. Never!..Bastards!...*

And now Rochine was her jailor anyway, so all that was left between them was a strange kind of 'armed' truce: Rochine would leave her alone...and she would not try to escape. And in God's Truth, she cursed silently, to where could they flee? And how?...They were almost in the middle of nowhere; three unarmed girls and three stray Arabs, only two of whom could fight! And mighty as Aquib and Aziz were...they could not fight all de Vere's men, half of whom were armed with bows.

And no man, no matter how big and strong he was, could take a bolt and stay upright for long. Look at what had happened to Gui? And the arrow that had struck him was tiny by comparison with a full size quarrel, especially one with a barbed hunting broad-head at its point!...*And where is he? Where is my Gui?...*And Sir Richard, and Father Matthew and all the other Lions whom she had set out with from home? Bones of the Saints...it was only a few weeks ago, yet it already seems like ages!...*Oh, my darling. I miss you so much. My heart can only take so much before it breaks!...*And she dashed away the sudden tears that had sprung unbidden to her eyes, making them glitter in the sunshine.

Are they even alive? She devoutly hoped and prayed so. She didn't 'feel' as if her belovèd Gui was dead...and she was certain she would *know!* That 'something' would tell her it was so...some dreadful lurch in her heart or sudden blackness of spirit would *tell* her she had lost him. And she had not felt that, yet, in any way. So she had still to believe and keep going...*But until when? Until the Château Grise? And the bloody Baron and his ghastly wedding plans? Until my cousin's wickedness gets the better of her and she really does try to kill me? Christos! What a dreadful tangle!...* How lovely to be Alexander the Great confronted with the Gordian Knot, who just took his sword and hacked the beastly great thing through in one great swipe of hardened steel and all his problems were solved!

And with another sigh of frustration, she had re-mounted and kicked on after her, determined that somehow they would get through all this without any further upheavals that would be likely to drive her cousin over the edge.

*

A nd now *this!*
Out of a clear blue sky, when everything seemed to be going so well...*this!* Some unknown terror about his sister that had so gripped poor Najid as to render him speechless with grief. And with a grunt of exasperation Soraya dragged the little man up the hill to find Alicia, and Aquib, and sort the whole beastly thing out!

Chapter 33...How Gaston de Vere ruined Najid's day.

Through Ortez, Pau and Tarbes they had ridden along the main roadway that led from Bayonne to Toulouse.

Staying in inns and small castles where they could, they had by-passed all travellers whom they met with studied indifference and forcefulness: packhorse trains, mounted armed guards close by; parties of pilgrims on their way to Saint James of Compostella; merchants on their way to Bayonne or Toulouse, beautifully dressed, with huge ox-drawn wagons of wine and olive oil; jongleurs, and acrobats in joyful groups, their clothes parti-coloured and often thick with bells; ladies in wimples and long capes, with their grooms by their sides; men trudging from town to town for work; scholars in black gowns; messengers on fast horses, thundering by in a blast of dust and fury...and young knights off to the wars in velvet caps brave with bright feathers, and flowing bliauts of orange, green and scarlet wool, embroidered with gold and silver, long capes billowing out from their shoulders and jewelled swords and daggers at their sides.

Sometimes on their own, sometimes in pairs, caracoling and titupping across the road in the joyous excitement of youthful high spirits, these young men boasted of the conquests they would make, the girls they would love and the enemies they would slay, often accompanied by small troops of armed men, brilliant in each family's blazon.

Then, at St Goudens they had cut across country to St Girons, across the ridges and along deep valleys that had seemed to twist all around them. Sometimes they clip-clopped alongside broad winding rivers, which in high summer were slower and lazier as they flowed towards the distant sea; not rushing wildly in a boiling mass of white foam as they were in the spring, when brown with silt and filled with melt water and spring rain, they made bridges dangerous and fords deadly. And sometimes they rode right across the very tops of high ridges from where it seemed you could see the whole world in a single glance: great vistas of open countryside, rolling wooded hills, great forests and simple patterns of vineyards, open fields of wheat and barley, broad pastures and tiny villages.

And so they had come at length to the town of Saint Girons, and its great stone bridge crossing the River Salat. Here the river was broad and deep, with shoals of great fish black and silver beneath the surface, fins and tails working to hold themselves almost motionless against the current, before dashing off to do the same thing further up the river, the sun sparkling off the rushing blue waters.

But as they approached the bridge of beautiful rose-coloured marble they found it was packed with people coming in for the Saturday produce market, bustling, jostling, chattering; every kind of food imaginable on the move towards the town, from live pigs and chickens, and goats on thick hempen cords, to fresh vegetables, scallions, shallots and lettuces, fruits of many kinds, strings and strings of smoked sausages, great bundles of herbs, cheeses, butter, breads...even costly spices in locked and painted caskets...everything.

Najid's eyes had lit up at the sight, and as soon as they had found a suitable inn, with space for their men and stabling for their horses, he had come running to Soraya to ask permission to go to the food-market that was even now taking shape amongst the tall plane trees that shaded the central square of the little town. And he had been boisterously excited, his Arabic so fast that even Soraya'd had to ask him to slow down, while Aquib stood by and smiled at the little man's enthusiasm for his cooking, and Aziz helped to field the pots and pans he had scattered off his packhorse in his burst of sudden enthusiasm.

"Mistress Soraya! Mistress Soraya! Did you see all those herbs and those chickens? And the fruit? Apricots as big as plums, peaches as big as..as big as my hand!" he had exclaimed, waving his hand at her and smiling. "And cherries and onions and beautiful bunches of red and orange carrots, celery too and fresh bread and butter in great crocks, and oil to cook with. I may even find some spices...and we need salt as well. Please, will you ask the La-dy Alic-ia if I may to the market go...and will she give me some silver as I have none left to buy with?" he had ended breathlessly, almost bouncing with excitement.

"What is all the to-do?" Alicia had asked laughing, coming up to them, seeing Najid almost hopping from one foot to the other.

"It is Najid, Alicia," Soraya said with a grin, laying her hand on his slender shoulders to calm him down. "He is most desperate for the food market; every Saturday here they hold it in Saint Girons. It is a market very good, I am told. And he has seen such lovely things for us, that he is most keen to go there, to see what he can buy, what bargains he can make. How for money are we today?"

"Oh, my Lady...Alicia," Agnes said pleadingly, her large hazel eyes wide as a fawn's. "This looks such a pretty place, and we have barely stopped anywhere for days. A market would be just lovely to go to today. Especially in all this sunshine, and the river and all those trees for shadow. I know we don't have much money, but I have a bit hidden and I know Sir Gui left you with some when we..we parted in Brest....Oh come on, Alicia," she pleaded, and seeing Alicia hesitate she took her hands and asked again, adding: "And Najid, needs things for us…and we need things for ourselves too!"

Alicia looked at all of them, at Najid, hopping about like a herring on a griddle, and at both Soraya and Agnes, their eyes shining, saying everything their mouths could not express half so eloquently…and she laughed again.

"Oh…very well! We will *all* go to the market, just as soon as Aquib and Aziz have finished sorting things out, and you too, my ladies," she added with a raised eyebrow. "Fun and games are lovely…but I don't want to come back to this inn and find our things in a mess. So bustle about and we'll meet here before the sun has passed the steeple.

"Soraya," she added, holding Najid back as Agnes hurried off. "Please tell Najid he must go to the market now…and not wait for us. I know all about markets, and some of the best things that he wants may be gone by the time you two have finished. I have a small purse of silver here which should be plenty. Gui also left me with a few gold coins as well…but they will not do here! Tell him to take a basket with him, and that if he can't find us amongst the stalls, we will meet him later…by the bridge we came across, by the time the sun is near the roof tops. Now, come on," she urged Soraya, as she spoke in swift Arabic to the little man, both laughing as he rushed to find a basket off one of the tilt carts, "Now…I simply must get out of these clothes!"

*

Unnoticed by everyone, all being so busy talking, Gaston de Vere, standing not twenty paces away in a deeply shaded doorway, had watched the whole little scenario play out before him: saw the little cook run off towards the tilt carts, and Alicia and Soraya turn back towards the inn, chatting happily together.

He grinned, his mouth crinkling in silent satisfaction, his eyes hooded. For some time he had been wanting to have words with that damned cook. But every time he had found the time to do so, the wretched man had either been with Soraya or Lady de Burley, or in company with the two huge men whom El Nazir had sent with Alicia to protect her. Now however, in the midst of this bustling, thronging market…and with his protectors all cheerfully busy elsewhere…now was the perfect time to put the frighteners on him…*give him a real belly trembler!*

Foix was the next substantial town and beyond that was truly wild country: sparse, tiny hamlets deep amidst thickly forested mountains; twisted

210

tracks, some little more than single trails; tangled open spaces, and even deep caves where broken people lurked and sheltered...*Foix will be the ideal place for flight, and if they know where they are going they can evade pursuit and capture until the last moment...and I know just where they should stay, and who will help them in that little town!*...And he smiled to himself, for it was exactly what he had planned with the Baron all those months ago!

Waiting until the girls had disappeared, he signalled with his eyes and a flick of his head to the Cousins who'd been waiting near an empty courtyard for his sign, before pushing himself away from the door he'd been leaning against and casually sauntered after Najid.

He, happily bouncing along amongst the stalls without a care in the world, beyond what to cook for dinner that night...the innkeeper pleased to hand over that responsibility for a change...was completely in a world of his own. A small Ali Baba basket strapped to his back for all the good things he was hoping to find, he was humming as he went, his dark brown eyes flashing with excitement and simple pleasure. So it was a terrible shock when he felt a tap on his shoulder, turned with a smile, expecting to see either the ladies or his two Arab friends...and found instead that he was looking up into the leering faces of Lucas Fabrizan and Jules Lagrasse, and found himself totally unable to speak.

"Here, you little *fucker!*" Lucas exclaimed harshly, grabbing him by the arm before he could bolt. "There's someone who wants a quiet word with you, you sodding little squit. So just come along with me and you'll be alright!" And he pulled him towards him, clamping his calloused hand over Najid's mouth so he couldn't cry out.

"*Ta'ala alaan!*" Jules growled at him, grabbing his other arm. "Come with me now! *Asre'!*...Hurry up!" and together they picked the little cook up under his arms and strode swiftly with him through the crowds to where the Baron's big Guard Commander was waiting in a grimy wine booth down a shaded side alley at one edge of the market, some stoups of wine in tin beakers and a dozen tired slices of soft cheese on a red glazed platter before him on a small table. And dumping their captive on a coarse wooden bench that lay against one side wall, the Cousins picked up the beakers de Vere had left for them and loomed over their prize, full of evil intent.

"Well, well, well," de Vere grated at Najid in his rough, accented Arabic, a wide grin on his heavy face, while the little man trembled, terrified, like a tethered goat before a tiger.

"Look who you've found, boys? How good of you to drop by. And so unexpected...especially as I have been wanting to have a quiet word with you for some time, laddie," he snarled, poking Najid in the chest with one hard

211

finger, while he looked into the little Arab cook's quivering face, his eyes wide with fear, before adding quietly: "It's about your sister, Najid, your little 'Far-i-dah!'" he said, annunciating every syllable with exaggerated care, and he grinned wolfishly as he saw the frightful shock that rushed across the little man's face. His soft words draining the colour from it till Najid looked washed out, almost grey with the horror of hearing those words from his mouth…almost fainting with it as he slumped back against the wall like a half empty sack of barley.

"Now, Najid," de Vere growled quietly, after Lucas had slapped him about to bring him to his senses. "You love your sister don't you? Don't want the aunt to kick her out, do you?" he went on remorselessly, watching Najid wobble about on the bench, nodding his head all the time, too terrified to speak. "That sour old witch. No! 'Course not. Don't want the old bat to go to El Nazir, do you? Ask him to sort her problem?" He snarled at him then, pushing his face almost right up against Najid's nose 'til the little man's eyes fluttered in his head, while Lucas smacked his face again, and Jules kept guard at the entrance to the booth.

"No, Master! No…please. Do not hurt my sister!"

"Hurt your little sister? Me? Do I look like a monster?" the big man said leaning back against the wall. "No, Najid. Not me," he hissed, thrusting his wolfish grin at him…"*The Lady!*"

"*No!…No!*" Najid gasped, his hands scrabbling in his lap, even his feet shaking. "*No!*…she will do terrible things to her. People talk, Master. I have heard. Please, I am a poor man. I have nothing to give you. No money. Nothing. Wh..what do you w..want?" he stammered desperately as de Vere leaned closely towards him. "I w..will do anything! *Anything!*"

"Now…isn't that good to hear, lads?" de Vere said, sitting back again and looking up at Jules and Lucas with a satisfied smirk on his face. "How loving! This poor lad will do anything for his little sister. Isn't that sweet? Ahhh!" And they all laughed, the sound harsh and brutal. Then, tapping the little cook on the shoulder, he grinned into his terrified face and in his harsh voice he snarled softly: "That's just what we wanted to hear, Najid. Isn't it, boys?" and he tapped him on the shoulder again. "Anything, Najid?" he queried heavily. "Rather than have me talk with El Nazir and The Lady about your little problem 'baby'? Anything? Yes?" He asked again of Najid, the little man's head bobbing frantically as he spoke. "She's just the right age now for The Lady to be interested in her. Your Far-i-dah…your '*Precious Pearl!*'"

And de Vere sat back and grinned again, as the tears sprang to Najid's eyes, and he bent his head forward and cried, his shoulders shaking. Then sitting back he dashed his hand across his face, eyes reddened and said limply,

utterly defeated: "Anything, Master. For my Faridah, anything! *I promise!*"
And he slumped back against the wall, exhausted.

"Right...now you listen carefully, my lad," de Vere said briskly, leaning forward again, his big face almost against the little cook's in his intensity. "And your little lass will be as safe as a castle in a storm," and reaching into the bag at his waist, he took out a small wooden box.

And while the two Frenchmen took up guard outside the booth, having kicked the owner out with a few well-chosen words and the threat of serious damage to himself and his wine booth if he didn't: '*Fucking, hop off!*' for a moment...Gaston de Vere told Najid exactly what he expected him to do.

Chapter 34...The Company of the White Rose decides to flee.

So...just as de Vere had predicted that long ago night on the barge... between bouts of sobbing and broken sentences, and with encouragement from everyone, Najid 'blabbed'...told them all he knew, and all that had happened to him at St Girons, while Aziz took his turn to stand guard outside their covered bivouac.

And as the little man's tale unfolded an intense feeling of anger, and dismay, flooded out from those who were gathered there that warm summer's night. An anger displayed in growls of suppressed rage, small cries of horror and clenched fists for what had been said and done to Najid...and dismay for its implications, and the added distrust that it would now mean between themselves and the Lady Rochine de Brocas.

A distrust only heightened when Najid finally showed them the box he had been given, and the black and cream speckled powder it contained, with its dark tangy odour and its promise of uncertainty at The Lady's hands.

Alicia looked at the powder in the box and shivered, goose pimples suddenly appearing along her arms...*Forgetting powder? Poor Najid. What was he to know of such things? What do I, come to that? But whatever it is...it is not going into anything we might eat...*If her cousin had had anything to do with it, it was safer to treat it like the poison it probably was. Try it on a passing stray dog if they ever found the time; meanwhile she would keep it safe! And without a word, her eyes slitted with disgust, Alicia took the box from him and held it closed tightly in her lap.

In the golden lamp light beneath the canvas sheeting over their camp-site, with the stars bright overhead, sparkling in the cool clear air of the mountains, the moon rising in glorious silver splendour, just a few days off being full, they sat on cushions and leaned back against their saddles. Wine to hand and light blankets around them against the cool night, they had listened as if spellbound as Nijad's tale of St Girons unfolded, and then finally came to an end, his voice trailing off into a profound silence; each one of them thinking about the full meaning of all that they had heard.

Soraya moved first to comfort poor Nijad, standing utterly dejected, tears in his eyes not just for his sister whose life was still in such danger, but also because of what he might really have done if he had been alone...and not with people whom he had come to care for, and who cared for him!

214

Then, as her face relaxed, Alicia had looked to them both, and smiling at Najid for encouragement, she spoke the words everyone was expecting: "Well…that's it! That's enough! We made a kind of bargain, my sweet cousin, 'The Lady', and I. She wouldn't raise a hand against me, nor any of my Household…and we wouldn't try to escape. But if she thinks I am going to sit by and do nothing while she uses her power to terrify one of my people into a possible act of mass murder with this 'stuff'…and God knows what it really contains? Then she doesn't know who she's up against!"

It was with an act of supreme force of will that she didn't hurl her goblet and the wooden box of powder into the night she was so angry. "That double-dyed, murderous, black hearted, wicked *bitch!*" And then she really did swear: "*Cette conne française!* Urrrgh! And to think I almost liked her! God preserve my sanity…but I could *murder* her!" And she gasped, her hand to her mouth, as she realised what she had said.

"So, my lady," Aquib rumbled at her, as she collected herself. "What do we do now?"

"Well…we can't fight them, Aquib," she said resignedly. If we had some bows we might have given that some thought…but we don't and none of us are trained in their use anyway. So…if we can't fight them…then we must run from them, and as fast and as far as we can before they find us missing."

"But where to, Alicia?" Soraya asked. "We are in the middle of nowhere here, and we have no friends nearby."

"And no-one knows where Sir Gui is," Agnes said quietly.

"Or even if he is still alive," Alicia finished for her, looking across at her with a sad smile. "I know, sweetheart. I know that *I* believe he is still alive, somewhere…*God keep you safe my darling*…but it isn't as if we can just set out to find him, as we have no way of knowing where to look. And I'm not forgetting your Allan either, Honeyone," she added as Agnes looked up at her anxiously.

"So, where, my Lady?" Aquib rumbled again.

"And when?" Soraya asked. "For once she finds Najid has failed them, they will surely kill us all anyway…and say it was outlaws or bandits!"

"Well," Alicia said, drinking from her goblet before shuffling her back up against her saddle. "And forgive me for this, because you will all think I have gone completely mad, but the only place we *can* run to, where we will truly be safe…and where Gui will *know* where to find is…"

"…Is to *Monsieur le Baron* in the Château Grise!" Soraya interrupted, her voice almost soundless.

"Yes! The bloody, murdering old bastard himself," Alicia said through gritted teeth...*Sweet Jesus, but I can think of nothing else that might keep us safe!*

"You *are* mad! "Agnes exclaimed, appalled. "After all that man has put us through, to throw ourselves on his mercy now seems...seems completely insane, my love. You have bats in your belfry!"

"No, Mistress Agnes," Aquib said calmly in his deep, gravelly voice. "Forgive me...but the Lady Alicia does not have the madness. She is right. Only the Baron can control his daughter. Our Prince said so. Only the Lord Baron can protect you all. Right now The Lady is racked with jealousy, and is acting without thought or reason. So she is doubly dangerous. Sadly, Aziz and I cannot fight all these men together, as the Lady Alicia has already said, much as we would like to. But they are armed with bows, and bows of great power...so we must run. And, as your lady has just said, there is only one place we can run to...and that is to the Baron's Château at Gruissan."

"*Sweet Jesus!*" Agnes exclaimed, horrified. "What may that man not demand in return for all of that?" she asked, her face suddenly drawn.

"What indeed, Agnes?" Alicia said, looking at her grimly over the rim of her goblet. "Let us hope it is not such a price as we cannot easily pay, because if he rescues us from this deadly peril...he will have earned it!"

"Well," Soraya said a little sharply. "You may be right in that, Alicia, but while *Monsieur le Bar-on* may be many things that are bad...you can at least reason with him. But his daughter? The Lady? She is of all things the most different! With her you cannot reason once she is started. If we are to flee...and I am sure that Alicia and Aquib are right in that, then it is to the Château we must go, if only because Lord Roger is the only one who can control The Lady when she gets like this. But then how are we to do it? And when? We are foreigners here, with no knowledge of where to go; no map and we can only go with what we can carry. And very little money!"

"Well," Alicia said quietly. "Actually money is the very least of our problems. Before Gui left us at Brest to board the *Mary*, he gave me a money belt..."

"But there was nothing like that on you when you were brought on board the *Morning Star*," Soraya interrupted, astonished. "I searched you myself."

"No...it was stitched inside my armoured jacket, which Aziz rescued for me before we left the *Morning Star* five or six days ago. Agnes did it, with Father Matthew's help. He is one amazing monk, that man....and don't have a go at Agnes," she added, as everyone turned to stare at her, now with her head down and blushing. "She was sworn to secrecy, and there are few oysters as close as my loving Agnes," she went on, throwing her a beaming smile.

216

"So…knowing that El Nazir would not just throw anything of such good use away, I guessed it must be somewhere safe and it was, hanging in the armoury. And, '*Insh'a Allah*'!" she exclaimed softly with a smile and a subtle nod to Aquib and Najid. "There should still be a hundred and fifty golden bezants hidden within it…" And everyone just gasped, for in very truth it was a huge sum of money.

"No wonder it was so heavy, my Lady," Aquib said with his quiet grin. "Because it was to me that Aziz gave it after Mistress Soraya had changed you."

"Thank you, Aquib. Agnes, can you bring it to me please?" she asked her friend with another dazzling smile. "It is in the bottom of the clothes chest that came off the *Morning Star*…beneath yours, which Aziz also rescued for me. So…Soraya," she said grinning at everyone's confusion, as Agnes bustled off. "How are you with sums? One bezant at home is equal to two silver shillings, and there are twelve silver pennies in each silver shilling. So…how many silver pennies does that give us for our one hundred and fifty gold bezants?"

"Plenty, my Lady," Aquib said with a laughing growl, watching the tortured look on Soraya's face as she struggled with the strange figures, while Agnes brought in Alicia's armoured jacket; handing her a small pair of beautifully made spring shears as she did so.

"See!" Alicia crowed softly after snipping at the back of it. "My money belt!"

And pulling out a long canvas belt into which had been stitched tiny pockets, each one containing a hard disk, she looked around at everyone and with a great smile she cut one open and squeezed out a beautiful golden coin that simply glowed with rich, fat colour in the soft lamp light. "*See! Abracadabra! One golden bezant!*" and she held it out on the palm of her hand for all to see.

"But I'll not take out any more…that'd be the quickest way to start losing them. But they are all there, and that actually gives us…*three thousand six hundred silver pennies!*" And she was delighted with the further gasps and looks of complete amazement on all their faces. "So, as I said, money is not really the problem! And as for the 'when' you have asked me?…then…" she hesitated, looking round at them for a moment. "Then…I think we must leave from Foix; in three mornings' time. But we need a proper journey plan and a good map!" she added as they flustered at her decision. "So, tomorrow, when we get there and have settled in for the night…and we are not going up to the castle so de Vere tells me…which I hear is magnificent…

"…Why not to the castle, my Lady?" Soraya interrupted.

"Because, Mistress Soraya," Aquib chipped in with his dark, rumbly voice. "The Lady would have to answer a lot of very awkward questions about you all to the Count of Foix, who is no fool, or to his Seneschal in the Count's absence…and neither are lovers of her father either. The Count supports the Crusade ,which the Baron has refused to go on…and he is neither deaf nor blind to what goes on in Gruissan."

"You are well informed, Aquib?" Alicia said, surprised.

"I am a good listener, my Lady," he chuckled deeply. "With Sheik El Nazir, you learn to be!"

"As I have learned to be also, with The Lady!" Soraya exclaimed softly. "As I told you all on the *Morning Star*."

"Well, that is actually better for us, isn't it?" Alicia said looking around at them. "Getting away from a town with lazy town guards is infinitely easier than getting out of a powerful castle with sealed gates and efficient professionals to keep them safe. No, my friends, outside the castle is infinitely better, and if we can find good stabling for our horses near the ford out of Foix, then so much the better.

"Anyway, once we are well settled in we can all go into town, and have a thorough mooch about the place. So, keep your eyes sharp and ask questions. And we will need tougher clothes than these to flee in. Leather kirtles, chausses and jackets and simple woollen cloaks at least; all sorts of things I expect. We have to get to Carcassonne and onto the main roadway, the old Via Aquitania that runs from Narbonne to Bordeaux. Once on that and we should be safe from outright attack, and away from these small roads and distant country places…yet we will also have to go across wild country to escape easy pursuit…and to get there.

"One thing is for certain…the moment we are missed there will be a frightful uproar, and de Vere and his men will be on us like wolves after sheep. If we set off up any main trackway, they will have us as quickly as chasing deer at home with a pack of rache hounds!" At that moment Aziz put his head around the wide canopy that had been stretched over their bivouac. "Be warned! There's movement over by The Lady's encampment. Some men are leaving and De Vere is arranging his guards."

"Right, Aziz," Alicia said quietly. "Council of War over." And turning to Aquib, she touched his arm: "It is your turn to take over the watch: Aziz must rest. But call us if there is anything you are concerned about. He will relieve you later. And remember," she added to them all. "Tomorrow, we do everything exactly as normal. Everything, and Najid, you must continue to be miserable," she gestured with a long face as if her eyes were weeping. "Because for certain they will be watching your every mood. Especially de

Vere and those two bloody Frenchmen…so if he suddenly becomes cheerful again," she said to Soraya, "they will surely smell a rat and we will lose the advantage. So make it clear to him, please.

"And all of you…don't get caught in dark corners when we get to Foix…stay in pairs! That was always Gui's advice to his lads whenever they found themselves in an unknown place. Soraya, tell Najid he is to stay with either Aquib or Aziz at all times…and he is to decide what he must take with him when we go, and what he can most easily leave behind. And remember, I have that box of powder which we will need to keep hold of until we can give it over to the Lord bloody Baron himself in Gruissan! Now…sleep all of you. We have a lot to do tomorrow. I don't know about you?" she said to them with a weary smile and a stretch of her shoulders. "But I am feeling exhausted!"

Chapter 35...Foix!

Foix!
A lovely, ancient walled town nestling in the space between two rivers, the Ariège and the Arget: the Arget on the western side of the town, crossed by an old wooden bridge below the castle; the Ariège on the east side by a ford close to the ancient Benedictine abbey church of Saint Velusien that had stood there for nearly three hundred years.

Both crossings had their own gateways into the town and abbey through the walls where they ran beside the two rivers; and to the south, facing Spain, where lay the greatest danger of a swift attack, a further long battlemented wall, with its own strong gateway, that ran back to join up with the town's western entrance below the great castle of the Counts of Foix. High on its massive pinnacle of rock, its twin towers linked by curtain walls and surrounded on two sides by foaming water, the great fortress was impregnable, and had dominated the town and countryside since the Romans first built there over a thousand years before.

Battlemented town and castle; abbey, church and bustling market...truly Foix was a little gem.

The narrow, winding streets of shops and timbered houses, their red pantiles glowing in the evening sunshine, were broken up by little squares with trees scattered amongst them for shade and beauty, stone benches to sit on and a lovely open square next to the ancient abbey church of St Velusien. Here, every Wednesday, it was packed with traders, farmers, pedlars and local villeins come in to sell their wares, a market so popular it spread out amongst the twisted streets around the abbey church, and would be held the second day following their arrival.

Lady Alicia de Burley, paused on the high ridge overlooking the long valley that led to the distant town, was breathless both with the view and the excitement of their coming escape. From where she was seated on her horse, she could see for miles: great rising ridges dark with forests, and a wild panorama of distant mountains and twisted valleys, blue smoke from the tiny settlements hidden amongst them winding upwards, and nearby the flash of sunlight off the two rivers between which Foix had been built. And far to the south the vast high mountains of the Pyrenees, snow-capped and shining, that marked the barrier between the lands of the Franks and those of Moorish Spain.

High up above the town, its crenellated walls seemingly built into the very rocks themselves, stood the mighty fortress of the Counts of Foix, its two great square towers rearing up into the summer sky, just as they did on the Count's own Great Seal. With the massive mountains of the high Pyrenees far to the south, their snowy peaks just glinting in the evening sunlight, it was like an eagle's eyrie, from where the Count of Foix, Raimond-Roger II and his lovely wife, Philippa of Montcada, could view all that moved for miles around them.

*

All day they had travelled along the high ridge on which La Bastide de Serou had sprung up, stopping only for food right on its crest, and to enjoy the fresh breezes that flowed around it, cool as the great mountains away to the west from whence they came. A welcome contrast to the crushing heat of high summer, that all around them had burned the grasses brown. Alicia and her little Household fed on what Najid could find for them, and The Lady Rochine and her guards on supplies that de Vere had gathered from the tiny auberge before they had left that morning.

With his troops ranging both far ahead and behind the tilt carts, and Almahdi staying close to the Baron's precious pigeons, de Vere had kept everyone moving at a steady pace, so it was just as the sun was beginning to slide down the heavens, that they had come at last to the old wooden bridge across the Arget. From there it was just a step to the stone gatehouse that guarded the western entrance to the town, as a gatehouse had done since the Romans first fortified the place when Caesar's legions carried their eagles through all of ancient Gaul.

On that Monday evening, still glowing with late sunlight, warm and golden, dappled with lengthening shadows, the townsfolk were already walking out to take their ease in the cool of the evening after a long day in the town's busy streets. And while the river slipped by in one long crystal stream beneath the great timbers that carried the bridge, bubbling and frothing amongst its piers, the handful of guards who lazed near the archway, their long spears propped against the warm stonework, chatted with them happily.

Others Foixians paused to look down into the clear flowing waters of the river to watch the ducks. Lovers strolled hand in hand, or leaned over the bridge sides to watch the fish that swam and darted in the crystal waters. Still others, with children and hounds at heel, walked and gambolled along the wide river bank, pleased to be away from the close, hot air within the narrow streets, rejoicing at the end of yet another hectic day…with all the excitement of the Wednesday market still to come.

Nothing could have appeared more peaceful as Gaston de Vere, The Lady Rochine and his whole command, pigeons and all, clip-clopped and rumbled over the bridge with a casual wave to the guards lounging there; just another small party of travellers coming for the Wednesday market. Yet despite the seeming calmness of their demeanour, there had already been a further violent clash of wills between Rochine and Alicia over arrangements for their brief stay in Foix, which had come just as they were setting out.

*

"So! Almost packed and ready I see, cousin?" Rochine had sneered, sidling her horse close to where Alicia was helping Agnes and Soraya to sort out some of their things, while Aquib and Aziz loaded up their tilt cart and Najid packed his panniers ready to move off.

"Well, Rochine," Alicia had replied tersely, looking up at her cousin, her hands on her hips. "You have twelve men to run about and do your bidding. I have three, including Najid, who is as sulky as a bear just now - I have no idea why - and is almost worse than useless," she added, looking sideways at her cousin's face. "So I think we have done rather well. By the way, I understand we are not staying beneath the Count's roof tonight. Why is that? We have stopped in far smaller castles than Castle Foix before now. And it is supposed to be magnificent."

"It does not suit me to do so!" Rochine had stated baldly. "We shall stay in *L'Auberge du Rocher*…the Rock Inn. It is spacious and I have stayed there before with my father. There will be no problems about rooms. And we will all stay together there. I cannot allow you to be on your own in the town. It would cause comment."

Alicia looked up at Rochine sitting comfortably on her mare, looking self-possessed and supremely conceited and had an almost irresistible urge to seize her elegant booted foot and pitch her straight out of her saddle onto her elegant pleated backside! Instead she simply said dangerously: "Cannot allow? You dare dictate to me? No!"

"No?" Rochine said astonished. "You will not comply?"

"Comply? No, cousin! I will not 'comply'!" she answered tersely with a toss of her head. "I do not intend to stay anywhere nearer to you and your men than I can throw a stick! Foix is a very well organised, smart little town, and

222

though its ruler may not be present, as I can see no house flag waving above the castle, his Seneschal certainly will be. If you will not accede to my request for separate accommodation, I will instruct Aquib to accompany me directly to the castle and throw myself on his mercy."

"The Seneschal of Foix? Hubert Le Grange? That old fool!" her cousin mocked her, her eyes twitching sideways at Alicia. "My father bought him years ago. Why else do you think we are here? He will not lift a finger to help you!"

Alicia looked at Rochine and shook her head. "I do not believe you, cousin. The Count has a reputation for straight dealing, fidelity and honour. No man such as you suggest would last in his Household for five minutes. And if not the Seneschal...then there is always the Abbot! Mother Church would not turn down anyone who could claim the Holy Father's protection!"

"*Fough!*" Rochine snorted with disgust. "Now *you* lie! You have no such protection. You were searched, remember...to the skin, cousin; which is as wrinkled as an old prune and as withered as your parts!" she snarled. "The Abbot would not let you near him."

"Try me!" Alicia said in deadly earnest. "Just try me...and we will see who lies and who tells the truth."

"You would not *dare!*" Rochine ground out through gritted teeth, her face suddenly fierce with anger. "I would have de Vere seize you immediately. You would not get twenty paces."

"And what then...*cousin?*" Alicia sneered at her. "The moment you try to do that, Aquib and Aziz will defend me. Your men are no match for them at any price...they will be slaughtered."

"No...they won't. If those two infidels draw their swords, or attack my men, I will have them both shot!" Rochine snapped back, flourishing her whip, making her horse rear its head and shuffle its hooves. "And you, I will have bound in chains as I have always wanted."

"My men shot? Me in chains?" Alicia laughed at her, arms akimbo, eyes flashing. "Then what, my *so* clever cousin?" she sneered at her again. "This is no wild, empty countryside, Rochine, where such vile murders might be hidden," she railed at her, waving her arms around her expressively. "See, this is a well-travelled trackway in a well-ruled land...and murder will out! Two arrow-riddled bodies in the Count of Foix's domains, and one English noblewoman, Royal ward to King Richard of England, in chains to the Baron Roger de Brocas's daughter? I think not!....*She really is mad if she thinks like that!*...And what on God's Earth would you say to the Seneschal about *that*, my fair Lady? And when his men arrest you for bringing death into his town, what then? Do you think I will stand there mute? And how will you explain their deaths to your father? And to Sheik El Nazir? You, dear cousin, are an arrant *fool!*" And she laughed up at her, one eye on her booted feet, while Rochine almost foamed at the mouth with frustrated rage.

"Don't you *dare* laugh at me you...you *bitch!*" she hissed down at her venomously, whisking her hand up to strike at her with her whip, immediately pausing to lower it again as she saw both huge Arabs take a determined pace towards her. "Fine!" she snarled viciously, then wrenching her horse's head round as she spoke. "Have your wretched accommodation then, if you can find any at this late stage in the day. Wherever you please. It is *nothing* to me what gossip you arouse with your dusky Arab followers. But you still have to get to my father *cousin!* And *I* rule him, Not you, my *sweet!* And one day...one day, I promise you, I will give you the thrashing you deserve!"

And viciously twisting her horse around, she thrust in her heels, pulled the poor beast onto his hind feet, spun him around and thundered off, while Alicia mocked her back with a brazen: "Oo Hoo!" and a sway of her body, with her hands on her hips, such that all her Household laughed.

"My Lady, you push her too hard," a harsh, gravelled voice quietly admonished, and Gaston de Vere pushed his horse forward from behind her. "The Lady is not used to being crossed...and she is not easily reasoned with," he added. "There is only one man who can control her...and he is not here. Be advised, Lady Alicia de Burley. Do not lock horns with The Lady. That way always leads to bitter sadness." And with a shake of his head, and raised eyebrows, he gave her a look almost of pity and then, after a pause, to her complete astonishment, he leaned over her and said softly: "*L'Auberge de L'Abbaye*...The Abbey Inn, is said to be very good," and with a slight bow, and sardonic smile, he turned and cantered slowly away, leaving all three girls open-mouthed.

Chapter 36...How the Company escaped from Foix.

T wo mornings later and Alicia and her small Household were ready to leave at first light by the ford that ran across the Ariège from just below the abbey. From there they would turn up river and travel south towards Tarascon-sur-Ariège and the Spanish border, away from the main route north to Carcassonne and Toulouse, and from there into the wilderness beyond.

Here, they had learned, a narrow trackway ran right beneath the huge escarpment that loured over the town and then stretched eastwards for miles across the broken countryside. A narrow twisty trackway it was, little more than a broad cattle trail, hidden by trees and bushes and known to few, that linked a tiny string of spring-line villages with Foix. And a good day's journey along which lay the village of Roquefixade, their first stopping point.

There the village was overlooked by a remote stone fortress built on the very crest of huge limestone cliffs, where eagles flew and only mountain goats could find a way.

From Roquefixade they would journey through the edges of the great Corret Forest, completely by-passing the usual roadway by miles and miles...and then away towards Lavalenet, Chalabre and Limoux. And from there into the wild forested mountains that shielded far distant Carcassonne, their first goal that lay astride the ancient Via Aquitania that would carry them safely to Narbonne and so to the Château Grise, the Lord Baron Roger de Brocas's feudal home at Gruissan.

*

I t had been a day and a half of intense activity carried out under the very noses of de Vere and the Lady Rochine's guards; when bit by bit they had gathered all the things they needed into the large room that Alicia had hired in a small inn close to the ford itself, opposite the open square on the south side of the lovely stone abbey church of St Velusien, where the market would be held, the many stalls and booths spilling into the narrow streets all round it.

Close by, the walls of the town curled towards the stone gatehouse that guarded the eastern ford across which everything moved, goods, animals and people, both to visit the abbey and to enter the town itself. While this was nothing like the great gatehouse that guarded Castle Malwood, it was sufficient for Foix; for the walls were thick, the ashlar smoothly laid, and all properly crenellated, the merlons rising strongly above the wide parapet walkway that stretched around them. The defences were completed round the northern end of the town by the abbey walls themselves as they curved past the confluence of the two rivers. And to the south, she glimpsed the further battlemented wall that ran between the two rivers, with a stout gatehouse midway along it to protect the entrance to the city, and the great southern highway that ran through it, from any possible attack from Spain, still held by the Moors at that time.

Alicia, viewing the defences as a whole, as Gui had taught her, sighed. Altogether it was a really tidy little town, only somehow they would have to get out of it, and Alicia silently thanked the Good Lord that indeed they were not in the castle.

She smiled.

Clearly the place was confident of its own safety, otherwise the town guards would have been much more circumspect towards any travellers entering its walls, market or not... but they had been relaxed and sloppy as she had suspected they would be, employed by the town rather than by the Count himself...*They should be grateful that they are not at Castle Malwood, Sir Richard would have had them hopping about in no time!*

Castle Foix, however, would have been a very different matter altogether, with guards and careful checking everywhere...*Not good. And it is just as well the Count is not at home, because he would have been bound to have wanted to meet with us, and as he is allied to the Count of Toulouse, himself an ally of de Brocas and no friend of King Richard's either, we might well have ended as hostages to his favour...and I might never get back home.*

Better Lord Roger de Brocas, from whom she might escape, than the Count of Toulouse from whom such a thing would not be possible at all!...*God willing, the town guards will be just as relaxed and sloppy on Wednesday morning?*...And armed with that thought she had made her way back to their inn.

*

L'Auberge de L'Abbaye...was typical of the town: red pantiles, white plastered stucco on lath between tough oak frames and built on two floors, the second storey leaning out over the ginnels that ran between the other houses and over the church square with its drainage channel down the sides running towards the river. There was a small set of stables, hay barn and outhouses, with well and kitchens at the back, and the usual midden in a far dark corner.

After what de Vere had said, there had been quite a free discussion amongst them, with much general dismay and complete amazement that so kindly a suggestion could have come from such an unexpected source. It was as if a wolf had shown a sheep how to escape his pointed teeth!

And while Rochine and her party had settled into the Rock Inn almost beneath the castle, as she had said, they had tried to find a different place to stay other than that suggested by de Vere. But in vain, as with the market opening early on the Wednesday morning, almost everywhere else was full. So, in the end, the Abbey Inn it had had to be, and Alicia was surprised to find a large room still available for herself and her two ladies, and good stabling for her horses and room for her three men.

But it had been quite strange, too, because Monsieur Gérard, the *aubergiste*, unlike the other innkeepers she had approached in Foix, had been surprisingly willing to deal with Alicia and her companions…almost as if he had been expecting them! Not seeming to find it odd that three such ladies of obvious quality should be out on their own. Indeed, it was only when his doorway had actually been darkened by the appearance of Abdul and Aziz behind her that he had appeared truly startled. As Soraya said laughing to the others later, she had heard one local merchant say to the innkeeper with a broad smile: 'By God's Teeth, Gérard. It looked as if the tower of Saint Velusien itself had walked into your bar today!"

But at least the place was theirs to command, and they did not continuously have to check on Rochine's whereabouts, because she came with de Vere to check on theirs; sweeping in behind him later that evening, two of his men left outside as guards. Wearing a long cloak of azure damask lined with sky blue sarsenet, its very hem weighted with discs of gold and silver, and pinned to her shoulders by great ouches of burnished gold, the centre of each holding an enormous garnet, she was the very image of arrogant hauteur.

Seeing the surroundings Alicia had chosen she laughed with derision, even more so when she saw the people amongst whom her cousin had been forced to stay: visiting pedlars and common market traders, and several farmers with special produce to sell like cheese, pâté de sanglier and foie gras for which the area was famous.

"My dear cousin," she had mocked. "How positively rural! And the smell…so disgusting. Of swine and the byre…and no bathing facilities either, I should think!" And she gave a tinkling laugh that reeked of utter disdain. "But then it is no wonder you are happy here, cousin," she had said, turning to Alicia with an angelic smile, adding with dripping venom. "So like that pigsty my father and I had to endure at Malwood…just asking to be burned down, don't you think? Along with the common farmers who owned it!"

And smiling at the rage that suddenly suffused Alicia's face, she ignored her cousin completely while Aquib seized Alicia's shoulders in a vice-like grip to prevent her attacking her, watched by Rochine with a curling lip from beneath an arched eyebrow, and a smug smile that Alicia just itched to smash off her mocking face, before turning away with a shrug of elegant disdain to de Vere: "Post two of your men to watch this…this *midden*, and the three fat sows within it! They are to report to you morning and evening." And she had swept out again, leaving Alicia more angry than distressed, tears flooding into her hands as she buried her face in them and wept, the pain of Rochine's vicious comments about the murder of Gui's parents sweeping over her…while Agnes and Soraya rushed to comfort her.

But the *aubergiste* and his plump wife, Mathilde, who'd heard what had been said, did their best to make up for Rochine's wickedness with small kindnesses of their own and much understanding, and the food had been good…food they could all eat and enjoy And that last night a delicious lamb ragout had been served, with green vegetables, shallots and some of their precious rice that Alicia persuaded Monsieur Gérard to allow Najid to cook for their final meal before leaving; followed by a wonderful deep peach and apricot pie and custard from Mathilde, who had beamed at them when she had presented it.

That last day the girls and Aquib had scoured the little town for more suitable clothes to wear: leather hats and chausses against the rain that could come sweeping down the mountains, tougher boots, warm cloaks and woollen chemises against the cold mists and sudden thick fogs that were sometimes a problem in the high lands, even in summer, where cool air off the mountains met the warmer air off the land. Meanwhile Aziz and Najid sorted things out at the inn, and kept de Vere's two guards busily occupied with all their comings and goings until the two wretched men had no idea who was doing what, when and with whom. Indeed, in the end they gave up trying and placed themselves at the front of the inn where de Vere had originally left them.

But though Alicia and her people managed to plan some kind of route across the countryside to Carcassonne, it was only sketchy at best. Nowhere near as specific as they really needed, so by late afternoon they were seated together on a stone wall above the river across the cobbled inn yard as they pooled their knowledge, all feeling pretty grim.

"Well, we have all that we need…except any sort of map!" Alicia muttered darkly. "We can't take the tilt cart…but we can take the two horses as pack animals, and I have quietly purchased some pretty ancient panniers off

Monsieur Gérard, along with the crooks to hold them and the leather harnesses the horses need to carry them which, after Rochine's little display yesterday, he was very happy to do. The panniers are a bit tired to say the least...but Aquib has had a good go at them with some of the wicker we bought this morning, and he says they will be fine. Yes?"

"Yes, my Lady," the huge man replied, in his calm manner. "And I have replaced the worst of the leather strapping," adding: "Something I am used to doing after my travels through so many places in the Persian wilderness!"

"And Madame has agreed to give us all a pack-up meal to take with us," Agnes chipped in brightly. "All wrapped in damp linen to keep it fresh, and half-a-dozen old wineskins we can fill with water. She was really sweet," adding lightly, "especially as I did my best with her language, poor love. She even gave me a kiss!"

"I have found some old sacks we can use to muffle the horses' hooves," Aziz said quietly. "We can cut them up and tie them on with some of the twine Mistress Soraya bought for us."

"Actually, Aziz, I don't think we'll need them," Alicia said, laying a hand on his arm with a smile and a swift word of thanks. "It is the market tomorrow, and people will be flooding in from all around here from well before dawn to set up their stalls and be ready for the market bell at 8.00 o'clock. There will be carts, drovers, pack horses, loose animals and people everywhere. It is the very best thing for us...for who will notice just one more string of travellers amongst so many?"

"What about the gatehouse, my Lady?" Aquib asked quietly.

"I cannot see any problem there. I have looked at all the defences of this town, as Sir Gui has long taught me. The town guard here are wholly relaxed and undemanding. No-one asked us for papers when we came in. Didn't even bother to check us, and I am sure that leaving will be no different. Agnes and I have also been watching them down by the abbey gateway. The men there are a disgrace by Malwood standards, they've even put out a bench for themselves to sit on, spears propped against the walls, helmets on top. Sir Richard would have them skinned alive were they at home!"

"That's right," Agnes chirped up as she saw the men's eyebrows rise. "Alicia and I went down to check things out. Very cheerful guards, completely relaxed. Oh, don't worry, we didn't talk with them! We just sat around and listened, and threw pebbles in the river. Just like home really," she added wistfully.

"According to all we heard, the Count and his wife are away with their children visiting family," Alicia said, looking around her. "And there's no alert anywhere nearby. We must have been there a good hour, and they didn't bother

229

to stop anyone. Crack of dawn tomorrow," she continued, stretching her shoulders, "there will be many others crossing that ford, both coming in for the market and leaving to get away before it becomes too crowded. We will just be some of many."

"But still no real map!" Agnes said.

Alicia sighed: "No, sweetheart. Soraya and I searched everywhere, and asked as well. But no joy. What we really need is…"

"…Is a friendly pedlar, *milady*," Mathilde said coming across the yard in a floured apron, dragging a surprised young man with her, an enormous pack across his shoulders, stuffed with every imaginable trinket one could think of: bundles of brightly coloured ribbons, rag dolls, carved wooden soldiers and horses on sticks, clumps of wooden spoons, kitchen knives, little silver charms, and rolls of parchment, quills for pens and small pots of black ink sealed with waxed corks.

"This is Louis," she said, giving Alicia a big smile. "He comes from Carcassonne every year, across country, through Limoux and Chalabre and often stops off at some of the smaller places along that route that don't often see a pedlar. He will help you I am sure…the more so if you buy him his supper tonight!" And she gave the man a playful cuff across the top of his head.

"But Madame," Alicia said shocked. "How…"

"…How did I know you were a real 'Lady?'" she asked with a smile. "Because of how you *are*, *Milady* Alic-ia. The way you speak with people…*sans hauteur*…without pride. And the way they look to you, your own people, and how you walk…head held high and shoulders back as if you owned the place. Nothing escapes the eyes of Mathilde. Nor Monsieur Gérard…and after that one yesterday? *Pouf!* No-one, but no-one insults this house like that but I do something about it! Yes? A pigsty indeed!" she exclaimed enraged. "She is *une cochonne…une truie!* So…I help you, *Milady*. It is the pleasure of the house. Now, Louis," she said briskly, these people need your help and you are to give it, yes? Good! *C'est bon!*" And without giving him the chance to object, she turned and walked swiftly away rubbing her floured hands together, leaving Louis seated on the ground, a piece of rolled parchment spread across a large flat stone, a fresh quill in his hand and a screwed-up expression of great concentration on his cheerful face.

*

230

And now the moment had arrived at last and they were really leaving. Escaping, just after cock-crow, with the stars still shining from a clear sky and the light grey, dull, everything formless and without colour, hidden in a fine mist rising off the river as the day slowly inched into life. Around them the dawn chorus was just breaking out, and as they prepared to leave, so a host of others were already beginning to flood into the town for the Wednesday market.

Up in the stables the two guards whom de Vere had left at the inn to keep watch were laid out flat, unconscious from Aquib and Aziz's gentle ministrations: rough wine forced down their throats and poured all over them, gagged with strips torn from one of Alicia's kirtles, trussed like chickens, old sacks over their heads and hidden behind a huge stack of hay. Also ready were their rounceys and their two pack horses, panniers stuffed with all they had decided they must take with them, including the armour that both Alicia and Agnes had worn on the *Pride*, with the precious money belt firmly stitched back in place.

While Najid and the girls were dressed in simple country clothes, Aquib and Aziz wore their half armour under their plain woollen cloaks, bought the previous day, their monstrous swords in their deep scabbards strapped across their backs. Hilts and quillons hidden beneath their cloaks, their hoods pulled well over their heads, their obvious Arab faces were properly shielded. There was no chain mail to chink or suddenly sparkle in a stray shaft of light, and once safely mounted, their great size was not so obvious.

In her saddle bag, carefully rolled and tied with scarlet ribbon, Alicia had the precious map that Louis had drawn for them with such care. On it were the names of the places they must go through, a track to follow with simple directions...and Louis had added well advised cautions: places that were dangerous or absolutely to be avoided, places to beware of...and places where they could be sure of a ready welcome. The little map was a joy, and much joking and laughter had gone into its creation, with little drawings of special features and stick people doing funny things. And they had invited Louis to join their little farewell meal in heartfelt thanks as well as giving him two silver pennies for his pains. To Monsieur Gérard Alicia gave one of their precious bezants and to Mathilde his wife, for her daughter, all the fine dresses she could not take with her...for which she was more than delighted, thanking her a hundred times.

So, with simple caution, they swung up into their saddles and gently clip-clopped on their way as they pulled out of the Abbey Inn's little yard towards the small gatehouse that guarded the ford across the Ariège, the river bubbling in a rush of white water over the bar of rocks that marked it, black and white in the pre-dawn. The tall rushes and yellow irises still closed up for the night stood swaying in the current, a pair of swans paddling majestically against the current, dipping their long necks into the clear water as they searched for food. And as they passed under the arch, the two men on guard looked up and smiled, calling out 'Good Morning' in their thick Frankish, and shouting to be careful as the river was higher that day due to rain further south in the mountains.

So, with a casual wave, their hearts hammering as they gently urged their horses forward, fearful at any moment of a wild shout for them to stop, they pushed forward into the rushing stream. But no call came. And so that morning they left Foix behind, splashing through the ford already busy with traffic: horses, carts, driven animals and people. Many flooded in to the town as Alicia had expected, as people did everywhere there was a market…and many others left also, as many did on market day.

Faces blurred by the early mist, cloaks wrapped round them against the morning chill - they were just another string of riders on the move with packed goods for sale elsewhere, and once across the river they turned up-stream, away from the town, and about a mile or so later they left the main roadway altogether. Kicking-on up the narrow, isolated trackway they had chosen with Louis' help the day before, the pathway masked by trees and thick bushes, the dense wayside sedges muffling their hooves, they turned their backs on Foix and silently disappeared.

*

With unexpected help from good people they had slipped their leash at last, and were on their way towards the tiny villages of Caraybat, Soula and Saint Cirac; riding along the base of the vast escarpment that ran steep and craggy above them right across the countryside as far as the eye could see, with little more than goat tracks leading up it: and thence to the village of Roquefixade below its rock-bound fortress.

Then, in the grey pre-dawn tomorrow, after a simple 'Roman breakfast' as Gui would say, and a hard ride through the Forest of Corret, they would re-join the distant roadway that today they were avoiding, that would finally lead them to Carcassonne, still a fair week's journey through the wilds.

Alicia leaned back in her saddle and jagged her heels in with a smile. De Vere would need a good lymer to catch them now…a really good scent hound…and she knew he didn't have one!

*

From behind one of the great stone buttresses that held up the walls of the Abbey church, despite the ghostly mist off the river, de Vere watched them leave and grinned.

Soon it would be time to find those two fools he had left on guard and rescue them from wherever they'd been dumped. And rubbing his hands with quiet satisfaction he went to join Louis, Mathilde and Monsieur Gérard for breakfast, and pay them for the arrangements he had made with them for room and board and Louis' expert help.

It had gone well.

The Baron would be pleased. What he needed now was some of Mathilde's fresh baked rolls, with butter, apricot jam, fresh peaches and a glass of wine. Lovely. And he smiled.

Next the message to the Baron: '*Your pigeons have flown! Make for the Fox and Goose at Rouffiac-d'Aude. 4 days!*' And then to tell The Lady, who would be livid. *Wine first and Rochine second...*and he laughed.

It was going to be an interesting day!

Chapter 37...The Company flee into the wilderness.

All that day they travelled hard, and as fast as it was possible to go along the twisted trackway that ran along the base of the enormous escarpment they were following.

Aquib led, with Alicia close behind, then the other two girls, Najid with one packhorse and Aziz behind him at the trail with the other; both tough beasts, with shaggy fetlocks and strong hindquarters. They had been good on the tilt cart, and were excellent as pack horses, delighting in having panniers evenly weighted, and not the great, heavy yoke from which the long shaft of the tall-wheeled tilt cart would have been fixed between them.

And as the morning progressed so the sun burned off the early mists and they began to climb up the sides of the first ridge below the great escarpment that would take them all the way up the deep, flat bottomed valley to Roquefixade. Past fields of golden wheat and barley; cattle on the lower pastures and flocks of sheep scattered like stray bundles of wool across the hills, their bells clonking as they moved: every horse stride taking them further from Foix...and further from the hot pursuit they were all certain would be raised against them.

At first they looked often behind them, but soon concentrated more on covering the ground safely than worrying about anyone who might be following, and as the sun rose higher so it got hotter, becoming harder on man and beast as they kept moving. So it was with enormous relief when they reached Caraybat that Aquib called a halt, both to water their horses and to fill the empty wineskins that Mathilde had given them with fresh water. This from the deep well in the centre of the village, that was fed by one of the many springs that bubbled out from below the escarpment.

But though it was intended to be only a brief stop, enough to run cool spring water over their faces, wash off the dust and eat soft rolls, fresh baked by Mathilde early that morning before they had left...they'd had to wait while others used the well first, for by the time they reached the village, the world was waking up. Colour had flooded back into their lives with the light, the sky turning from blush pink to scarlet and gold as the sun leapt up into a clear, cornelian sky in one gorgeous bound.

First the women came out to draw water for their families, and while some men left for the fields, their bait in simple carry-sacks over one shoulder, others came in from milking. Some also brought small flocks of sheep to water at a great stone trough put there for just that purpose, while the communal goats and geese were herded out to pasture under the watchful eyes of a handful of small boys whose job it was to guard them.

And all looked at the six strangers suddenly come amongst them with a mixture of awe and fear, the dark faces and hawk-like eyes of the three Arabs stunning them to silence.

Aziz laughed. "They don't know whether to run or make friends. I am sure if I said '*Boo!*' really loudly, and flapped my arms they would all flee like monkeys up a tree!"

"And that, of course, dear friends," Alicia said with a wry smile, leading her rouncey to the water trough at last, "funny as that would be…is also a problem because we cannot just melt into the local background. You are all too noticeably different. However, as we move further south that should be less of a problem, as the people there are more used to having Moorish traders amongst them. Up here you three stick out like blackbirds in the snow. Very handsome blackbirds, I hasten to add…and I am *so* glad you are with us," she added, gripping each huge man by the arm with a smile. "But…you are still…noticeable!" And they all laughed, including Najid as Alicia smiled at him also, just to be certain that he was not allowed to feel left out in any way.

"Hot work, my Lady," Aquib said as he led his rouncey to the water. "And like to get hotter," he added looking up at the sun. "We must be careful not to push these beasts too hard in these empty hills. We have a long way to go, and no spare mounts. We may have to stop more often."

"How far have we come?" Agnes asked coming up, wiping a cold, wet rag over her face and around her neck. "My haunches are feeling worn already."

"About a dozen miles," Alicia answered. "Maybe more. It is hard to tell with so many twists and turns, and so much woodland around us…I could wish it were twenty! We must have been missed by now, and we are not nearly as far forward as I had hoped. We have had to travel such a wide loop to get here."

"That is true, my Lady," Aziz said coming up to them. "But from what Louis said yesterday the next bit of the journey is fairly straight all the way to Roquefixade."

"But higher up this enormous ridge!" Agnes exclaimed, tearing into a roll with her neat white teeth. "And it is so hot. Can we not take off our cloaks now? I am roasting."

"Aquib?" Alicia asked. "You are our guide and leader on this journey."

"It is a pity we don't all have *djellabas* to wear," he sighed. "Arab cloaks of light cotton, or wool depending on the season. Light brown ones right now would be ideal both against the heat and to hide us against all this

235

rock. Especially as we go higher. So, we must keep cloaked-up for the moment, until we have gone further. At least to Saint Cirac, which according to Louis' map is the last but one village before Roquefixade. By then the sun will be right on top of us. The main roadway to Lavalenet and Laroque-d'Olmes runs behind that long ridge on our right. While up here we are several miles distant and moving slowly. Anyone riding as if *Shaitan* himself was after him will show as a plume of dust; but of us they should see nothing!"

Alicia sighed and shuffled her shoulders under her cloak. "Right, if everyone has watered themselves and their rounceys, let's get going again before anyone plucks up the courage to start asking questions; lunch when the sun is right above us. Kick-on, Aquib, before we all melt into pats of greasy butter!"

*

In fact it was about the time that Alicia and her small company were leaving Caraybat that Rochine was told that her birds had flown their coop...left the inn she had visited and disappeared into thin air.

No-one had seen them leave, and no-one knew in which direction they could have gone either. With the Wednesday market now in full swing, and people coming and going everywhere, trying to find anyone who knew anything was an impossibility...and The Lady was incandescent with rage! Not only had she trusted the little *conne anglaise*...but the guards she had put to keep watch over them all had failed her. Like two soused herrings pickled in alcohol, they had been found trussed like chickens for the market behind a huge stack of hay! If she could have slit their throats then and there she would have done so; as it was she had to satisfy herself with watching de Vere flog them with a stirrup leather until their backs were bloody.

As for the inn, '*L'Auberge de L'Abbaye*', she ordered de Vere and his men to turn it inside out, and string up Gérard to one of his own rafters by his wrists and submit him to the *bastinado*, tie his big toes together and beat the soles of his bare feet with a thick rattan, while his wife was forced to watch...and was even more angry when de Vere refused to do so!

"You cannot do this, my Lady," he had said calmly in the face of her tumultuous rage. "The *aubergiste*, Monsieur Gérard, is an important citizen of Foix. How do you think the people here will react to such a brutal act? The Abbot himself is in the market today...and no matter what you may have said to Lady Alicia, Sir Hubert will have you and me arrested immediately word reaches him, and we will all be imprisoned. And do you think he will release us because your father asks him to? Or the Count of Foix? No, my Lady…let me question them, and I will see what news we can gather elsewhere." And he had marched off before she could say a word, leaving her biting her leather quirt and stamping her feet with rage, and shouting at everyone in her household.

Calm de Vere may have sounded, but he had rarely seen The Lady in such a fury, and there was cold sweat on his brow as he thought of what would happen if she discovered the trick that had been played on her. Worse…that he had assisted in her captives' escape and even now knew where they were headed, and what tracks they were taking to get there. He might indeed be the Baron's Guard Commander, but even he would not countenance any harm coming to his daughter…so God help him if he ever actually had to draw steel against her!

Still, Almahdi had sent off his message, as he had arranged with Lord Roger. The next thing was to send out his men to scour the gateways and the roads: north towards Toulouse; back the way they had already come towards St Girons and, of course, east towards Carcassonne across country, but along the main roadway towards Saint-Antoine and Celles and Canalot…and not the tiny, almost hidden trackway south of the town that led towards the huge escarpment that ran for miles.

Eventually, of course, he would have to do so. But fast messengers sent along the three most obvious routes for them to have taken, given their obvious ignorance of the countryside, would keep The Lady on side for a while. By the time he did 'find' the correct route they had taken, Lady Alicia de Burley and her party would be at least a full day ahead of them, maybe more. And unless something drastic happened, they should meet up with Lord Roger this side of Carcassonne, and all would be well.

He just had to keep all his balls in the air…and gripping his crotch lightly, he grinned. Except those of course…the air was the last place he wanted them to be in, and certainly *not* on a silver platter cooked like doucets with roasted garlic and a sauce of white wine and cream, when the Lord Baron would then expect him to eat them!

Chapter 38...The White Rose and her command reach Roquefixade.

J ust as the dusk was settling around them, with swifts screaming on scimitar wings both high and low across the darkening fields as they hunted for moths and insects still a-wing in the soft dusky light, Alicia and her small company reached Roquefixade at last.

The castle, perched like an eagle's nest high above the village, marked the place beyond question. Its battlements part-lit by flaring flambeaux stood out stark against the last light from the western sky as the first stars blinked into life.

Those last few miles had been almost the hardest, the three girls drooping in their saddles by then and all exhausted from their early morning start, so they were delighted to have got to the Castle Inn...*L'Auberge du Château*...at last. Clean and bright, with rooms for all to share and, because of the castle, a warm welcome: the *aubergiste*, Monsieur Legrand, a man as jolly and round-faced as his name, with a voice to match, was used to stray travellers, and to travellers from hotter climes than his, so their little Arab entourage did not startle him.

They had time to settle their horses, curry their hides, check their shoes, and relax a while before their supper which was excellent: delicious baked rabbit pieces beneath a crusty topping of cheese and herby breadcrumbs with fresh greens and peaches to follow. A simple meal that left them all pleasantly sated and very ready for an early rest for which they were desperate, having had little break all day, except a short time when the sun in all his glory was right above them and they had stopped at Saint Cirac.

*

A nd Saint Cirac had nearly been the end of them all!

There Aquib had taken pity on them and had at last allowed them to take off their cloaks, and they had flopped in the shade of the nearest group of trees just above the village, almost panting like hounds on the chase, while with a big smile Nijad brought round tin beakers into which he poured cold sherbet made the night before from the last of the oranges off the *Morning Star*. For everyone there were chicken thighs boned and stuffed with cheese

238

and herbs, wrapped in lettuce leaves and savoured with fresh scallions; with hard boiled eggs, also cooked that morning by Mathilde, and the last of the rolls; all double wrapped in cheese cloth and damp linen in the middle of his food pannier…together with a fresh apricot pie as tasty as the one they had so enjoyed the previous evening.

"I know you told us Mathilde had given us a pack-up to take with us today," Alicia said to Agnes. "But I was expecting a cheese roll at best…not a real diner's delight like this…and no bones in my chicken to bother with either. Delicious!"

Seated right up against the slope of the hill, the main roadway between Foix and Lavalenet that ran below them about a mile away was perfectly laid out for them to see, and though traffic was moving along it, it was more solid wheeled farm carts and groups of peasant workers, with the occasional horse litter accompanied by a groom or man-at-arms, than a furiously riding messenger with a plume of dust behind him. For nearly an hour they sat and lazily lunched there, while their horses cropped the grass around them and the bees buzzed amongst the wild marjoram, bell flowers and wild carrot that were growing in profusion all around them, with blue cornflowers, scarlet poppies and brilliant corn marigolds dotted about throughout the wheat fields below.

With the hot sun casting dappled shadows through the trees, and a soft breeze blowing up the long valley below it was hard to remember that they were on the run from real enemies who were seeking their deaths, rather than their safe delivery to the Château Grise…and they all drowsed.

For Alicia, lying back in the long grass gazing sightlessly up at the blue sky, it was a delicious break from the frantic past few days and she could easily have lain there all afternoon…what she wouldn't do to stay here and not get back up onto that damned horse! But time was passing and much more of this and they would all fall asleep…*and then where would we be?*…So, with a grunt of effort Alicia dragged herself to her feet just as Aquib was coming across to rouse her, Aziz helping Najid to pack up his food pannier again, and everybody stirring from their midday torpor.

"Next stop, or little market we come to, we must buy some sturdy buckets, my Lady," Aquib rumbled at her in his dark voice. "Aziz and I have watered the horses as best we can with the help of two of Najid's pans. But that really won't do. Like today at Caraybat; if we'd had buckets we could have been on our way much more quickly. And for us, time is something of which we have very little to spare."

"You are right of course, Aquib. In all the rush to get away, no-one thought of it. When we stop for the night, I will see what can be found. Sweet

Jesus, my bum is sore!" she exclaimed to laughter as she rubbed her buttocks briskly. "If I don't get moving again soon, I may never want to!"

Minutes later they were on their way again, dropping down fifty yards or so from where they had rested and back onto the long twisted trackway that led first to Leychert, and finally to Roquefixade with its castle poised right on the very edge of huge limestone cliffs that overlooked the village, and which could clearly be seen against the horizon, still miles away, made dusky blue by the distance.

Then, when they were less than half way towards Leychert, just as they were negotiating a sharp bend in the track, they heard what they had secretly been dreading all morning: the faint thunder of hooves in the distance. At once all looked towards the main roadway, at that point a bare half mile distant below them, closer than it had ever been since setting out. Here the ground was sloping open pasture on fallow land, a mass of flowers and long grasses, with a great open field of swaying barley, golden in the sunshine just beyond, hiding flocks of small birds that whirred from one part of the field to another as the fancy took them. And they were all in plain sight.

Immediately, Aquib threw up his hand and they all stopped.

"Everyone, off your horses, fast. Aziz, Najid, run your packs back down the track, and shelter them behind that huge hedgerow we passed a few minutes ago, no-one will be able see you from the road through that…but hold their muzzles. Everyone else, pull your horse's heads and make them lie down. Then lie across their faces, eyes and ears particularly. If they can't see they won't struggle and they won't call out. And once you're down stay down until I say move. If he's one of de Vere's men he won't be looking for us here, he's going too fast for that. If he was ambling I would be far more concerned. But that is a pounding, furious gallop. Now…down you go! I will help you…and whatever else you do, keep your pale faces away from the road!"

In fact it only took moments once all three girls were out of their saddles. While Alicia had done it before with Gui, not so Agnes or Soraya…but with Aquib's great strength to help, there was no horse on earth that was going to resist him, his own included, and with less than a minute to spare all four were down, their riders lying across their heads, their faces buried into their horse's manes.

Closer and closer the hooves raced 'til with a muted thunder they rushed past below where they were lying in a whirl of dust and disappeared into the distance. Then suddenly they slowed…and stopped, and with the wind blowing towards them up the valley, they could all hear the rider clip-clopping slowly back along the road. Something must just have caught his eye: some flicker of movement, something out of place that had made him stop and walk his horse back to try and find it.

Even though they were lying flat in grassy wasteland, the track they were on was on sloping ground above the line of sight of anyone on the road below…especially if they were mounted, and to say their hearts were racing was to put it mildly, Alicia especially as she had the most to lose.

"What's he doing?" she hissed to Aquib, who was lying across his horse's withers, face towards the road.

"I can't see, my Lady. There's too much grass in the way. But my face is dark, and I am shielded a bit by those bushes behind us. I will take a slow look." And raising his head very gently he lifted his eyes above the tall grasses all around them.

*

Beyond the fallow pasture sloping away from him was the huge open field of golden barley that almost swept down to the road where a man on horseback was stopped, his hand up to his eyes as he looked up towards them.

At first Aquib felt sure he was looking directly at him, but just at that moment he moved his horse and it became clear that the man was searching a different part of the field. For quite a while Aquib could not, for the life of him, see what it was that had caught the man's attention, and in fact he had to kneel up in the end to find out, his head and shoulders draped with his cloak swiftly pulled from his pack to disguise his shape. And then he laughed. A quiet chuckle that almost drove Alicia mad, because she could not see anything funny to laugh at!

Below them to the right, a very rough cart track from just beyond Saint-Cirac ran down one long side of the barley field, and two thirds along it, part hidden behind a clump of trees was an ancient tilt cart, one solid wheel in a ditch, its horse happily cropping the wayside flowers while the two boys who should have been on it were thrashing around in the barley chasing pigs! This way and that they fell, their wild shouts now coming clearly up to them on the wind…now they had one, now they didn't… as the wretched animals dived this way and that to avoid capture, rushing between their legs, standing still, then dashing in opposite directions, and squealing as only pigs can, giving the two lads after them the complete run-around.

Down on the road the rider was falling about with laughter, almost out of his saddle, as he rollicked from side to side, his great hoots coming faintly up to them on the wind, then, clearly wiping tears from his eyes, he kicked on his horse, picked up speed and hurtled on his way once more.

"Pigs, my Lady Alicia!" Aquib exclaimed, laughing properly, pulling his rouncey up as the horseman disappeared from his view. "Listen! You can hear their squeals now! And look!" he pointed, and in moments she too, and the others who quickly joined her, were all in stitches at the desperate activity going on below them. Doubled over as the two young lads desperately hunted down their escaped charges, and finally carried them kicking, wriggling and squealing back to their tilt cart, furiously arguing as they did so. Both were completely unaware that they had reduced a small group of adults to a state of hilarity, tears rolling down their faces, hands clutching their bellies and gasping for breath as they mimicked the wild antics of both pigs and boys...

So...by the time they reached Roquefixade, and were finally seated for supper, with wine and cold lemon water to hand, it had been a long, long day, the first of many; and the first of many early starts, too, before they would reach their journey's end.

Chapter 39... The Lady and de Vere take up the chase.

For Gaston de Vere in Foix the initial turmoil had settled down to a more controlled wait as his messengers came and went throughout the day, and the Lady Rochine, after her opening burst of violent rage, had also settled down to await results, her anger cold but none the less potent for being so!

The Rock Inn was ideally placed to be such a headquarters, as the crossing points over both rivers were easily accessible, being well within the town wall that joined them up along the south side. And while there were gatehouses in front of both crossings, and to the south, with the market in full swing, and the guards wholly relaxed in their duties, their comings and goings had not caught the interest of the town commander; especially as de Vere had expressly told his troopers *not* to gallop their mounts within site of the castle for any reason. Not even if all the devils in hell were after them.

But by the evening, of course, there was still no news, and by then The Lady was getting very restless indeed as messenger after messenger returned with nothing to report. No-one had seen any such party leaving; at neither gatehouse had anyone passed over of their description, and along all the obvious routes leading north, east and west, for miles, no-one had seen anything either. Travellers and market traders had been asked, innkeepers questioned, and stables along the way had all been searched. Their tilt cart lay abandoned at the Abbey Inn, and almost all their clothes. They had paid their shot the night before and simply disappeared.

Monsieur Gérard and his plump, cheerful wife, Mathilde had appeared as mystified as anyone else: they had been quiet guests, kept themselves to themselves, been polite, and their Arabs had slept in the stables with the horses. No...they had not talked with anyone else they could think of. They didn't know anyone, did they? The ladies were all very pretty. The one called 'Alicia' especially so. Very kind to her servants. Very like a proper Lady. Had they been ill? From her food? *'Non! Non! Non!'* The very idea! *'Quelle horreur!'* Yes, they had paid. The money was in their rooms, and a bit extra. *'Formidable!'* One moment they were there...the next, *'pouf!'* they were gone. Like magic, like witches on broomsticks! And she and her husband had laughed at the idea.

So it was a gloomy, frustrated gathering that had met for food that night, de Vere sharing a table with The Lady in a room separate from the rest of their company, she in glowering silence; he contemplative and aloof. Her anger was not so much because de Vere had defied her earlier, but because his men had found no sign of her fugitives! Dead was one thing…but alive, and on the run? Maybe even to her father? That was a prospect far from pleasing, unless that ridiculous cook used the 'spices' that she had poured into his box…in place of the powdered toast crumbs that de Vere had given him in St Girons.

Or thought he'd given him…and she suddenly looked at de Vere from the corner of her eyes, happily stuffing his face with foie gras on toast and lettuce…*What an ignorant bumpkin the man is. Look at him stuffing his face as if there was no tomorrow!…Did he give that box to him as my father had arranged?* And then she laughed…*Of course he did! And Just suppose that idiot cook really does give that 'forgetting powder' to that scum he is travelling with? Now that would be good!…*and she suddenly chuckled again, her eyes sparkling at the thought of what de Vere had actually given the little Arab in his plain, wooden casket…*One good spoonful of food with that in it would do for the bloody lot of them! And that puffed-up idiot thinks he has given them toasted breadcrumbs!…*and she smiled again.

"You seem suddenly more relaxed, my Lady," de Vere said, wiping his mouth. "What has amused you? I could do with a good joke just now. This day has not been exactly glorious!"

"No, Gaston," she grimaced, her smile disappearing. "It has not. Those fools of yours should surely have found something by now? They must have been looking in all the wrong places. And my smile? Just thinking how horrified those thrice damned *canaille* will be when we catch them. That rabble…that rabid pack of dogs! Now what is all that noise?" she demanded fiercely as the men eating their meal in the Great Room nearby suddenly burst into raucous laughter, beating their hands on the tables and stamping their feet. "What do those idiots have to be so amused about? Go and find out. They are disturbing my meal!"

But it was not necessary. Almost as swiftly as the noise had erupted, it had fallen away again, and moments later there was a knock on the door and de Vere's second-in-command stepped into the room.

"I am sorry to disturb you, Sir…my Lady, but one of my lads may have stumbled on the very news we have been seeking all day."

"You know where they are, Sergeant?" De Vere asked his troop leader tersely…quite sure he didn't!

"No, Commander. But I think I know where we should have been looking today."

"And where is that, Sergeant Duclos?" The Lady demanded of him, menace in every word.

244

"The lad we sent to search towards Lavalenet, Pierre Rouge, saw something that caught his eye on the long stretch of road just past the hills near Celles…"

"*What?* What did he see, Duclos?" Rochine snapped at him, exasperated.

"It's not what he saw, my lady. That was just riotous…what we have just been laughing about. It's what he didn't see, my Lady…"

"*What he didn't see?* Gaston, is this man drunk or mad? What stupid riddle is this you have brought me tonight Sergeant? Get out of here!"

"No, Sergeant!" de Vere crisped at him. "Stand your ground, and explain. We will listen."

"Well, Sir," the man continued somewhat abashed. "His eyes were drawn to two young men catching pigs in a barley field close to the road…"

"*Sacrébleu de dieu*, Gaston!" The Lady snarled. "God's Holy Blood!...Do we have to listen to more of this drivel? Now we have pigs!"

"Please, Sergeant," De Vere said calmly, ignoring Rochine's outburst. "Continue with your report."

"Well, Commander…Milady. Pierre also noticed they had a tilt cart with them…and that there was a very faint trackway leading up the hillside, away from the road, to what looked like a small settlement high above them. Since coming back he has asked questions…and there are a whole string of tiny spring-line villages, nestled right up against the base of that huge escarpment, all linked by a single rough track that runs all the way from Foix to the castle at Roquefixade…"

"*Nom de Dieu!*" The Lady Rochine cried out, slamming her fist on the table. "That's where those bastards went. No wonder your men could find no trace of them!"

"Well done, Sergeant, well done," de Vere said, grim faced, but clapping the man across his shoulder none the less. "And well done to Pierre Rouge. Three bottles of the House's best…on me!" he added, tossing the man a coin. "But be advised we will be on the move at first light. So…now we know," he said to Rochine as his Sergeant left. "That is good."

"Yes, Gaston. Certainly that is good. But they could not possibly have taken so remote a passage without help. Your men searched all the likely places that a small group might have taken who were ignorant of the countryside. To take such a twisted trackway up into the hills shows greater knowledge than they could possibly have had. So…someone helped them. Either from the inn…or from elsewhere," she added. "Even from one of us maybe?"

245

And giving him a penetrating stare, she tossed back her wine, rose from her table and swept out of the room. De Vere smiled and shrugged his shoulders. He had done his part, the hare was running, now it was up to the Baron to catch her if he could...before his daughter got there first!

Chapter 40...Last chance inn for the Company of the White Rose.

Chalabre, and the end of their second day on the road.

A small town a good thirty miles further from where they had spent the night at the Castle Inn and another long, hard day's travel albeit on a better road than the poor trackway they had been on that first day. And with their arrival came a sign that the weather was changing, the sky filling with more cloud, and there was a wind that had teased them all day, picking up weight as the long hours of travel had passed, channelling its gusts up the valleys with the sound of distant thunder in its wings.

Chalabre, and their last chance of a good night's rest under a solid roof before setting out for Limoux along the steep valley that led to the village of Montjardin...and from there up into the dense forests that covered the Peche Laurague and the Col du Bac, and all the other mountains of that untamed region. With its steep scarps and mist-shrouded valleys, twisting roads and sharp bends that doubled back on themselves, serving a handful of tiny hamlets that lay scattered amongst them, it was dangerous country. Each tiny settlement a flickering beacon of life in a tree shrouded wilderness where fell beasts haunted the mountains and brigands, thieves and murderers lurked in the depths and fastnesses, ready to pounce on any traveller who was not of a strong, well-armed company.

Louis had told them it would be the most frightening part of their journey. Where danger lurked everywhere; not just because the road was rough and twisted as it climbed into the mountains, nor because the forests and high hills hid bandits and outlaws, men who had lost their livings as Soraya's father had done, as well as those who had been cast out of their villages for crime or wickedness...but because the whole area was so remote. The people of the forests were themselves sometimes a little strange; there were few if any wayside inns and they might have to seek the help of villagers if they wished a bed for the night at Saint-Benoit, half way into the mountains...or at La Bezole, an even smaller hamlet of not more than half a dozen houses. But if the weather closed in on them, then they might have to bivouac in the open, and even in summer there were wolves in the high mountains, and if they had cubs at foot they would fight to the death to protect them.

That night they discussed how best to move on, and quicker though it might have been to leave their pack horses behind in order to push on harder, all agreed that to do so was just too much of a risk, for if they did get stranded the following night they would have no way of either feeding or protecting themselves against the changing weather.

"This is hard going, Aquib," Alicia moaned quietly as they waited for the vegetable broth and meat pottage they had asked for, dipping the bread they'd been given in local olive oil and Italian balsamic vinegar while they waited. "And another early start tomorrow, I suppose. You are a hard overseer, my large Arab friend!"

"We escaped by a whisker yesterday at Saint Cirac, my Lady. I hadn't seen that track when we were riding by. Had he had his wits about him, and not been in such a hurry, that fellow could easily have ridden up it and we'd have been right in his lap. Oh, I'd have killed him…but they would have been on to us the moment he was missed."

"So…it will be another early start tomorrow! Never mind," she sighed with mock resignation. "One day I shall lie and watch the dawn bounce into life without seeing it from the back of a bloody rouncey, and think myself in heaven!"

"God willing we get that chance, Alicia," Agnes replied in a cheerful voice. "You with your Gui and me with my Allan!" And she blushed.

"*Insh'a Allah*! Mistress Fitzwalter," Aziz said with a wide grin and a shake of his finger. "*Insh'a Allah!*" And they all chuckled at her confusion

"What is your plan, Aquib?" Soraya asked, a moment later. "Where do you want us this time?"

"Tomorrow, my Lady," he said, turning to Alicia. "You and Mistress Agnes must wear your armour, helmets and all. And Najid too: I have brought his with me in one of the panniers."

"I didn't think he could fight?" Alicia said, astonished.

"*All* those who serve The Prince must fight, my Lady Alicia," Aziz said quietly in a very matter-of-fact tone. "No matter what their real job may be, all must be able to use a weapon of his choice. Our Najid may not be a powerful fighter like me," the huge man added with a grin, putting his massive arm across the little cook's shoulders, "but he is a good comrade and a very *Shaitan* with a knife, and in war he is never far from his *khanjar*. Not as fine as that worn by the Lord Prince of course, the one you saw at Bayonne; but a fine blade nevertheless, and he can move like a cat. He may be soft-hearted in some ways but in others he is …*usama*, a Lion!" And he gave the little man a great smile and a friendly shake.

"Why the armour, Aquib?" Soraya asked.

"One, because I do not want to let everyone along the way know that we have three women amongst us. I think that would be inviting trouble. Two…apparently there is a band of naughty outlaws that haunt these

248

mountains sometimes, led by a man called Paul Grillade, the 'Griller', whom no-one can catch. If we are seen to be well armoured-up and bristling with weapons, they may choose to leave us alone rather than attack. Wild bandits are after money...not hard knocks!"

"'Naughty' outlaws, Aquib?" Alicia asked, astonished, smiling at his use of language. *"Naughty?"*

"Well, my Lady," the big man said with a smile, in his dark rumbly voice. "It is better to think of them as 'naughty'...rather than 'wicked' or 'evil': less scary, don't you think? Then while still keeping your eyes and ears open - you..er..won't be so anxious!" And they all laughed.

"Anyway, this way we will be five well-armed men escorting one woman...so both Aziz and I will be fully armoured-up. And in truth I have missed my full war harness, so it will be good to wear it all properly. You two ladies will have to lead a pack-horse apiece, but I want you in the middle all the way. Aziz will cover behind us, and Najid will be out up-front, ahead of me. He is as expert a tracker as he is a cook...and has a 'nose' for things. That's why he is so good with his skillets and his spices!" And as they laughed at his comment, so their food arrived and with much busy chatter they tucked in, no-one knowing when they might get another such occasion again. Nor did anyone linger after their meal, all going up to the two rooms they had hired for the night, intent on what rest they could get before their early start the next day.

This could be their last chance of warmth and safety for some days...and no-one wished to waste a moment of it!

*

But in the morning they awoke to a completely grey-white world, for during the night the wind had dropped, and the clouds had come so low that they filled the valleys, hiding the slopes and tops of the hills with a wet blanket, the fine mizzle making everything drip water. Everything was covered with fine droplets that hung like tiny teardrops from the tips of the horses' manes and even from their long eyelashes, making them shake their heads and hurrumph in the chilly dampness.

Another 'Roman breakfast' followed, food for later wrapped in the saddle bag each horse carried, along with a flask of watered wine, or watered fruit juice in the case of Aquib and his friends; and before anyone else was stirring they slipped out, all wearing long black cloaks to cover their armour, and all with mail coifs beneath their steel helmets and chain mail mittens with

249

leather palms. Only Soraya was different, wearing a dark leather hat with a wide brim pushed firmly over her long hair, her hands in supple leather gloves lined against the chilly wetness, dark green leather chausses thrust into thigh-high leather boots to protect against chafing as she rode along, and a dark blue cloak drawn close around her.

In moments they were mounted and with Najid going ahead, they kicked-on into the mist, eyes straining to see their way, their horses' hooves deadened as much by the dripping trackway on which they were clumping as by the thick mist by which they were surrounded.

At first it was easy to keep in close touch with each other, but as they moved further up the valley the mist changed as the wind moved through it, so that sometimes it was almost quite clear while at others it seemed almost impossible to see beyond their horse's head. Sometimes even less, the reins disappearing into a thick opaque, clammy wall. Sounds also came and went in the mist. Hooves clomping right ahead of them on the track one moment then seemed to be miles away, or right beside them, the next. And calling out was of little value, the wet, cloying air seeming to swallow all sounds into itself, dampening one's shouts as if through a wet flannel pressed close against the face.

And as they went higher the mist grew thicker, and an hour into their journey they found themselves stumbling like blind men into the tiny hamlet of Montjardin, a handful of simple houses clustered around the track that ran through it, before it turned left handed and upwards into a steep valley that was completely blanketed in mist, the trackway running up the left hand side of it, a handful of fields along the valley bottom from which cattle moaned plaintively through the white blankness, their voices hollow and echoing as they pushed higher.

*

All around them the great forest leaned and swayed, the trees ethereal in the drifting mist, long dripping fingers, like leaf covered hands, dabbing at their heads and faces as they rode by, sometimes even brushing their shoulders. All around them was an eerie, kind of pattering 'silence', their horses hooves making little sound as they walked along, any kind of speed being impossible to attempt, only the sighing wind and dripping leaves and branches any accompaniment to their journey.

Now they were climbing higher all the time, both up the valley and also up its steep sides, leaning forward in their saddles to help balance their rounceys as the track wound its way upwards in a series of deep loops and bends, at one point actually doubling back on itself the way was so steep. They thanked God they did not have the big tilt cart with them because they might never have got it up the road. It was when the trackway made a second great twist, deeply right-handed, that Aquib finally called a halt, pulling his gelding off the track and onto a kind of flattened clearing to one side of the road, so that everyone else could gather safely together.

"By *Allah*, this is miserable stuff," Aziz moaned, wiping the wetness off his face. "What has happened to the weather? This is high summer."

"This is just cloud, Aziz," Agnes Fitzwalter said, laughing. "It can be like this in the high mountains, especially when there is no wind to blow it away. Tomorrow it could all be as clear as a bell, and you'll see for miles. You should live in England...it is often like this at home."

"No thank you, Mistress Agnes," Aziz replied, his face a picture of misery. "I would rather hunt lions with a kitchen knife than live in your damp island of fogs and rain storms. How about something warm, Najid? If I make a fire with my flint and tinder could you make us some soup, or broth?"

"Oh that would be lovely, Najid," Soraya said, wrapping her cloak around her. "Anything to get this wet chill out of my bones. Where is Alicia? I haven't seen her since we stopped."

"I don't know," Agnes replied, sudden concern in her voice. "She was in front of me when Aquib stopped us. Did she go on? She can't be far!" And running a little way up the road she called: "Alicia! *Alicia!*" And was hugely relieved when a moment later Alicia came trotting back down towards them out of the mist.

"Where have you been?" Agnes started to say, when Alicia rapidly swung off her horse, held up her hand and stopped her.

"Shh! Be silent, all of you. Not a word, until we are all close together." And gathering her cloak, she led her horse swiftly to where Aziz was coaxing a fire to life, the twigs and other kindling nestled in a bed of stones on the edge of the trackway where someone else had obviously once had the same idea, Agnes almost running beside her to keep up.

"What is it my Lady?" Aquib said quietly as he moved to join her, the others following, except Najid who was rustling about in his food panniers.

"*We are being followed!*" she said, dropping her voice to a husky whisper. "*Someone, or something, out there is tracking us!*"

"So...my Lady, you noticed too?" Aquib said quietly.

"You knew?" Alicia gasped, gripping his arm urgently.

"Yes, my Lady," the big man replied calmly. "Najid told me an hour back. I wasn't sure myself for a while. But he is right. That is why I have stopped us here to light a fire, and not just for food. Fire is a great protection in the wild; not even a lion will brave fire unless driven to do so."

"A Lion?" Agnes asked, quavering. "Surely, Aquib, there are no lions in France?"

"No, Mistress Agnes, no Lions," he smiled, putting his huge hand comfortingly on her tiny shoulders. "Only Najid! He is *usama!* Remember?" and he gave his deep rumbling laugh. "Now, my Lady," he said quietly, turning to Alicia. "What was it that alerted you?"

"It was the pattering!" Alicia said, her voice shaking. "At first I thought it was just the wetness from the trees. But when I stopped…it stopped also. It was like this in the great forest at home when I fled from Rochine and her father the last time. Only then it was a stag that was following me. This is very much the same, only now my horse is frightened. I can feel her pulling, and she has been tossing her head and snorting."

"Mine also," Soraya said. "I just thought it was the rain in her eyes."

At that moment, leaving a big pan across the fire, now burning well, Najid came across and joined them and he, Soraya and the other two men exchanged a rapid burst of Arabic while Alicia and Agnes quietly waited. A moment later Najid went back to his cooking and the others came to join them.

"Well?" Alicia asked Aquib. "What did our Number One tracker have to say?"

"He says that there are men out there, he has heard voices. Very quiet in all this mist. But he says that there is also some kind of great beast. He does not know what. He has smelt something harsh and strong on the air, but it is not wolf, that he knows. He says this is different, rank and powerful, and it moves quietly. That is what has frightened the horses…mine too. Few things scare Najid in the wild. But this time he is afraid."

Such knowledge was dark and frightening, and the three girls shivered and drew close together, their hands reaching out instinctively for one another, suddenly desperate for human contact in the face of an unknown terror.

"It will be *un sanglier énorme!*" Soraya said boldly, with a sudden high-pitched laugh, clutching Alicia and Agnes's hands. "A wild boar enormous; like the one that killed my mother maybe? Najid will not know *les sangliers*. They have a very strong smell. Very!" And she held her nose and smiled.

"Perhaps it is a dragon!" Agnes said, her voice trembling. "St George slew a terrible dragon that ate girls. It is in all the stories. And dragons are terrible, great beasts. Oh…my lady. Pray God it is not a dragon!"

"Agnes, don't be such a big silly," Alicia said sharply, giving the girl a shake...privately hoping that it really wasn't a dragon! "There are no such things as dragons today. St George killed the last one centuries ago!"...*Didn't he? Of course you never really knew with dragons - perhaps they were immortal? No, Saints were immortal...dragons got slain! Dear God, I am getting as bad as poor Agnes!*

"Come now, girls," she said brightly. "I am sure that Soraya is right - and that what Najid has smelt is a great wild boar. They stink to high heaven wherever they are. Even worse in autumn and winter time when they are looking for mates, and this part of France is noted for them! Now...I don't know about you...but I am starving! Come on, let's eat!"

And holding Agnes's hand firmly in her own, Soraya's arm crooked around her elbow as girls do, she walked across to where Najid was stirring a great pan of chicken and vegetable soup, the smell of which was making her mouth water.

Moments later, when she was cupping in her hands the wooden beaker that Najid had given her, Aquib came quietly across to join her by the horses, his huge figure shadowy in the thick mist, more like a wraith than a living man.

"I don't like this, my Lady." he rumbled at her softly, drawing her away from the others. "Men we can deal with...even outlaws. They are always just a rabble. The very debris of society who will flee from true warriors like Aziz and myself, so I do not fear them. But if there is a great boar out there we have no spears to hold it at bay, least of all a boar spear; nor hounds to drive it. When we start off again, a short distance up the track, Aziz, Najid and I will slip away from you..."

"*What?*" Alicia exclaimed, horrified. "*Abandon us?* But that will leave us completely unprotected! Najid said he heard men's voices. What if we are attacked? Or seized on the road? What will happen to us?"

"We are not abandoning you, my Lady," he said urgently. "*No!* You must not think that! Nor will you be unprotected, I promise you, *on the beard of the Prophet*...as I promised my Prince, remember? Aziz and I will be close by. But if we are surprised in this...this *muck!*" He growled forcefully, gesturing around him. "Then it will be very difficult to defend you - especially if the enemy have bows. We need space to move in without...forgive me, Lady Alicia," he added sweeping his hand over her and towards Agnes and Soraya..."without any hindrances. If there is real trouble we will attack any enemy who may be out there – and, *Insha'Allah*, it will be devastating, I assure you. But you must trust me, my Lady Alicia. Please!"

"Oh, Aquib!" she exclaimed sounding desperate. "You are asking a great deal of me," she said, looking him full in the face. "And of Soraya, and poor

Agnes Fitzwalter who does not have half my courage. But we will do as you suggest. Only pray God you do not lose us in this mist...nor yourselves fall victim to some fell beast from the forest, that you and I both know to be out there!"

"*Insh'a Allah*, my Lady. We will be close." And seizing both her hands in his enormous grip to reassure her, he added fiercely as he squeezed her hands: "My heart and soul on it!"

"Well, Aquib...just make sure your *Allah, Insh'as* it properly!" And she gave him a smile. Tremulous maybe...but still a smile as she walked back to where Najid was already packing up his things....*Please God, that man knows what he is doing!*

Chapter 41...*They seek her here, they seek her there...they seek the White Rose everywhere!*

Away near Gruissan, Baron Roger was already on the move north-west towards Carcassonne to catch up with Alicia at last.

With his full Guard Commander, Gaston de Vere, assisting his daughter, it was to Sergeant Xavier Le Brun, his huge Officer Commanding the Castle Guard, to whom the Baron now turned for the men he needed to mount a rescue of his intended bride.

Two dozen hard-faced troopers, well-armed and mounted, and only carrying saddlebag supplies for three days, had left with him at their head the day de Vere's message had reached the castle pigeon loft. His great house flag carried proudly beside him all along the way, the wind of their passage made the green standard with its great black Boar's Head stream behind them, its scarlet tusks and tongue looking as dangerous as ever they could if they were real: every armoured man upright in his saddle, the Baron, on his great black charger, Charlemagne, in the lead.

But despite the news from de Vere, it was a grim look he carried on his face as he cantered along the old Via Aquitania, forcing others off the road as his command forged westwards, for no message had yet come through from either de Courcy or Bertrand de Vernaille...and he now feared the worst. That somehow Gui de Malwood had escaped his trap. And he growled with anger, banging his clenched fist against his thigh.

This time he would make sure that Sir Gui's precious Alicia did not evade his net! And digging in his spurs he picked up the pace, leading his men in a plume of dust towards Carcassonne and the English Lady he had determined would be his bride.

*

Two days behind Alicia, The Lady Rochine and her escort had also caught the scent and like a pack of Rache hounds, was now hot on her trail. Having first arranged for both tilt carts, especially the one carrying the Baron's precious pigeons, to leave with hired drivers, fresh horses and the Cousins as their escort on the long north-eastern road towards Toulouse,

Narbonne and Gruissan, Gaston de Vere, followed by The Lady, led the way out of Foix with his men and gave chase.

By then the sun was rising, and having splashed across the ford they turned south until the guide they had found took them east along a narrow trackway that led towards the base of the huge escarpment that ran right across the countryside to the castle of Roquefixade and beyond. At first The Lady had been doubtful that Pierre Rouge had been right at all, as the further they went along the track, the further away from the escarpment they found themselves. But when they swung back and reached Caraybat, the first village since setting out, she soon got the confirmation she had been seeking.

"This is the right direction, my Lady," de Vere told her after one of his men had questioned two of the local women. "A small group of riders stopped here two days ago to water their horses. Three men and three women, with two pack horses. The men with dark faces…they frightened the children! There can be no doubt. It's them alright!"

And after watering their own beasts, they kicked-on sharply along the narrow trackway. They were two days behind their quarry, and the dust of their passage billowed out behind them.

*

Far to the north, Sir Gui de Malwood and his battered command were still two days from Bordeaux and pushing hard. Their tilt carts rattled and bumped along the road, as fast as the surface and their injured could bear the pace, for they were behind time now from when they had left Nantes, and every minute counted.

The battle at Saint Jean d'Angély had cost them time and good men too!

While Allan-i-the Wood and Dickon Fletcher had slaughtered de Courcy's men with their arrow storms, de Vernaille's bowmen had wreaked havoc amongst his command before they had been cut down or forced to surrender, and over a dozen of his Lions had been killed or injured in one way or another. Seven had been buried in the town cemetery, five more were badly wounded, with sword cuts or arrow strikes, but would still travel with them, and three more were so badly injured that they might well never fight again and would have to be left behind.

Father Matthew had done his very best for all of them, but the tilt carts bore witness to the fierceness of the fighting, and the limits of even his surgery; though without him they would all have died.

The two Vernaille brothers might not have been up to much, but some of their men who had fought bravely until forced to surrender, did not deserve such poor leadership. Of those whom Gui had spared a dozen had asked to join his command, including their big sergeant, Martin Riberac who had fought like a tiger, and after a stiff examination from Fitzurse in weapon craft and obedience to orders, they had been duly sworn in under his simple leadership, exchanging the Golden Lion and Stars on Blue of Vernaille for the Rampant Scarlet Lion surcoats of Malwood, stained with blood as they were…and felt privileged to have been allowed to do so.

As Fitzurse had said: "Those lads did well, My Lord. That sergeant even managed to take a chunk out of my shield, the cheeky varmint! I'd rather have 'em with us than against us!"

But in the end it had taken two days to get themselves sorted out: letters to the King on his way to Marseilles on all that had happened, and letters to Sir James Bolderwood in The Forest; the dead stripped and buried; live horses gathered and dead ones burned; spare weapons and good armour saved and the wounded tended. And three left behind in the Abbey Hospitarium as too injured to travel further, with money for their welfare, their horses and their armour left with the Abbot, and orders to follow on if they could…or return to Malwood if the Abbot deemed them beyond further warfare.

Then they had left, and as Alicia and her small coterie fled into the mountains pursued by The Lady, and the Baron left Gruissan to capture her…her own leal man was still two days out of Bordeaux, with a week's hard journeying from there to Narbonne ahead of him, driving himself and his men with unrelenting vigour and determination. Sir Gui de Malwood did not carry the Lion Rampant on his chest and on his flag for nothing!

*

And all were seeking the same goal…the Lady Alicia de Burley!

Chapter 42...The Company of the White Rose are attacked in the forest.

With a shiver Alicia re-mounted her horse, shook her shoulders beneath her armoured jacket to settle them more comfortably and eased the sword at her waist.

Agnes, sitting there shivering in her armour, as much from fear as the cold, watched while Soraya fussed with her hat and cloak, making sure her hair was well hidden beneath them both. Then, with the slim French girl safely between them, Alicia and Agnes both took the long leading rein for a pack-horse each, and with Aquib in front, Aziz at the rear and Najid ahead of them all, they kicked back onto the road and began to climb the steep right hand bend that had stopped them earlier.

Sixty or seventy yards further up and the roadway began to level out, before dipping away towards a sort of hollow, then rising again...and it was then that Alicia suddenly realised that she could no longer see Aquib ahead of her in the thick mist. The faint blurry outline of horse and rider had simply vanished, yet she had heard nothing. One moment he had been there...the next gone!...Aquib had warned her that they might; she had just hoped they wouldn't! She had never felt quite so alone since El Nazir had seized her...*Dear Lord, Agnes will be terrified! Well. Kick-on, Alicia, and hope for the best*...And feeling frighteningly vulnerable, not daring to look behind her in case she unnerved the other two, especially Agnes, she pushed on along the track.

She had not realised before just how much she had been relying on their two huge Arab guardians. Facing Rochine with the men close by was one thing; being suddenly alone in a deeply forested, misty wilderness in a foreign land, where bandits might be out and about...and some fell beast might be stalking them, was just terrifying! And her whole body shuddered with fear of the unknown, dimpling her arms and making the hairs stand on all along them.

Then, just before the roadway dipped down, the whistling started.

First on one side of them and then the other: one moment very faint, and seemingly far away, the next almost right beside them...before dying away to nothing. And there were eyes in the mist. Huge, yellow tigers' eyes, the pupils striped and barred, that moved as she moved; making her heart turn over and her hands flutter with terror. Her gelding also tossed his head and snorted with fear, his brown eyes rolling madly as he strove to see what was happening around him, so that he scrabbled his hooves sharply on the track and violently jerked his head up, almost tearing the reins out of Alicia's hands as she fought one-handed to control him, the other still holding her pack-horse.

"*Alicia!*" Agnes shouted wildly from behind her, her mare also jittering beneath her "What's happening? What's going on? *I'm frightened!*"

"Close up on me, Agnes. Soraya too," she shouted out behind her. "And keep your nerve. This is just some awful silliness going on around us...*Dear God, I am terrified!*... Keep your horses well up to the bit and don't let them bolt. We must try and keep together!"...*This whistling makes my belly quake!*... And she turned to loosen her sword in its scabbard.

"*Where are the men?*" Agnes screeched at her a moment later. "I can't see them in all this mist. I can't see Aziz behind me...he was there a moment earlier. Now he's gone! And where is Aquib?" she cried out again, panic in every word. "I can't see him either! I can't see anything! *Alicia, what is happening?*"

"Calm down, sweetheart," Soraya called out then, allowing Agnes to come up along her right side, reaching out to stop her jibbing at the reins by taking the hand still desperately clutching the packhorse rein in an effort to comfort her. But at that moment Agnes screamed out: "*The horse has gone! The horse has gone!*"

And so it had, leaving just a fallen section of leading rein in her hand, cut through as cleanly as if someone had been slicing beans at home for supper. And then she screamed again, piercingly, as a great figure with antlers strapped to its head bounded, roaring out of the mist, and disappeared behind her, the stolen pack-horse running by his side as the whistling reached a sudden piercing crescendo.

Then silence!

Hearing Agnes scream, Alicia dropped her leading rein to give her greater freedom, and turned her rouncey hard left to swing back alongside Soraya and sandwich her between herself and Agnes, drawing her sword at the same time, as Gui had taught her long ago. But with Agnes still screeching in terror on the far right side of the track, like a rabbit in a weasel's jaws, and Soraya pressed up against her sword arm she was unable to wield her weapon properly. So seizing Soraya's arm she shouted: "*Dismount!* We cannot defend ourselves from the back of these horses...they are not trained destriers. They don't know what to do. Get off, Soraya! *Get off!* Agnes...*get off your horse* and come to me! Leave the bloody thing. God willing we can catch them up later."

In moments all three girls were huddled together in the middle of the track, now at the very bottom of the slight dip they had been riding down, the

259

ground rising around them, the great trees further apart and the undergrowth not so dense.

"Soraya, can you use a sword?" Alicia called urgently. "Agnes has no skill with weapons."

"A little. The Lady has taught me a few passes."

"Then take Agnes's sword, and her mailed gloves! Quickly, girl. They will be upon us in a moment, and bring her here, now. Good! *Good!* Agnes, lie down at our feet, quickly, and we will stand over you. It is what Gui told me I must do if ever he had occasion to defend me. Now, Soraya, brace yourself and sell your life dearly. It will be soon now. I can feel it!"

And the noises all started again!

All around them in the thick mist, the trees distant dark shrouded pillars, their leaved branches like mighty arms drooping towards the ground, wild figures leapt and shouted their war cries. Sometimes they rushed by them with shrieks and screams, their heads like those of wild beasts - boar and bear and lordly stag - appearing and disappearing like maddened wraiths, almost without human form. While at others they stood still, frozen statues in the dank murk, curled ram's horns to their shapeless faces, groaning like bulling heifers, *Hwooooooooooo! Hwooooooooooo!* The noise going on and on and on without remorse, coupled with the heavy beat of great thudding drums hidden deep in the misted forest.

And then, with a single mighty roar of noise and thunderous drum beats...there was complete silence!

Eerie in its suddenness, terrifying! Making the belly gripe, the heart race and the lungs pant, as the girls stood over Agnes and circled her in the sodden white-out, mouths dry with fear, peering into the billowing mists, their swords twitching, Alicia's mind racing...*Sweet Jesus! When will they come? When will they come?*... Then more whistling, soft at first and all around them, rising and rising to another wild, insane crescendo...and with that came the first brutal attack. Two men rushed in upon them out of the blank wetness, long iron studded clubs in their hands, and screamed their war cries as they came, faces screwed up in murderous rage, one on either side of them.

With no shield on her left arm to ward off a blow, Alicia remembered what both Sir Richard and Father Matthew had said to Gui so often... *'Use the point, dear boy, more than the blade. Use the point!'*...So as the first man reached her and raised his hands to strike her down, she leaped within his swing and slipping her right foot forward she drove her long blade upwards into his armpit with all the strength she had, her razor sharp steel piercing his ragged clothes and splitting his shoulder and neck apart so that he fell screaming beyond her, blood pouring from his wound as he thrashed about, his feet scrabbling frantically for several moments before he gave a dreadful groan and died. The other, seeing what had happened to his friend, fled screaming past them into the mist...and all around them the forest howled and hooted.

"*You killed him!*" Soraya cried out, her face white with the shock of it. "You killed him! How did you do that?"

"Gui taught me," Alicia rasped, straining for breath, her face sweating beneath her helmet, her heart hammering. "He showed me how to defend myself. And I listened to Sir Richard and Father Matthew. You and I do not have a man's strength to wield a blade for long," the words almost falling over themselves to get out, "but you can use the point, as I did. Step forward and thrust, and hope the forward rush will do the rest!"

"*I cannot!*"

"You *can!* Soraya...you *must* try...*here they come again!*" she shouted at her. "Imagine it is The Lady you strike at and don't hold back."

And with that the next attack came rushing in, and this time Alicia and Soraya met it back to back, their legs straddling Agnes, her small body curled up in a tight ball beneath them, their swords held low as they waited to see which way they should move. One was the clubman whose friend lay dead just beyond them. The other wielded a great curved sickle, and both were wild with rage, advancing slowly, shouting and roaring, but without any real weapon skill, just flensing their weapons furiously backwards and forwards across their bodies with every step.

"Cock your sword, Soraya!" Alicia called out sharply. "Over your right shoulder, two handed! No thrust will work here, you must try and cut down on their weapon arms. These men are not trained, but they are deadly. This will all be in the timing. I will take the sickle, you take the club. When I say *jump!* Spin round and go for it!"

And all the time she was watching her chosen enemy stride purposely towards her, his wicked curved blade on its thick wooden handle, swishing backwards and forwards, and up and down his front as he moved; determined to slice her as he would a sheaf of wheat, each empty blow enough to cut her head off.

Dancing from side to side on the balls of her feet as Gui had taught her long ago in the castle garth, Alicia watched and waited as the ragged man advanced, feeling Soraya matching her every movement, hoping that somewhere nearby their guardians would be waiting to make their move, but concentrating solely on the two men now intent on killing them. Left! Right! Their weapons swayed. Left! Right! Left!..."*Jump!*"...Alicia shouted and leaping sideways, she brought her sword down two-handed in one great swingeing blow that hewed the man's sickle arm off at the shoulder. A

261

massive, single blow that sliced through his bones and sinews as if they were paper, his blood spouting upwards into the wetness that pressed down all around them, covering her face and armour as with a terrible howl of agony he fell writhing at her feet.

And spinning with her momentum, she followed through, sweeping her blade backwards with a vicious reverse cut that almost severed the clubman's head, his left arm already on the ground where Soraya's blade had left it, his horrified shriek of pain immediately stilled as the blood from his neck fountained upwards, spraying everything with hot scarlet drops that steamed in the chill damp air. And once more the forest rang with shouts and howls.

"*Well done,* Soraya!" Alicia gasped, clasping her briefly, both now badged with blood on arms and faces, and all over their clothes and armour. "You were brilliant!"

"I closed my eyes, Alicia!" Soraya cried out, the tears flooding out. "*I closed my eyes!* And then he screeched and his blood ran hot all over me. It-it was horrible!"

"Yes! It is h-horrible," Alicia stammered also, her heart pounding, resting on her sword; her words running together as her chest heaved, the breath almost painful in her throat. "But we expect our men to do this for us all the time. It is only when..when you've done it yourself...as we have today...that you can understand how a man feels when he kills!"

"Is it over now?" A small voice queried from below them. "Have they all gone?"

"No Agnes," Alicia said firmly, reaching down to clasp her hand. "No. Not yet, I fear, sweetheart. This is only a pause. We have hurt them but not enough to stop them. Stay down where you will be safer. But I will take your helmet for Soraya. She needs it."

"What now, Alicia?" Soraya questioned urgently, as she tore off her leather hat, settling Agnes's helmet over her long hair, while Alicia fumbled with the straps, her sword thrust into the ground before her. "And where are the men? Where have they gone?"

"First we bargain...if we can. And as for Aquib, and the others? I don't know. But I do know that they are not far away. So we must try and buy them some more time! How does that feel?"

"Better," Soraya said strongly, shaking her head to make certain her helmet was secure. "I just wish I had her armoured jacket as well. No matter," she added flexing her arms. "But how do we buy the men more time?"

"Well...suppose we stir this lot up a little?" Alicia said grimly, waving her hand towards the thickly mist-shrouded forest full of calls and whistles and formless capering figures.

"*Are you mad?*" Soraya snarled, horrified. "Listen to them…they are worse than a pack of howling wolves! What are you going to say?"

"This," she said quietly, and then raising her voice she shouted into the opaque mist still swirling around them in the wind: "So…you *canaille!* You have our horses - and we have killed three of your men. How many more will fall to our blades before you slink back to your caves, or the holes in the ground where you live like the animals around you. Why seek death, when what you have already taken can give you life?"

"Because it pleases us!" An answer came fiercely out of the mists. "Because the real robbers around here are not us, but the heartless bastards who prey on our lives every day. Who keep us sweating and swinking in their fields for no return," the voice continued, making Soraya jump and glare ferociously into the mist. "And they use armed scum like you to carry out their orders!"

"*Excuses! Excuses!*" Alicia bawled into the opaque murk, pulling her blade beneath her arms to clean it, then whirling it around her head, the thick wetness making her voice harsh and hollow. "You prey on others like the reeking filth you pretend not to be!" She shouted towards the distant voice. "You murder whom you please; rape and pillage at will…and then seek to blame others for your wretched plight! You are no better than the ravening wolves that steal your sheep from their folds and tear their shepherds to pieces!" She added, her words deadened by the mist: "You are all just wild beasts!"

But before she could say another word, there was a great shout from somewhere up in the swirling blankness ahead of them, and a wild mob of ill armed ruffians rushed out upon them from the thickly shrouded forest round about, some with great flaring flambeaux, some with thick quarter-staves, others with weapons of iron and bone, some even with just their bare hands: all baying and rowling, capering like demons from the Pit, in a whirl of rags, tags, leather armour and chained steel.

And Alicia and Soraya fought them as fiercely as they could, while Agnes screamed in fear beneath them, her body drawn into a tight quivering ball.

Twice the girls cleared a space around themselves with their blooded swords. Parrying blows on their blades, as they whirled and flicked them from side to side; now thrusting forward with the point; now cutting sideways at any leg, arm or shoulder they could strike at. Ferociously they defied the mob that leaped and twisted about them like dervishes, all trying to strike down the two fighters who were so famously defying them.

And three more times Alicia and Soraya killed with fierce thrust or cutting edge, while maiming others. The swords they had brought with them from Malwood, edges still like razors, hewed through bones and sinews as if they were mere faggots bound with string: the dead lying in twisted heaps, the maimed dragging their blood-boltered bodies from the desperate scene, writhing and crying out with pain and terror.

But it could not last.

There were just too many of them, and quite suddenly the strength simply drained out of their arms and wrists, and with the bandit leader roaring for them to be taken alive, their blades were finally knocked from their hands, themselves beaten about their heads and shoulders and hurled to the ground in bitter defeat.

"*Stand them up!*" A harsh voice shouted out from a small mist-shrouded hillock further to the left that dominated the dip in the trackway where they had been attacked. "And let us see what we have caught for our amusement today. What fat piglets have been sent for us to roast squealing on our spit tonight?"

And stepping forward, dressed wholly in black…padded gambeson studded with iron, black mailed chausses and boiled leather vambraces strengthened with strips of forged steel on each forearm…came a man of medium height, with broad shoulders, strong thighs and a square face across which a terrible scar ran from his left eye right across his nose and face. Both ears had been hacked off, only the black holes they had once shielded showing though the lank hair that trailed around his shoulders, and he carried a sword.

"I am Paul *Grillade!*" he shouted as he strode towards where his men had pinioned Alicia's arms behind her. "I like my meat grilled with the blood running free! I am Paul *Cauchemar!*"…he roared down at poor Agnes, cowering between two of his men, stabbing at her with the point of his sword as she wriggled and whimpered in terror on the bloodied ground. "Your worst living nightmare!"

And whirling his sword he turned and raged at Soraya, where she stood, helmet torn off, clothes and arms smeared with blood all over, head down and utterly dejected: "I am Paul *Le Mort!* The death to all who defy me!" And his men bayed and howled their pleasure at each shout, like a pack of ravening wolves.

But suddenly, violently shaking herself free of the two men on either side of her, unprepared for any such action, Soraya rushed forwards and looking up she stared at their leader with bitter rage. Her eyes seeming to stab green fire, she brought her hand round with every remaining bit of her strength, and slammed him across his face with her mailed gloves as hard as she could.

264

Chapter 43...How the Company of the White Rose escaped the Outlaws.

"NO!" she shouted at the top of her voice as she hit him, the solid *smack!* ringing out across the mist-laden clearing as his head shuddered with the weight of her blow. "*NO!* You are Paul Fermier, murderer and hunted criminal; arrested and slighted," she shouted, jabbing at his empty ear sockets. "Cast out and driven from your village for your crimes...our village; it was you who beggared our father and shattered our family. You are Paul Fermier," she cried out again in rage..."*My brother!*" And she spat in his face.

White with shock, the mark of Soraya's hand livid across his cheek, his flesh scraped open by her mailed mittens, the outlaw leader was struck dumb by what she had said, clutching his scarred face where she had struck him, all around him equally stunned by what had happened. Then, with a cry of fury he strode up to her, seized her long hair in his hand and twisted her head so he could see her better, and snarling with rage he shook her like a tree in a gale, while Alicia struggled to break free from the two men who had fiercely gripped her by her armoured shoulders.

"By God's blood, so you are!" he sneered, dragging her round to face his leering followers. "The silly bitch is right! This is my little sister!" he roared out, shaking her head at them until she was dizzy. "The famous family beauty! So like our dear Infidel Mama," he raged at her. "That's why Papa loved you so much! Always *you!* You always were his pet, his *petite choute!*" He spat at her. "His 'little darling!' But I fixed you both good and proper, *little sister*," he snarled, straightening up. "Good and proper! The Lord Baron and I. Showed him where all the springs flowed, bartered the lands and sold you off! You and our poor Papa both!' He sneered again. "Yes...I fixed you good and proper, you screeching bitch!"

And while Soraya stood there, shocked to the very core of her being by what he had said, bereft of sound or movement, he struck her fiercely across the face, then back-handed her even more so, a vicious blow that raked her face with his knuckles, her teeth tearing them open even as they split her lips and hurled her almost senseless to the ground.

Then, swooping down on her, he seized her by her long chestnut hair and dragging her upright he tore her clothes apart, then hit her again so her head snapped backwards with the force of his attack, hurling her in a crumpled mess almost at Alicia's feet, half naked, her breasts and shoulders spilling out of her ravaged clothing into the damp, chilled air that still swirled around them. Agnes, who had been dropped by the men holding her when their leader had first roared out, scrabbled on her hands and knees across the torn glade to cover Soraya's nakedness with her own body and comfort her in her unspeakable distress.

Leaving Soraya sprawled, sobbing on the ground, he turned to Alicia, still armoured, her helmet still firmly tied beneath her chin with leather straps, her shoulders gripped and her arms pinioned behind her by two of his men, blood all over her face and hands.

"And who are you, little man?" he sneered at her, his bloodied hands on his hips, his men gathered all around them in a ring of hardened, leering faces. "A stupid soldier boy who carries out the orders of those who drive families out into the wilderness when they cannot pay their rents; take the best of all we have when we die; rob us of our livelihood and burn us out with their wars?" And he smiled at the jeers and howling that his words had delivered for him.

"Let go of his arms!" he ordered her guards with a vicious smirk across his mutilated face. "Let us see what this lump of shite is all about, eh lads? This stupid soldier boy, whom the good Lords of Chalabre and Limoux have sent to us today! Whose twisted guts we will use for bowstrings and whose blood we will drink with the wine we took off the Bishop last month!" he added to rough shouts of brutal humour.

"That'll go nicely with his fucking balls!" someone shouted with a bark of laughter.

"It did with the Bishop's!" Another crowed. "Shame he didn't like them, and after Raoul had taken such pains to cook them too!" And they all roared with laughter.

"And they'd go well with the goat's cheese we had off those fucking nuns!" another shouted out.

"Not half as bloody good as those nuns were for fucking though!" yet another man bawled out. "They were the tastiest fucking dishes we've had for *months!*" And another gale of raucous laughter swept round the men gathered there, convulsed with the coarse, ribald wit they'd just heard, while Paul Fermier stood in front of Alicia and laughed the most at the wretched look of shock and disgust that ran across her face, ghastly white and blooded from her fight.

Then, tossing off the hands which had held her, Alicia unlaced her helmet straps with studied care, not a single tremble in her fingers, and taking off her casque, and pushing back the steel coif beneath it, she shook out her golden hair to a gasp of surprise, causing all about her to take a sudden step backwards as it suddenly fell in thick waves around her armoured shoulders.

266

"No! You scum, *Fermier!*" she spoke out then in words of crystal glass, shaking her head to clear her eyes as he, too, stepped back amazed. "I am no stupid 'soldier boy'," she sneered. "I am the Lady Alicia de Burley, a woman grown, and your sister's friend. And a fighter who can wield a blade with her well enough to slay half a dozen of the disgusting *rabble* you have gathered around you," she mocked, gesturing to the bodies still lying where they had fallen. "For soldiers they are not! And I have maimed others who will never fight again!

"You piece of choice *filth!*" she snarled, stepping fearlessly towards him…her heart almost leaping out of her chest. "You strike down an unarmed, defenceless woman and boast of your wickedness as if you were a hero. But where were you, Paul *Cauchemar*? Paul *Grillade*?…when your men were fighting?" She railed at him. "Hiding in the mists in your fancy clothes and calling out your orders, while two girls, with little skill but great courage, cut your pathetic *mop heads* to pieces! Then, when it is all safely over, here you are," she sniped at him, "O mighty one…a carnival figure in black with a big sword! A mountebank if ever I saw one!" And she laughed in his face, as the voices so loud around her moments before suddenly faded away, and their mouths fell open in amazement…*Now, just keep gawping you scum! That is my sword over there. They must have dropped it there. Now…if I can just get close enough?*

"You, Paul Fermier, *Le Mort*…The Death…are no more than a common bully!" She chided him with icy disdain. "A nasty, slinking coward who makes war on priests and women, and then boasts of his brave deeds in the ale house!" she added, her eyes locked on his, while subtly moving sideways towards her fallen sword as she spoke, now just a few feet from where it had been thrown down when she had been captured. "You are no better than the beasts amongst whom you live!"

Spell-struck by her words, and the sheer forcefulness of her tirade, Paul Fermier was forced backwards with every phrase she spoke. This man, known for his wickedness and vile brutality, seemed to wilt before Alicia's forcefulness, her face and armour still stained with the blood of those she had cut and slain. While his whole command of wild killers and gutter fighters, seemingly also mesmerised by her words, and by her utter contempt for their leader, were unnerved, silent and did nothing…Alicia edged her way closer and closer to where her sword lay discarded on the torn ground and bloody ground.

It was at just the moment when she felt close to make her move, that she became intensely alert to some form of wild movement in the murky treeline behind Paul Fermier's shoulders. There, where the mist seemed thinner, saplings were quivering, and bushes being thrust aside, everything becoming

267

wilder by the second, and choosing her words carefully she suddenly bawled out in English. *"Come to me quickly! Soraya and Agnes are alive. I cannot hold these men much longer. Aquib, Aziz, Najid! Come to me! Come to me!"*

Then taking one more sideways step from the big bandit leader, now stunned into immobility by the words she had just shouted out in a language he recognised but could not speak, she mocked him mercilessly one more time: "Thank God I am English, *Fermier!* We do not creel like sick babes in England when our lives are tough! Mewling and puking and seeking our mother's tits for comfort! You ignorant peasant! *Vous cochon! Vous maquereau!*...We fight to the death!"

And seeing the fierce flash of wild anger rip through him at being called a '*pig*' and a '*pimp*', Alicia at last dived for her sword as she had so often watched Gui's men practising at home: running, tumbling and sweeping her weapon up into her hands as she moved, to roll up perfectly on to the balls of her feet, crouched down and sword held out...just as a roaring, coughing hell hurtled towards them from the forest edge behind her, hotly pursued by Aziz and Najid both wielding huge flambeaux in one hand and their own chosen weapons in the other.

It was a bear!

A great Pyrenean she-bear from the High Pyrenees, like a Rocky Mountain grizzly, galloping as fast as a horse, with a terrifying coughing roar across the glade, eyes red and mouth agape, saliva dripping from her massive jaws, while from right behind Fermier came Aquib, his huge scimitar in one hand, a flambeaux in the other, and driving two cubs before him, both creeling in terror as they fled, the stink of them almost enough to make her eyes water.

And pandemonium followed! Howling panic and desperate fear.

"Une Ourse! Une Ourse!...A She-Bear! *Courez! Courez!*...Run! *RUN!"* And run they did, in all directions like headless chickens, screaming in fear and terror...but for many not nearly fast enough...and Paul Fermier not at all. Appalled by the sudden dreadful change around him, he stood rooted to the ground for just that moment too long...and when he did turn to run it was too late!

Rearing up on her massive hind legs, enormous forepaws held open in front of her, both armed with great fistfuls of huge black claws, mouth agape and fearful teeth glistening, the she-bear came roaring and foaming with rage. Towering over the petrified outlaw leader, with a single vicious *bat!* of a mighty forepaw, she knocked his sword aside as if it were a harmless pin, and seizing his head in her jaws and his body with her massive fore-claws, she first cracked his skull open and then, with a single massive tear, ripped him into

268

bloody pieces, ribs and offal flying in all directions as he was literally dismembered.

Pausing a moment to savage Fermier's shattered carcase and grabble at his entrails with her teeth, she hurled it away from her...as desperate to reach her cubs as they were to reach their mother. Rushing on, she attacked her next howling victim without pause, her great muzzle now dark with blood...and then onto the next, and the next, coughing and roaring as only a wild and angry bear can. Her great hind quarters bunched behind her, she strode and rolled from side to side amongst her fleeing enemies, galloping one moment, rearing up on her hind legs the next, her mouth running with blood, her ravening claws filled with torn flesh and sinews. Some she swiped with her huge front paws, disembowelling them as she passed by, others had their faces ripped apart, or their arms torn off, as she savaged with tooth and claw every terrified fighter she came upon.

And where the bear led, Aziz and Najid followed, Aziz with his scimitar and Najid with his great curved khanjar, both with great flaring torches of spitting, snapping pine and resin...and as Aquib had promised, they wreaked havoc.

Aziz struck left and right with his huge curved blade, slicing heads, arms and bodies in bloody profusion as they came; some he even split from crown to navel. Also they thrust their great flambeaux in the faces of their enemies, burning out their eyes, setting their hair on fire, making them howl and scream with pain...and while Aziz hacked them down across the neck or shoulder in a spray of blood and splinters of bone...Najid thrust and sliced with his wicked curved blade into their hearts and bellies. And both shouted and roared: "*Allah Akbar! Allah Akbar!*"..."God is Great! God is Great!"...as they ran, their dark Arab faces and their wild, foreign war cries causing almost as much terrified panic as the bears!

And the noise was appalling! Demonic!

Screaming, howling men: crying, bleating cubs: roaring, snarling she-bear...and the fierce clash and sizzle of steel, as fighting men and brawling beasts reeled backwards and forwards through the swirling mists and battered undergrowth; while Agnes wrapped her arms over Soraya and Alicia who had dropped to the ground beside them the moment the bear had started the attack. Shielding them both with her body, she pressed them all into the cold, wet grassy track, hiding her face from all the battle-rage going on around her, and praying for it all to stop.

Aquib, driving the cubs before him with his flambeau, singed their brown rumps as he bounded forward, making them leap and bleat and cry out in terror, their fur smoking and flaming. And he was just as merciless with his blade as

269

either of his friends. Flensing his enemies with the strength of four, he hewed through bone and steel with the ease of hacking melons, and with the same sound, also roaring out *"Allah Akbar! Allah Akbar!"* at the top of his voice, his armour running with brains and blood until they dripped onto the ravaged ground with every step he took

Then, in the middle of the small clearing, mother met cubs at last, and with a coughing roar she fell onto her huge forepaws, and with her two cubs close beside her, still crying out in fear, she galloped roaring off with them into the forest, crashing away through the thick bushy undergrowth as desperate to escape the flame and fury of that desperate fight, as the remainder of Fermier's outlaw band, and just as swiftly.

And then, suddenly it was all over…and as if at a signal the mist cleared away at last, blown free from the high tops and deep valleys by a warm westerly breeze as the sun broke through in great shafts of golden light that shimmered amongst the trees, returning colour, warmth and light to all around them.

It fell on Alicia, Soraya and Agnes struggling up onto their knees, gasping for breath and shivering from the aftermath of all they had gone through, tears in all their eyes as reaction set in. It fell on Aquib, Aziz and Najid, chests heaving from exertion, blood from their own wounds and those of their enemies running down their arms and off their armour, dented and torn in places, and on their blades encrusted with blood and hair.

And it fell on the ghastly chaos of the dead scattered all around the dipping roadway: heads, arms and torn bodies; brains, entrails and scattered offal… upon the brutally injured, some clutching their bowels in their hands, others their shattered limbs and butchered arms and hands, groaning, whimpering and swearing as their lives ran out in scarlet streams across the forest glade.

And it fell in glimmering shafts upon Paul Fermier's shattered carcase, ripped and torn by tooth and claw, utterly savaged by the she-bear's violent attack, his skull shattered into broken shards where her great teeth had crushed it, his body in torn pieces, only recognisable by the shreds of black leather and torn armour he had been wearing; the whole now lying in a great pool of blood

Then silence! Both sudden and complete, without the sound of bird or wounded, almost as unnerving as the noise of battle, and at first no-one spoke.

Then, with a grimace, Alicia staggered on to her feet and stumbled, like a drunkard, across to where Aquib was standing looking around him. Calm as always, his massive chest still heaving, he looked down at her with a smile, while Aziz strode off to recover their horses, now quietly cropping some distance away along the road, and Najid walked softly amongst the injured.

270

His great khanjar now safely returned to its curved sheath, its fine blade of shimmering blue steel held sweetly in its usual place, he now grasped a narrow bladed poniard firmly in his right hand, a lethal needle of razor steel.

"Well,…*Afdal Sadeaky*…my best friend…" Alicia said with a grimace as she flexed her shoulders. "What kept you?"

"The bears, my lady!"

"Mmmm…The bears? And what were you trying to do with these bears, oh *Afdal Sadeaky*? Eat them?"

"No, my lady. Stop them from eating us first! Then help them to eat your enemies."

"But our enemies almost ate *us*, Aquib! Where were you…oh my Guardian of Guardians?"

"Up a tree!"

"*Up a tree?* Were you mad? Bears climb trees, Aquib! That's one of the things bears can do…they climb trees."

"So I discovered, my Lady," he said with his rumbly laugh. "I have not fought bears before…but we learned…very quickly!"

"So I can see," she replied with a sudden grin. "By the fact that you are here and they are not…and nor are most of this bastard's bloody gang, either," she added, going across to where Fermier's mangled body lay already covered with flies. "What do we do about this bloody shambles?" she asked, gesturing around her. "And about the wounded?"

"The dead, my Lady? Leave them, as they would have left you; as a terrible warning to others of their kind. The crows, the wolves and foxes, and the rats, flies and beetles will devour them. *Allah Akbar!* As for the wounded? There will be no wounded, my Lady."

"No wounded, Aquib?" Alicia queried sharply, raising her eyebrows and waving her arms around her to where there were a slew of men groaning and rolling in agony on the ground, with many others propped up against the trees…*What does he mean, 'No wounded?' There are dozens of them!*

"No, my Lady," he repeated in his deep, calm, gravelly voice. "There will be no wounded! Najid is gently seeing to their needs."

"But…" she began to exclaim, shocked by the simple brutality of his solution…*Good God! He means to kill them all! Do I care?*

"We cannot take them with us, my Lady Alicia," he said, looking into her deep, blue eyes. "We cannot stop to explain to any authority how all this happened. We do not have the time, remember? The Lady will surely be pressing us hard. And we cannot leave them here in their agony untended. Nijad's 'needle' will solve their pain and they will feel nothing.

"Needle?" She queried, eyebrows up again…"*What needle?*

271

"His next most favourite blade, my Lady," he said in his rich, gravelly voice. "Eight inches of finest tapered Toledo steel, with a gold wired ivory hilt and golden quillons...he took it from an angry Spaniard in Algiers."

She opened her mouth to speak, but he simply shook his head: "Don't ask!"

"Very well," she said quietly, looking up at him from the corner of her eyes. "No prisoners!"...*And that's that! And, no!...I don't care. They are all bastards who deserved to die. Every last one of them.. I only wish I'd had enough courage to have killed more myself!* And she surprised herself by bursting into tears.

"Do not grieve for a single one of them, my Lady Alicia. They are all worse than infidels!" And he smiled down at her mischievously, seeing she was one. "*Allah* will deal with them as they deserve, and they will all be free to join their bastard leader in Hell where they all belong."

"I do not weep for them, Aquib. They all deserved to die. I weep for myself...that I, a woman, have been forced to take life...and for my friends that I did not do more to save them from so terrible a morning."

"My Lady...Truly you are '*usama*' today," and he put his massive arms round her slender shoulders. "No Arab girl could have done what you have done today. Aziz and I are honoured to have shared our steel with such an Angel of God. *Allah* Himself surely led you and protected you today. No *djinn* could have been more terrible." And he took her hand and kissed it. "When he hears of all this, my Prince will be proud that he sent us to guard you. Your courage today gives honour to us all." And she was astonished.

And looking all around the clearing they turned their faces back, each to the other, and with a broad smile..."*Insha'Allah!*"...they both said together, with sudden wicked grins..."*Insha'Allah!*"...Aquib adding in his dry way. "At least we have just saved this area the cost of hanging them all!"

"Aquib is right," Soraya said quietly, coming up beside her, her face horribly swollen, one eye almost closed. "I heard what he said Alicia. He is right in *all* things!'"

"But your brother...?"

"You saw what my brother was like! Saw what he did to me...and what he has done to others, and ordered others to do. He wrecked our family. I knew about the money...I told you on the *Morning Star* that Papa had to find extra. When he went to the Baron for it? But I didn't know until much later why he had needed so much. Poor Papa, no wonder he was broken by all that happened. I shall shed no tears for *him*, my love," she said, spurning Paul's shattered carcase with her foot. "This is the best way for that...that *bastard* to go...food for the wild things of the wild. Let him rot as he let others. And may

272

God show him some mercy…for I never shall!" And burying her head in her hands in almost unbearable sorrow, she turned into Alicia's open arms and wept, her whole body shaking.

And putting her arm around her, Alicia led her away to where Agnes was standing, a rather forlorn little figure surrounded by fly-covered corpses, and with soft cloths in her hands with which to bind wounds and wash Soraya's face.

Chapter 44...How Alicia and The Lady were divided by a Bunch of Grapes.

hey left within the hour beneath a clear sky.

The threatened storm from yesterday had long since blown away with the morning's mists, the forest steaming in the warm sunshine as it dried out, and with the mist melting away they were able to pick up the pace. Najid rode far ahead along the twisting trackway, all the others following close behind at a fast canter, rounceys and pack-horses all bouncing busily along the forest roadway.

Now at last they were able to make up for time lost during that dreadful morning, and by midday were dropping steeply down into the tiny hamlet of Saint-Benoit, placed at the head of a violently sharp bend that doubled right handed completely back on itself. Here they were astonished by the welcome they received from the forest dwellers as they arrived there, for the whole village came running out to meet them, men, women and children crowding round them with shouts and smiles and laughter.

"We have heard you have slain the outlaws! That foul hornet's nest of robbers and murderers led by Fermier *Grillade*. Many called him *Le Mort!* He has been a terrible scourge upon us for years. Yet no-one could finish him, until you!"

And while the children petted the horses, and the men gathered around Aquib and Aziz, fascinated by their dark faces, their outlandish armour and fierce weaponry, they were all offered food and much kindness...especially poor Soraya who was offered soft bandages for her wounded face, with a fresh poultice of comfrey leaves, and liniment and tinctures of arnica that she could use afterwards.

But they could not stay long and were soon back on the narrow track, always pushing forward, always worrying how close their pursuers were, knowing that by now The Lady and her soldiers, led by Gaston de Vere, must be hot on their trail; but with no knowledge of how close they might be they felt driven to move onward with all possible dispatch.

With the weather holding, but clouding up again from the north-east they passed through La Bezole in the late afternoon, once more enjoying the intense scrutiny and hearty welcome of the tiny community who lived there. Delighted to help them water their horses, the children were fascinated by the dark skins of their Arab guardians, daring each other to touch their skins to see if the colour would rub off on their fingers! Then with a wave of their hands and

274

shouts of goodwill from that tiny community, they were off again, now riding out of the mountains and forests at last to take to the plains that stretched all the way ahead of them to Carcassonne.

And at the small village of Ajac, surrounded by acres and acres of vineyards, green and fruitful in the evening sunshine, they halted for the night at *Le Grappe de Raisins*... The Bunch of Grapes'...a low slung building of yellow painted plaster beneath red pantiles. Here the tall *aubergiste,* with great moustaches and a ringing laugh, Monsieur Le Bon, came striding out to greet them. Wreathed in smiles that so famous a party of unexpected visitors should come to his house, he was determined to do his best to make his inn welcoming and his village proud.

His wife, Annette, as petite as her husband was large, with liquid brown eyes and a warm heart, clucked over Soraya's injuries with lots of hands thrown up bore her off to her kitchen immediately with many *'Quelle horreurs!'* to wash out her eyes and replace her comfrey poultice with something special from her own cupboard.

"This is St John's own plant," she said in a hushed voice, taking out a jar of beautiful, rich red liniment. "St John the Baptist. We call it 'St John's Wort'. It is a plant from the golden cornfields, with beautiful yellow petals that grow like a halo. You pick the flowers on the 24th June...St John's birthday, and when you prick the petals they bleed!" she almost whispered. "Great crimson drops of blood like he did, when that wicked Salome had his poor head chopped off. You put the petals in olive oil and leave them, and this wonderful liniment is born. Take this, *Petite Lapine*, and massage it into your poorly face and if you have a goodly heart, *ma chérie*, St John will heal you...and make you *feel* better, too! It is truly wonderful, *ma petite*. It will do you so much good!" And she had given Soraya a great hug and a kiss on her other cheek, and packed her off with the jar in her hands to find Agnes.

So, with a bright smile, Soraya had tripped off to find her, and Alicia, and ask them to help her with her face, and see if somehow the blood that had sprayed all over their clothes that morning could now be washed off.

But within moments of their arrival it seemed as if the whole village was cramming into the inn to meet them; to thank them and to gift them with a night of laughter and tales. Everyone wanting to hear how Alicia and Soraya had fought the outlaws in the hollow; how she had dared to defy Fermier *Le Mort* before his own men, and how their huge guardians had rescued them with a sleuth of ferocious mountain bears and great swords of power from distant Araby, on magic carpets that had flown them all round the world!

And, of course, how the wicked Paul Fermier...*Grillade! Cauchemar! Le Mort!*...had come to the dreadful death that so many had longed and prayed

275

for. How he had been ripped in pieces by the teeth and claws of a ferocious she-bear, clearly sent by God, along with their new friends, in answer to their many prayers to cleanse their mountains of his evil.

The wine had flowed, and so had the juice of many fruits for their Arab guests, the first infidels that most had ever seen. The food had been wonderful, everyone bringing something to the inn; Najid using the last of his precious rice to present a fantastic lamb ragout, made with some of his precious spices, such as no-one had ever tasted before. And with shouts and cries of eternal goodwill and best wishes, they had all finally staggered to their rest long after the moon had risen over the silent fields and vineyards all around them, where screech owls on silent wings of white feathers sought field voles among the long rows of vines, from which their grapes hung in huge bunches, swelling beautifully in time for the autumn harvest.

After such a terrifying start to their day they had all been delighted to find such good comfort and warmth at Ajac, especially Agnes. She had been most affected by the desperate fight in the forest, and had at last begun to recover her spirits. Bitterly ashamed that throughout their horrific ordeal in the clearing she had been unable to do much of anything except scream, she had been unusually withdrawn.

But as Alicia pointed out to her with much love and kindness: "Not everyone can wield a sword in anger, sweetheart. I didn't know that I could, really. But I was brought up to it, more than ever you were. But you were always there for me, Agnes, when I was small and needed a caring shoulder, especially when Gui went away to the north and I realised how much I missed him!

"Today, you may not have stood out with a shaft of steel in your hand, Agnes, and your heart in your mouth…but you were there for Soraya, when she most ever needed you, and you truly hazarded your life for her when you covered her nakedness with your body, and then shielded *both* of us when that bear attacked. It is easy in the rush of fighting to be brave, honeyone…but to do what you did takes real cold courage…and that is far braver. Oh, dearest Agnes," she wept then, flinging her arms around her and hugging her fiercely. "I am *so* proud to have you as my friend!"

So that was that, and they all slept that night with warmth in their hearts and a smile on their faces for a night's rest well earned.

One more day's good travelling should see them onto the Via Aquitania at last, and well beyond the great walled city of Carcassonne itself. Then, just a half a day's journey to Narbonne, with a dozen miles further to Gruissan, and with Fortune smiling on them, they should be beneath the Baron's walls in two days' time…and safety!

Meanwhile, in La Bezole, just ten miles from where they were sleeping, The Lady Rochine and her men were also stopped for the night, having forced the pace fiercely all day to catch up with their desperate quarry.

Not stopping as Alicia had done at Roquefixade two nights before, they had pushed further on to Lavalenet, arriving there almost as the moon was rising, and managed to force a meal and a bed for the night from the *aubergiste* of *Le Sanglier Noir*, Monsieur Thomas: Rochine deciding that as a black boar was her father's blazon it had to be the best place to stay.

But Monsieur Thomas had not been too pleased with The Lady's typical high-handed demands, nor by her threats and raging…but with a good fistful of silver from de Vere and a quiet word with the Cousins who promised to '*fucking drown him in his own fucking pig shit*' if he didn't find a meal and rooms for the night, he soon did…even though it had meant moving himself and his wife out of their room and into Harry Ostler's simple quarters above the stables.

As for Harry Ostler, he and his doxy had to sleep with the horses in the stables along with de Vere's command, and a very busy night they all made of it too! Harry's doxy, Marie-Anne, particularly so…and while Harry came away with a nasty lump on his head and a surprise headache when he finally awoke…she was left with a good pocket full of silver to show for the stalwart exercises his men had put her through, never really appreciating until that evening quite what 'Good Service' really meant!

Then, up before Lauds in the morning, they had all left at first light, still following the trail Alicia and her Arabs had left, simply by virtue of their being different. Better still, by the time they reached Chalabre for breakfast, the mist that had so bedevilled Alicia's company earlier was even then clearing from the distant tops and valleys. And before long the whole tale of how the notorious bandit, Paul Fermier '*Le Mort*', had been famously slain, along with his whole outlaw gang that very day, by a small party of armed strangers…was rapidly acquiring both heavenly and heroic status...and was on everyone's lips, only making their chase easier.

By then it seemed as if half the countryside was on the move, all wanting to see the sight of the famous battle…especially as the bodies were still supposed to be there for all to see! So their trail then became more like a procession, with the whole world and his wife busily expressing their opinions as to what had really happened in the thick mountain mists…not least because no-one had been able to deal with this man and his gang of murderous thieves and vagabonds before.

Of course the moment Rochine heard Fermier's name she realised exactly who the dead, murderous outlaw leader might truly have been, and was as eager as her Commander to push on into the mountains and see for herself what had really taken place. She was deeply intrigued to learn how six people, three of them girls, had actually managed to slaughter so many terrifying fighters, let alone their ferocious leader!

And when they finally got there, impressive it surely was…and very puzzling also as the wounds and torn bodies were more like those made by a tempestuous madman, a completely insane murderer armed with an adze and a sharpened garden rake, so hacked about and mauled some of the bodies were. And there were so many of them, their eyes and tongues already pecked and torn out, and bits of them too had been scattered everywhere. And there were no wounded. Those propped up against trees had all been throat cut; those who had crawled away with frightful wounds had been heart stabbed with a fine blade slipped through the collar bones to pierce the heart as neatly as you please.

Rochine shook her head and snorted with disgust.

She was not at all surprised that the man whom her father had helped all those years ago, and who had helped him with the Fermier lands, and with the elder daughter, should have come to so vicious and violent an end. He had always been a boastful fool. A pity he hadn't managed to kill his precious sister…and that bitch shielding her. Now that would have been providential! And she kicked her horse on, a grim smile stitched across her lovely face as she did so, still astonished at how much killing had taken place with so few men to carry it out!

*

With the weather now more helpful, and all around them drying out most pleasingly, they had pushed on at a fast canter, passing through Saint Benoit in late afternoon, with more ballyhoo about the deaths of Fermier and his outlaw band from all the villagers. They, only too willing to tell all they could about those who had cleared their mountains of such a

278

frightful scourge, were also full of how smashed up one of the girls with them had been, the one called 'Soraya'...which pleased Rochine mightily!

Here, at last, they also learned about the bears that had come down from the high mountains, and how the Arab men had so cleverly used them. And The Lady ordered de Vere onwards again, her anger bubbling, her heart seething with jealousy and spite for what Alicia had achieved. Eaten by it, consumed by it, she urged her men onwards, sparing nothing, despite de Vere's advice to slow the pace.

But with every expectation of catching up with their errant runaways by the end of the day, she refused to listen...until her horse suddenly threw a shoe and de Vere's went lame, and they were forced both by the lateness of the hour and the lameness of their mounts to call a halt to their pursuit at La Bezole.

Here there was no inn, but there was good stabling and a forge, the only one for miles, and the villagers were hospitable enough to offer simple accommodation which Rochine loathed on sight...and de Vere rather enjoyed, along with the comely wife of one of the villagers who was delighted to keep his bed warm for a fair consideration, as her man was away up in the high pastures with the sheep, and she was lonely!

In the morning she and the other hamlet dwellers fed them all well; the blacksmith sorted out The Lady's gelding; de Vere's horse had remarkably recovered from its lameness, and leaving a goodly purse of silver for all his hostess's pains, which she had thoroughly enjoyed being a lively, cheerful girl, de Vere led Rochine and her men back onto the track and down towards the plains that led at last to Carcassonne.

Chapter 45...How the White Rose was saved by the Lord Baron, Sir Roger de Brocas.

The night that Alicia was in Ajac, and Rochine was in La Bezole, the Lord Baron Sir Roger de Brocas was just beyond Carcassonne towards Limoux, in the village of Rouffiac-d'Aude.

There he was resting in *L'Auberge du Reynard et de L'Oie...*'The Fox and Goose', where de Vere had advised him to be when he had sent his last message, knowing where Alicia and her party were aiming for...as of course he had suggested it through Louis at Foix.

But Lord Roger who had set out so precipitously from Gruissan had already been there a day, and was now getting frustrated, anxious not to miss his quarry - and equally anxious that Alicia should run headlong and panting into his arms and not into his daughter's, when there was no knowing what the outcome might be, given how deeply jealous Rochine was proving to be and how uncertain her temper could be when jealousy gripped her.

The inn was both old and well-appointed and the *aubergiste*, Monsieur Hugo Perdrix, was as plump and homely as the game bird whose name he carried, as was Céleste, his equally plump and cheerful wife, and like the French partridges for which his country was famous, and he was named, he too liked to wear red leggings: cotton ones in the summer and woollen ones in the winter. Thanks to his lady, his inn had become famous for both its cuisine and for the comfort of its half-a-dozen rooms upstairs where visiting gentry could always be sure of the warmest welcome. Where the sheets were dry and of good Egyptian cotton, the covers of best English wool and there were no fleas or rats!

In fact it was a far better place to stay than in any of the *auberges* in Carcassonne itself, except the castle of course, for the city was always noisy, and pretty noisome as well, with its narrow twisted streets and huddled shops and houses, no proper drainage, the ginnels not paved and the cobbles often choked with filth...everyone waiting for a really good storm to wash the city clean.

The place was bad enough in winter...in the summer it could be vile beyond description...and from all his contact with Sheik El Nazir and his many Arab traders, Lord Roger had come to value cleanliness most highly.

So he was more than an occasional visitor, and the *aubergiste* knew the Baron of old, and when he saw how smartly he had dressed that morning after breaking his fast in his room, and the size of his escort who were putting up with others in the village. Even the Officer Commanding his Castle Guard was not staying at the inn, and his full Guard Commander was not with him either...So Monsieur Hugo smiled to himself and thought...A girl! No, maybe not this time...a real Lady?

All knew the Baron needed an heir, and that meant a bride. So perhaps a bridal was in the air for the Lord Baron of Narbonne and Gruissan? And he smiled and louted low, offering Lord Roger his best Burgundy, kept only for the most special occasions...and in the Baron's favourite silver-gilt goblet without which he never travelled. And he smirked at the way the man twitched his clothes and stamped around his chamber as he drank it, becoming more restless with every passing moment.

Finally the great Lord of Narbonne and Gruissan, the ally of powerful counts and the friend of kings and princes, could stand it no longer. Tossing his empty goblet to the *aubergiste* as he passed him, he stalked outside to find his escort already drawn-up for his inspection. Each man had polished his steel helmet and his chainmail armour till it shone in the fresh sunlight of the new day, where a cooler breeze now blew up from the north-east, brocading the sky with clouds. Each horse had been beautifully groomed until its coat shone and its tail floated in the ruffling air, hooves oiled and gleaming, fetlocks trimmed, manes brushed out...and the Baron paused to growl his thanks to Xavier Le Brun, massively waiting at the side of his men, and to his stalwart troopers, for their splendid turnout.

Then without further delay, Lord Roger swung up onto Charlemagne's back, his saddle shining, his enormous destrier's coal black coat beautifully smooth to the touch, neck arched proudly, the whole great beast looking magnificent, and with a shout and an imperious wave de Brocas ordered his men to move out, Le Brun beside him, one of his troopers carrying the Boar's Head standard rippling behind them.

*

Meanwhile, though Alicia and the Company of the White Rose had risen early as usual, they had all decided on a real breakfast for a change with fresh fruit, hard boiled eggs and new baked rolls, local butter and comb honey, all washed down with hot lemon water from Nijad's hand, his very last lemons from the *Morning Star*.

And so with a proper meal inside them for once, they had set out cheerfully on almost the last leg of their long journey slightly later than expected, but as they had done at the start, with Aquib leading, the three girls next, Soraya still the only one not wearing armour between them, and Najid and Aziz at the rear with a pack-horse each on a long rein.

Overhead the sky was a blue silk patchwork of clouds, the wind light but cool, and with a wistful sigh as she thought of Gui still out there somewhere, she called Najid for a swift leg-up, dropped herself down into her high saddle once more, and with a brief scrunch of hooves Aquib led them out of the small inn yard, and with a flick of tails and a toss of heads their rounceys bounced onto the track and they were away.

"How far to Limoux, Alicia?" Soraya asked her, stretching her legs in their long stirrups, the leathers creaking as she put her full weight onto them.

"About an hour...maybe less if we kick-on a bit. It's about twenty two miles altogether to Carc'. We should do that easily today. More I hope. I don't want to get caught in a city I don't know, and where I can't see round corners!"

"Do you know the way through Limoux?" Agnes asked her then, a little anxiously. "It would be awful to get lost now!"

"Don't worry, sweetheart. Louis' little map is quite clear, and Aquib knows where we have to go. There are only three main routes in and out of Limoux. We are on one, coming in from the west...from the mountains. Of the other two, one turns slightly south of east, to the right of the big river and the other one north, to the left of it. That's the one we want. Stop fussing, honeyone. We will be alright! Now...let's crack on!"

And digging in their heels they cantered gently off, picking up speed as they bounced onto the roadway itself, the horses on long reins lifting their heads as they ran, doing their best to avoid the dust thrown up off the dry road which plumed away from them to the north-east, borne on the wind that was keeping their faces clear.

Ten, fifteen, twenty minutes' good riding followed at a comfortable canter, all desperate not to break into a full gallop with such a long way still to go. The road was quite empty ahead of them running all the way to Limoux: rolling miles of vineyards on every side, spaced with wide open fields of wheat and barley, swaying golden in the wind that blew around them; scattered olive groves with flocks of hardy sheep and goats belling happily amongst them.

And it was exhilarating, the air in their faces cool and fresh as if the world was new, the hammering of iron hooves along the beaten ground, the nodding of their horses' heads in tune to their rushing speed, the power of every muscle working beneath them as they pounded along the track...each rider knowing that every horse had more to give if it was asked for, for no-one yet was galloping. Nevertheless it was a beautiful morning in high summer, they were nearly there to Carcassonne, and Alicia felt like shouting!

*

Four miles behind them de Vere saw the distant plume of dust and his heart sank.

That it was Alicia and her party he had no doubt...but just as he was beginning to think Rochine had not seen it too, as it was so like faint smoke from a farmer's cot, she called his attention to it herself.

"What is that, Gaston?" she challenged him as she rode beside him at the head of the column, all going at a fast canter. "Is that a fire or riders on the track ahead?" she queried again, pointing over his shoulder.

"I don't know, my Lady," he replied, and before she could say another word he threw up his hand and brought his command to a panting halt, the dust swirling up from their horses' feet as they bounced to a standstill.

"Just smoke from a cottar's fire, I think!" he said, shielding his eyes with his hand as he searched the distant skyline, twice passing it by in his apparent efforts to see more clearly.

"No, Sir!" one of his men called out, standing up in his saddle shielding his eyes from the glare of the morning sun just then rising up ahead of them. "It is riders, away ahead of us. Look, my Lady, you can just see them as they go, lit by the new sun. See! Their helmets are flashing in the sunlight."

"You have keen eyes, Pierre Rouge!" de Vere growled at him, silently cursing the lad's youthful eagerness.

"How many are there, soldier?" Rochine snapped at him.

"Eight...no! Six, my Lady...and two horses on long reins. They are a long way off...but the sun lights them well in this clear air."

"By Christos, Gaston! It's them! *It's them*," she shouted out exultantly, standing up in her stirrups. "A golden bezant to the first man who can lay hands on the Lady de Burley!" And after swift adjustments to their gear, and with a great shout, led by de Vere, The Lady's whole command sat back in their saddles, dug in their spurs and leaped off up the road at the gallop; arms, legs and heels working furiously to bring out the best speed in every horse, some even using their reins to lash their beasts to even greater efforts.

Above them rose a great plume of dust and flying debris off the track that could be seen for miles.

283

It was Aziz who saw them first.

"We have company I think, my Lady!" he called out tersely. "There is a sudden great plume of dust behind us. Some miles I think. But coming fast. Do we stand or run?"

"*Run!*" Alicia called back behind her. "But gently at first, we still have a way to go. Our horses are fresher, and we have not pressed them so hard," she added as they all clustered round in the middle of the track. "Now my friends...let's see who best stays the course this day! Aquib, lead off! We will keep pace with you...and we will stay together. And if we have to fight then fight we will together, as we did yesterday, on the ground."

"Ready, my Lady?" Aquib asked of her.

"Yes! Ready!"

"Then here we go! Steady at first, no more than a fast canter. But do not spring your horses until I give you leave." And with those words Aquib led off up the track, looking back to see where their pursuers were, making sure they were not yet gaining on them more than he wished them to. Planning for them to tire before he ordered his small group to clap in their spurs and ride *vent à terre*, 'wind to the ground', away from their pursuers, leaving them to eat their dust with every stride their horses took.

*

Ahead of them all, Baron Roger rode at an easy amble, leading his troops to where the northern road passed closest to the river across from which the town stood connected by bridges.

Riding on further they came to the point where the three routes around Limoux all met...and there he waited, looking down the long western road, up which two palls of dust were already rushing up to meet him, and with a lazy smile on his hard face, he waved his command forward.

With his great house flag fluttering and flashing in the brisk morning breeze, he kicked Charlemagne into a striding walk, and then a fast, loping canter. His body stiff and upright against the tall cantle of his saddle, long legs thrust out before him, hands relaxed, he rode superbly, wholly at one with his enormous coal black charger.

And as the Baron rode out towards them, so Aquib gave the order for his small command to be prepared to ride like they had never ridden before, and as Rochine's men came racing up behind them, hallooing and waving their swords in the air like lunatics, convinced they had them in their bag...so Aquib, Alicia and all her small company sprang their horses at last.

They dropped their reins, stabbed in their heels, and sat back as their rounceys bunched up their great hindquarter muscles, snorted, tossed their heads, dug their hooves into the ground and took off up the trackway towards Limoux like rache hounds after a deer when the scent is strong, the day is cold and clear and the blood is hot!

"Harrow away! *Away!*" Alicia shouted out as if she was at the chase, a wild grin on her face as she hurled her gelding up the road, stretching her body down along her rouncey's withers as she had with Sunburst when she had fled away from The Saracen's Head through the king's forest the night of the fire,

"*Tarooo! Tarooo!*" de Vere's men roared back at her, from the backs of their mounts, now visibly tiring, as they watched their quarry steadily pull away from them, Alicia's final taunt: "*Gone away! Gone awayy!*" almost lost in their groans of disappointment as they finally pulled up, their horses totally spent. After three days of intensive riding, and a wild final chase, always pushed to the limit, now their withers were streaked white with foam and sweat; blowing hard and their heads drooping, they had no more to give.

Beside herself with frustrated rage, caracoling and titupping her horse all over the track, The Lady berated them all as feckless, hopeless, pathetic cowards, mindlessly striking out with her leather quirt at men and horses alike, until de Vere snatched it out of her hand and shouted: "*Look! My Lady, look!* Your father is out along this track too, and he has her now for certain. Your job is done." And with a final look around him, and a secret smile in his heart, he said tersely: "Now we can all go home!"

And captured her the Baron had, for even as Alicia and her household broke away from their furious pursuers...so she came upon him again at last, much as she had seen him at Malwood that very first time, seated on Charlemagne, his great prancing charger, dressed magnificently in black and gold. With a certain look of hauteur and calm pleasure on his sardonic features, the noble Lord Baron, Sir Roger de Brocas, Baron of Narbonne and Gruissan, leapt off Charlemagne's back and opened his arms to his intended bride as she rushed to him off the back of her own horse, leaving its reins trailing and its feet stamping sparks off the hard roadway.

Giving a subtle bow and a twitch of his black brows, and with a broad smile on his face as he caught her, he said: "Welcome to France, my Lady; I see I am come in good time!" And as Alicia looked up at him, suddenly lost in

285

his fierce black eyes, he bent and gently kissed her lips. Stunned by the sudden contact, her arms goose-bumped and her whole body shuddered, making the Baron breathe deeply in satisfaction. He had achieved his aims, and with Alicia in his arms he turned a moment later to face his daughter.

Rochine, seeing the two of them together, knew a moment of all-consuming jealous fury. A moment when she could have drawn cold steel, leapt from her horse and ripped Alicia's life out of her in a spray of crimson blood. Instead she gritted her teeth and forced a smile onto her lovely face, still flushed from the chase, her eyes glittering like frosty stars.

Her time would come, of that she was certain. She already had plans in place for her cousin of which even her father knew nothing. That *conne anglaise* had no idea just how bitter her end would be at her hands, when all she had arranged fell into place.

Let him enjoy her for now…he would not have her for long!

HISTORICAL NOTE

In this part of the story there is much talk of a 'fother'. This was a well-practised device for covering a hole in a wooden ship and was inspired by a description in C.S.Forester's book, 'Mr Midshipman Hornblower', where Hornblower attempts to save the *Marie Gallant*, a French vessel seized after being fired on by his ship, the *Indefatigable*. The whole process is brilliantly laid out and is well worth a read, as are all the Hornblower novels.

Gemstones, in the days of Gui and his companions, could not be given the sparkling facets we see today. The technology did not exist until the fifteenth century. Square cutting was possible but nothing more. So usually the stones were simply polished ovals or circles, a process called 'cabochon', and then set in gold or silver. Faceted diamonds were not possible until the 19th Century.

The great tower at Saint Jean d'Angély certainly exists, and the town was very heavily assaulted by Henry II, as stated in the book. But the tower was not there in 1190! It was built much later, in the 14th Century by the merchants of the town to show off their wealth. During the Hundred Years' War Saint Jean was the Black Prince's headquarters for much of his expeditions against the French at that time.

Crossbows, unlike long bows, have a flat trajectory, fire a short thick arrow called a bolt, or a quarrel, often with leather fletching, from a composite bow strengthened with steel. This the archer had to bend down to wind up, his foot in a kind of stirrup, because the bow is too stiff to be pulled by hand. It fires like a gun from the shoulder, and in professional hands it is a deadly weapon! *But*…it takes time to reload, and in the time a crossbow archer is rewinding his weapon…a long bow archer can fire off half a dozen shafts. The range of both weapons is about the same…but a longbow archer can kill men hiding behind walls and battlements by arching his arrows up and over them…a cross bow can only shoot in a straight line. Its single great advantage is that recruits can be taught to use it with very little instruction. To be a longbow archer takes a lifetime of practice! Read Ronald Welch's book, 'Bowmen of Crécy', and you will find it is all wonderfully explained..

I know this part of the story may read rather like a travelogue, but all the places are real and can be visited, and so are the named mountains, and 'though the various inns along the way are very much my invention, the food is not. All is pertinent to the period, especially the Chouchen cider they enjoyed in Nantes. Sadly 'elf an' safety have done for the bee stings…but it is still good stuff! And while they did have rice, turnips, lettuce and spring onions…of course there were no tomatoes, peppers, chillies or potatoes. They all came from the Americas which, in 1190, were still 300 years from being 'officially' discovered!

In films, and TV programmes of this period you often see women riding sidesaddle. Very pretty, very demure…and completely wrong. In the twelfth century women still rode astride! The first known use of a sidesaddle in Europe was not until the fourteenth century, accredited to Anne of Bohemia in the 1360's, but it was not until the sixteenth century that one was developed that allowed the rider to control her horse effectively. So Alicia and Rochine, and Agnes and Soraya, rode astride which is why their riding costumes were actually split front and back to their waists, as were the long chain mail hauberks of the men who accompanied them. Remember…there was no gusset in those days either!

In this story I have William de Forz as ruler of Niort in the Vendée, which he was, but in fact he was with Richard's fleet as his High Admiral at this time, not in his castle when Gui arrived there. His wife was called Hawise, and his eldest son was another William, but, as far as I know, he did not go on any pilgrimage to Saint James of Compostella for whom the sign of a scallop shell remains a most powerful symbol. Remember that St James, Santiago in Spanish, was Jesus's brother.

Finally, bears! When I wrote that part of the story I so wanted to introduce a real 'fell' beast into the southern French mountains, but was not sure whether bears would still have been around at the time Alicia and her companions were fleeing for their lives from Foix. But, to my joy, I discovered that not only were there bears around in 1190…having disappeared from England shortly after the Conquest…but that there are still wild brown bears in the High Pyrenees to this day. Very much like the grizzlies of the American Rockies, the Pyrenean brown bear can be just as devastating. They kill sheep and goats every year, and the French farmers are very well compensated for the damage. The French government are trying to increase the numbers with imported brown bears from Eastern Europe, a move not supported by French farmers.

BOOK III... 'The White Rose Betrayed.'

Chapter 1...Gui arrives at Bordeaux.

Nine days after leaving Nantes, and two days after leaving Saint Jean d'Angély, Gui and Sir Richard brought their whole command down to the teeming city of Bordeaux at last.

Dust covered and bone weary on exhausted mounts, they were all pleased to have arrived safely at last. Lancers, bowmen, heavy foot and spearmen, their gisarmes over their shoulders, long swords by their sides; their two tilt carts, laden with their gear and their wounded, Father Matthew in close attendance, all worn down and saddle sore. And at the back, behind Gui's and Sir Richard's chargers, now on leading reins, rode the two Vernaille brothers on their own destriers but under close arrest.

Twice they had tried to escape by falling off their mounts and once by running away at night. But each time they had been re-captured swiftly, the last by one of their own men. So on entering Bordeaux, Gui had ordered them to be tied to their saddles, with two men on either side of them with orders to strike them down if they tried anything further!

And in all truth, with their moaning and whining about discomfort, sparse food and being, 'belted knights', Gui and Sir Richard had had enough of both of them, and were delighted to bring them, still bound, to the High Constable's Officer of the Guard and his men in their tough mailed hauberks and nasal helmets.

Simple bindings of cord now replaced by chains, and preceded by Gui and Sir Richard, Father Matthew close behind them with his big leather scrip, they were brought before the High Constable of Bordeaux himself, Guard Commander and overall military ruler of the greatest city on the western seaboard of France, where the Golden Leopards of England bravely flew from every gatehouse...the Lord Baron, Sir Hugh Willoughby.

A man of enormous presence, a former Commander of the North during Gui's time on the Borders before his knighthood, and now King Richard's High Seneschal of all Aquitaine, he was the most powerful man in this whole region of France. As they were ushered into the great man's Chamber of Office, ahead of his prisoners, Gui knew they would be amongst friends for the next few nights at least.

Sir Hugh, square faced and of medium height, with great strength in his broad shoulders as you would expect in so practised a fighter, rose to greet them with a smile as they were ushered into the room.

Steel-blue eyed, as befitted his Norman ancestry, clean shaven and with a fine head of dark brown hair, he had broad hands but fine tapering fingers; more those of an artist than the great swordsman he truly was. He greeted Gui warmly - this young warrior whom he remembered with affection from their days together on the Scottish borders, when Gui was still only a squire learning his knightly ways.

Both had served under the fierce auspices of Baron John de Methley, that bold knight whom Old King Henry, Richard's father, had put in charge of England's northern borders under the Lord Earl Percy of Alnwick, the great Earl of Northumbria, the King's plenipotentiary in the North. Who ruled over those bleak, misted lands where Scotland marched beside England along the wild Cheviot hills, from Northumbria to the lakes and mountains of the west. It had been the great Earl himself whose sword had knighted Gui before the young man had returned to his estates around the King's New Forest in Hampshire. And Sir Hugh was delighted to see him again...though not the two Vernailles, and especially not Sir Bernard whom it was quite clear had lied to him from the outset...*And I will make him rue the day he ever did so!*

Coming from behind the massive desk that filled one corner of his great room, where three monks were seated amidst a pile of parchments, heads down, their quills busily scratching away, he came and stood before the two disgraced chevaliers and glared at them, hands on hips, his long bliaut of red and green wool, belted with golden leather, swirling as he moved.

"On their knees!" he growled with a sharp gesture to the burly escorts who had followed Gui and Sir Richard into his high ceilinged chamber. "On their knees!"

Lit by tall lancet windows that threw brilliant shafts of golden light across the polished oak floor, with beautifully crafted stone work in the corners, the chamber was in stark contrast to the dishevelled figures forced down before King Richard's Chief Justiciar and Seneschal of all Aquitaine. He now stood over them, the very harbinger of Death itself. His flowing robes and clean cut mien, his athletic movement around his chamber and the strong aura of power that emanated from him made the two men at his feet seem no more than the strutting popinjays they truly were.

"I have heard, and read, all I need about your wicked attempt on the lives of these worthy knights," he said quietly, holding up the detailed parchments that Matthew had sent forward from the abbey at Saint Jean d'Angély. "One of whom, Sir Gui de Malwood, is King Richard's chosen man...and of those who

290

follow them," he added, his voice deadly in its soft intensity, every syllable clipped and perfectly delivered. "And of your close liaison with the Lord of Narbonne, the Lord Baron, Sir Roger de Brocas, the King's declared enemy, and whose warrant for arrest for High Treason, with the King's Great Seal upon it, Sir Gui carries with him."

"Sir Geoffrey and I did not know..." Bernard de Vernaille tried to say, any arrogance he might have displayed stripped from him, his face now pale with fear, sweating, his voice trembling.

"*Do not lie to me!*" Sir Hugh rasped, in a voice of iron. "I have had enough of your dissembling and your lies, you miserable wretch! This time it is not a 'pass' out of the city that is at question...it is your very lives!" he went on remorselessly, as they both gasped with horror.

"Do not mumble to me that: '*You did not know!*'" he seethed at them with biting scorn. "I am my Lord King's Chief Justiciar and Seneschal in all Aquitaine...a fact which seems to have eluded you completely in your planning. I see and hear *everything!* I hold the power of life and death over every soul within these Marches...*Of course you knew!*

"Do not attempt to lie to me. Of course you had full cognizance of whom you were attempting to kill. And why, you fools? For greed...and Philip of Valois' royal favour? For hollow promises that never would have been kept? And that your father, whom you so disparaged in your ignorance and folly, never would have entertained for one single moment...how he must be spinning in his grave over your venal stupidity. Least of all would he have accepted promises from a vile mountebank, whose hands are thick with the blood of others; in whom 'honour' is a foul joke for the simple minded, and whose word means *nothing!*

"Yet it is with this man of blood, the Lord Baron, Sir Roger of Narbonne and Gruissan, whom you have chosen to ally yourselves! This ignoble, deceitful robber baron," he went on relentlessly, "who has murdered Sir Gui's family, slain his soldiers, burned his home and kidnapped his betrothed Lady, Alicia de Burley, King Richard's own Ward...the penalty for all of which treachery is death...as it should be!"

"*But we did not do those things!...*" Sir Bernard pleaded, bringing his hands together with a rattle of chain.

"No! You *snake!*" Sir High snarled at him, his voice rising as he spoke. "You didn't! But...you *crétin*, you chose to ally yourself to the one man who *did!* And have since carried out his orders to make a further attempt on Sir Gui's life, which has now failed. And tomorrow, at dawn, you will both pay the ultimate penalty for your stupidity..."

"*No!*" Both men cried out in terror.

291

"*Yes!*" Sir Hugh shouted, his face twisted in disgust for their behaviour. "You will pay in full for your greed and for your treason to your King…to whom you swore allegiance for your lands before me in these very chambers after your noble father had died, and whose honour you befoul…*at dawn tomorrow beneath my headman's axe!*" he added in ringing tones of utter finality:

"*No!*" They both cried out desperately again; Geoffrey de Vernaille scrabbling across the polished oak floor to grovel at Sir Hugh's feet.

"And, as declared traitors," he snarled down at them, spurning the wretched man's appeal with his foot, "henceforth *all* your lands will return to the crown. *No appeal!* Sergeant," he called out to his own officer standing nearby. "Take them down!"

And as their escort dragged them off their knees, still pleading their innocence and begging for his mercy, and hauled them to the door with tears in their eyes and faces grey with shock and terror, he turned his back on them with a chilling lack of remorse.

Then they were gone…their cries and struggles fading as they were marched away, while Sir Hugh turned to his secretaries and ordered them to draw up the necessary documents for his signature and his seal, before ushering them out of his room, requesting his guards by the door to send in two of the castle varlets to wait on him as he did so..

"In truth, Hugh? Their execution?" Gui questioned him after the door had finally been closed, surprised at the swift ruthlessness of his decision.

"Yes, Gui. *In very truth!*…But it does not please me to do so," he sighed. "The fact is that those two have been on the edge of such disgrace ever since their father, Rupert de Vernaille, died a few months ago. He was a man of great integrity and honour; served the Old King all his days and was always known as the 'Old Lord'. He was a true leal man to the crown, and one of the first of the Poitevin barons to swear his allegiance to Richard Lionheart after King Henry died at Chinon last July. He would have *hated* what his sons have done. He was a fierce old man and would have sent them to the block himself! "But those two?" He gestured at the closed door with disgust. "They are prime articles of malice and treachery. Bernard far worse than Geoffrey, but both weak, dissolute and greedy.

"I have had my eye on them for some time. I was certain that they were bound in with de Brocas…but could find no proof of it! But this," he went on, smacking the message Gui had sent ahead of his arrival with the back of his hand. "This is exactly what I have been waiting for. And they are one tentacle of that foul octopus in Gruissan that I shall lop off!"

And banging his hands together for a job well done, he ushered both men across the room towards where a number of great padded armed chairs stood loosely scattered around a fine oval table of polished walnut, beneath a pair of tall windows overlooking the city and the great Garonne River that wound its way through it.

"Now…you young cockerel," he said with a shake of his shoulders and the broadest of smiles, after Gui had properly introduced him to Sir Richard L'Eveque, and to Father Matthew, whose hands he warmly clasped. "The last I heard of you, before this *débâcle* with de Brocas, you were high in King Richard's esteem and off to seek your fortune with him in the Holy Land. I saw your name on the lists of knights who had signed up to travel with the King to Marseilles…heard you had done well at the Christmas joust in London too? Knocked our Good Lord and Master clean out of his saddle and onto his royal arse no less!" he added with a great guffaw of good humour. "My boy, you are famous!"

And shouting for wine and food to the two tabarded servants who had quietly entered just at that moment, he flung himself down into a chair, gesturing for Gui and his companions to join him; and in a moment they were all settled comfortably in four of the huge padded chairs that graced his apartment, their long legs stretched out in comfort for the first time since leaving Southampton.

Glossary

Abigail	An 'abigail' is the generic name for a young female servant, but most 'abigails' often became highly valued close personal servants, even much loved companions as Agnes did with Alicia.
Bailey (The)	This was the courtyard, sometimes huge and often down to pasture, that lay within the encircling walls of a castle. Some big castles had two baileys, an inner and an outer one.
Baldric	The belt that carries a sword.
Ballista	Roman style stone throwing machine, could also fire a heavy iron-headed bolt: a torsion machine worked by ratcheted arms and twisted animal sinews.
Blazon	The heraldic beast, or device, worn by a knight with its heraldic background.
Bliaut	Long over gown of differing materials, often pleated, worn by both men and women.
Borel folk	Illiterate country workers.
Byrnie	A tough leather coat to which metal plates, scale armour or chain mail has been fixed. Sometimes just thick boiled leather with loose chain mail on top.
Cable	A 'cable' is taken from the length of an anchor cable in the days of sail, usually 100 fathoms. Six feet to a fathom; so, 600ft in imperial measurement, about 200 yards. Officially one tenth of a nautical mile!
Cantle	The high back to a medieval saddle.
Casque	The round dome-topped helmet that came in around this time, sometimes with a nasal protector, sometimes with a perforated faceplate when it was known as a 'salt cellar'.
Chausses	Trousers, usually leather, but could be any favoured material. Often overstitched with chain mail.
Chemise	An under shirt, or blouse, Worn by both sexes.
Christian mail	This was much thicker and heavier than Eastern mail, often reinforced across the chest and back. Syrian arrows could not pierce it!

294

Courser	A strong horse used for fighting, different from a destrier, which was bigger, or the rouncey which was a Spanish work-horse very popular for most purposes.
Crenel	The gap between the merlons, the 'teeth', of battlements.
Crenellations	The technical name for 'Battlements'.
Cyclas	A knight's long over dress, only ever worn over armour, that carried his blazon, usually of white material.
Demesne	The Lord of the Manor's Home Farm.
Destrier	A trained war horse, or charger…bigger and stronger than a courser and hugely expensive.
Devil Wind	Today this is called 'La Tramontane' and blows violently from the North West down the Pyrenees towards the Mediterranean, sometimes with torrential rain. It howls and rages and can drive people mad, hence its name!
Djinns	Muslim Spirits of fire, we call them Geniis. Can assume human form, often hideous and sometimes found in bottles!
Doucets	The testicles of a deer: a delicacy when cooked in a white wine sauce.
Doxy	A low born mistress, or woman of uncertain morals, often found in ale-houses…what today might be called a 'tart' or a 'slag'. One up from being a whore!
Drudges	Menial servants, usually women, who worked in the kitchens or about the castle, doing manual labour.
Ermine	The white body and black tail of a stoat in its winter colours; very exclusive and very expensive. Also a 'fur' used in heraldry.
Fewmets	The droppings of any hunted game animal, but especially of deer.
Friars	Wandering monks, usually in brown habits. The Franciscans wore grey.
Furlong	A measurement of land, still used in horse racing today. One eighth of a mile - 220yards. A cricket pitch is one tenth of a furlong!
Gambeson	Like a thick eiderdown, split to the waist between the legs for ease of movement. Usually worn under a knight's chainmail armour to protect him from the battering effect of weapons in combat.
Gavelock	A form of throwing spear…heavier than a javelin.

Garderobe	A loo. Great things to look for when out castling.
Gisarme	Basically a billhook on the end of a long pole, the end of which was cased in metal. Very nasty!
Gralloch	The gutting of a deer after a kill.
Greek Fire	A truly horrendous medieval weapon that remains a real mystery even today. Made a terrifying roaring noise when fired towards you. Water spread it and it could only be extinguished with sand, vinegar or old urine!
Guerdon	The reward to a knight from his lady for his courage and his chivalry, as a symbol of her love.
Hauberk	A knight's full coat of chain-mail or overlapping scale armour. Could weigh over 80lbs of interlocked, riveted iron rings.
Heater shield	Shaped like the bottom of an iron. Easier to use than the kite shaped shield of earlier years: came into fashion about this time.
Herne the Hunter	Mythical God of the forests, probably of Celtic origin.
Jacks	Leather 'Jacks' were the tankards of the Middle Ages. Only in England were they successfully made waterproof!
Kirtle	A woman, or girl's skirt.
Kist	A large wooden chest, for clothes or armour…or money. Often dome topped to keep off the rain!
Liripipe	A long tail of material attached to a hood, that acted like a scarf in foul weather.
Lymer	A scent hound, like a bloodhound, but wholly different in shape from today.
Mangonel	Light artillery. A siege weapon, sometimes like a giant crossbow on wheels, sometimes with an upright bar against which a throwing arm could strike. Effective between 300/400 yds. Could throw a 50lb weight.
Mantling	What a bird of prey does to protect its kill, by drawing its shoulders…its wings, right over the prey object. Bats do the same thing.
Marchpane	What we call marzipan.
Mark	A Mark at this time was NOT a single coin. It was an actual sum of money, in English terms, 13/6d, in old money! Roughly two thirds of an old pound, 20s. Could be weighed out and then paid in gold or silver bullion.

Mazeling	Someone not in their right mind, either from disease or trauma, or from a mental defect. Such people were believed by some to have been 'touched by God', and so were known as 'God's own children'.
Meinie/meisnie	A knight's personal armed followers...by oath. All kings/earls/barons have to be knights.
Mie	Your lover: could be used for a much cherished child.
Mistral (Le)	Violent cold wind that blows down the Rhône valley from the Alps into the Mediterranean basin.
Mercury/Hermes	The winged messenger of the gods. Wings on his hat and on his sandals. Son of Maia Maiestas...the Goddess of Spring, the most lovely of the seven sisters that make up the Pleiades...and Zeus/Jupiter, and god of trade, merchants, travel...and liars! A lie goes round the world before the truth has got his boots on! Our month of May is named after her.
Merlons	The upright 'teeth' that make up the battlements of a castle.
Messuages	Those lands and buildings immediately around the Lord's homestead or castle. Still used in conveyancing today.
Meurtrières	Murder holes in the roof of a castle gateway passage through which boiling oil or any kind of missile could be poured or hurled upon an enemy below.
Nemesis	Traditionally the daughter of Zeus and the distributer of Fortune and Retribution, neither good nor bad necessarily, but each in due proportion to what was deserved. Often seen as the implacable distributer of Divine Retribution against Hubris...human arrogance before the gods!
Orphrey	Beautifully intricate embroidery, often with gold and silver thread, very expensive and very popular at this time.
Ouches	Great brooches of intricately worked gold and precious stones most used to pin a cloak to the shoulders.
Outremer	This word literally means...'beyond the seas'...and could apply to anywhere beyond the borders of one's own country; but by the time of this story it had come to signify the Holy Land.

Palfrey	A light riding horse, little bigger than a pony and usually ridden by a woman. Infinitely more delicate than a destrier, or even a rouncey.
Paynims	A very medieval word for a heathen, a pagan, or any kind of Muslim infidel.
Pommel	The high front of a medieval saddle, or the weighted handle end of a sword, iron or steel, sometimes with a fancy jewel set into it.
Quillons	The cross piece at the top of a sword or dagger: could be chased...incised... with gold or silver.
Rache hound	Like a modern fox hound: hunted by scent and sight.
Revetted	Earthworks, usually moats or dry ditches, lined with shaped stone.
Rouncey	A breed of Spanish horse that was most popular at this time as a 'maid-of-all-work'. About fifteen hands, so not a large animal, but sturdy and strong in work. Spanish horses were considered by many to be the best, In Spain they had retained much of the Roman skill with horse breeding, especially crossing mares with Arab blood, and with that of horses from Germany. Remember that southern Spain at this time, was still dominated by the Moors.
Sabatons	Steel boots that could be worn over the foot mail.
Sarcenet	A thick silk material used for lining garments.
Scorpion	Similar to a small mangonel, sometimes with a sling: a weapon for hurling rocks at a castle or a ship. Often ship borne weapons.
Sendal	The finest of silk material used as a lady's light over gown or negligée. Soraya's yashmak would have been made of sendal.
Sanglier	The wild boar, big and dangerous, especially around mating time in the autumn. Still hunted all across France. A big male can weigh over 600lbs!
Seax/Scramaseax	A long-bladed Saxon stabbing knife.
Seneschal/Steward	A hugely important post on any great estate and usually a member of the knightly class, like Sir James at Malwood, and often a family member who 'ran' everything.
Sheets	In sailing, 'sheets' are ropes for handling sails or spars.

Sherbet/sherbat	A deliciously refreshing drink made with fresh fruit and spices, still very popular in Muslim counties today.
Shoats	Young wild boar; prettily striped in ochre, chocolate and cream for the first six months or so.
Sounder	A group of wild boar, usually sows, young males and babies. Adult males are much more solitary except at mating time in the autumn when, like rutting stags, they are at their most dangerous.
Sumpter	A horse used especially for carrying goods in boxes or wicker panniers carried on either side on a special frame called a 'crook'. Like the rouncey, not a big horse, but strong in work. What today would be called a 'pack horse'
Talbot	A very large pure white scenting dog for hunting game. The heraldic beast of the Earls of Shrewsbury: like a big dalmatian...but with a heavier jaw and without the spots. Norman, very popular with the Conqueror.
Times of Day	Matins: Midnight; Lauds: Cockcrow...3/4.00am; Prime: 6.00am; Terce: 9.00am; Sext: Noon; None: 3.00pm; Vespers: 6/7.00pm; Compline: 9.00pm.
Trebuchet	The heavy artillery of the Middle Ages. A huge stone throwing machine that could hurl a 300lb stone, or a dead horse, over quarter of a mile, 440yds! The finest example to be found in the UK is at Warwick Castle...and they have never tested it to its fullest potential!
Trencher	A large, thick piece of stale bread that served as a plate on which your meaty meal could be served. A good 'trencher man' was one who finished off his meal by also eating his 'plate' having already eaten everything else!
Trumpet sleeves	Long deep sleeves, sometimes almost to the ground and often trimmed with ermine. The sleeve hung down from the upper arm, often lined in a contrasting colour, complemented with a tightly sleeved undergarment called a chemise.
Tushes	A wild boar's fighting tusks...up to six inches long, and usually curved.
Vassals	In the Middle Ages a Vassal was *anyone* holding land from, or owing allegiance to, someone else. Peasants

were vassals of knights; knights were vassals of lords; lords of barons; barons of the king, the king of the pope and the pope of God Himself.

Verderers Technically they were what today would be called 'Gamekeepers', but in the Middle Ages they were also Officers of the Law; and given tough powers of life, mutilation or death over poachers!

Vexin (The) This was a small buffer 'state' between Normandy and the lands ruled directly by the King of France. A constant bone of contention between the two kingdoms.

Wimple This was usually a very simply made woman's headdress held in place with a fillet of precious metal, or a different piece of material. Not the hugely elaborate headgear that came into fashion in the fifteenth century!

Withers A horse's shoulders.

Wolves Typically a European timber wolf...They were a real menace in the Middle Ages, especially if the winter was cruel, forcing them to seek food from the farms and villages.

Zeus The Greek king of the gods, the Romans called him Jupiter... hence 'by Jove'

Very Simple Heraldry

Armed Claws, teeth, tushes or antlers, coloured or metalled.

Blazon The whole coat-of-arms, including any heraldic beast, on its field. Sometimes the 'beast' only.

Colours Azure: blue; Gules: red; Vert: green; Purpure: purple; Sable: black.

Heraldic Beasts Too many to mention. I have used several, including dragons: here are the four principals from the story:
Lion Rampant...upright on his back feet, forward facing, paws up...De Malwood.
Lion Rampant-Gardant...upright on his back feet, paws up but looking at you...Richard L'Eveque.
Stag's Head Erased...just the antlered head of a stag looking at you...De Burley.
Boar's Head Erased: Just the tushed head of a wild boar looking forward and upwards...De Brocas.

Fields	Background colours, metals or furs on which the principal blazon, or just the beast, of any family is painted.
Furs	Ermine: White with black 'tails'…the stoat in its winter colours. Vair: Squirrel…uniquely patterned and usually in alternate colours. Either furs can be used as a whole field.
Langued	Tongues coloured or metalled.
Metals	Argent: silver/white: Or: gold/yellow: White and Yellow as whole Field backgrounds.